SOME CAME BY SHIP

CATHY A. LEWIS

978-1-7370267-2-3 for Paperback
978-1-7370267-3-0 for eBook

Editorial Team: Emily Conlin, Christine Schaub, Jenn Giffels
Credit: Musician photo on back cover—London Orlins
Cover Design: BookCoverExpress.com
Interior Design: BeAPurplePenguin.com
Author photo: photographer Amiee Stubbs,
taken at Ron and Becky Sohr's home.

Library of Congress Control Number 2025917154
2025 Copyright Registration Number TXu 2-490-207
Lewis, Cathy A.

www.cathyalewis.com

SOME CAME BY SHIP
6 Years Later, Germany 1939

CATHY A. LEWIS

Author Disclaimer

Some Came By Ship—6 Years Later: Germany 1939 is a work of historical fiction inspired by actual events. While many incidents, dialogues, and characters—aside from a few well-known historical figures—are products of the author's imagination, they may not be entirely accurate. When real-life historical figures are included, the situations, incidents, and dialogues related to them are either entirely fictional or based on actual events, enhanced by the author's creativity. These elements are not meant to depict actual events or alter the fictional nature of the work. Research has been conducted to validate certain aspects of the story, ensuring that the historical elements remain faithful to history. Any resemblance to actual persons, living or dead, or real events is purely coincidental. Some names and identifying details have been changed to protect individuals' privacy, while some real names are included for storytelling purposes.

In Loving Memory of the family I never
knew, because of the Shoah.
This is for you, Mom, whose Jewish name
Malkah was changed to Matilda.

For my sister, Melissa Lewis Bell, with whom I
share family history and countless memories.

"There is no possession more valuable than
a good and faithful friend." Socrates

I dedicate this book to my good and faithful friend, ALB,
who has made everything possible for me as an author.

Extreme gratitude for the goodness of God,
who makes all things possible.

For the survivors of the S.S. St. Louis — your courage
endures, and your legacy will never be forgotten.

Author Thanks

To my Beta readers. It's been a long road getting here. Thank you for your input and support of my writing. Melissa Lewis Bell, Alisa Dillinger Smith, Elizabeth Marquis Cooper, Adele Locurcio Kandanada, Benjamin Lewis Bell, Richard Arthur Bell, Jennifer Giffels, Cathy DeSimone Piciulo, Tom Vincent Ricco, Nancy Peterson Hearn, Becky Sohr, Diane Baltadonis.

Special thanks:

Dr. Jacob Silverstone, Vera Karliner, Robert Krakow, Executive Director of the *S.S. St. Louis* Legacy Project Foundation.

Tina Pavlis, Toute Suite, aka Hollenious and the irascible KiKi.

Jenn Giffels, your editorial input and insights were incredibly valuable.

Ben Bell for early guidance when I needed direction.

Special thanks to my friend Alisa Dillinger Smith who made my author photo shoot possible.

Much gratitude to Susan Siebert Daly, Melissa and London Orlins. Many thanks to Jim Strowe for his photograph of London Orlins.

I want to give special thanks and shout out to all of my family and friends, who mostly understood why I didn't attend events or when I said, "I'm writing." Your encouragement is priceless. Thank you for your support.

And to my readers, I am forever grateful you read my books.

*Now the serpent was more subtil than any
beast of the field which the Lord God had made.*

—Genesis 3:1

*"No matter how noble the objectives of a
government, if it blurs decency and kindness,
cheapens human life, and breeds ill will
and suspicion, it is an evil government."*

—Eric Hoffer

CHAPTER ONE

The Beginning—
Operation Sunshine

MAY 12, 1939, HAMBURG, GERMANY

A MAN CALLED FRITZ matched his breathing to the rhythmic thud of his boots on the shadowy, wet cobblestone street. The reverberation of his jackboots on the stones echoed eerily off the empty buildings and large structures.

Intermittent rain fell, and an aroma of ozone permeated the air, intermingling with the scent of the day's fresh catch, the smells of a city, and the droplets carrying the essence of dirt, salt, and sea. He inhaled the salty, desolate emptiness of the late night and shuddered as a chill swept over him, reminiscent of walking through a graveyard. Fritz paused to wipe the sweat and rain from his eyes, squinting at his watch. It was nearly midnight.

As he trudged through the dense mist and light rain, his feet heavy, the moisture seeped through the collar of his trench coat, trickling down his spine and settling at his belt. A bolt of lightning jolted near him, prompting him to pick up his pace. The streetlights cast fragmented, dim beams of light onto the sidewalk, merging with the shadows of the surrounding buildings and trees. The sky was dense, dark, and devoid of clouds. Finding a hiding spot would be effortless if necessary.

Thirty meters away, the glint of a door lamp on a two-story

warehouse caught his attention. He gazed at the flickering light, noting its rhythm, and exhaled a sigh of relief. He'd reached his destination. In the distance, a bell from a tower chimed, resonating across the unsettled skies.

Fritz stood at the front of the building, where the lamp illuminated the entrance. Before him was a sturdy, wooden door with an elaborate, brass eagle knocker. Adrenaline pumped through his veins as he lifted the weighty eagle and tapped out the code given to him by his contact. The lock turned, and the door opened.

A balding man of medium stature stood inside, dressed in a deep red smoking jacket and luxurious satin slippers. The light behind him created a silhouette. He gestured for Fritz to enter while he scanned the outside area. "Were you followed?"

Fritz shook his head. *I would not tell you if I was.* Water ran off him, creating a puddle where he stood.

The man squinted at Fritz, scanning him from head to toe, disregarding the water pooling at his feet and trickling across the grooves of the stone floor. Locking eyes with Fritz, he delivered a stern warning. "Let me make this crystal clear. This Abwehr operation is under my command. Failure is not an option."

Fritz nodded, standing at full attention beneath a dazzling crystal chandelier. "I assure you, sir, I will not fail."

The man paced the Persian carpet as if to gather his thoughts. He stopped and fiddled with something in his pocket, then cleared his throat. "Your mission is to travel from the Hamburg port to Havana, Cuba. Upon arrival, you'll disembark from the ship to meet your contact, Robert Hoffman, a counterintelligence operative for the Abwehr. His cover is an assistant manager position at the local HAPAG office in Havana. HAPAG stands for the Hamburg-American line of ships."

He handed Fritz a small, bent photograph. Next, he gave him a pocket-sized, leather-bound black diary with a swastika stamped in gold on the front alongside the initials F.E..

Fritz took both, glancing briefly at the little book, and slid them into his pocket without further inspection. "The initials, a nice touch."

His host returned to pacing and smoked his cigarette down to a nub before grinding it into a porcelain dish. He lit another cigarette while Fritz watched, then began speaking again, so low that Fritz had difficulty hearing him. He leaned forward to listen.

"There is something you must be aware of, something so critical."

Fritz clasped his hands and nodded.

"Remember that the information you transport could significantly impact the Reich's plans in the coming months. It could even sway the course of a potential war. This mission is a top priority for Berlin. Our agents have crucial information pilfered from the Americans and the British. The Reich is counting on receiving it as soon as possible." The host stopped speaking, fixing his gaze on Fritz, who shifted uneasily in awkward silence.

His host continued, "You will be responsible for transporting films and newsreels made by Reich Propaganda Minister Joseph Goebbels. You will carry these in a suitcase. Once aboard the ship, you will transfer the films to Steward Otto Schiendick, the Nazi and Abwehr representative aboard the ship. He will come to your cabin to retrieve them."

The man hesitated, then offered a word of caution about Schiendick. "He's intractable. He'll be furious with you for doing what he thought was his job, even though you were hand-picked for this assignment."

His host stopped and tilted his head, eyeing Fritz with suspicion. "I don't know who got you into this position, but they must be powerful to supersede Schiendick. He's a favorite of Admiral Canaris," he said, speaking of the head of the Abwehr.

The man glanced at Fritz. "How well you perform will determine whether you receive a reward or a punishment. Do you understand?"

Fritz nodded once more.

"A man of few words. Even better. Do you have any questions?"

Fritz focused intently on his host, committing his features to memory. "I require information on where to obtain the films and newsreels, and details about the ship and my orders while on board."

"The *S.S. St. Louis* is a luxury liner that will transport 937 German Jews to Havana, Cuba, tomorrow, departing the harbor at 8:00 p.m.. The ship can be found at Shed 76. Your accommodation is a second-class single cabin. The crew is 100 percent German; most are members of the Nazi party. Captain Gustav Schroeder is a puzzle who has yet to commit to the cause. That is why we chose him for this *special voyage*. He is above suspicion."

His host continued, "Your conduct will be as such. You will keep to yourself, speaking to no other passengers beyond 'hello.' While aboard, you'll have meals in your cabin. Regarding the films, you'll pick them up along with your credential packet tomorrow at 6:00 am at the Speicherstadt near the port. Look for the first building on the right after entering the series of warehouses from the north entrance.

"Once you arrive at that first warehouse, go directly to the entrance door marked with a swastika, identify yourself as

'Fritz,' and flash your ID to receive the reels and credential packet. Board the ship as soon as possible and go directly to your cabin. Once you board, Schiendick will retrieve the reels from your cabin. Are you with me so far?"

Fritz nodded.

His host continued, "Upon arrival in Havana, look for Hoffman waiting on the pier in a green Tyrolean alpine hat with a red feather and a Leica camera hanging around his neck. He will be easy to spot. He will cancel the mission if he suspects his cover has been compromised. If you can't locate him, then you can be sure he aborted. But the chances of his cover being blown are minuscule."

Fritz smirked. *A green Tyrolean alpine hat with a red feather and a Leica camera hanging around his neck? Could the contact appear any more obvious?*

His host got up close to Fritz, their faces just inches apart. "Did I say something funny?"

"No, sir."

"I'm telling you once. Don't screw this up."

His host handed over a small metal swastika pin to affix to Fritz's shirt collar. He whispered, his voice raspy, "You will dress as you are now, in civilian clothes, a suit and tie, and a trench coat." His gaze rested on Fritz's boots. "Get rid of those.

"Now, you'll retrieve the intelligence, reboard the ship immediately, go to your cabin, and await departure. Upon returning to Hamburg, you will report to me here to hand over what Hoffman gives you."

"Yes, sir." Fritz shifted his weight impatiently.

As his host opened the door, allowing the wind and rain to enter, he grabbed the lapel of Fritz's trench coat, pulling him close. In an ominous tone, he said, "One last thing. We will be monitoring your every move. Heil Hitler!"

CHAPTER TWO

A New Life For All

FALL 1937, ROCHESTER, NEW YORK

IN SEPTEMBER 1933, an American lawyer named Raymond Wellington, who worked for the US State Department, began the adoption process for four friends he and his son Buster had met in Munich during Buster's summer Boy Scout trip through Europe.

Motivated by a strong desire to safeguard them after learning of their dangerous situation, Raymond worked tirelessly to ensure their safety, as staying in Germany posed a serious threat. The group included Polish citizen Maddie Turetsky, seventeen; German citizen Stanislaus Birnbaum, forty-five; Frederick Wolferman, thirty-six; and his son, Wolfie, seventeen. Buster and Wolfie were the same age. Because their lives were at risk in Germany, Raymond negotiated with the US State Department for the legal adoption of both minors and adults. They would all take the last name Wellington. Raymond expedited the process by using the US State Department-issued identification, visas, and medical clearance provided by the German Embassy for each individual, allowing their entrance into the US.

While Raymond finalized legal documents during a conversation with his longtime friend, former US Ambassador to Germany William Dodd, the man remarked, "Timing is everything. What a stroke of luck you adopted when you did.

With Breckenridge Long in charge of doling out or withholding visas and immigration papers, it's good that his appointment began after you completed the process. He would have shut us down in no time."

Raymond nodded. "When things go as planned, you have to stop and thank God for the miracle."

Raymond assumed full financial responsibility for the four and ensured they would never be indigent. The adoption took a year to finalize and was completed in the fall of 1934, its speed thanks in large part to Raymond's connections in high places.

After moving to Rochester, Frederick, Stani, Wolfie, Maddie, Buster, and Raymond all lived together in Raymond's residence. Frederick and Raymond established a small used car import dealership, utilizing Frederick's skills as a mechanic, fulfilling his dream of working on imported sports cars. Stani, who had been Maddie's first violin teacher while they both lived in Munich, had retired. He loved to cook, and kept the home, cooking and cleaning for the family.

Raymond enrolled Maddie, Wolfie, and Buster in his alma mater, the University of Rochester. Maddie would pursue musical studies, concentrating on violin at the Eastman School of Music and taking general subjects at the U of R. The boys focused on general studies, concentrating on chemistry and math. They would continue to live at home after college began, while Maddie would live near campus. She was an extraordinary beauty and gifted violinist, and both Buster and Wolfie competed for her attention, captivated by her brilliant smile, deep cobalt eyes, long dark hair, and shapely figure.

The Wellington residence at 420 Rugby Avenue in Rochester was a sprawling English Tudor home dating back to the turn of the century. It featured a steep, pitched gable roof, brick exterior, hand-hewn half-timbering, stonework, and windows lined with leaded glass. The house was a showpiece, boasting exquisite gardens, a spacious yard, and five bedrooms. It offered ample living space and privacy. Still, clashes often arose between Buster and Wolfie, many of them over Maddie.

"Buster, you drag your feet too long, and someone will come and sweep Maddie off her feet and take her from you," Wolfie told him.

Buster scoffed at Wolfie's thinly veiled threat. "Who will do that? You? I met her first, don't forget that. And, after all, she knows how I feel. I owe you no explanation, but we have plans for the future. Sorry if it's not following your timetable."

Wolfie rolled his eyes in response. "I'll believe it when I see it."

———❖———

Regarding the name change to Wellington, only Frederick objected at first. Two weeks before the adoption was confirmed, he told Stani and Raymond after supper, "I don't want an Anglo-Saxon name. My name, Wolferman, is my heritage. It is my ancestry and Wolfie's. What do you have without your name? I've lost my country, everything. Now my name." Frederick slurped his coffee and continued to gripe while his cat, Hollenius, pawed at his hand for a scratch behind his orange tabby ears.

Stani kept silent, busying himself with the dishes, while Raymond tried to make light of things. "What say you, Hollenius? Will you accept the Wellington name?"

Frederick wagged his finger at Raymond. "You leave my cat out of this!" He scooped Hollenius into his lap, and the cat rubbed his head against Frederick's flannel shirt. "You tell him, Hollenius. If losing my name's not bad enough, they don't even have German food or beer here!"

Always rational, Stani reasoned with Frederick, "One day, on the other side, all believers will get a new name, so I'm okay with this earthly name, Wellington. It's a good name, a fine one." Still, Frederick fumed.

Raymond, as always, tried to smooth over the situation. "If you were to ever travel back to Germany with your name, it could be dangerous," he told Frederick. "Nazis have very long memories, and they document everything. Does blowing up a garage at Dachau and stealing one of Hitler's cars ring any bells for you? Do you think the Nazis will forget your name or Stani's? I dare say, resoundingly no. So, you're back in Germany, and your name is recognized. Then what?"

Frederick's shoulders slumped. "I know, I know," he said, resigned. "But my brother and sister-in-law are still in Vienna with the Wolferman name. We must get them out, too."

Wearing a plaid skirt and a pretty sweater, Maddie strolled into the kitchen. She'd been practicing her violin while the boys ate supper. Pouring a cup of coffee, she said, "I don't care for the name change either. Turetsky is fine. Why can't I keep my name?"

Raymond sighed. "Maddie, look at it this way: you'll be able to tour Europe, play in the greatest symphony halls, and you won't have to fear the Nazis or the threat of being sent to a concentration camp if discovered. You're under the protection of the Wellington name, like an umbrella to shield you from the pelting Nazi downpour. You won't have to run and hide under a hotel bed, like when we first met you in Munich. You won't have to worry that they'll murder you if they find you, like before. Look what they did to Elenena." The Nazis had murdered Maddie's former teacher and beloved friend before the group left Germany for the United States.

Maddie's nostrils flared, and her jaw tightened. Stani

observed her closely; knowing Maddie's quick and searing temper, he feared an explosion. Hoping to soften the conversation, he reminded Maddie, "You're adopted. You have no historical tie to your birth name, so what's the problem? After all, when you marry Buster, you'll take his name."

Maddie wouldn't look at Stani. "Who says I'm going to marry Buster? Is that a foregone conclusion?" She stomped out of the kitchen, slamming the porch door.

———❀———

Stani found Maddie sitting on the porch swing. The cool night air rustled the fallen leaves, creating the platform for a symphony. The crickets sang their evening song, and a neighbor's dog barked in the distance, adding to the harmony of the high-octave buzz of the yellow porch light. The air carried the scent of the coming autumn: leaves and apples from the orchard less than half a mile from the house, where Stani and Maddie liked to pick fruit.

Stani sniffed, breaking the silence. "The air smells crisp tonight. May I join you?"

Maddie scooted over on the swing, wringing her hands and fingers, as she often did when angry. He scolded her, "As an artist, you're not doing your hands and fingers any favors. They're as vital as the strings on your violin! Be kind to your fingers."

When Maddie didn't respond, he tried again. "Doesn't the air smell like apple cider and doughnuts? Oh, I'm obsessed with American doughnuts. Those brown, chubby, coated-in-sugar delights that smack of heaven. Two doughnuts and coffee for fifteen cents? Now, that's a bargain. You'd think they'd charge more. They should be illegal, they're so delicious! Ah, well, I could talk about doughnuts all night." He lit a cigarette. "American cigarettes are so much better than the ones I used to smoke in Germany."

Stani waited, peering at Maddie to see if his talk of doughnuts had made her smile. When her expression didn't change, nor did she speak, he tried a different tactic. "Would you like to discuss anything? How about the fact that you now have the possibility of playing in Vienna in eighteen months? Mrs. Genhart mentioned that." Maddie's violin teacher at the Eastman School of Music had tutored her during the spring and summer before the university started classes, and had immediately recognized her immense talent.

Maddie's temper warmed her voice as she jumped to her feet, her body rigid. "Do you want to hear what I say, or will you try to smooth everything over? Perhaps pretend Raymond didn't just wipe away my heritage like the Nazis do? Please don't do that."

Stani attempted once more to change the subject. "Do you want to discuss…"

"I'll tell you what I want to discuss. It bothers me to give up my Jewish identity. I agree with Frederick. Why would I choose an Anglo-Saxon name? And, with the rise of Jewish hatred worldwide, I feel even stronger about it. Does Raymond think being Jewish is just a name?" She huffed. "Change the name, and you're no longer Jewish? If it were that easy, why would Nazis want to murder us?" Maddie stared into the night, pulling at a loose thread on her cable-knit sweater.

Stani fidgeted with his cigarette, knocking off the ash, then took a long drag and blew smoke rings. "It's based on rational pragmatism. As Raymond said, the Wellington name will provide cover and protection, especially while traveling in Europe. You're not giving up your Jewish identity. Remember, you're more than a name."

Maddie gave Stani a look of doubt, her eyebrow raised sharply. "I like my name as is. I'm not ashamed to be Jewish.

Are you?"

Wincing, Stani looked away from her. "Maddie, I know you don't mean that. You wouldn't intentionally try to hurt me."

Maddie sank back onto the swing and rested her head on Stani's shoulder. They sat silently until Maddie gave a sad sigh. "I didn't mean it like that. I'm just confused. I know it was the deal Raymond made, and we have no choice, but it doesn't mean I have to like it. Since Raymond adopted me, it only confirms my feeling like an orphan. I have no country, no home, no identity. I don't fit in or belong anywhere."

Stani turned to face his precious Maddie, his right hand on her cheek. He cradled her face like it was the most precious thing in the world—and to Stani, it was. Studying her expression while the fading light enrobed her and looking at her with all the tenderness he could employ, he said, "You have your life and the world before you. Fitting in is not all you think, but belonging is. Remember I said that."

Then, taking her hand in his, Stani reasoned with her, "One day, you will come to appreciate the gift of this name. The Wellington name has served this family well. We are here in this great land solely by the goodness and benevolence associated with that name. You should be grateful for it, rather than railing against it because it's not Jewish.

"Being Jewish *is* more than a name. It's who we are inside, and it's the blood that runs through our veins. That is your identity in the highest heaven and here on earth. We are part of the family of God, chosen. No one can take that from us." He lifted her hand to his lips, kissing it. "Remember I said that, too."

———❖———

The benevolence associated with the Wellington name in Washington, DC, and the US government served Raymond well—until it didn't.

While Raymond maintained a close relationship with President Roosevelt, changes were taking place within the State Department. These changes reflected an ideology Raymond disagreed with when it came to helping the Jews of Eastern Europe immigrate to the US. He couldn't continue in his current position as a matter of principle. He felt deeply about this issue of immigration for the Jews—his wife, the late Rachel Stein Wellington, had been Jewish, making his son, Buster, Jewish as well.

In January 1936, Raymond retired from full-time employment with the State Department. At the behest of President Roosevelt, he assumed a minor role in the administration, acting as an advisor to the newer legal counsel who worked with Secretary of State Cordell Hull and his undersecretary, Sumner Welles. Hull viewed Welles as an enemy, envious of the family connection between the Roosevelts and the Welles's, causing the president to rely more on Welles than Hull. A former senator from Tennessee, Hull was a lawyer and did not see the need for extra counsel. However, the president insisted on it, against the wishes of his secretary of state. President Roosevelt knew he had a trusted advisor in Raymond, who had an unrepentant love for the United States.

While in close contact with Roosevelt's administration, Raymond discovered Hull's and Welles's simmering dislike for European Jewry, especially those hoping to immigrate to the United States. Rumor had it that Hull even agreed with some of the Nazi programs. To make matters worse, Hull's undersecretary, Breckenridge Long, a former ambassador to Italy from 1933 to 1936, was an admirer of Benito Mussolini and purported to be an antisemite.

Long became the administration's key figure in establishing

refugee policy. The United States failed to update its refugee program, maintaining an antiquated one dating back to right after World War I. Long erected a maze of bureaucratic barriers that made it impossible to fill the immigration quotas, thereby blocking thousands of Jews who were fleeing the Nazis and contributing to their certain death.

Raymond's friend, Ambassador to Germany William Dodd, had direct access to the emigration figures. He knew the plight of the German Jews and had witnessed it firsthand during his tenure in Berlin. Dodd confided in Raymond, "Indeed, they'd be able to admit more, even fifteen to eighteen thousand easily." The Jewish population in the United States wanted to support Roosevelt but felt that he lacked political courage and failed to address the issue of European Jewish immigration without prejudice.

But there was little change. While Roosevelt made thinly veiled attempts to help, publicly claiming support for assisting immigrants, his actions were non-existent.

CHAPTER THREE

Hopes, Dreams, and Plans

FALL 1937, PULTNEYVILLE, NEW YORK

IN 1899, WHEN Raymond was ten, his parents visited friends in Pultneyville, a hamlet in Wayne County, New York, sixty miles west of Syracuse and twenty miles east of Rochester. Although the drive felt quite long during his childhood, the 1937 cars made quick work of the twenty-mile journey.

Pultneyville occupied a warm yet painful place in Raymond's mind and heart. Before they married in 1915, Raymond and Rachel spent summers at the town's lake. She thought of the grand possibilities they could enjoy—fabulous picnics, bonfires, swimming, fishing, and camping. Rachel reveled in the stunning Pultneyville sunsets that painted the skies with fierce reds, streaked pinks, and dusky purples. One of her favorite summer activities was kissing Raymond under the vibrant hues of a lake sunset, surrounded by a symphony of buzzing fireflies and croaking bullfrogs. He promised her that they would someday buy or build a place there.

Now Raymond rarely spoke of Rachel, who died after giving birth to Buster in August 1916, nor did he mention his parents, who drowned in a boating accident on Lake Ontario two years after Rachel passed away. Later that year, compounding his sorrow, the Wellington home in Rochester burned to the ground, destroying all the family history, photographs, and letters of communication with relatives in

Europe. Raymond's mother's oil paintings also perished in the fire, cutting him deeply.

For years after their deaths, Raymond nearly buckled at the mere mention of his parents or his wife. Grief gripped him at the slightest memory, awakening a terror that chased him like a specter during sleepless nights. Yet, looking at him, one would never surmise the extent of Raymond's broken heart. He masked his pain behind a polished exterior, carefully constructed through money, education, and culture.

After semi-retiring from the State Department, Raymond purchased a summer home in Pultneyville. Departing from the murky slime pit of Washington, DC, he sought refuge during spring, summer, and fall weekends on Lake Ontario's quiet shores.

❈

The sleepy village of Pultneyville is situated on the southern shore of Lake Ontario and frames the mouth of Salmon Creek on the town's northern border. The area is surrounded by farmland speckled with apple orchards. Stoic Eastern white pines, sugar maples, and red cedars line the lake's edge, and quaint homes and estates dot the shoreline. This welcoming and pleasant town has a strong sense of community, people know their neighbors.

Along with the residents and neighbors, the persnickety Miss Ada Berk, the town historian and librarian, welcomed the Wellington family into their community. They were happy to have a new and affluent resident like Raymond, who bought banking businessman extraordinaire Tom Black's lakefront colonial house on Lakeshore Road.

He enhanced the pine-shingled, rustic home, beginning with insulation for the chilly spring nights and autumn mornings. The renovation added two new bedrooms, totaling five luxurious and elegantly appointed rooms, plus a flagstone patio that extended to a three-car garage. With a spacious kitchen and a large dining room boasting a mahogany table for twelve, there was ample room for everyone. In the den, Raymond showcased a thoughtfully curated collection of historical fiction and non-fiction titles and a study area with a reading lamp on a Victorian-style desk. A proper parlor was available for entertaining guests and hosting formal events.

The yard in Pultneyville required new landscaping, and Maddie took the initiative to research the area's indigenous trees, plants, shrubs, and flowers. Since immigrating to the United States in 1933, she'd taken up gardening as a hobby. She pored over landscape and gardening books at the West Avenue Library, two blocks from her apartment. From her research, she formulated a proposal. She rendered a sketch while explaining her vision for the Pultneyville yard to Raymond, who agreed, voicing confidence in her designs, but recommended that she meet with Miss Berk for more insight into the indigenous shrubs and trees.

On a Tuesday, Maddie was off from school for fall break. Having scheduled an appointment with Miss Berk at the library, she borrowed one of Raymond's cars and drove to the lakeside village for their meeting.

Miss Berk welcomed Maddie into her office. Books lined the walls, reminding Maddie of Raymond's study. She ran her fingers over the leatherbound spines of hundreds of literary works. Marveling at the colors and sizes, she spotted a red leather, thumb-sized version of the *Psalms and Proverbs*. Nothing was out of place, even Miss Berk's pencils.

"Age teaches you things," quipped Miss Berk after Maddie commented on the order of the office.

Two Victorian-style sitting chairs faced each other, with a marble-top parlor table between them, pre-set with a silver tea set, two porcelain cups and saucers, two silver spoons, and embroidered linen napkins. Miss Berk scurried to the table, pouring tea. "Milk or sugar?"

"Both, please."

Miss Berk beckoned to Maddie. "Be seated, dear. Now. How can I help?" She glanced at Maddie over the top of her wire-rimmed glasses. The lines on her face showed years of care, and her intense, cornflower-blue eyes searched Maddie's face.

"Well, this certainly isn't the most exciting of topics, but I'm curious about the weather patterns of Wayne County, and how they influence planting flowers, shrubs, and trees."

Miss Berk clapped. "You've come to the right place! We get strong winds off the lake in early spring and winter. In spring, we call it 'pruning time' because the wind shakes loose debris, small branches, and such from the leafy trees, which is how God prunes them. Fall is the only time to plant bulbs, flowering trees, and regular trees and shrubs. They must store enough energy during winter to bloom in spring and summer. Here's a list of indigenous trees and shrubs that grow beautifully in our region."

She handed Maddie a typed list. Looking it over, Maddie commented, "I find it fascinating that some things grow well here, while others don't."

"God knows what He's doing with the earth, doesn't He?"

Maddie considered the statement, unsure of its meaning. She took long to respond, earning disapproval from Miss Berk.

Her stern voice prodded Maddie. "Well, He does, right? God knows what He's doing!"

Maddie squirmed. "Uh, I guess so. I can't say I know if He

does or doesn't." *Why is she asking me about God?*

The tea ended at once.

Following Miss Ada Berk's directives, Stani, Frederick, Wolfie, and Buster pitched in on a few weekends during the cooler fall months, working with Maddie on the landscaping. She directed the placement of shrubs and trees. They planted lush, deep green arborvitaes along one edge of the expansive lawn. The trees shielded the patio and backyard from the winds Miss Berk described as "the northeastern winds of spring and winter."

Through the fall, they planted a plethora of bulbs, spinning the color palette to include all colors of tulips; paper-white Narcissus; lilies of the valley; yellow to almost sunset-orange daffodils; yellow, violet, and dark-purple irises; flowering pink crabapples; oak leaf hydrangeas, lavender and fuchsia lilacs; magenta peonies; and four varieties of sweetheart roses.

All the trees benefited from "winter clothing," as Maddie called it. They wrapped each young tree and shrub with burlap, some at their base, some around the circumference, to protect them from the extremes of winter. Stoic old trees that had braved many a frigid and bitter season stood in the yard: a willow in front, two stately white pines sentries at the driveway's edge, and four sugar maples in the back, front, and both sides of the house. They provided shade in the summer and a little cover in the winter, breaking up straight-line winds.

The house in Pultneyville was where the Wellingtons gathered for special occasions during the spring, summer, and fall weekends. The fall brought on a spell of melancholy for Raymond, and with every passing season, he lamented how it seemed like the family only gathered together on holidays. He became known for saying, "The older you get, the faster time goes. It is fleeting."

After Thanksgiving, when winter arrived with its blustery winds, ice, and snow, Raymond closed up the house. The days were shorter, and nights came quicker in the north. Homes on the lake left their dock lights on at night year-round, and the docks closed until the first signs of spring revealed themselves. Until then, the lake and all its inhabitants prepared for the cold. Not yet frozen, the lake lapped at the shore, slapping at the rocks. Birds chirped to herald the day, squirrels scrambled up trees, and crows called distantly to one another. During the colder months, the dock lights glowed eerily, reflecting a temperature change that came without warning, as fast as a switch being flipped. A fog resided over the lake.

Tradition and the *Farmer's Almanac* stated that spring formally began at the end of March or the beginning of April, or, as Miss Ada Berk believed, "the sign of the first robin," which could appear as soon as the first week of March. No one had the fortitude to argue with Miss Berk about when spring began. She claimed, "Robins know better. After all, God's creatures are the best communicators of such things."

During fishing season, which started the first Saturday of April, everyone in Pultneyville focused on the lake and the enjoyment of lake-style living. Raymond, Frederick, and Wolfie had a blast catching salmon, bigeye chubs, and smallmouth bass. Stani never hid his delight when one of the boys brought him a fresh catch. "While you love catching fish, I love cooking them!"

On a late summer Sunday afternoon, Stani stood at the side of the dock, listening to his young German friend, who tried his patience. Wolfie told Stani that he passed Buster and Maddie on the way to the dock, overhearing them talking about taking the boat out for a last spin before nightfall. In a high-pitched voice, he mocked them, "'It is a beautiful time of day. The sun takes its time to go down. It's so romantic.'"

Wolfie rolled his eyes. "I'm so sick of those two. They ignore me, like I don't exist. Do they think they're the only ones that like to take the boat out at sunset?" Wolfie picked up a rock on the dock to skip across the water. It didn't skip. Instead, it sank. "Well, that sums it up! I wish I could go off with Maddie on the boat. She's my friend, too."

Stani lit a Marlboro. "And, of course, all you're interested in is friendship, right?"

Wolfie huffed, "You're no help," and turned on his heel to walk away, but Stani grabbed him by his shirt sleeve.

"Hey, what's with the temper?"

Wolfie trudged back and sat down, dangling his feet over the side of the dock. "The water looks cloudy today. It must be the algae. Or that's what Miss Ada Berk says."

Both men chuckled, and Wolfie said, "Honestly, after we first met, I thought there might be a future for Maddie and me. Buster's so slow to move or make a decision. Maddie and I've been good friends now for years. And there's always been a spark between us."

Wolfie picked at a rotted piece of wood on the dock as Stani pressed him, "Come on, out with it. Tell me what's on your mind."

"Okay, okay. I'm in love with her! There. I said it. I hoped our friendship could grow into something more, more... meaningful. But Buster has ensured that won't happen. And now I rarely get to see her." He lit a cigarette. "You know, being European, we understand each other. Sometimes, I stop by the library on campus on the chance I'll get to see her without Buster hovering over us."

Stani frowned with disapproval, tapped Wolfie lightly on his back, and asked, sparse on condemnation, "Who met her first?"

—❖—

Buster and Maddie explored the lake's hidden inlets and deeper waters by motorboat. She loved observing Buster steering the boat with confidence and contentment, kneeling on the captain's chair and holding the throttle with one hand as they rendezvoused at sunset, their favorite time of day to be on the lake.

As the setting sun splashed orange and red across the almost cloudless expanse, Buster mused, "Would you look at that sunset? It's like the daytime is protesting its end, hoping to burn, if just to fend off the darkness."

"Wow. You're feeling poetic tonight. You seem so content. Are you?"

He shot her a warm smile. His teeth were so white and perfectly shaped. Maddie thought he had the most beautiful teeth and smile in the world.

"I'm content when you're by my side. But I'll be more so if you come here and kiss me."

Maddie came in close for a neck nuzzle and covered Buster's neck and face with small, soft kisses, then deeper ones. She slid onto his lap. With a mischievous grin, Buster told Maddie in German, "Yes, ma'am, mmm. More, please."

Maddie blushed in the glow of the setting sun. "What's happened to you?"

He flashed a coy smile. "You happened to me, that's what."

They reveled in their intimate moments of pleasure away from Wolfie and Raymond. Under a glorious sky, redolent with red, pink, and purple, their skin caressed by the lingering warmth of the day, captured in the waning dusk, the world's cares melted away. Nothing mattered but the moment they shared as the engine purred and the boat cut across the serene lake.

——❋——

Later that evening, Buster insisted on speaking about the future while they lay together on a flannel blanket under a sweeping star-filled sky. Maddie commented, "The stars seem so close, you could reach up and grab one." Buster pointed out various star formations and constellations and shared how the Boy Scouts taught him about astronomy.

He pointed out Orion's Belt and Taurus the Bull. "How different the skies look from when I first experienced the Hungarian skies in 1933. I've learned so much more about astronomy since then."

"I never noticed the skies as much as I do now because of you." She leaned over to plant a kiss on his cheek.

Buster pointed upward. "See that? That's the Big Dipper, and if you tilt your head this way, you'll see the Little Dipper."

Maddie sighed with contentment. "You amaze me. You know a little bit about everything. You're brilliant, and I love you for it." She planted a big kiss on Buster's lips, and the two snuggle together as the evening chill descended. The sounds and vibrations of the lake hovered around them, and the wind carried the song.

Buster leaned in and kissed her, hoping to communicate his love for her through his kiss. He gazed at Maddie, admiring her beauty, delicate features, prominent cheekbones, and deep-set cobalt eyes.

Pushing a lock of her silken hair back from her face, he said, "My love, I'm dreaming of our life together here in the States, one that I think will prove better than anywhere else."

She kissed his lips, pressing into his to stop him from

speaking. She'd told him multiple times, "One step at a time. Please, let's not rush."

He always countered, "I feel like our relationship is more like a geological study, one of slow-forming pressure and time."

Around midnight, Maddie drifted into the kitchen after everyone except Stani had gone to bed. Sitting at the kitchen table with a cup of coffee, he offered her some. Maddie shook her head. "Won't that keep you up?"

Stani smiled, then became serious. "The only thing that keeps me up at night is worrying about you and your choices, decisions, or lack of them."

Leaning against the kitchen counter, her hair pulled back in a soft knot, Maddie blurted, "Okay, here's a choice or a decision. I don't know if I'm in love with Buster. I just don't know. I'm conflicted." She hesitated, and then added, her tone spiked with defensiveness, "I'm not ready to settle down in a small town and have a bunch of kids and a boring married life."

Stani tilted his head and peered at her, like he so often did. "Do you think it's that, or are you afraid of commitment? Or perhaps you love Wolfie?" He said this half-smiling, more to goad Maddie than meaning it seriously.

Then he posed a solemn question, "What about the nightmares? Do they still trouble you?"

Maddie whipped around and put her hands on the table, her face inches from Stani's. "Very funny about Wolfie. He has a crush on me, so what? I think it's sweet. I know my mind! And I'm sick of everyone asking me about marriage!" She marched out of the kitchen, leaving Stani wondering what happened.

Yet, no more than a week later, Buster pushed the issue

even further, asking his dad, Raymond, for Maddie's hand, seeing he was her legally adopted father. Raymond suggested Buster not rush, and to give Maddie time.

As Buster's anxiousness grew, the unspoken pressure caused Maddie to withdraw. Twice in one week, when he asked her for a date, she replied, "No, not tonight, Buster. I must focus on my violin as I have an exam soon."

Maddie suggested they finish their respective educations before deepening their relationship, marriage being the next step. Buster agreed, but less than wholeheartedly, knowing demands would push Maddie away. He brooded in silence; her rejection triggered a reaction, and Buster made a rash decision. *I'll join the Army now and serve my time. I don't need anyone's permission. But do I need to worry about Wolfie swooping in during my absence?*

Maddie asked herself, *Is Stani right, as usual? Do I have a problem with commitment, or is it more? Is it my past, at the orphanage? I haven't thought about that for so long. Will the nightmares continue to hold me prisoner? Ugh, the dreaded nightmares. If I remember them one more time, fully acknowledge what happened, feel the pain, and press into it, will it heal me? Stani says Yeshua wants to heal me of my broken places. But he says it takes faith to believe. And I don't even know where to begin with that. I don't even know if I believe in God.*

As Stani prepared the vegetables for soup, Buster meandered into the kitchen and stole a carrot off the table. Lost in thoughts and visions of Maddie, his full-time obsession, Buster munched on the carrot and posed a question, asking Stani why Maddie wouldn't commit.

Stani chuckled when Buster asked, "How can Maddie be at once hot and cold?"

Stani said, "Buster, you have much to learn about women."

He pointed out the window to two brothers playing soccer in the street. "Reminds me of when we all first arrived. You and Wolfie would do the same thing." He sighed.

"Yeah, so what's your point? What does that have to do with Maddie?"

Stani shook his head. "It doesn't. But look, whatever you do, don't chase her. Maddie knows her mind and will tell you when the time is right. You must trust that. What else can you do but trust?"

Stani scooped the vegetables into a bowl and set it to the side of the stove. He poured oil into a pan, turned up the heat, and added the vegetables when the oil was hot. They sizzled, and steam and aroma rose from the pot.

Buster swiped another carrot off the table, dropping his head in resignation. "Well, yes, I'd have to agree. Trust plays a big role, and I need to work on that. But what if Wolfie swoops in? How can I even compete with Wolfie? He's confident and good-looking and shares a European background with her. And if that's not enough to add to my worry, Dad is getting closer to him, too. It's like I don't exist!"

Dejected, Buster sat at the kitchen table, one arm on his leg and a fist under his chin, posing like Rodin's *The Thinker*.

"You know Dad favors him. Don't tell me you don't see it," Buster told Stani. "He's always talking about 'Wolfie this, and Wolfie that, and he's this and that.' It turns my stomach! Not only do I have to compete with him for my father, but also my girl. Where do you stand?"

As Stani went about his business of soup-making in silence, Buster grabbed a cigarette from the pack on the kitchen table. "These yours? I'm taking one." He lit it, breathing a sigh of relief. "Good thing I don't drink in excess. I'd be hammered all the time if so. I walk around bunched up in knots, angry because of Wolfie and his not-so-subtle encroachment on everything mine. Remember how close we were when we first met in Vienna? I would have given my life for Wolfie."

———❖———

Meanwhile, Raymond remained unaware that his son was wounded by such praise for Wolfie. One day, Buster overheard his father talking with Frederick about Wolfie. As he listened, his face burned red with anger.

"With his can-do spirit, fearless attitude, and innate sense of leadership...Wolfie's raw and a risk taker, but he'll fall in line with training."

Frederick chuckled, "As if I don't know my son? Thank you for sharing your praise of him. So, what have you done about plans for Buster?"

Raymond hesitated, lowering his chin to his chest. "Uh, well, nothing. Not yet."

Frederick blew Raymond a sarcastic kiss and quipped, pointing to his watch, "Time is wasting!"

CHAPTER FOUR

The Nightmares

SPRING 1924, THE ORPHANAGE IN BARANOVICHI, POLAND

MADDIE TURETSKY'S BIRTH name was Matryona Nadia Turetsky. Although her first name meant *diminutive*, the Polish-British headmaster of the orphanage changed it to *Maddie*, hoping the simplified name would help her be adopted more quickly by a childless European couple.

But that didn't happen. No one wanted a six-year-old girl who, despite her size, revealed herself as a spitfire ready to fight anyone who came too close. For six weeks after her arrival at the Baranovichi Children's Home, she remained silent during meals, chores, prayer time, and wash-up. She didn't engage in conversation or complain about anything until a ten-year-old boy named Mikhail, who only spoke Russian and not Polish like the other children, arrived from a border town close to Russia. Hearing the boy speak Russian jarred Maddie's memory.

Maddie recalled the Russian words she'd learned, possibly from her mother or the woman who brought her to the orphanage. Baranovichi had a history of occupation by Russia and, at other times, Germany. She observed the other children teasing Mikhail, making gestures to provoke his response. Maddie intervened, sitting beside him as the other children formed a circle around them. She greeted him in Russian, saying, "Privet, kak dela?" which translates to,

"Hello, how are you?"

The boy's face brightened upon hearing his language, yet he eyed her suspiciously. The other orphans closed the circle around him and Maddie, and he got up, pushed past the others, and bolted from the room. He ran down the hall to the dimly lit cavernous chamber where the children slept, then threw himself on his cot and began to cry.

Maddie followed him. She walked up to his cot and sat on the edge. He turned around and blushed, tears staining his cheeks, then asked earnestly if Maddie spoke Russian. She nodded and said, "nemnogo," which means "a little." His face relaxed, and he smiled, extending his hand and asking if she'd be his friend. "Ty budesh' moim drugom?"

She smiled back. "Da." They shook hands, forming a bond.

Over the next two years, a nun from a Catholic church in Poland, originally a missionary from the United States, came to the orphanage three times a week to teach English. The orphans learned to read, write, and speak rudimentary English. Maddie had an evident competency in languages. She took to the English language like a fish to water and loved writing notes and slipping them to Mikhail when no one was looking. He asked about her past, but she refused to speak of it. "Don't ask me about it. I have no answers."

Mikhail and Maddie were inseparable. She protected him fiercely, even though he was four years older. When other children attempted to pick on him, calling him "soft-brain" and "stupid," or if the older boys wanted to fight him, she'd step in front of Mikhail and dare them to hit her instead of him, and they wouldn't. They knew she wasn't afraid to threaten them with slitting their wrists in the middle of the night or poisoning their food. But over time, once Mikhail turned thirteen, and Maddie was nine, the headmaster separated them and wouldn't allow Maddie to be alone with Mikhail, and she couldn't understand why.

One day, Maddie and Mikhail's group were assigned to pick weeds on the grounds. Mikhail edged his way toward Maddie and asked her about her background. "Why won't you tell me how you got here? What's your story?" He focused on the earth beneath his body and dug with his hands to get to the root.

"Hey, what's wrong? Why won't you talk?"

Maddie didn't answer.

He shrugged. "I grew up in orphanages. My mother left the only thing I have: this." He reached a dirt-stained hand into the collar of his shirt and retrieved a silver necklace with a Star of David on it. "I guess this means I'm Jewish."

Maddie reached to hold the Star and inspected it. Her eyes narrowed. "You're lucky no one stole it from you, especially as a baby."

Mikhail laughed. "You have a criminal mind, the way you think."

Maddie said softly, "No, it's how I stay alive." Even with Mikhail, she was cautious about revealing anything about herself. The enigmatic nature of her past was as confounding to her as it was to strangers.

One winter day, the state pulled a surprise visit to the orphanage. Maddie and Mikhail were on high alert, using one of their hiding places chosen especially to spy on the headmaster. They hid behind the wall divider that separated the parlor from the dining room. From their vantage point, they saw the state inspector sit at the dining room table and hand the report to the headmaster.

The other children took their afternoon naps while Maddie and Mikhail heard every detail and accusation about the headmaster's diabolical workings, a front for all kinds of felonious activity. The state inspector detailed the headmaster's scheme: He told the state he paid money to the nun for her to teach English and expected reimbursement. But the nun charged no money. The receipts were fake.

Nothing came of the inspector's findings. There were no changes.

When Maddie turned ten, the food rations dwindled, and a frightening number of children suffered from malnutrition; some of their bellies extended from the buildup of gases within their little bodies. That's when Maddie began planning an escape for her and Mikhail. She called it Plan A.

In the pantries of local townspeople, the inspector found state supplies and foodstuffs designated to feed the children. The items were being sold out the orphanage's back door. Twice weekly, townspeople lined up from 5:00 a.m. to 7:00 a.m., bringing cash, silver, or sometimes gold jewelry to trade for rationed food. After observing this practice, the inspector insisted on a cut of the money the headmaster took in.

Maddie had a knack for being at the right place and time when it came to discovering the dastardly secrets of the orphanage. One day, while snooping around the headmaster's desk, Maddie discovered that the drinking water was in short supply, falling below the state minimum requirement. At most, each child received only a few milliliters daily. When the state tested the water, the findings indicated that it was tainted. Then, the headmaster's secret black market adoption ring was exposed by a state inspector, who confronted him. Maddie overheard the exchange, hearing there were many buyers in Berlin, an epicenter of black-market activity. Inexplicably, the state did nothing to correct these significant issues. The inspectors were in on the take, too.

That's when Maddie began formulating a plan B, in case plan A failed. Her ten-year-old mind churned out ideas, adding details until she felt it was complete. *Both plans are ready to deploy at a moment's notice. Now, to get Mikhail on board.*

After their reading lesson, she scribbled a note to hand him at prayer time. His expression curious, he asked, "Why are you looking so serious?"

Maddie shook her head and turned, holding the note against her side. Inconspicuously, she passed the note off to him, then walked away. Unbeknownst to her, he dropped it, and another boy, Ernst, picked it up.

Ernst slid the note into his pocket, then held a fist to Mikhail's face. "C'mon, Ruski, are you afraid to fight now that your girlfriend can't protect you?"

Ernst was three inches taller and twenty pounds heavier, Mikhail glared at Ernst. "You have no idea what I'm capable of. You had better back off."

Ernst turned to walk away, then spun and caught Mikhail square in the jaw with a right hook, delivering an uppercut with his left. Mikhail stumbled back, and a group of boys held him while Ernst beat him unconscious. He spat on him. Then, bending over his limp body, Ernst felt inside the neck of Mikhail's shirt. "I know he wears it."

Ernst retrieved what he sought: a silver Star of David on a chain. He ripped it from Mikhail's neck, breaking the chain.

Standing, Ernst clenched the chain and Star of David in his hand and proclaimed, "He's a Jew—a Ruski Jew, even worse. I bet his girlfriend is too. You know how those Jews stick together like rats." And the five boys all spat on Mikhail's unconscious body.

Ernst took charge, ordering the boys, "Put him in the back

room behind the shoe racks." The boys did as he said while Ernst retrieved the note to read it. *M, meet me in the cellar after prayer time before the evening meal. —M*

Behind the two-story brick orphanage, shrubs lined the fence surrounding the property. On one side of the building were stairs to a seldom-used root cellar. It was there that Maddie and Mikhail rendezvoused and talked. Maddie always went first and waited for Mikhail, leaving the door slightly ajar. The orphanage was so poorly run that the children would escape if it weren't for the nine-foot-tall chain-link fence topped with razor-sharp barbed wire. The only way to escape was out the front door. That was where Maddie's plan A began and ended.

Maddie heard footsteps coming down the stairs, and the light from the late-afternoon sun shone in, silhouetting the bulky figure of Ernst Braun, a fifteen-year-old boy built more like a man. Later, she recalled nothing except the pain he caused.

Her nightmares started after Braun's attack. The terror-filled dreams led to frantic nighttime screams.

Two days later, Maddie decided it was time to enact plan A.

CHAPTER FIVE

Reminders

*APRIL 1939, DACHAU CONCENTRATION
CAMP, DACHAU, GERMANY*

WHAT'S IT LIKE being Jewish in Germany?"
"It's something you're reminded of every minute of every day."

In the spring of 1938, Stefan Soutine, a twenty-two-year-old Frenchman whose mother was a German Jew, was the chef de cuisine at Café Moritz in Paris. One night in December of 1938, after dining at Café Moritz, the German officer Dietrich von Dorsten and his wife Huberta convinced Stefan to come to work for them, promising three times his salary. Stefan thought, *They are Nazis. How can I do this?* Pragmatic thinking won out. *It will allow me to save money. Money can buy freedom. And food.*

In March 1939, the von Dorsten family asked Stefan to move to Munich. Since saving money was his priority, he agreed to relocate with the family. Stefan visited a local beer hall on a night off to relax and unwind. After his beer and supper, he sat at a table, writing some cooking ideas on a paper napkin. At the same time, a commotion outside spiked his attention. Soon, the beer hall emptied, and Stefan followed.

Brownshirts—Nazi troublemakers—clubbed anyone who looked the least bit Jewish, bearing down on a peaceful protest and gathering of Jewish men who were protesting the

Nuremberg Laws.

"Arrest them all," was the battle cry of the Brownshirts. Almost every man on the street near the square was arrested, some bloodied, all bruised. Stefan found himself in the wrong place at the wrong time. A Brownshirt screamed in Stefan's ear, "Juden dreck"—Jewish garbage—while pushing Stefan toward the truck where protesters were held.

Stefan pleaded in German, to no avail. "Please, check with Major von Dorsten. I'm his chef. He will vouch for me!"

Stefan and two hundred other men were sent to Dachau that fateful night.

———❋———

After three weeks of little to no food, a drafty barracks with wooden bunks for sleeping, and manual labor for eighteen hours a day, Stefan began to lose hope, horrified by the treatment of Jewish prisoners. He watched a guard circumcise prisoners with an eighteenth-century warrior sword, just one of the many cruel and unusual punishments. *How am I going to survive this?*

One day, a month later, a kapo in charge of prisoner counts asked every man about his trade before Dachau. When the kapo came to question Stefan, he answered simply, "A cook."

He didn't dare call himself a chef, fearing the kapo would take offense, assuming Stefan thought himself better than the other prisoners. One thing was sure at Dachau: you didn't give the kapos or guards a reason to beat you. They didn't need a reason. Some enjoyed abusing prisoners. It took a certain kind of personality to enjoy performing such acts. Kapos at Dachau could be described as some of the cruelest, misanthropic types. They were prisoners, non-Jews, who gained the trust of the guards serving at Dachau.

The kapos' job was to monitor the prisoners and line

them up for day and evening counts. They did the dirty work of beating prisoners and took part in the cruelest torture of Jewish men. The most significant offense common to all men was the lack of food. What they called food insulted Stefan's sensibilities.

Stefan became a chef in part to ensure he'd never go hungry, as he did where he grew up, in an orphanage. Here, he was hungry again, cold and weary. Stefan lost count in that first month of how many days the prisoners went without food. Not even a scrap of bread. His beatings were less severe than those of the other prisoners because the guards assumed he was German due to his perfect dialect. While this treatment troubled Stefan, there wasn't a thing he could do about it. *It is an unjust world here, and the weaker pay the price in a concentration camp.*

Manual labor took up almost every minute of sunlight and waking hour. Rock carrying was a detail assigned to newer prisoners. Prisoners who still had strength or youth. One day, while carrying rocks, Stefan battled the tormenting hunger harder than ever. All he could think about was food. Some prisoners cried over the lack, and the kapos beat them for it. Stefan wouldn't give in to tears, at least for now. The weather was pleasant; the winds blew a crosswind, cooling the men as they labored under a persistent sun that sat above the low-hanging, puffy clouds.

Another prisoner told Stefan, "Be happy you're not here in the winter, when the vilest practices occur."

Stefan smirked at the man. "Who says I won't be here in winter? How can it be worse than I've already witnessed?"

"You have no idea."

The two men dropped the rocks at the ravine's edge and walked back for more. Stefan glanced around the area. "Look, the guard. He's gone. Tell me."

The man eyed the general vicinity, fearful of being called out. His eyes darted side to side. In a low, gravelly voice, he said, "Okay. Well, in the winter, when the temperature drops way below freezing, and your breath comes in short gasps because of the cold, if you fall asleep or fall to the ground during the day or night counting, the guards will strip you of your clothing, then string you up with chains by your wrists between two metal poles. Then comes the fun for them."

He checked the area to make sure no one was listening in, then continued. "They turn on a firehose full blast, soaking the naked offender over and over until the man becomes encased in ice. The guards leave him up until he's dead. It doesn't take long. They suffocate. They'll choose a weak and infirm prisoner to try and transport the body to the pit. It's a game they play, placing bets. The weight of the dead man encased in ice is too much for even a strong man to carry. The prisoner falls, crushed and killed by the weight of the ice-man. More amusement for the guards. They place bets for various challenges."

He stopped, peered over his shoulder, then continued. "For example, they win money or cigarettes for whoever guesses how long it will take before the man under the body dies. They'll leave both men on the ground until the carrier is dead. Then they'll pry the dead men apart, hang up the ice-man again, respray him to refreeze the broken ice, and then choose another prisoner for the task only to obtain the same result—those sick bastards. May they split the gates of hell wide open when they die." The prisoner snorted, then spat on the ground to underscore his hatred.

One day, the kapo again asked the prisoners to name their

trade. He reported their answers to the attending guard and then the officer.

Stefan and three other men who claimed to be cooks were taken to the showers and instructed to wash with lye soap to disinfect themselves. Each was given a clean prison uniform, the kind with stripes. Then they were marched to the annex, the private compound of the camp commandant, Theodor Eicke.

Stefan's eyes grew large at the sight behind the barbed-wire fence and twelve-foot-high brick walls. Meticulously maintained gardens and lawns surrounded the stately brick, two-story home that housed the camp's commandant and his family.

It's like another world behind the fence. No, it IS another world.

Stefan followed the kapo, afraid he'd be reprimanded for stopping to admire the property. Once inside the house, they came to a white-walled, spacious, windowed kitchen. Stefan marveled at how fresh and clean everything looked and smelled.

A six-burner gas stove with twin ovens sat against the back wall, and small white tiles lined the wall behind it. Four stations, complete with a fork, bowls, and a skillet, were set up for the men to cook. No knives were present anywhere in the kitchen.

The men were all given the same ingredients—veal, flour, egg, breadcrumbs, salt, pepper, and oil—necessary to make wiener schnitzel. The camp officer who attended them said, "Whoever makes the best schnitzel will have a special assignment."

The men submitted their versions one by one. Behind a swinging door were Commandant Eicke, his wife, Bertie, and their fourteen-year-old daughter, Irma: the judges of the contest.

They tried the first three submissions with few comments. Stefan, who cooked last, made his Schnitzel golden brown and puffy as a classic Schnitzel should look. When Eicke tried it, he exclaimed, "Yes! This one knows what he's doing. See how thinly he pounded the veal, unlike the other three."

Irma peeked around the door, viewing Stefan while he stood tall and at attention. "Daddy, please pick the handsome one. Not only can he cook, but he's easy on the eyes, even with a shaved head."

Bertie agreed. His wife and daughter persuaded the commandant to choose Stefan. He would have selected him, regardless.

After an interview with Eicke and a phone call to Major von Dorsten, it was decided that Stefan Soutine would be the commandant's family chef. Commandant von Dorsten agreed to release Stefan to cook for Eicke only because von Dorsten had been assigned to a post in Vienna and did not require a cook at the new location, as an entire staff was already in place.

"Lucky you," says Eicke, "I'd take a post in Vienna in a second."

Commandant von Dorsten questioned Eicke, "Why don't you release him? He was arrested without cause." As a major, it was within his command to offer advice as he saw fit.

Eicke assured the major, "I will in time. A transfer is in the works for me."

"Ah, yes, I heard about that. Best of luck. Auf wiedersehen. Heil Hitler."

Eicke hung up the phone. "Damn it." He pulled at a hangnail until it bled. "Damn it." He wrapped his handkerchief around his index finger and dialed with his other finger, calling his wife with the news. "We have him for a time, at least until my next assignment. We might as well enjoy his talents." He withheld the evidence that Stefan should be a free man.

Stefan would still sleep in the camp compound at night, but spend his waking hours cooking and baking at the Eicke's home. He would no longer work in the rock pits or dig new roads.

Bertie Eicke was in charge of picking menus and pinning the assignments to a board in the kitchen. She decided on French and German recipes, aiming to exploit her new chef's skills. Bertie ordered the ingredients and had them in the kitchen every morning at 7:00 a.m., before Stefan began work at 7:15.

Stefan's food tantalized and tormented him, and the aroma alone deepened his already bottomless hunger pangs. He was forbidden to eat the food he cooked or the delicacies he baked, and the smell of apple strudel, chocolate eclairs, buttery croissants, stout rye bread, perfectly seasoned and broiled meat, and roasted chicken with potatoes and carrots came close to driving him mad.

During Stefan's duty, there was always a kapo in the kitchen, to ensure Stefan didn't eat or abscond with any food. The kapo warned him, "Eyes are everywhere, and if we catch you eating, you'll lose your tongue. We will cut off one of your hands if caught a second time." The kapo demonstrated just where the amputation above the wrist would occur.

Stefan shuddered at the thought. But the kapo was in the same situation as Stefan, not permitted to enjoy the fruits of his charge's labor. After two weeks on the job, the kapo requested that the guard speak to the officer in charge to inquire if he would transfer him to another assignment, telling the guard, "The smell of the food is causing madness in me; I can't take it anymore. It's too much." The guard showed no sympathy, and the kapo came to resent Stefan as the perpetrator of his insanity.

On a Monday, with a predictable sour mood, the kapo begged Stefan for just a tiny taste of the chocolate he used to make a cake. Feeling sorry for the man, Stefan dropped a small piece of the dark, shiny chocolate by the man's shoe.

The kapo moved his foot, covering the chocolate. He bent down like he meant to tie his shoe and extracted the tiny taste of heaven. His eyes flitted back and forth as he pretended to cough while he slipped the thimble-sized chocolate into his mouth.

The kapo smiled for the first time since Stefan had come to the compound. His eyes rolled in reaction to the silky feel of the chocolate melting on his tongue, and his body trembled from the blissfulness of the taste. From then on, he was less aggressive toward Stefan.

During the later days of spring, Stefan tended to Bertie's herb garden before entering the kitchen for work, coaxing the herbs to grow fuller for his cooking. He spoke to the herbs in French with love: "Bonjour, mi petite ciboulettes, tout de suite!"

Stefan picked some parsley and thyme and headed toward the house. That's when he spotted a small, black diary with a swastika stamped in gold and the initials *JG* on the cover, to the left of the kitchen steps. It looked like a pocket diary but smaller, with a pad. Thumbing through it quickly, he saw many words scribbled on it, including the name "Operation Sunshine."

He glanced around the grounds and at the house's windows, hoping no one was watching him. The coast was clear, so he picked up the diary and shoved it into his pants.

That's when Stefan detected the unmistakable scent of gas.

CHAPTER SIX

Life + Hollenius in a New World

FALL 1937, ROCHESTER, NEW YORK

ON A BRISK, late-October day in 1937, Wolfie strolled into Raymond's office at the house, after Raymond's request to "sit down and chat for a moment."

After taking summer school classes for credit, Wolfie had one semester left before he graduated in January. He gazed at the rows of books before him, taking his time to peruse the vast array while Raymond finished a phone call. The book-lined walls of Raymond's office provided a stunning insight into his intellectual acuity. He'd read almost every book in his possession. Raymond even created an inventory list to loan out books to family and friends, hoping to increase their knowledge and encourage them to read for pleasure.

Raymond finished his phone call, then extended his hand to Wolfie, greeting him warmly. "Please, have a seat."

Wolfie settled into the leather club chair that faced Raymond's mahogany desk. Behind the desk was a picture window with a panoramic view of the meticulous gardens and yard. The leaves on the maple, chestnut, hickory, and oak trees were past their autumnal peak, but still colorful. "Would you mind if I smoke?"

"Be my guest. Need a light?" Raymond offered Wolfie the

silver lighter on his desk, a gift from the former ambassador to Germany, William Dodd. Nodding, Wolfie reached into his shirt pocket and extracted a cigarette from the pack.

After a moment of silence to collect himself, Raymond began. "The time has come to start thinking about your future and the direction you see for yourself. I've given it some thought and would like to discuss this with you if you're open to it."

With his usual easygoing, casual nature—some would call it nonchalance—Wolfie smiled. "Say on, Counselor." He slouched back in the chair, draping a long, lean leg over the arm, then took a drag off his smoke.

"With your intellectual understanding and steady nature, you'd do well in service of our country. You've mentioned your desire to serve and repay the United States out of gratitude. I have great respect for your aspirations. Serving would satisfy that desire. We are not at war now, so getting in early before a conscripted draft would seem appealing. Officers have a good life and receive solid treatment as long as they obey orders and keep their noses clean. Knowing the right people helps, too. What say you?"

Wolfie took a puff and exhaled. Sitting up straight, he placed his elbows on his thighs so his hands supported his chin, and made direct eye contact with Raymond. "To be honest, I've thought of that myself. But not as a foot soldier. I have no interest." Wolfie weighed his words. "Espionage and counterintelligence work is something I can see myself doing." He sat back and concentrated on his adopted father's face, unsure of his reaction.

Raymond's lips pursed and brow wrinkled, and then a broad grin stretched across his face. He smiled at Wolfie. "That's right. You wrote a piece for the *Times Union* on the Dreyfus

Affair! You spoke of intrigue, treason, international espionage, and the failed efforts of the French at counterintelligence. You've read Sherlock Holmes, for God's sake! Of course, you'd be interested in this line of work." Raymond stood behind his desk with his hands on his hips, shaking his head.

"Here I was thinking more like a pilot or something that has to do with engines or speed. Look at you, and you've already thought this through. Impressive." Raymond walked to the front of the desk, resting against it. He focused his eyes on Wolfie's; they were as blue as ever, clear, crystal blue. His blond hair. His classic German features.

"You need an aptitude and passion to excel in this line of work. Greatness requires both. As you might imagine, on the world stage, espionage and counterintelligence play a significant role in the strategy and the setting of policies within countries and nations. With your blond hair and blue eyes, you are the image of what Hitler worships: an Aryan. You could fit well into a counterintelligence program with the proper temperament and training. There are tests for that. And you don't need a war to do your job. How many languages do you speak, four?"

Wolfie shook his head. "That would be Buster. I speak two."

Raymond ran a hand through his thick, graying hair, then snapped his fingers. "I've got it. I know the perfect place for you. Wait, though. Allow me to research before I reveal the idea."

Wolfie jumped to his feet in protest. "No way. You have to tell me now. You can't bait me like that!"

"Bait you, like what?" said a third voice.

Neither man had noticed Buster slipping inside the office.

Buster leaned against the wood-paneled wall with his suit coat open, exuding his meticulous brand of understated elegance. He addressed Wolfie, his tone neutral. "Who's baiting who here?"

Wolfie side-eyed Buster. "No need to get agitated, Four." When he wanted to get under his adopted brother's skin, he called Buster "Four" after the Roman numerals at the end of his last name: Wellington IV. "Your dad and I were discussing my future after college, just like you do with him..." his voice trailed off.

With a snide smile, looking down at the floor, Buster drawled, "Now, why would you think that? Just because he has a conversation with you, you assume he must have already had the same one with me. Well, here's the scoop. We haven't had any such talk, have we, Dad? We have deep talks so often, don't we?"

"Now, son. You find problems with everyone but yourself."

Buster jammed his hands in his trouser pockets. "That's where you're wrong. You don't hear the conversations I have with myself. But it's okay. I know I'm always the problem. You can blame yourself for everything if you think about it long enough."

Conflict hung over the three men like a thick vapor. No one made eye contact. The ticking of the mantel clock was the only sound.

Buster broke the silence. "Supper's ready. Stani sent me to tell you."

Raymond heard the familiar sound of the screen door opening and slamming shut.

"Is anybody home?" Frederick peeked around the office door. He assessed the men and atmosphere. "Who died?" he smirked, an unlit cigarette hanging from the corner of his mouth. He sniffed the air. "Smells good. I think it's time for supper. Let's go." Leaving the men to their musing, he headed toward the kitchen.

———※———

Frederick entered the kitchen and greeted Stani, asking about the delicious aroma. Stani shared his menu for the night: "Chicken paprikash, spätzle, braised red cabbage with apples, and challah." He checks the oven. "Now, where is everyone? Get them in here."

Frederick shrugged. "Oh, they're in the office, the three of them. Someone is brooding, maybe all of them. Who knows?" With a big grin, he asked, "Can we go ahead and eat without them?"

Stani scowled, placing the dinner plates on the counter. "You know the answer. Now go drag them in here!"

Cued by Frederick's voice, Hollenius entered the kitchen, still warm from lying over the heat vent, with matted fur to prove it. No one knew Hollenius's backstory. He took residence on the front porch three years ago and never left.

"You hear everything in this house, all conversations, because you're sneaky like a spy. And aren't you fancy with your new collar? Did your daddy Frederick buy that for you?" Stani admired the wide brown leather collar. "Are you carrying secrets or microfilm in that collar? I wouldn't be surprised if you were!"

Hollenius yawned and looked away, apathetic. Stani chuckled. "Oh, excuse me, am I boring you?"

The cat sat, observing Stani's every move.

"Go ahead and judge me, like you do everyone except for Frederick." Stani rechecked the oven and extracted its contents: a perfectly golden-brown challah bread. "Is there anything better than fresh-baked bread, Hollenius? Can you smell that? You don't know what you're missing. I know what I'm missing. I'm missing Maddie."

Hollenius circled the chair where Frederick would sit, narrowed his bright lime-green eyes, and yawned with a full tongue roll. He made himself comfortable on the braided rug atop the oak hardwood floor, his substantial motor purring.

"Well, at least someone is happy here, even if it's just you, Hollenius! Maybe your happy mood will become contagious. From direct observation, those four Neanderthals sure could use some happiness."

The phone broke the silence. Stani answered it on the second ring.

"Maddie. How are you? I was just discussing you and the boys with Hollenius. He's as fractious as ever. So. Tell me. When will we see you? Okay, that sounds good. Yes, they're all here. We're going to sit down for supper. Chicken paprikash and spätzle. I wish you were joining us. All right, my darling. You'll do fine. Believe in yourself, remember? God has already supplied all you'll need. Just thank him for it and be grateful. I know, you know. It doesn't hurt to be reminded. I will pray for your imminent success! I look forward to hearing about it. Yes. See you then. Shalom to you, too!"

Oh, Lord, help Maddie pass her violin practical with flying colors. Thank you.

Buster cruised into the kitchen and to the stove, lifting the lid of a pot. He bent his head and inhaled the savory aroma. "Ahh, heaven. You're getting good at this. I'll miss your cooking next year."

Stani walked over to Buster, now a full-grown 6'1", standing six inches above him. "What do you mean, miss my cooking next year? Where are you going?"

CHAPTER SEVEN

Brothers in Arms

FALL 1937, ROCHESTER, NEW YORK

WALKING IN BEHIND Buster and overhearing his son's words to Stani, Raymond asked, "Yes, where are you going?"

Buster whipped around. "Do you even care? You've essentially ignored me ever since Wolfie became your new son. I've decided my future. I'm twenty-one; I can do that."

"Boys, it's time to eat," Stani said, trying to bring peace between them. "After that, you can continue your discussion wherever you want, except for the kitchen. This place is sacred and my workspace. No arguing or fighting allowed. If you want me to cook for you, you must follow the rules!"

"They started it," Buster said. "I'm here just to hold my ground."

His flippant attitude angered Stani, who despised conflict even more when pride was causing the issue. He slammed his apron onto the counter and looked sternly at the men. "What happened to our family atmosphere? I see a lack of caring, growing jealousy, simmering distrust, and no empathy. And each one of you knows better. That's what's so painful."

Stani studied each face, but none of them apologized or answered his question. He grunted, turned on his heel, and left the kitchen. His voice trailed off as he walked away. "Well, no answer is an answer. Let me know when you're done. I'm through here. You can stay or come with me and find some peace, Hollenius. Stay here, and the minutes will fly like hours." The cat meowed and followed Stani out of the kitchen, leaving the four men to marinate in uncomfortable silence.

Buster was the spitting image of his mother, who had fine features and green eyes. He was dressed in a stylish glen plaid suit and silk tie tailored to fit his athletic build perfectly. For shoes, he'd chosen wingtips. He took pride in his appearance and appreciated a well-made suit's classic look and feel. In contrast, Wolfie was dressed casually in a t-shirt and dungarees, with a bandana tied around his neck like a sailor.

Buster side-eyed Wolfie, shaking his head and muttering under his breath, "Only a German would be shoeless in late October."

"What's the problem now, Four? What have I done? Spit it out. If you've something to say, say it." He half-glared at Buster. "I hate when you pussyfoot around and don't say what's on your mind."

Buster sniped back, "Yeah, well, I'm not as fast on my feet as you, brother."

"What are you talking about? More of your mealy-mouthing?"

Buster clenched a fist, ready to knock Wolfie in the teeth; instead, he spoke his mind. "Your fast feet are cutting into my territory, and if you can't figure that out, then, well, I can't help you."

Hoping to defuse the rising pressure in the room, Raymond said, "I think I need something to drink—Frederick, boys, can I get you anything?" After receiving no response, he said, "No? Fine. I'll be right back."

Frederick grumbled, "What the hell happened to dinner? I'll be in the garage if anyone cares," he said as he left the room.

Raymond walked from the kitchen to the living room and headed straight for the discreet bar in the corner, rising from a glass and mirror table. This brief separation from the kitchen chaos gave him time to reflect on his parenting. *Have I neglected my son in favor of Wolfie?*

Raymond poured himself a bourbon. He returned to the kitchen and approached his son with a quiet and conciliatory tone.

"Buster, I apologize. I didn't realize that my actions bring you pain. Why didn't you come to me with this issue earlier? You carry this resentment without communication, allowing your anger to contaminate everything you touch."

Raymond continued, defending himself, "It's not like we have copious amounts of time together. I rarely see you. We are like two ships passing at night."

Buster's face grew redder by the minute, and he tapped his index finger on the kitchen table, waiting for his father to continue apologizing. But Raymond didn't, and Buster slammed his fist on the table, making the silverware and china rattle.

"I play varsity soccer and belong to Debate Club; I pledged Phi Psi Epsilon, your fraternity; I sing in choir; and then there are my studies! How much time do you think I have?" he roared. "I did much of this activity at college to please you, following in your footsteps. But while I'm busy trying to please you by being a dean's list student, Wolfie only wants to work on cars and goof around with you."

They stood in silence as the stinging words sank in. Raymond broke it, directing his question to his son. "Well, will you tell us your plans, or must we tie you down and force it out?"

Buster rolled his eyes. "Miserable comforters are ye all,"

he said, quoting from the Book of Job. "I've enlisted in the United States Army. I've already completed enough credits to graduate with my degree in January. I begin my enlistment ten days before Christmas. I'll complete Basic Training, then I'll attend Officer School the third week of February, and then they'll ship me out. The army has dwindled to just under 180,000 men on active duty. I'm enlisting for two years and will serve the country through non-conscripted enlistment. If I like it, I may stay."

He reached for Stani's cigarettes, extracting one, and lit it. "Please, let me break the news to Stani and Maddie. Wolfie, that means you, too. I will tell Maddie."

Wolfie made eye contact with Raymond; they stared at each other intensely before Wolfie nodded toward Buster. "Tell him."

"Tell me what? What are you keeping from me?"

Crossing the kitchen to face Buster, Raymond took a deep breath. "I think Wolfie should enlist in the military after graduation as well. I would have shared this with you sooner, but you beat me to it with your surprising news. Are you sure this is what you want?"

Buster sighed with resignation. "Yes."

Frederick meandered back into the kitchen. Impassively, he said, "Hmm. I see you're still arguing."

Raymond clasped his hands. "Well, that's that!" He shrugged and nodded at Frederick, sharing the boys' future plans. "What do you think?"

"Good. Problem solved," Frederick replied with his usual ornery candor. "We ship them both off, and then we can finally have peace around here." After a second, he added, "Perhaps you should ensure the boys are linked and must depend on each other for survival. Handcuff them together for good measure; that would fix them. Now, for God's sake, can we eat?"

Raymond snapped his fingers. "Say, you might be on to something."

Frederick laughed. "Always happy to contribute!" He left the kitchen to bring Stani back for supper.

With that, Buster excused himself, departing through the front door, car keys in hand.

First, I'll tell Maddie, then Stani. Since we agreed to hold off on anything serious like marriage until we're mature enough and ready, she shouldn't have a problem with me being gone six or seven months at a time. Maybe Stani and Maddie could tour while she plays in symphony halls like she's dreamed of. She spoke about an opportunity in Vienna. She'd be safe with Stani. She's so self-sufficient that she'll barely notice I'm gone.

CHAPTER EIGHT

Good Timing

APRIL 1939, DACHAU CONCENTRATION
CAMP, DACHAU, GERMANY

STEFAN WASTED NO time. He ignored the choking panic spreading over him like fire and hurried into the house and kitchen, careful not to turn on any light switches. One spark could ignite the gas and blow the house to kingdom come.

The commandant and his wife sat in the dining room, overlooking the gardens, glancing at the daily papers and drinking coffee. They awaited Stefan's arrival. Every morning at 7:15, Stefan arrived, and his first order of business was to cook breakfast. The kapo arrived at eight.

Under other circumstances, Stefan would never have considered intruding on his employers by entering the dining room uninvited and addressing any of the family. If he did, he could assure himself that a severe beating would follow.

Usually, the family gave him orders, and he nodded in response. But today, he had no choice; he had to address them and speak in a calm, level tone without panic, even though he wished he could scream at the top of his lungs and get out of there. Stefan began to shake; he told himself, *Calm down, take a deep breath. It's okay—it's all going to be okay.*

He entered the dining room just as Eicke pulled a cigarette from his silver case and reached for his lighter. Stefan starts to raise his hand, but instead yelled, "Stop! Sir, forgive me..."

Eicke's face darkened as he slammed the cigarette on the table, jumping up from his seat. "Why are you addressing me?" he barked.

"Sir, forgive me. The smell of gas is evident outside the house, at the stairs. There must be a leak."

Theodor Eicke towered over Stefan. "Is this a ploy of some sort, part of an escape plan?"

Stefan's eyes widened with fear as he shook his head. "No, sir. Please check outside if you wish. I caution you not to light your cigarette or turn on any light switches, and, of greatest importance, we must move the women from the house to safety as fast as possible."

Eicke sized up Stefan. "If you're lying, I'll shoot you myself."

"Yes, sir, I would expect nothing less."

He ordered his wife, "Bertie, awaken Irma. You both get out of the house as fast as you can. No light switches. No turning on anything. And for God's sake, don't light a cigarette! Just go. Go to the garages and stand watch. Go now and get Irma. Hurry."

As if he were walking a tightrope to the kitchen door, Eicke opened it and sniffed the air, stepping to where Stefan first smelled gas. The commandant's nose twitched. "Good God, you weren't kidding."

Moments later, Bertie and Irma, still in her nightgown with bathrobe and slippers, with sleepy eyes, came out the door and ran down the steps, then the fifty meters through the expansive green lawn to the garages and the stable of cars. When the women were halfway through the yard, Eicke clapped and yelled, "Run faster!" causing his wife to trip and his daughter to squeal in fear. He looked away in disgust.

Captain Zollinger, Eicke's assistant, came upon his boss and Stefan. He clicked the heels of his jackboots and saluted.

"Heil Hitler." He sniffed the air, his nose wrinkling at the strong scent. "Sir, is there a gas leak?

Eicke pointed to Stefan. "He found it."

"I'll call the engineer to immediately cut off the gas supply before we're all blown to bits," Zollinger said.

The commandant nodded. "Definitely." He grabbed Stefan by the arm. "You, come with me."

The two headed to safety, trotting across the lawn as the sun rose, bathing them and the grounds in light. Once they reached the edge of the garage, Eicke pulled Stefan aside. "You could have run for your life and not warned me. I could have lit my cigarette, and the rest would be history. Why didn't you run?"

Stefan blinked aware he could have done just that. He swallowed hard. "Sir, the thought never crossed my mind. My conscience would never allow me to see a wrong and not do anything about it when given the opportunity."

"You have impeccable timing and saved our lives. Are you German? Speak freely."

"Thank you, sir. My mother was German. My father was French."

Eicke contemplated his words. "Hmm. French. I still can't get over you not running from here. You know, I could let you go."

Stefan's eyes watered at the thought. "Sir, if you would consider that in return for saving your lives, I think that would be reasonable."

Eicke's eyes narrowed as he squinted at Stefan, reminding him, "One German life is more valuable than ten prisoners' lives."

Stefan countered with, "Not to sound impertinent, sir, but while that is true, it only took one prisoner's life to save three German lives."

Eicke pondered, deliberating what to do with the man before him. "I can't decide whether to slap you for that comment or laugh." Remembering his wife and daughter, he waved at them, and they returned the wave. "My wife and daughter adore your cooking skills, and we've yet to have a better chef. However, I'm told I'll soon be appointed Waffen-SS's commander. My wife and daughter are moving to Berlin to be with her parents soon. They employ indentured servants; needless to say, there will be no place for you."

Eicke paused again and looked back at his wife and daughter. He softly said, "In all truth, yes, we have you to thank for our lives, and it would only be right of me to release you. Major von Dorsten gave you an upstanding review and said we would be lucky to have you. He did mention you were not a rabble-rouser and believes your arrest to be a mistake. Also, considering your mother's German heritage, it may be appropriate to show some leniency."

While some might have unleashed anger at the knowledge of being held when not guilty of a crime, all Stefan could do was revel in his good fortune. *Is he going to release me?*

Eicke pauses. "Stay put. I'll be right back."

Stefan watched as Eicke trotted toward his wife and daughter. Captain Zollinger and a driver appeared with the family automobile; Zollinger stood, ready to open the doors for Bertie and Irma. Eicke ordered, "Go to your mother's house and wait until I call with the 'all clear' sign, okay? See you in a few days." Eicke kissed his women goodbye while Zollinger relayed instructions to the driver, and the car departed.

"What about him?" Zollinger inquired, nodding toward Stefan.

Eicke scowled. "Hmm. Let me think about it. Release him to his kapo and allow him to return to the barracks."

Captain Zollinger did as instructed. As Stefan stood in a corner of the barracks, he scanned the plain wooden bunks.

To his surprise, they were all empty. He crawled into his bunk, craving sleep like a person deprived, knowing the kapo couldn't punish him, seeing he was ordered back to his barracks by the camp commandant. He slept soundly, but awakened to a commotion. *Count. It must be evening count! Oh my God, I've slept the whole day! But boy, I feel good!*

He only had a moment before he'd be late for the count. Then he remembered—the small pocket diary. *I've got to see what this is.* He pulled it out of his pants.

The room was dim, with little to no light peeking through the stained, cracked windows. Once more, he scanned his surroundings cautiously, hearing every creak and sound. The dilapidated wooden structure moaned when the wind blew. His hands revealed his nerves. They shook as he thumbed through the diary. He dropped it just as the door flung open, and a kapo screamed, "Count."

Panicked, Stefan looks down and strained his eyes to find the book; he found it and stuffed it in the back of his pants. The kapo screeched at him to hurry up, and Stefan did, walking with intention right past the kapo outside into the waning dusk light.

He stood with the other men in a row as they waited for the count to begin. They might stand there for five minutes or five hours; it depended on the mood of their captors. It was part of the psychological games the kapos and guards played with the prisoners. They might prolong a count, like tonight, when it was a half hour before dinner. If they prolonged the count for more than an hour on a night like tonight, then there was no dinner.

Stefan dared not look at the pocket diary while waiting for the count to begin, for fear that another prisoner might call attention to it or try to take it from him, hoping for a favor or food from the kapo or guard, like a piece of sausage. Some prisoners would do anything at all for food. They would sell you out for a scrap of bread. If you could imagine it, it had been done in Dachau. Hunger and desperation will lead a man to do things he vowed he'd never do—another form of Nazi psychological warfare, the game of humiliation.

That night, Stefan and the men stood for five hours for the count, and three men dropped. Since it wasn't winter, they'd be dragged off the line and shot in the head; then, some poor soul would be tasked with taking the bodies to the dreaded, deadly pit to drop them on top of the other bodies, where the dead remain in Dachau, in various states of decomposition.

The following day, while on his way to report for work, Stefan pulled out the diary and peeked at the first few pages. He began to understand: this was a plan for a ship to fool the public, a propaganda campaign, and the transport of vital information purloined from American forces. *Whose is this, and what do I do with it?*

Wheels in Motion

LATE MARCH 1939, BERLIN, GERMANY,
REICH CHANCELLERY

JOSEPH GOEBBELS WALKED with a limp, shuffling behind his escort down the hallway of the Reich Chancellery toward the meeting room where the Führer awaited. Nervous, he wiped sweat from his brow as he dragged his shriveled leg and clubbed foot over the expansive imperial rugs while admiring the exquisite works of art lining the hallway and the opulence of the crown moldings and ceilings.

Goebbels's two-year affair with Czechoslovakian film star Lída Baarová had damaged his marriage and his performance within the Reich. He was aware of the Führer's expectation that he demonstrate genuine remorse. The best way to show this was to produce a brilliant plan, proving that he completely controlled and was in command of the plans to achieve the Reich's goals and desires. He talked to himself, trying to build courage by rehearsing his objectives. *Operation Sunshine has to succeed. This has to work.*

The escort rapped on the massive wooden door, then opened it and announced, "Reich Minister Joseph Goebbels to see the Führer."

Goebbels bowed and scraped, saluting the man he hoped to manipulate. Filled with bluster, he disguised it as enthusiasm; he clapped his hands and locked them together to hide his nerves. His palms sweated. So did the back of his head, where his hair was thin. His neck was soaked. He was a bundle of frayed wires with an electrical current running through each one.

Goebbels began, "My Führer, you look like the picture of health, vitality, virility, and power. Thank you for seeing me. I requested this meeting to bring you a plan and a solution to the Jewish problem, one plan with two central goals to accomplish. These goals will help us achieve our end."

At the head of a table with ten heavy, high-back chairs on either side, Hitler was seated, sipping tea. He wore his customary drab beige-brown military surplus shirt, a black tie, and a Sam Browne belt across the front. A Nazi armband adorned his left arm at the bicep and jodhpurs and jackboots completed his ensemble. His thinning black hair was pasted to one side of his forehead, and his trademark splotch of a mustache was fortified with black dye.

Hitler's voice was raspy as usual, resulting from amphetamines and the Eukodal that his physician, Theo Morell, administered to him by injection. The drugs contributed to Hitler's already short fuse. "Are you done with your blathering? Or will you go on and tell me your intentions?"

Goebbels's face twitched. His voice trembled. "Yes, well, certainly, I will continue."

As Goebbels stood before the Führer, his polio-affected leg throbbed under the weight of his slight frame. He hoped he'd be offered a chair. When no offer came, he gritted his teeth and resigned himself to standing.

He began explaining his entrapment plan, waving his hands for effect. He bent and contorted his body while he spoke, raising and lowering his voice, using all the theatrics he could think of to convey excitement.

"To the rest of the world, Germany looks like the benevolent benefactor, releasing one thousand German Jews to leave the country. On a *luxury liner*, no less. Can you believe it? The foreign media will eat it up. Here's the caveat: to leave, the Jews must surrender and release all their wealth, belongings, and property to the Reich for reappropriation. They will sign a form giving up their rights as German citizens, promising, under the threat of death, never to return."

Hitler nodded, his face locked in his usual glassy but steely-eyed expression. "Go on."

Goebbels's voice soared with jubilation. "Imagine the art collections; you'll have your choice of exquisite works, in past times unobtainable. They become the Reich's property at surrender. Concerning the ship, each passenger aboard will have a nominal amount of money, not enough to begin a new life elsewhere. The beauty of this particular voyage is this. The ship is set to sail to Havana under great fanfare, with the passenger ship being used as a cover for transporting top-secret information. Abwehr operatives will be waiting at the Havana port to hand over the information to our Abwehr operative aboard the ship."

Goebbels paused, but no reaction came from Hitler. He prattled on.

"The passengers will not be allowed to disembark. A month before the ship sails, we send ten or fifteen Nazi SS and plant false information among the Cuban citizenry to portray the passengers as the worst kind of people with questionable character at best, saying many are thieves, liars, murderers, ex-convicts, and concentration camp prisoners. We spread false rumors about these asylum seekers, that they will come and steal Cuban jobs and threaten the Cuban way of life. Cuba becomes the victim, not the homeless Jews.

"By doing this, we cause unrest and sway the public's opinion. We will stage a rally and protest the landing just days before the ship arrives at port. We hope to gather upward of forty thousand protesters. We'll offer the protesters money if needed to ensure vast numbers of people participate. The Cubans will be easy to persuade. We will have pre-printed protest signs for them to carry, and the television cameras and reporters will promote our agenda unwittingly. We will coordinate and state a narrative to share with our contacts in the media so they all tell the same story and spread the same information, false as it may be!

"Our newspaper and magazine contacts will publish stories that we approve of before publishing, of course. We'll do the same with our radio contacts. They will trumpet the news to the residents of Havana, telling them that their city is about to be inundated with the scum of the earth. Who would want the Jews to land? The ship will not be permitted to do so. We've gauged the temperature of the public around the world. No one wants the Jews; we've shown the world what they are: homeless sub-human indigents."

Hitler recalled the Evian Conference held last summer, organized by the American president but, strangely enough, not attended by him. He stood and walked toward one of the floor-to-ceiling windows that looked out over Berlin.

Hitler replied, "You know, the American president did not attend the conference he set up. What a coward. He fears facing the thirty-two countries that attended the Evian Conference. I guarantee you he will do nothing to save the Jews. Re-election is his priority; he won't rock the boat. While the world may have sympathy for the plight of the Jews, there are thirty-two world leaders not willing to expand their refugee programs. They say the American public isn't warm to the idea of Jewish immigrants from the Slavic countries."

Goebbels's face lit up. "My Führer, as you are aware, not one country from that conference was willing to include the rising number of people hoping to emigrate from Germany. Because of the world's complacency toward the Jews, the world leaders and the general population will have no stance on which to pass judgment over our treatment of them." Goebbels's expression bordered on delirium. He was so excited that his bladder released a little. Breathless, he explained his vision.

"We will have the basis for the final solution you hope to achieve. We have successfully illustrated to the world that no one wants the Jews, and what else can we do but the best thing for the world? Exterminate them. With the rejection of this ship in Havana, the world arbitrarily gives us the green light to proceed to the next step of our plans: to rid Germany and Europe of this Jewish evil.

"I spoke of two aspects of this special voyage. The second part of the plan is the transporting of vital American secrets. Since our Abwehr operatives were discovered in the United States by Army Intelligence, specifically in Miami, they now use Havana exclusively as a haven. Transporting the documents vital to the Reich will be easy. After the ship is refused in the port of Havana, the ship will turn around and come right back to Hamburg with the Jews and the secrets!

"The voyage of the *S.S. St. Louis* is a bonus for the Reich. We will accomplish so much. And for the ship and crew who face a lagging industry, this will be a bonus for HAPAG, as the ship was previously unscheduled and just happened to be available for our purposes." Goebbels sucked in his limit of oxygen, giddy with excitement.

Hitler put his hands together as his head bobbed up and

down and then side to side, as if to loosen a kink. His index fingers extended like a steeple as he presses them to his lips. He pondered the plan, seeking flaws or potential hindrances.

He croaked, "I don't foresee any problems with this plan. There are many benefits to be gained. However, I remember a conversation about Kristallnacht. While the plan produced modest results, it was not enough. You gave an assurance that the Jews would leave in droves. They didn't. So, can we really call that plan a success? And today, we have this problem. What to do with the Jews. We must find a way to rid us of this blight. This latest effort better produce more, especially since the news that the Americans have heard about the camps."

The Führer eyed Goebbels as if he was solely responsible. After Kristallnacht, the Nazis had been sure all the Jews would scatter like rats and leave Germany by any means possible. The Reich had severely underestimated the strong bond that German Jews felt toward their country. They loved their country despite everything that had happened in its storied history. Goebbels's bowels reacted to that implied responsibility. He'd need a bathroom soon.

Hitler turned toward the door and extended his arm to show Goebbels out, ending the meeting with these words: "Proceed with your plans, then. Keep me updated on any potential inadequacies. I expect an inventory of all artworks and collections obtained. I expect separate receipts of acquired wealth to be deposited in our specified accounts. I expect day-by-day intelligence reports of the voyage. That is all."

Goebbels saluted, clicking his heels like an obedient lap dog. "Yes, my Führer. Heil Hitler."

———※———

Later that night, after numerous shots of schnapps, Goebbels spoke with his wife about the meeting. "It's a brilliant plan. But he didn't commend me on its brilliance or strategy. Is he unaware of what this means for the Reich? I cannot understand the man. What more must I do?"

He sipped his last schnapps and said, "You know, the thing is, there's no one in that administration I trust. They're all power-hungry ghouls who want more power."

Magda Goebbels, the statuesque, blonde, blue-eyed wife who had produced six children for him, hoped to assuage her husband's anxiety. Married to him for eight years, she made excuses for his extramarital affairs, blaming them on the constant pressure he faced from his position. She had no such pressure but made excuses for her dalliances anyway. Sitting up and reaching across the bed, she handed him her snifter of brandy. "Darling, you've got to trust someone sometime, don't you?"

He tossed back her brandy and slurs, "I would, but you see, I've run out of people, and you're the end of the line." He smiles at her sweetly.

"Joseph, you know your worth to the Reich even if you're not recognized. Remember, he's given you free rein over policy, the media in all its forms, and the film industry. And if he's consuming as many drugs as you say, his days are numbered. I've heard talk among the wives and other officers that some would like to take him out."

Goebbels resists the urge to question his wife. *Just how* do *you know what other officers think?*

"Now, you stop this gloom and doom and come over here." Magda sprawled across the nineteenth-century antique bed, pilfered from a Jewish banker's home, spread with a velvet comforter over silk sheets of the finest quality. She pulled the tie to her silk robe, swinging the tasseled end and winking at her husband. Her robe opened, revealing her magnificent body.

She extended her hand, hoping to relieve her husband's stress and worry. However, his mental state remained unyielding, and her romantic notions failed to deliver.

CHAPTER TEN

Maddie's Grand Invitation

APRIL 1939, ROCHESTER, NEW YORK

VIENNA'S NEO-CLASSICAL CONCERT hall, Wiener Musikverein, is home to one of the world's greatest orchestras, the Vienna Philharmonic. They take great pride in their place in the world of classical music. Principal conductor Wilhelm Furtwängler was known to be a conscientious objector to Nazis' rule, especially when it came to choosing artists to perform.

In 1936, the statue of famed composer Felix Mendelssohn was destroyed in Leipzig, signaling the end of Jewish performances in Austria and Germany. By early 1939, more than two thousand conductors, soloists, concert masters, and singers were banned or expelled from teaching positions and stages because they were Jewish. Furtwängler opposed the regime's policies of excluding Jewish artists, leading the Nazis to label him a "cultural Bolshevist, a spiritual non-Aryan."

When the Anschluss occurred on March 13, 1938, and Germany occupied Austria, Maddie feared she'd never have the opportunity to perform on stage with the Vienna Philharmonic and Conductor Furtwängler. She had to perform in Vienna to be considered a true virtuoso. While it was the loftiest of goals, Mrs. Genhart and Stani favored it, and they encouraged Maddie to dream big and reach for the highest star.

All prodigies long to perform under the guiding hand of the most renowned conductor, with the reputed world's greatest symphony, a dream of Maddie's since her days under Elenena's tutelage in Munich. In her fifth year of the master's program at the Eastman School of Music, Maddie became suspect when an opportunity arose for her to play with the Vienna Philharmonic. The selection confounded her. After their weekly Bible study, Maddie told Stani about the selection, explaining she didn't understand why she was picked.

Stani's response was what she'd expect from him: ever-cheerful and positive. "Your talent is worthy of such a selection. I say this with no bias. As a student of the Eastman, in the master's program, you've performed at numerous competitions. You've earned this!" But Maddie still didn't understand why she had been picked.

After her final lesson for the week at Mrs. Genhart's apartment, she asked a similar question. "Why would they pick me?"

Mrs. Genhart huffed in exasperation as she leaned forward in her chair. "Well, you earned this, my dear. Your performance at the QE Competition in Brussels was nothing short of mesmerizing. Don't you remember the applause, people shouting 'Brava!'? The world of classical music embraced you as a native daughter that evening, falling in love with you and your tremendous talent."

Maddie shook her head. Ever since the August night in 1933 when the SS had abducted Stani, and she'd fled for her life, she'd struggled to recall specific details. She shared this with no one, afraid to be judged and labeled unstable or emotional. She labored to remember anything specific from the performance the previous October but could not. "I only remember getting through the piece with relief, and my hands were sweaty."

The piece she was referring to is Tchaikovsky's "Violin Concerto in D Major, Opus 35." The music is euphonious and affectionate, and the score for strings is exceptional in beauty. It is the only concerto Tchaikovsky penned for violin.

Mrs. Genhart assured Maddie that she more than qualified for the opportunity, listing her past achievements, including sold-out performances at the Eastman Theater with the Rochester Philharmonic, in New York at Carnegie Hall, and her earth-shaking debut at the QEC, also known as the Queen Elizabeth Competition. QEC was the newest and most demanding of all international competitions.

Maddie scowled, fidgeting with a pencil. "I'm not worthy of such praise." She bristled when called a "virtuoso" and pointed out two other talented students in the same master's program. "Why weren't they considered? Is it because they feel sorry for me, the orphan immigrant?" She turned away to attend to her violin, carefully wiping and polishing her instrument before returning it to its case. Elenena gifted it to her. She whispered, as if speaking to heaven and to Elenena, *Until next time, I love you.*

"You're not the only one who misses her. I do too; she was my friend as well," Mrs. Genhart said, her eyes becoming misty. She wiped them and then headed to the kitchen to prepare tea.

Maddie's cheeks burned as a single tear escaped the edge of her eye. Emotion welled in her chest, and she breathed deeply, then exhaled, hoping even temporarily to release the pain. She whispered the same refrain she'd spoken one hundred times in her mind.

Oh, how I miss you, Elenena. I never had a chance to say goodbye. Why did your life have to end that way? How will I make it through without you? Stani tells me to trust in God, but somehow, I can't. Why would he allow you to die like you did? Why would He do that? Stani says you are a loving God, and we are your children. Yet, you allow your children to die in the most brutal ways. I don't understand.

Maddie closed her eyes and leaned into the chair she uses during lessons, hoping to ease the intense cramping in her abdomen. Mrs. Genhart reentered the room, setting down the tea service; she rushed to Maddie's side. "Child, are you well? You look pale." Putting a hand on Maddie's head, she said, "You're not hot. Hmm. Here, have some tea."

"I'm sorry, I get like this sometimes." Maddie decided not to share that she hadn't had her regular cycle that month. She brushed her dark tresses off her slender neck, twisted them into a knot, and secured it with a bobby pin. With inauthentic enthusiasm, she clapped her hands. "There. All better!" She clenched her jaw, praying the pain would pass sooner rather than later. It finally did.

Pouring a cup of tea, Mrs. Genhart took Maddie at her word and wasted no time getting down to the business of travel. She explained, "You'll leave New York on April 24th and arrive first in Bremen. Then, you'll travel to Vienna by train on the thirtieth. You'll have five days to practice with the symphony orchestra, culminating in a dress rehearsal on May 5th and a performance on May 6th. You will perform the same piece you played at the QE competition. After your concert, you'll have free time to spend in Vienna or travel if you wish." She hesitated, adding, "I have one small request."

Maddie was only half-listening, caught up in trying to absorb the travel details. She snapped out of her fog and answered, "How can I help?"

"There's a friend of mine from my days at the Conservatory. He's written to me, asking if I could come to Hamburg. He's dying of lung cancer and has something to give me. He didn't say what it is."

Maddie raised her eyebrows, trying to think of what it could be. "Could it be an instrument of some kind, a violin or viola? Or perhaps a priceless vase from the Ming Dynasty?"

Mrs. Genhart chuckled at the thought. "Werner Kempler traversing through the mountains of Mongolia to find an artifact from the last imperial dynasty while reciting Neo-Manchurian doctrines. Oh, dear! I'm not quite sure and truly have no idea. It could be a violin; if my memory serves me well, it may be his Nicoló Amati."

Having a love of timeless and priceless pieces, Mrs. Genhart became sentimental as she explained to Maddie the finer points of the craftsmanship of the chordophone-lute-bowed, unfretted violin, which was crafted in Cremona, Italy, in the mid-to-late 1600s. "It is more like a piece of art than the spruce and maple violin itself. It produces a unique and distinguishable sweet tone," she said.

"It's said that Amati apprenticed under three geniuses of lute-making: Antonio Stradivari, Francesco Rugeri, and Jacob Stainer. Stani calls the violin 'the Amati of Angels,' having experienced a magical evening where Kempler was the soloist performing with his Amati in Berlin during the days of the Weimer Republic when artists everywhere were flocking to Berlin." Mrs. Genhart's eyes reflected sorrow instead of joy as she recalled the memory.

"I'd like you and Stani to travel to Werner's house in Hamburg and pick up whatever he has for me. I'll have a letter for you to bring to him. You'll be able to come home directly from Hamburg. I'll speak with the school about the travel arrangements, including your departure from the Hamburg port. How does that sound?"

Maddie was agreeable, yet a knot formed in her throat at the thought of traveling through Germany. Her mind raced ahead while spinning new fears.

Mrs. Genhart interrupted her thoughts. "Now, do you have any questions about the overall political climate in Austria? I know you're interested in this. Stani says you spar with him over his interpretation of the news and current events, trying to persuade him to stop being so, ah, as he put it, 'happy-go-lucky and upbeat.'"

Maddie snickered at the thought of Stani telling anyone about her complaints that his optimistic outlook on life lacked objectivity. "It's true. We do spar," she admitted. Stani frequently called her a 'curmudgeon,' and she called him a 'marshmallow' in return.

Maddie added that she'd never had an optimistic outlook on life but could be persuaded with a fact-based argument. She masked her fear with a regal smile. "While I'm nervous about returning to Europe, even more since the Nazi Anschluss of Austria, I'm also very excited to play on the stage in Vienna with the symphony and the master, the superb Wilhelm Furtwängler."

To calm her nerves, she sipped her tea and asked, "What's your take on the goings-on?"

Mrs. Genhart was an expert on all things Austria; she was born in Salzburg in October 1900. At age seventeen, she'd entered the conservatory in Vienna, focusing on music theory and violin. After graduating with her degree, she'd begun teaching and giving private instruction in Berlin, where she'd first met Stani and Elenena.

During the last days of the glorious Weimar Republic, everything creative had emanated from Berlin. The end came in January 1933, when Hitler became chancellor of Germany. She'd read his autobiographical tome, *Mein Kampf*, dictated to Rudolph Hess in 1924 during their 264-day imprisonment at Landsberg for their involvement in a failed coup d'état, the Munich Beer Hall Putsch of 1923. After reading the book, her mind had become illuminated as to what lay ahead.

Relying on her instincts, after much paperwork and a genuine offer of employment, Anatolia Genhart had emigrated to the United States in the summer of 1932, accepting a prestigious position at the Eastman School of Music. When another position opened at The Eastman, Anatolia Genhart had recommended her friend Elenena Laurent for the position.

Mrs. Genhart kept informed of changes and updates in Vienna, where friends resided. Not much was known about her life before or after her time in Berlin. She never spoke of it.

"Knowledge is power. This is why the Nazis control the media, so the people of the world won't know what's happening there, allowing Propaganda Minister Joseph Goebbels to spoon-feed his lies to the masses while distracting from and masking the critical issues facing Austrians and Germans alike.

"The economy is still reeling from the Great Depression. Austrians face unstable commerce and industry, along with a high unemployment rate. Despite holding gold and foreign currency reserves, unused factories remained idle as a wealth of skilled workers remained unemployed.

"Austria is rich in resources. These are the resources that Germany needs if it's going to fulfill the goals of the Reich. Greed drives this unification. While the Treaty of Versailles forbids unification of the two countries, Hitler thumbs his nose at the Treaty."

Maddie nodded, wagging her index finger. "We must have similar news sources. I've shared such information with Stani, yet he continues seeing everything through a lens of optimism without basis!"

Mrs. Genhart agreed, "Yes, then perhaps you're familiar with Hitler's Four-Year Plan of 1936, which increased military spending while he exploited Austria's raw materials and riches. This plan allowed Germany to prepare for what could be on the horizon. War? Perhaps. This remilitarization and German rearmament can and will shift the balance of power in Europe. Can I warm your tea?"

Mrs. Genhart poured more tea for them both and then set the pot down. With bitter contempt, she said, "Meanwhile, Britain and France stand by, allowing the Reich's agenda to proceed. The abdicated king of Great Britain, Edward VIII, who married an American divorcée, is courting the Führer and Joseph Goebbels, working to negotiate a deal. Will Great Britain help Poland, not if but when Hitler invades? Or will Great Britain capitulate to the whims of the Reich?" She shrugged, shaking her head. "I just don't understand. Why do they hate Jews so?"

Maddie said nothing, but the telltale sign of a wrinkled brow and a full frown gave her thoughts away.

Mrs. Genhart reached out and placed her hand on Maddie's. "Now, I'm not saying this will happen. Yet, the political climate is ripe for such an invasion. Hitler rants about insufficient land or territory for Greater Germany to expand. The cities are crowded and overflowing with citizens. The Nazi machine will deliver on the plan of Lebensraum, or *living space*, by invading Poland for a land grab. I read about this in his book. Should Britain and France continue to sit on their hands, to ignore what's taking place across the channel, or if they fail to respond promptly should an invasion of Poland occur, within twenty-four hours, the Nazis will destabilize the entire block of Eastern Europe."

Maddie bit her lower lip; the wheels turning in her head were almost audible. "But what if that happens while I'm in Vienna?"

"Assembling and executing plans takes time. You needn't worry," Mrs. Genhart replied. "But can one remain blind to the imminent outcome? No. The Nazis can steamroll Poland in a matter of weeks, and there are millions of Jews living there. What about them? Who will rescue them?"

CHAPTER ELEVEN

The Letter From Buster

APRIL 5, 1939, UNDISCLOSED LOCATION

My Dearest Darling Maddie,

Hello, my love. I have a few minutes left before it's time to hit the hay. I'm bushed. How I long for you! Wolfie and I were on maneuvers all day. We were grateful for our assignment; it was much easier than the poor chaps that had to hike twenty miles out and back today. It's hot, too. I'm afraid those boys will be shipped to a place where the weather is blistering.

Today, our maneuvers were more related to the unique training we're getting here. Dad's friend is looking after us. Please tell Dad he's sincere, kind, and helpful. He's also patient, even with Wolfie's antics. Wolfie says Stani mentioned in a letter that you might visit Rolf and Cecile. He asks you to please convince them to move to the US once and for all. He says, "Remind them what the Nazis did to Josef and Minka." We're hoping they'll listen to you and Stani. Tell Rolf his little brother Frederick misses him!

I want to know all about you—how are you? Please tell me about your thoughts on the Bible studies with Stani. I want to know all the details, so darling, please write to me and lift my spirits. I miss you like the dickens.

Do you feel closer to me knowing I'm thinking of you at

10:00 p.m. every night and asking God to watch over you and protect you?

I also ask Him to inform you how much I adore you. I count the days. Life here isn't too bad; the food here is okay, but I miss Stani's cooking more than ever.

I won't be able to see you until after deployment, and this mission concludes. After that, I'll be home. Our commander says, barring any issues, I should be able to come home in late July for a two-week leave. Then, it's back for the next mission. Wolfie and I will have a different leave, he hopes to use his time to go to Vienna and help Rolf and Cecile pack and move. Get ready, baby. We'll go to Pultneyville. I'm sure Dad will be there most of the time. Of course, you'll be expected to stay in your room.

We'll be able to relax with minimal distractions. We have some significant things to discuss. Please tell me you won't be traveling or on tour then! I know we have to compromise. It doesn't matter where we are as long as we're together.

It's lights out for me, my darling. Be good to yourself, never forget how much I love you, and count the days until I can hold you again. Forever, your Buster.

After receiving Buster's letter, Maddie brought it to Raymond's house to discuss and go over the plans with Stani for their upcoming European trip. The Eastman School made all the travel arrangements and would provide a stipend for travel expenses. *Maybe Stani can help me clarify my feelings for Buster. I love him, yet at times I still feel conflicted. What does he mean, significant things to discuss?*

The sunshine offered warmth, so Maddie walked to Raymond's

Rugby Avenue home. As she continued down the tree-lined street, filling her lungs with the vernal air, her mind was full of details, information on the trip, and questions about the curious request from Mrs. Genhart.

Maddie stopped, her eyes soaking in the grandeur of blooming trees, shrubs, and flowers that line the avenue, then continued her quick pace. Springtime in Rochester was more lovely than she could have imagined. It truly was *the Flower City*, a moniker given to Rochester because of Highland Park. She'd discovered that Highland Park was home to the world's most significant varieties of lilacs. She and Stani would miss the coming Lilac Festival held each May. They'd be in Europe.

Highland Park was Maddie's place of solace. Whenever she felt sad or lonely, she strolled along one of the many trails that weaved through the spacious one hundred and fifty acres. A bus from the University could take her down to the park entrance on Reservoir Drive. She favored the stairway on the northeastern side of the park; it led to a rock garden perfect for contemplation or a romantic rendezvous with Buster. But he wouldn't be home until July. The park would be packed, with no quiet space to escape.

I can't think about anything until the concert is over. Maddie stopped her fast pace. Cramps in her abdomen caused her to double over. She pressed her hands against her belly, then straightened and took large strides to distract herself, focusing on something other than the pain. That effort was futile, so instead, she recalled the words of Buster's letter, having read it ten times.

I'll write him back today. How I wish I could see him before July! I hope the time will pass without me noticing how slow it goes.

And what about Mrs. Genhart? Why would that man gift such

a priceless piece to her, if that's indeed what it is? There has to be more to their history than just students at the Conservatory. Were they lovers at one time? I'll have to ask Stani if he knows. I'd be afraid to ask her such a personal question.

Maddie arrived at the house and strolled down the winding sidewalk leading to the front door. Marveling at the lushness of spring grass—how deep green and hearty for April— she recalled a conversation with Miss Ada Berk: "Northern snowfall has mystical powers. When it melts, it's chock full of nutrients and minerals, restoring health to Mother Earth and bringing color to our winter-drab world. Our Indians in this region spoke of this time, saying when Young Man Spring comes, it will defeat Old Man Winter."

A smile formed on Maddie's lips as she remembered the terms Miss Berk used, like 'Old Man Winter.' She spied a few conspicuous weeds and squatted to pull them out. Standing back, she admired her work and the dividends paid by the group effort of labor performed at last fall's bulb-planting party. On either side of the front door were garden beds. To the left and right, tulips, just sprouting their heads and gaining height by the day after a lengthy winter's rest, would provide a dazzling array of color once in full bloom over the next few weeks.

Planted in groupings were a mess of daffodils and narcissus, sharing their happy blooms and cheering anyone who saw them. They sprang up from the insidious ivy, the most encroaching of all ground cover in the garden beds. Nestling up to the house's side gardens were lilies of the valley, and their subtle fragrance pleased Maddie. She adored the simplicity and exquisite beauty they possessed. A scripture Stani shared about them pops into her head; it's something like, *A rose of Sharon, a lily of the valley.*

Stani observed Maddie through the kitchen window, where he was washing dishes in the sink. He dried his hands on a towel, and as he did, he spotted Hollenius perched atop the china cabinet in the corner. The cat extended a paw.

Stani slowly blinked, gazing into the cat's eyes, and Hollenius repeated the same action. "Good. Now I know you love me!"

Stani trotted out the kitchen door to greet Maddie. He half-skipped toward her. Just seeing Maddie brought joy to his heart. "Inspecting your work?"

Maddie turned. "Hello!" She hurried across the yard into Stani's waiting arms.

They gave each other a kiss and shared a warm embrace. "My sweet, how beautiful you look. You smell like the sunshine, fresh air perfumes your cheeks. To what do we owe this privilege of a visit?"

Maddie bent to pull another weed and huffed, "Ugh, these weeds! They spring up right before me, daring me to pick them! The unmitigated nerve!"

Stani laughed at her feigned disgust. "Are you aware that weeds are an outcome of Adam's fall? God cursed the earth after Adam and Eve disobeyed his command not to eat of the tree of knowledge of good and evil."

Maddie shook her head. "Does everything have to do with the Bible? I mean, really." She rolled her eyes, stooping to pluck more weeds.

Stani laughed, "Of course it does! Not everyone has eyes of faith to see it."

"Well, I guess I need to acquire new eyes because I just don't see it."

Stani knew Maddie like a book. He wouldn't press her, knowing that no good would come from it. Instead, when she stood and faced him, he cupped her chin. "Some things one must learn through experience, and when it comes to faith, it has to draw you, not vice versa. I know that's hard to comprehend, but know this. The scriptures tell us, 'You are loved with everlasting love and drawn with loving kindness.' Now. Tell me, to what do I owe this grand visit? Let's have some coffee and catch up. Come with me."

Relieved, Maddie still ruminated. *Does everything really have to do with God or the Bible? I cannot understand this perspective.* She walked next to Stani arm-in-arm, and they entered the kitchen.

Maddie sniffed the air, noting the sweet notes of cinnamon and sugar. "Oh, it smells so good in here. What have you cooked or baked today? It smells like kugel!"

He spun around and did a little jig. "Good nose! Right, you are, my darling."

Stani poured coffee and placed a piece of lokshen kugel before Maddie. She proclaimed it as "the best!" Between bites, she said, "I have the travel arrangements for our trip and news from Buster. Which would you like to discuss first?"

Finishing the kugel, she put the plate and fork in the sink. She admired the new spice rack on the wall next to the sink, which held Stani's favorite spices and herbs.

"Frederick built that for me, under the watchful eye of Hollenius," Stani said while eyeing the cat, still perched above the china cabinet. Maddie sat down and patted her lap, hoping to lure the cat down, but Hollenius stayed put.

"Tell me about the news from our boys afar. Did Buster mention how he and Wolfie are getting along?" Stani's face scrunched in horror. "Please tell me they haven't murdered each other yet!"

Maddie giggled. "No, not yet. They are going on a mission

soon; he says it's tied to their training, which I know nothing about. Raymond connected the boys to an impressive man who oversees their training. Buster says, 'Wolfie has not pushed the man to the limit,' at least not yet. You know how he tests everyone, pushing until they blow? Why he does that, I'll never know. Buster says he'll be home on leave in July. He never details where he is, his mission, or who he is with. You know I love those details."

"Neither Buster nor Wolfie will ever be foot soldiers. It's not uncommon for military personnel to not disclose location or mission." Stani scratched his forehead. "What else did he say?"

"Oh, not much else, but I'm interested in what you said. The more I think about it—they're both in the Army! Wouldn't they start as foot soldiers? Isn't that the normal course? If they're in intelligence...Buster, yes, I can see it; he's brilliant. But Wolfie? He gets by with his charm and dazzling good looks." She shrugged, expecting Stani to agree.

Instead, Stani guffawed. "Dazzling good looks, you say? Ha!" Stani wagged his finger at Maddie. "You don't give Wolfie enough credit. He's a crafty one, quite brilliant. The humor and tricks are his cover. You know that, don't you?"

Maddie sipped her coffee. "I guess so."

"And regarding the boys starting as foot soldiers, no. They're college graduates. They qualify for Officer School. From there, they are assessed, and it's determined what would be the best fit. Raymond had input with their path, but who knows what they're doing? And both have flat feet. They would never serve as foot soldiers." Stani poured more coffee. "More kugel?"

Maddie shook her head, still considering Stani's words. "Wait. What do flat feet have to do with being a soldier? Well, anyway, I doubt I'll hear from him again until we return from Europe at the end of May, and that makes me sad."

Maddie finished her coffee and shared the itinerary. "The school has us traveling by ship to Europe, leaving on the 24th of April. We arrive in Bremen and take the train coming to Vienna on the thirtieth. We have five days of practice, with a dress rehearsal on May 5th and the concert on May 6th. After that, we are free to travel. We will visit Rolf and Cecile. We know what Wolfie wants, for us to convince them to emigrate, but I don't know. According to Wolfie, Rolf and Cecile Wolferman seem so set in their ways. What do you think? Can we convince them?"

Stani lit a cigarette, drawing the smoke deep into his lungs. "Oh, I don't know—separating an Austrian from Austria is about as tough a fight as you could want. But the Anschluss may have changed that for them. Rolf appears to be more stubborn than Frederick."

They both laughed at the thought. Maddie added, "Is that even possible? But I have something else to ask you. Do you know Mrs. Genhart's friend, Werner Kempler? He has a fragile gift for Mrs. G. It can't be shipped, so she would like us to travel to Hamburg and pick it up. Who is this man? Do you know their history?"

A slow smile made its way across Stani's lips, and the corners of his mouth turned upward, like a Cheshire cat's. "Ah, the Amati of Angels! If that is what we are to pick up, it is most fragile, made in the late 1600s, and quite priceless, a collector's piece of mammoth proportions." He took a slug of his coffee. "I suppose that is what we are getting. She didn't say for sure, did she?"

Maddie shook her head. "No, she didn't say because she doesn't know. But I'm curious. Why would a man leave such a gift to a friend unless there was more to their relationship?" She eyed Hollenius, awaiting Stani's response. "Was there anything romantic between them?"

Stani took a drag, stubbing out the cigarette. "I have no idea. A woman's heart is like a deep ocean. Many secrets are hidden, like mysterious caverns beneath the sea or rooms in a mansion awaiting discovery. Mrs. Genhart has always played her cards close to the vest. I know very little about her life in Germany. After all the years we've known each other, I cannot say I know any more about her than you do."

"Maybe she leads a double life. Maybe she's a secret agent for the Nazis?"

Stani chortled. "My dearest, your imagination knows no bounds, but I suppose in this day and age, anything is possible."

He watched Hollenius climb from the cabinet, leaping into Maddie's lap. "Well, hello, you," Maddie greeted the purring kitty, scratching behind his ears while his motor ramped up.

"Good thing Frederick's not home. He'd be jealous." After a moment, Stani asked, "Maddie, is there anything else you'd like to discuss? You seem upset by the news of Buster's letter. Is it something he said?"

Maddie bit her lower lip. "Well, Buster said, 'We have some important things to discuss,' and then doesn't say what the things are. I'm dangling above a precipice, not knowing when I'll drop."

Stani sympathized, "I know you like everything wrapped up, neat and tidy."

"Indeed! I'm not sure how I should feel. I adore Buster and I think I see our life together in the future, in the distance, but how do I get through now until then? What do I do with all these emotions, like missing him? I feel like loneliness is eating away at my insides."

Stani focused on Maddie's luminous blue eyes, peering into them to see if they would reveal more of her feelings. "Still not in love with Buster, huh?"

She ignored his comment, as if he'd never spoken.

Stani walked over to the sink. He gripped the counter's edge, planted his feet, then leaned back and pulled himself forward, causing his lower back to expel an audible crack. A wry smile crossed his face. "Ahhhh. That feels good."

The crack startled Hollenius, and he jumped down from Maddie's lap. He sauntered toward the hall, returning to the heat vent as Stani gazed out the window at the garden below. "You've done a fantastic job with the gardens. I can't wait to see the tulips, their colors, and the variety in the petals. The diversity within a flower is all so interesting. It causes me to think how no two snowflakes are alike. A Maine farmer proved that around the turn of the century."

Unimpressed, Maddie sat quietly, her hands folded in her lap. She offered no insight.

Bored with the heat vent, Hollenius returned to Maddie's lap, watching Stani's every move. Stani turned around and sat back down so they were face-to-face. "Okay. So. I have thoughts about how to deal with those emotions and feelings. Would you like to know?"

Maddie sighs. "Yes, of course, please."

"I've shared this with you before, but you chose not to follow my advice for some reason. I'll repeat it if you take to heart what I share—know that I say these things because I want you to soar as high as possible. You have limitless talent. But it must be unleashed. When you take what I've taught you, the hole you feel in your heart will be filled. This results from pouring every bit of your indescribable gift into your practice and performance."

"I know you've told me before, but tell me again. I promise to listen and apply whatever you tell me." She struck a familiar pose, sitting up, back arched, eyes straight ahead as they taught her at the orphanage in Poland, then nodded at Stani as if to say please begin.

Stani stood and used his hands to express the weight of the words as he said, "Fear is your greatest enemy. Fear causes you to play stiffly and technically. Just as I've said in the past, emotion is lacking in your performance. You may hit every note to perfection, but without that fire—and not just fire, but the full complement of emotions—what do you have? A technical interpretation of the piece that's perfect?"

He flubbed his lips, emitting a 'phwwwhhh' sound, then shook his head, telling her, "You are meant to be more than that, so much more. You cannot hold all that you feel locked inside, pent up with no release. It has to come out. For the love of God, let it out through your playing."

Stani paused, lighting a cigarette, then tilted his head, peering so profoundly into Maddie that he could almost see the wheels turning in her head. He shook a finger at her. "This is the most valuable information I could ever bestow upon you. I will not go further unless you promise not to interrupt or question me until I finish. Agree?"

Wearing a solemn expression, Maddie nodded.

"Take this to heart. You will be an artist when naked, free of shame and judgment, and 100 percent vulnerable before your audience. That is being authentic and illustrates what being an artist is all about. You funnel all that emotion, heartbreak, passion, energy, sadness, joy, turmoil, and love into your practice and music." Stani waited, pausing so that what he says would sink in.

"This comes through when you perform; it's all that passion. Weave it between the notes on the page with your perfect execution of a piece, and you will captivate and hold your audience; they will adore you for it. The greatest performers used the sufferings of life to augment their playing. The Tchaikovsky violin concerto you play is a perfect example, especially considering the devastated place within the man who wrote it! Music without emotion is flat. Music incorporated into your heartbreak, your pain, released into your interpretation of a piece, makes it yours. Own it with all your being. Focus on that."

Maddie sat quietly, absorbing her mentor's words.

"Listen, when you perform, it has to be more than just technically perfect, which you are. Your schooling has taught you well. You are technically very good. But good is the enemy of great." Stani's voice softened, and he grasped her hands between his, crouching beside her chair while Hollenius dared him to move closer.

"Look, I'm not faulting you. I just want to encourage you to dig deep. You know this. We have had this discussion. But still, you do not follow what I share or instruct. Perhaps now, before such a pivotal performance on the world stage in Vienna, you will apply this knowledge, and I pray it doesn't fall on deaf ears."

Maddie was very still, digesting Stani's wisdom. She stroked Hollenius, telling him, "Wow. That's not pressure, now, is it?" She glared at Stani, but then her face relaxed. "I know you mean it for my good."

Reaching up, she pulled at the band holding her dark tresses, unleashing them to cascade over her shoulders. She massaged the back of her head, hoping that she could unleash the courage to speak the truth.

"Thank you for telling me what I need to do; you're right. My playing is too pedestrian—safe. I've never thought of playing in the way you speak of, funneling my emotions." Maddie's voice caught. "I-I know you've told me this before, and Elenena did as well, but it does not penetrate for some reason. I do not apply it."

Her hands dropped to her lap. "The truth is, I'm afraid of nuances like I am shadows. I grew up knowing little about life while being raised in the orphanage. I knew nothing about the in-between, the hidden, or the gray areas of life, where corners are dark, decisions are complex, and where it's not safe to expose emotions. I've lived programmed to run at the first sign of danger.

"It is my biggest fear and challenge to stand before people and play, yet if I don't perform, I feel like I will die. But to play wholly emotionally naked before the audience? I don't know if I can do that, Stani. I'm afraid of that place, of going there. What do I know about funneling my emotions into music? Throughout my life, I've only known how to survive."

CHAPTER TWELVE

The Speicherstadt

MAY 13, 1939, THE WAREHOUSE DISTRICT, HAMBURG PORT

A S INSTRUCTED, AT 6:00 a.m., the man named Fritz went to the exact location where he would pick up the film reels and credentials for boarding the ship. He brought an empty suitcase for the reels, hoping it would accommodate them, but he had no idea as to their size.

Once he found the correct door, he knocked. The door opened, he gave the name Fritz, and he received the films—not in reels but in round aluminum canisters and a packet of documents for his travel. There was nothing more to it.

Relief.

If he weren't so exhausted, he'd take the time to admire the red brick towers and nooks of the Neo-Gothic Speicherstadt. The warehouse complex, the largest of its kind, was comprised of many multi-storied buildings with entrances on land and water, supported by thousands of oak poles in the Elbe Riverbed. The district was crossed by what were known as fleets—canals that were flooded depending on the tides. The Speicherstadt was built within part of the extensive canal system that spread across the city like a spiderweb.

But this was his second day without sleep or food. Hunger roared in his ears, gnawing at him with a gutting, hollow ache. His imagination ran wild, tormented by the idea of eggs, fried potatoes, bacon, and a steaming cup of coffee. Something, anything to help overcome the dead-man-walking feeling that had absorbed him.

He spent the night tucked away inside one of the warehouse sheds among the varied, large stationary containers. *Rats, why rats? Of course. Water. Containers. Damn it. Why did I ever think I'd get rest here? Did I think I'd catch forty winks?* The rats were the size of his shoe. Rats have, by nature, destructive intentions. They refuse to sleep. Why should they, when an unusual cuisine lies before them?

The rats' constant shucking around, sizing up their catch, jarred him from the pitiful state of altered half-sleep. He stretched his lean body, trying to straighten his back, cramped from dozing, while wedging himself into a space well out of sight from the dock workers. They hurried about, some on official business, the evidence of such being a clipboard and pencil.

He yawned, aware that no sleep was possible now that the sun was up. The overarching smell of saltiness from the sea permeated the atmosphere, awakening his nasal passages. Fritz contemplated how he would spend the next half-day while awaiting the ship's boarding. The four propaganda films added thirty pounds to his suitcase, jeopardizing its handle's reliability. Snagging his duffel bag, he walked to the back of a storage shed, where he spied a place to leave his belongings. He grabbed his Gestapo-issued black trench coat, devoid of his rank emblems and the usual red-and-black swastika armbands. He had only a badge given to him by the Gestapo for identification.

Various seafaring birds, gulls, ducks, and geese of many varieties occupied the rafters, squawking at his arrival. Something caught his eye as he walked toward the front of the shed. He noticed a young man sleeping as he had been, buttressed between the containers, and it appeared he had no concern with being in view. He must have been beyond tired—he was sleeping so soundly. Or perhaps he was drunk—or both.

Fritz observed the man's shaved head—covered with a cap—and ragged clothing. As if sensing someone watching, the cap-wearing man's body twitched, and he opened his eyes wide, as if seeing an approaching tidal wave. They stared at one another in sweat-inducing silence until the man in the cap asked, barely squeaking out the words, if he needed to present his papers. Clearing his throat, he said in German, "I'll present my papers."

Fritz nodded and beckoned, flashing his Gestapo badge. "Yes. Come forward. What is your name?"

A wind swirled, causing debris to blow. The cap-wearing man rubbed both eyes and stood straight, handing over his papers. "Stefan Soutine."

Fritz repeated his name. "Why are you here? Are you waiting for someone or something? Tell me everything, and there will be no issue. Now. Out with it."

Stefan's spine straightened, knowing that lying to a Nazi could cost him his life. "I am awaiting the *S.S. St. Louis*, in shed 76, sailing to Havana tonight. I'm a former prisoner at Dachau Concentration Camp. Commandant Eicke agreed to free me if I signed a paper stating I would leave Germany and never return. If I do, I will be shot."

Fritz considered the bold statement. "Why is that? Why would you be shot? I don't see any markings showing you're Jewish."

Nervous, the ex-prisoner looked side to side, then said, "I don't know why, sir. I was accused, judged guilty, even though I wasn't, and put in Dachau by mistake."

Fritz smirked. "Are you telling me that Nazis made a mistake, that they are wrong, and you are right?"

"Yes, sir. That is just what I'm saying." He half-winced, awaiting a punch, kick, or swing of the baton. But one didn't come.

It was almost like he hadn't spoken out loud.

"You speak perfect German. Where are you from?"

"I'm French. My mother was German, and I lived in Germany for a while, first in Berlin, then in Dachau, Munich, as a chef, cooking for Commandant Eicke and his family."

A maritime horn blew two stout, distinct blows, signaling the approach of a steamship on the starboard side of another vessel. Stefan asked the time, "if you wouldn't mind, sir," and Fritz peeled back his cuff to look at his Patek Philippe watch.

"Six-twenty a.m." The man reached inside the breast pocket of his coat, retrieving his cigarettes, held in a silver case with initials inscribed on the front, impossible for Fritz to make out. It wouldn't be proper for a former prisoner to ask the name of a German officer. Stefan gauged that the man must be affluent by the look of his suit, watch, shoes, and cigarette case.

Stefan took the offered cigarette, and the man lit his first, then Stefan's. Taking a deep drag, Stefan noticed a distinct difference from his usual cheap German cigarettes. Since the men were sharing a casual smoke, Stefan took a chance and spoke to the other man as if he were chatting with a friend. "That is one smooth smoke. Are these French cigarettes?"

Fritz shook his head but did not reveal their origin. Instead, he asked, his tone laced with suspicion, "Where is your suitcase? Have you no belongings?"

Puzzled by the officer's lack of knowledge, Stefan stated, "While I risk sounding impertinent, sir, as a prisoner, we come into Dachau with nothing and leave with even less. Most don't leave; if they do, they leave this life for good."

The man didn't react to the extremity of the statement. Instead, he asked, "What kind of chef are you? Are you a chef trained with much experience and credentials, or do you have a repertoire of ten dishes and call yourself a chef? There is a difference."

Stefan said with authority, puffing out his chest, "I was trained since a young boy, growing up, doing stáges in many of the greatest kitchens in Paris. I was chef de cuisine at the St. Moritz when Nazi Officer Dietrich von Dorsten hired me to cook for him and his wife. That was in Berlin. So, yes, I am truly a chef."

Fritz took one last drag and then stubbed out his cigarette with the heel of his shoe. "Do you think you'll be killed if you go back?"

Stefan's face went dark with confusion. He stepped back from the man, shaking his head and raising his hands. "Wait a minute, are you trying to trap me or something? I haven't done anything wrong. I was minding my own business when you approached me, and you have every right to, but I have done nothing wrong. If you don't mind, I'd like my papers returned, and I will go about my way if that's acceptable to you, sir."

A curious smile crossed the man's face. "What's the rush? The ship won't depart for hours. I'll keep you in custody until boarding time."

CHAPTER THIRTEEN

False Flags

MAY 13, 1939 , PORT OF HAMBURG, GERMANY

PERSECUTED AT HOME and not wanted abroad, the German-Jewish population in Germany hoping to emigrate had nowhere to turn. A ray of hope came in May 1939 when a luxury liner docked in Hamburg: the *S.S. St. Louis*.

The vessel was available for service, and the Nazis chose it with the intention of transport based on one factor—its captain. Danish-born German Gustav Schroeder, a thirty-seven-year veteran of the seas, became captain of the *S.S. St. Louis* last year. He was the perfect choice due to his stance on Hitler and his policies. Schroeder loathed the Nazi ideology and opposed the vitriolic Hitler doctrine. Goebbels picked him because "the captain is above reproach. He cannot be branded as one of us."

Schroeder was circumspect in behavior and kept his opinions to himself while onboard. With a record void of blemishes, he was known for being stoic and a leader of men. Almost all of his well-trained crew reflected his high standards and attitude of complete professionalism, except Abwehr courier Otto Schiendick and his gang of "firemen," who chose to be contentious objectors to the captain's stance on Nazi policies.

The firemen were onboard at the request of Schutzstaffel Chief Himmler in case of a "sabotage attempt," but it was a false flag. In reality, they were onboard to help Schiendick harass the Jewish passengers. The Nazis had succeeded with such tactics, starting with the Reichstag Fire of 1933 and Kristallnacht in 1938.

Staging the fire at the Reichstag, as well as the Paris shooting of German diplomat Ernst von Rath, were the perfect pretext for the Nazis to implement new restrictive, exclusionary laws and pay retribution. The Gestapo had marching orders to mount violent reprisals throughout Germany and Austria, staged to appear as "spontaneous demonstrations." Vengeance poured forth from rioters, paid to appear and commit acts of violence. Synagogues, homes, and businesses were burned to the ground. In Germany, every glass storefront was shattered, and the night became known as the "Night of Broken Glass"—Kristallnacht.

More than one thousand synagogues were burned or damaged in two days and nights. Rioters ransacked and looted more than 7,500 businesses—all Jewish-owned—and thirty thousand Jewish men were arrested and sent to concentration camps. Ninety-one men died. At the last moment, police were told to allow the perpetrators to wreak havoc and allow for destruction while arresting innocent victims—and placing them in the concentration camps of Dachau, Buchenwald, and Sachsenhausen, among others.

Goebbels, the Minister of Propaganda, had become so deft at using every tool available to him that he was now a master of staging riots, marches, demonstrations, and acts of violence. Even the Führer was confused about what was real and what was staged, and requested prior notification of such actions rather than being unaware.

Ships were a favorite tool of the Abwehr, to transport secret documents, gather counter-intelligence, and poll the average passenger. They accomplished this by staffing intercontinental passenger voyages with spies. An intercontinental journey was a perfect guise for their motives. They were onboard for a long trip, mixed in as first-class passengers. After a few days aboard, familiarity would take over, and discussions would go beyond the casual. Spies aboard passenger ships had proven effective at gathering information for recording and gauging reactions to statements made during informal chats. The results were passed on to the Reich and added to the information collection from spy and SS sources.

When paired with Nazi radical ideology, the propaganda was then manufactured, and narratives became policies custom-made to stoke the fears of the general population. The Reich recognized the public's gullibility, and if propaganda was used strategically, it could convince the people of any belief that those in power chose. They cooperate fully and work in concert with print media, publishers of books and materials, radio programming, and film industries.

Colleges, universities, and all aspects of education were overtaken by Nazi doctrine, complete with fabricated myths of a master race predicated on the manic dreams of a megalomaniac. Paid agitators riled up college students, causing them to protest and then riot. Recognizing the vacuum created by the educational system and that their young impressionable minds were ripe for brainwashing, the Nazis wasted no time indoctrinating them.

Every part of a German citizen's life was steeped in radical Nazi dogma. The Nazis learned that if you said an untruth enough and broadcasted it often, it would become truth to the public. After some time, lies became truth. And people didn't know the difference anymore. Their strategy was a simple one: Subject the public to it, a little at a time, then increase the amount of propaganda until the government gained complete control over the German people. The Nazis were brilliant, in an evil way, and confident in their schemes. They hoped the next one, Operation Sunshine, would play out as well as the others.

The Nazis confirmed the wheels to their plan were turning due to a third-party announcement that Operation Sunshine had begun. This confirmation came to the British consul in Havana via Robert Hoffman, after British sources intercepted a message from Joseph Goebbels to Hoffman at the HAPAG Office which doubled as an Abwehr base in Havana. Goebbels's message stated, *Operation Sunshine sails, the ship will return to Hamburg. More to follow.*

Aboard the S.S. St. Louis
Meanwhile, Captain Schroeder felt uncertain and anxious over the upcoming "special" voyage. The emphasis on a special voyage rankled his sensibilities. In his years on the seas, a voyage had never been labeled *special.* He was sure there were other forces at work, something nefarious, but he couldn't pinpoint what they could be.

Hours before departure, the captain received a message from the director of the HAPAG line, Claus-Gottfried Holthusen, who clarified that the ship and its "special voyage" would go as planned. He mentioned it would be best not to ask any questions for the captain's and the company's sake.

It was clear to the captain that the Reich, the majority shareholder of the HAPAG line, forced the director to comply with every request. The swastika flag of the Third Reich flew high on the tallest mast of every ship in the line.

The Gestapo kept its eye on such ships, watching the staff and crew, and recording questionable actions—like sending telegrams to family members in Europe and complaining about the "crew," who were, in reality, primarily spies for the Nazis. Schroeder hoped to rid his ship of such undesirable Nazi elements by lodging formal complaints, but these fell on deaf ears. It seemed like the zealots employed by HAPAG were overtaking the number of employees who weren't rabid Nazis.

In his message, Holthusen had informed the captain that he must use tact and follow his instructions if he wished to remain employed. He notified Schroeder that his ship would carry close to a thousand German Jews emigrating to Cuba, hoping to later relocate to the US. What Schroeder wasn't told was that the Abwehr would use this special voyage for a twofold purpose: to transport secret espionage documents from Havana to Hamburg and to show the world that no country wanted the Jews.

The Abwehr had formed an ultra-organized espionage ring that stockpiled American military secrets culled by agents in the US and sought safe means of transporting them to Germany. Steward Otto Schiendick, the ship's boastful Abwehr agent, used his little power as Abwehr's representative to influence and lead the Nazi cabal aboard the ship. His most significant ego-bolstering moment had come when he'd arranged for two members of the crew and its former captain to be removed from the vessel for expressing attitudes not in keeping with Nazi policy.

The captain had inherited Schiendick, along with the crew of the *S.S. St. Louis* when he took over command late in 1938. Standing on the bridge before the ship departed, the steward bragged about the great success of previous espionage operations, his voice sickeningly sweet and sarcastic. "Why, Captain, you of all people, a decorated hero of the Great War, I thought you'd be pleased to know you're helping the cause by transporting this ship of vagrants to start a new life. How philanthropic! Yet, you don't appear pleased. You seem depressed. Can I help?"

Overlooking the seas with his binoculars, Captain Schroeder didn't flinch a muscle as he said, his tone even, "You can dismiss yourself from my deck at once."

Schiendick was aware of the captain's disdain for the Nazi Party and had the nerve to warn Captain Schroeder that refusal to join the Party could result in loss of command. The threat shook Schroeder, but it wasn't the first time he'd been threatened. He remained steadfast in his refusal to join. Although he served as captain of the German ship, he didn't do it out of loyalty to the Reich.

Hours before a single passenger boarded the ship, as his first action as captain, Schroeder gathered the whole crew, all 262 of them, in the social hall, reminded them about important procedures, especially those in opposition to serving the Jewish passengers. The captain spoke with all seriousness, discussing his expectations to treat every passenger with respect and kindness, providing them the same service as any other paying passenger on a HAPAG vessel.

Despite his short stature, Captain Schroeder's stern presence commanded attention. He told his crew, "Anyone unwilling to participate with complete civility in the voyage to Cuba may resign at once. You will treat every single passenger with respect, honoring our reputation for high standards in all decorum and ceremony. They are paying customers, and you will treat them as such."

The captain glared at the greasy Schiendick and his cadre of Nazi firemen, aware of the intense hate these men held in their hearts toward the Jewish passengers. He scanned the room, looking for anything out of line. Then he spotted it. To the left of the piano at the front of the room hung a 36" x 42" framed picture of Hitler.

Schroeder's face turned red with rage. He narrowed his eyes and bellowed, "That picture is to be removed at once!" The captain points to a steward, telling him to take the photograph below for storage. "Our passengers will use this room for their worship services. Any attempt to cause discomfort for one passenger will result in the offender spending the rest of the voyage to Cuba and back in the brig. Now, go about your business, exceed expectations, devote yourself to doing your jobs, and let's have a good voyage. Dismissed."

Otto Schiendick took out his black leather pocket diary, the one with his initials inscribed in gold, and noted the threats Captain Schroeder had made. *I'll fix him.*

CHAPTER FOURTEEN

Uneasy Journey

MAY 5, 1939, VIENNA, AUSTRIA

Dearest Buster,

Our journey was smooth except for two days of rough seas that made me seasick. Of course, I thought of you and our voyage in 1933; you were so sick. I must have sympathy pains for you! It's curious how Stani never gets ill; he claims God made him that way so he could care for me when I do.

Today, after our dress rehearsal, I spotted him standing in the wings, brimming with pride as I was about to leave the stage. His eyes were shining, and he had a broad smile as he directed so much love toward me that I could feel it, and my heart received it. I cannot believe my luck in having someone like Stani to watch over me. What would I ever do without him?

The rehearsals with the symphony and Conductor Furtwängler this week went well, despite feeling a bit rusty initially due to not playing or practicing during the voyage, but not for lack of trying. We searched for a suitable place to practice with good acoustics and settled on the grand hall of the ship, which was available after luncheon. Stani stood beside me and held a bucket in case the boat swayed. We attempted to practice while seated, but it never worked as it caused me to tense my muscles. We gave up.

During my first full practice session here at the hall, I made a couple of squeaks and had to restart twice. I believe the excess resin on my bow, and nerves were the culprits. However, today's session was almost flawless. The Tchaikovsky piece is about thirty-five minutes long, with the second and third movements played attacca without a break. At first, I was concerned about my lack of stamina during the first few days of practice, given my recent journey. However, after a good night's sleep on Wednesday, I felt refreshed and prepared for the session.

The symphony and conductor were nothing short of magnificent throughout the week. When he takes command of the orchestra, it's not like he's commanding an army; instead, he brings a trembling state of heightened emotional awareness that is both irresistible and terrifying as he bridles the power of the music and each musician. With the bit firmly in place, he lifts his arms, and the journey of the Opus begins.

It's nothing short of thrilling; the piece accelerates, and it's madness! I'm lost in a mélange of notes, my body reacting to the harmonious blasts of perfection hovering around me. I'm moving without being conscious of moving.

When I played this piece at Carnegie Hall last year, my performance, while lauded, felt stiff and inauthentic. Since performing it numerous times, I know I possess the piece, and it possesses me. I'm ready. I know by the sensation I get before a performance. It's like a nervous confidence. I'm at peace and welcoming tomorrow. While anyone around me would never guess I have peace, I do. Stani has helped me so much, teaching me scriptures to memorize and rely on when I become intimidated or scared. I can't say whether or not the scriptures have helped me. I will search for evidence of its effect and report back.

How I wish you could be here for my performance. I'd look into the audience and see your handsome face in the front row, looking marvelous in your full-dress uniform; how it would cheer me. But it also would make me weak in the knees! How could I perform? I'd not be able to. I miss you so much.

I'm thinking about what else I wanted to share—yes! Let me tell you about this concert hall. It's even more beautiful than Carnegie Hall or the Eastman. The acoustics are incredible; they are the best I've ever experienced as an artist. Not that I'm an old pro. I'll read (write) you the brochure: "The Vienna Musikverein, built by Danish architect Theophil Hansen in 1870, boasts a facade resembling a Greek temple, reminiscent of the temples of music and heroes from ancient times. The Great Hall is renowned for its exceptional acoustics and luxurious interior that exudes classical Greek ambiance through various colors from antiquity. Everywhere one looks, there are reflections of Greece, including caryatids and columns. The room's shoebox-style proportions and sculptures allow for early and numerous sound reflections, making it the perfect venue for musical performances." It's even more impressive than it sounds. Maybe I'll perform here one day, and you'll be with me.

We will break bread with Rolf and Cecile on Sunday, the day after the performance. I've provided them with tickets to the concert. I'm looking forward to seeing them. Stani says we can help them pack; "many hands make light work," to quote him. I think that's rushing it a bit. But he told me Frederick said Rolf has already mostly packed up much of the house since the Anschluss, despite Cecile's complaints. Rolf will not disclose that a neighbor wants to buy their home as a gift for a newly wedded son until she commits to moving. We'll see what happens when we speak. Stani will be emphatic that they leave. "No time to waste." He believes Hitler will slam the doors shut at one point, and no Jews will be allowed to leave.

We are tasked with an errand, Mrs. Genhart has us going home through Hamburg, taking a different ship. Mrs. Genhart has an old friend who is dying and has a gift for her, and she wants us to retrieve it. She has no idea what it could be, perhaps a priceless violin he performed with, which Stani calls the "Amati of Angels."

Once we have it, we will scamper home, and not a moment too soon. The atmosphere here is frightening. We've seen people (Jews) beaten on the street, scrubbing painted words off the sidewalks while citizens of this fine city stand around jeering, calling them reprehensible names, and spitting on them. We've witnessed Nazis cutting off Hasidic men and boys' payos. Even more so now than in 1933, Nazi flags are everywhere the eye can see, as are swastika badges and armbands. The outpouring of love and affection for "der Führer" is something to witness.

Stani says, "Hitler believed fanaticism to be a virtue of the youth, so he capitalized on the ignorance of their young age, luring them into the Hitler Youth and, from there, the German Wehrmacht. Hitler figured out how to energize and passionately inflame millions." These Hitler youths marched through the streets like they did on the Konigsplatz in Munich the day we met. But now, they sing a song about an alleged martyr, Horst Wessel, a former organizer of prostitutes. He is the standard that the Nazis promote.

These Hitler Youth are nothing more than troublemakers. People are rabid with this Nazism—and they frighten me. We walk through the streets of Vienna guarded, keeping to ourselves, praying that our fear is invisible. Stani wonders how long before they demand everyone support Hitler or die. You have to show allegiance.

What about artists? Rules and laws: Jews cannot play or perform in German or Austrian Halls and may not be hired for symphony orchestras. Can you imagine if they found out about Stani and me? Trying hard not to get swallowed alive by that one fearful thought.

It's incredible how much has changed in six years. The Nuremberg Laws are enforced with an iron rod. Stani says, "Don't trust anyone," but I can't be like that, not here, in my continent homeland. I still strongly desire to perform for European audiences, but what would be the point if war breaks out? It appears that the people of Austria and Germany are eager for war, which I can't comprehend. Why would anyone ever wish for such a thing? Their leader, Hitler, is a creature who seems to have a massive appetite for conflict and greed for land and power. Stani reads all the papers and shares bits and pieces with me. There's a lot of talk about a program called 'Lebensraum.' I've heard it's about the German people needing more land to survive.

Speaking of Germans, we're told a large contingent of Nazis will attend tomorrow night's performance. It's not good to think about before going to bed when you aren't here to hold me; how I hate the nighttime!

I hate to say goodnight, but I must. Please be safe. I have no idea where you are or what you're doing. Raymond gave me an address in Buckinghamshire to send you letters. He said they'd find their way to you. I sure hope so. July feels like an eternity.

—Your Maddie

❖

For her performance, Maddie wore an elegant royal blue silk sheath that gave her a lithe appearance. Her dark-brown, shiny tresses were done up in a chignon, held in place by a pearl-studded hair comb Buster had given her for Christmas past, which she wore for good luck. She adorned her feet with white satin-and-pearl flat slippers, which were comfortable for performing. Her makeup was done perfectly, thanks to the ladies' maid assigned to her performance.

The maid, Elzbieta, made the room comfortable and decidedly feminine for Maddie, somehow setting up the room to her personal preferences: a chair in a corner where she could sit and read; fresh flowers, but not strong-smelling ones; and a teapot, cup, and saucer. Elzbieta also saw to it that the daybed was made up with new, soft, pink and yellow blankets and an assortment of pillows with a floral covering. She placed a cut-glass water pitcher and glass on Maddie's makeup table, along with a small, delicate, green glass plate on a doily. On the plate rested six Viennese butter cookies with lavender.

Maddie felt a kinship with the woman, who she'd learned was from Eastern Europe. Poland. Maddie tipped her generously, hugged her, and said in Polish, "Thank you, and God bless."

Elzbieta smiled warmly and squeezed Maddie's hand. Then she kissed it while repeating the same phrase. They whispered to each other in Polish, but after a minute, Maddie put her index finger to her lips. "Shhhhhhh. Please."

A loud knock on the dressing room door startled the women. The maestro strode in, and Elzbieta left the room.

The urbane Furtwängler dwarfed Maddie in the small confines of the "star" dressing room, causing a claustrophobic reaction. His presence, height, and bald head seemed so out of place in the ultra-feminine space. He held a full flute of champagne in one hand.

For the first time, Maddie noticed the size of his hands—not that she hadn't seen them before, but in the tight quarters, they seemed enormous. It looked like he could snap the glass in two, as easy as snapping his fingers. She worked to avoid staring at his hands or becoming obsessed with them. Needing something to focus on, she centered on his attire.

He was dressed in an elegant tuxedo with tails and a dapper cummerbund. He wore what little hair that remained slicked on the sides with hair tonic. Its smell made Maddie queasy and in need of fresh air. She fanned herself with sheet music, then smiled weakly while shaking his hand, her own hand limp while trying to overcome a sudden wave of nausea and cramping.

The maestro bubbled over excitedly, telling her, "You look marvelous! The audience won't be able to take their eyes off you! I can hardly take my eyes off you! How can you be twenty-three? You could pass for fifteen, and I mean that in the best of ways! How is our star doing? Are you ready? How about some champagne to loosen you up?"

He didn't wait for her to answer. "We have a sold-out crowd tonight. People are clamoring for tickets; they're even chanting your name! Maddie, Maddie, Maddie! I think they're as fascinated with you as the rest of the world. They want to know! Who are you? Where did you come from?" He paused, leaving Maddie puzzled. *Did he mean that in the literal sense? He's making me nervous. Please leave.*

Maddie placed her hands together and bowed her head as if praying. "Thank you. I'm very excited for tonight."

"Me too. We've had a sensational week of practice. I was pleased with everyone's performance. It's not an easy piece, and then there's your solo and that second movement after the cadenza. Wow." The conductor swayed back and forth. "That's a beast. You're going to throttle our audience. Cheers to you!" He raised his champagne glass and tilted it toward her. "After the performance, there will be people who want to come backstage and meet you. Please don't run off!"

The conductor moved close and stood in front of Maddie. He rested a giant hand on her shoulder and bent to whisper in her ear. She felt the warmth of his breath on her neck, too close for comfort. If she could only ask him to remove his hand. But she was afraid to insult the maestro. Instead, she backed away.

He didn't seem to notice. Instead, he drained his glass of the last drop of champagne and said, "You will be nothing short of magnificent. I believe in you! See you out there."

He turned to leave as Stani glided through the doorway. The men nodded to each other as Maddie collapsed in the chair. The ill feeling hadn't left.

Stani sat on the daybed across from Maddie; he searched her face, trying to read her emotions and gauge her nerves. "Was he bothering you? You seem annoyed."

Maddie remained silent, her expression blank, unreadable. But not to Stani. He noticed everything when it came to Maddie. "You have what's known as a poker face. Most would never know what's brewing beneath the surface, percolating. You are a blank slate to most, but not to me. Tell me, how are you? What's simmering, my love?" He pulled a small apple from his pocket and munched on it while Maddie decided whether or not to open up.

His question cracked the ice, and Maddie's lips pursed. Tears formed in her eyes. "'What's simmering' is an astute observation and question." She rose from the chair to face him. *Should I bring up the Nazis? How could I hide this from him? He must know. He's walked around Vienna enough to recognize that the whole place is inundated with them.*

She kept her thoughts calm, saying, "Usual nerves, but more so since I've been told the front rows will be filled with Nazis." She frowned and wrapped her arms around her body as if they would protect her. Apprehension filled her voice. "We don't need to worry, do we?"

Stani finished his apple, core and all, then lit a cigarette. "My dear, what else would you expect? As long as Germany occupies Austria, the Nazis will have the best seats for any performance of this caliber. Remember our first concert together, the Nazi elite with their wives, dressed in Jewish-made designer clothes, dripping with jewels and furs? That was six years ago. Expect to see even more tonight."

She shook her head. "It's not just that. Furtwängler posed a question; I didn't know how to answer, so I said nothing." Maddie bit her lower lip, ruining her lipstick.

"This is a new wrinkle. What did he ask you?"

Taking a drag from Stani's cigarette, Maddie said, "He asked, 'Who are you, and where did you come from?' What if someone asks me? We've never discussed that; how do I answer? What should I say? I feel like my insides are turned outside." Maddie's stomach began to cramp. The color left her cheeks.

"My dear, you look pale. Let me get you some water." Stani poured water from the pitcher on the dressing table and handed her the glass. He lifted her chin and looked into her eyes. "Please, tell me what's bothering you."

Maddie sipped the water, contemplating how to respond. Standing, she says, "How is it that you have no anxiety knowing Nazis surround us? I'm amazed at you. How do you just go on like nothing has ever happened? What if they discover us, or someone from the past recognizes us?" She turned from him and began wringing her hands.

Stani pointed upward to God and said, "Three words. The Wellington name."

Maddie stood up and turned on her heel. "What about it?"

He chuckled, which infuriated her. "You better have a good reason for laughing at me." Stani chuckled even more, prompting Maddie to throw a small pillow at him. "Stop it!"

Stani took Maddie by the hand, and they sat together on the daybed. "I said 'the name' for obvious reasons. The Nazis won't question 'Wellington.' 'Turetsky' would be questioned. The name shelters you. Remember? As for fearing them, fear makes itself known to the opposition. Not only do they recognize it, but even more subtly, they can sense it, smell it, and taste it. They pounce on the fearful; it's a sport for them. Therefore, we must appear fearless! Being fearful serves no purpose. I want you to memorize this scripture from the Psalms: 'At what time I am afraid, I will trust in thee.' You remember that every time you feel fear darkening your mind or thoughts. Remember, darkness has no place in the light. Light will always conquer darkness. The hand of God is on us, protecting us. Do not fear. You are here with a purpose. Faith comes by hearing the word of God. You have heard it.

"Now, let's focus on tonight's performance, and in the

meantime, why don't you warm up and play some scales? It will take your mind off of worry. Practice your breathing, too."

He stepped back and held an imaginary camera, like he was taking her picture. His voice softening, Stani said, "I want to remember everything about tonight, every detail, because you won't remember in the morning. But most of all, I want to remember how you look. Even more beautiful than Elenena. The world is your oyster, and tonight is all for you. You will be sensational."

Maddie blushed at the compliment. "What would I ever do without you?" With a twinkle in her eye, she said slyly, "Now, let me be so I can do what you recommend!"

Maddie practiced her scales to warm up her fingers. She said to herself, *At what time, I am afraid I will trust in thee.* The stage manager knocked on the door minutes later. "Five minutes, Miss Wellington."

Maddie's expression changed from calm to terrified, and she said to Stani, "It's time. Oh my God. It's time." She put her violin down and looked in the full-length mirror, then let out a lengthy sigh. *At what time, I am afraid, I will trust in thee.*

Her breath came fast; she began to take with deep breaths to regulate herself. In through her nose, out through her mouth. She adjusted her lipstick; her hand trembled a bit. *Calm, Maddie, calm. God help me.* She grabbed her bow and violin and, as was her custom, kissed it on the neck and whispered, "Elenena, I hope you can hear this tonight. I dedicate this performance to you."

Stani carried her violin case and held Maddie's free hand. He told her, "She can hear you, and will be with you tonight. God, too." He winked at her.

She smiled, squeezing his hand, saying what he already knew but loved to hear her say, "I love you."

The stage manager escorted them to the backstage hallway leading straight to the stage. Even surrounded by people, artists, stagehands, and managers, Maddie heard nothing but her breathing and footsteps. Her eyes were glued to the gold tapestry curtains; her breathing echoed in her ears, and time slowed down to microseconds; she noticed a piece of lint floating by.

She imagined a giant clock with large hands ticking. She was tied to the hour hand, and the minute hand moved its way toward twelve at a rapid pace. Her breathing quickened. When the clock struck twelve, it chimed Maddie's name instead of the hour. She closed her eyes when she heard, "Maddie Wellington," followed by deafening applause, and she floated on stage.

Maddie was lost in what felt like white noise. Her feet moved like they were driven by magic, leading her toward the front of the stage and her music stand. Despite trembling hands, she managed to hold onto her violin and bow. Like a majestic bird, the conductor stood tall on his stand, ready to lead the audience on a musical journey.

As he nodded, she approached her stand and assumed her position, prepared to play once the conductor signaled her. The orchestra's first notes pierced the silence, and she could barely hear their sound despite being surrounded by them. She kept time to the music and waited for her cue, wondering if her fingers would work. Then Furtwängler signaled her, and somehow, she started playing, dragging and pushing her bow over the strings, like an ebb and flow of life.

As she played, every part of her vibrated with sound, and the artist and instrument melded together like a rushing stream that flowed deep into her heart, passing through every vessel and vein as she poured all her energy, emotion, and loss into each note.

The first movement's main melody is one of such exquisite beauty that it doesn't merely move the soul. In allegro moderato, the music tells a story in a love language only a heart broken by loss or pain can recognize. Brought to life are the ups and downs of a relationship. Then, the musical pace ramps up, brilliantly illustrating the complexities of a failing marriage, transforming into an emotion-packed harmonic rhythm, building to a grand orchestral statement in which the main theme returns, stated in a powerful, heroic guise.

Tchaikovsky composed this three-movement "Opus 35 in D Major" in 1878, while recuperating in Clarens, Switzerland, from the aftermath of his failed marriage. The theme of this opus reflects that ill-fated period during the second movement, which disintegrates into unstable music, portraying the thrashing of emotions and the wearisome breakdown of the spirit, reflecting the intrinsic negativity that develops between two people at odds.

Each musician executed their part in this turmoil to perfection, leading to Maddie re-entering the piece, playing a delicate version of the theme, slowly building, swelling into orchestral proportions again, then leaving Maddie in the spotlight, playing alone, intense at times, accentuating the isolation one feels after a crushing breakup. Blithely, she moved into the cadenza full of intensity and high notes, ending with a trill, the signal for the orchestra to re-enter while the flutists, bassoons, and oboes played a reprise in allegro vivacissimo.

Meanwhile, Furtwängler led Maddie and the orchestra to race at a furious pace to the end of the movement in a stupendously thrilling coda. Maddie's passionate embrace of the piece was relentless as she extruded the final notes, which were abrupt, ending the piece and leaving the audience stunned and breathless. The hall was silent; you could hear a pin drop. Then, with thunderous applause, the audience jumped to their feet and shouted, "Brava, brava, brava."

For Maddie, time resumed in slow motion. She looked down at her shoes, ensuring her feet touched the ground, as the audience started tossing single long-stemmed roses to the stage at her feet. She turned to make eye contact with the maestro, watching him also applaud her, nodding and smiling.

A man approached her, carrying a grand bouquet of deep red long-stemmed roses. Another man took her violin and bow, replacing them with the roses for her to hold. *Oh, yes, I'm supposed to curtsy*. Maddie curtsied. She hadn't been able to see the audience throughout the performance because of the lights—they burned so bright. But now, with the stage lights turned lower, the audience came into better focus.

She began to breathe hard, and her hands trembled; her throat tightened and closed, and she'd scream for Stani if she could get the words out. The sight was shocking, reminiscent of six years ago in Munich. But now, the Nazi elite all stared at her, cheered for her. They wanted a piece of her. If, somehow, they could take something from her and make it their own. And it makes her sick to her stomach. *Oh, God, not that horrible feeling. These are not my people. How could I be so foolish, so prideful to think I'd come here and play for my people?*

Everything around Maddie was a blur. Someone took her by the arm; another took the flowers, while a third guided her through the crush. The backstage swarmed with a deluge of people—someone, perhaps the stage manager, whistled for help to get Maddie through the crowd unharmed. The crowd hummed like a busy hive, with hundreds of bees swarming.

People with no concept of space got right in Maddie's face, telling her how amazing she is— yelling "You're a genius," "Can I have your autograph? My name is Elise." The cacophony of sounds overwhelmed Maddie; her feet lifted from the ground like she was carried on a wave. She lost her footing, falling to her knees.

Someone yelled to clear the way. Men flanked her, lifting her off the ground and whisking her to her dressing room, with Stani awaiting her arrival. Clapping his hands for attention, he insisted, "Everyone, leave the room, and please give her ten minutes."

Stani closed the door as the last person left, leaning against it, though that did little to silence the roar coming from the other side. He adopted a comical expression, and Maddie laughed, despite feeling weak. His head dropped into his hands, and he shook his head. Sitting beside her on the daybed, still laughing, he said, "People must think Garbo is in here! This is madness! Understandable, but madness nonetheless!"

He removed her slippers and rubbed her feet. "The performance was beyond expectation. Otherworldly. Your interpretation of the piece is a paragon. But don't expect to hear that from this vapid group. They care about important matters, like fashion." He rolled his eyes for emphasis.

Maddie nodded, still feeling out of focus. The stage manager poked his head in the room and shouted to be heard, "They're going to want to come back here; can't hold them back." Stani said, "Give her five minutes. They'll feel special for having to wait. Tell them it's a privilege!"

He turned to Maddie. "Remember. You must be cordial, and I know how you feel even before you say it, but we must have a unified front to present, even though we are both filled to the brim with contempt." His voice lightened. "We will smile and be gracious. I'll give them fifteen minutes with you, that's it, then rush them out, saying we have to travel and a plane to catch. Okay?"

Maddie nodded. "Can you reach the butter cookies? Maybe food will help."

Stani jumped up. "I also have your tea ready. You just sit back for five more minutes. Then we'll get it over with."

The door opened without a knock. Three men dressed in jackboots and the traditional SS black leather trench coat entered and closed the door behind them. Shocked, Maddie stood, and Stani jumped forward, jaw clenched tighter than his fists. Taking a deep breath, he said, "Gentlemen, please, Miss Wellington has not had her required moments of rest before she receives any guests."

The shortest of the three men asked, "Why would you think we are guests?"

CHAPTER FIFTEEN

Nazis All in a Row

MAY 6, 1939, THE VIENNA MUSIKVEREIN

CECILE AND ROLF Wolferman had aged in the six years since the last time Rolf saw Wolfie and Frederick during the summer of 1933. Now, Maddie and Stani were their closest connection to Rolf's brother, Frederick, and their nephew, Wolfie. The Wolfermans were dressed in their best finery for the special night of music and family. Maddie and Stani were family to the Wolfermans, a family that lives too far away. On another continent, in a world without Nazis.

"Rolf, do you think Maddie will have time to see us?" Cecile's rhetorical question was answered, but not from Rolf's lips.

Rolf let his wife be. She got whipped up over the smallest of grievances.

Cecile went on. "Of course, she'll make time. It's more of a question of how we'll get back there. It's bulging with people, and here we are in the lobby, packed like pickles in a crock. How will we ever get backstage? I have so many questions."

Rolf yawned and then shrugged. He looked at his watch. "Worst case, we see them tomorrow as planned."

Cecile scowled at him. "That's not what I wanted to hear. Can you be any less excited? I wanted you to tell me we will find a way. Here we are, all dressed up. How can we not see her? She traveled a great distance to perform. She might think we didn't care enough to make the effort." Cecile fretted at the thought. "Oh, dear, we'll have to find a way back to her dressing room. Rolf, are you listening to me?"

It's not that Rolf wasn't listening; he was, but plotting a way back took focus, and Cecile was distracting him. "I'm working on it, dear. Patience is a virtue." He snickered to himself, knowing that the answer would prickle his wife. She ignored him in retaliation and stuck her tongue out halfway, making Rolf laugh.

He responded, "And this is my wife who sticks her tongue out at me!" Cecile blew him an imaginary kiss.

Rolf and Cecile attended concerts here yearly along with many other Austrians who loved their culture, especially music, which led to well-attended events. However, neither had ever seen such a packed house, so much so that Rolf wondered if they exceeded the occupancy limits.

Since the Anschluss, the number of Nazi elite attending events had skyrocketed, some nights making up more than half of the audience, much to the dismay of Austrian nationalists. The stress and fear stemming from the German Anschluss of Austria significantly impacted many citizens, particularly older Jewish individuals who were resistant to change. The Nazis' presence further exacerbated the climate of fear and uncertainty.

Rolf could almost see the wheels turning in his wife's mind as she sized up the crush of people, sucking up every molecule of air. To lighten the mood, Rolf tried humor. "I hope no one shouts fire!" His attempt missed its mark. Surrounding Cecile were just the kind of people she feared. The same kind of people who murdered her cousin Minka and her husband Josef. Nazis. Reich officials. Police. The SS. They were all cut from the same murderous cloth.

On their arms were insipid wives wearing designer fashions made by the hands of the people their husbands wanted to exterminate. Cecile whispered to Rolf, "They wear edelweiss in their hair, diamonds on their hands, necks and ears, furs draped over their bodies. They look harmless, when they are nothing but depraved murderers. I want to howl at them like a wounded dog in anguish over my cousin and her husband, over the loss of their precious souls. I want to shout *murderer* at the top of my lungs, loud enough for the whole world to hear."

Rolf reached for his handkerchief as Cecile's eyes watered and tears spilled down her cheeks. She said bitterly, "I know it's been years, but I can't get over it. I see these people right here, in my face, and it brings it all back." Squeezing her husband's hand and taking the handkerchief embroidered with his initials, she dabbed at her eyes and nose. "Oh, Rolf. I don't intend to spoil our evening; I'm sorry, my love. This is just too upsetting, all this," she said as she motioned at their surroundings.

"I never thought I'd say these words. But I think it's time. I cannot take this onslaught, daily confrontation of this in our face, overflowing into every aspect of our life, wherever we go." Her brow wrinkled as she whispered, "Nazis. Everywhere. I feel so helpless, alone. Since the Anschluss, Vienna has become nothing short of a police state for Jews."

Her voice choked with emotion, she spits, "I love this land of ours with all I am. It is a part of me. I have this fertile Austrian soil within my veins, under my nails, the very oxygen that fills my lungs. Austria is me, and I am Austria." Placing her gloved hand upon her husband's cheek, her eyes still moist with tears, she sniffled. "You know, my darling, it has been heaven on earth for me, living with you in our home, near the mountains, our glorious Austria. But what good does that do us? The Nazis will do the same thing to us that they did to Josef and Minka."

———✿———

Stani stood protectively before Maddie, asking the three SS men what they wanted and why they were there. Close to shouting, he said, "Who said you could enter?"

Ignoring Stani, one of the men said, "We have reason to believe you are in this country illegally. Please present your papers."

Thanks to Stani's six years in America, he was a formidable example of freedom, exercising his right to say no and push back. As if he needed help with that to begin with! Stani smiled at the Nazi, making his words even more inflammatory, which was his objective: to get under their skin. He feigned rage: "How dare you accuse us of such a thing. What proof do you have?"

The short Nazi had a facial twitch that appeared to activate when he sensed impertinence. He gazed at Stani as if he could see inside his brain. The expression on his face bordered disgust and intrigue. He removed his leather gloves, gripping them in one hand, then turned to Stani, inches from his face. "Let's begin again, shall we? What is your name? First and last."

Stani obliged, smiling the most irritating and cheerful grin he could manufacture. "Stanford Wellington, sir. And what is the Nazi obsession with standing so close? Back up, sir."

The Nazi's face twisted at the order. He stepped backward, pondering how a Jewish-looking man could have such an Anglo-Saxon-sounding name. He shook his head. Stupefied, he asked Stani again, his voice shrill, "What? What is your name?"

Stani offered an enormous smile while repeating his name with pride of ownership, like when someone asks, "Is that your car?" Standing proudly, he stated, "Stanford Wellington. But my friends call me Stani, sir." He gave the Nazi a Chaplin-style exaggerated wink and, for emphasis, blew a kiss.

Maddie reached to touch Stani on the arm but fainted, falling onto the daybed. A sudden rush of blood poured from between her legs, to the shock and horror of the men in the room.

❖

Cecile whispered to Rolf, pinching his arm, "Rolf, slip one of the ushers some money and see if he can get us to her dressing room." She nudged Rolf, who scowled.

Seconds later, a man came running, screaming, "Ambulance! We need an ambulance right away!" Then, "Is there a doctor in the house?"

A corpulent man pushed through the throng, looking for the hall's manager. The buzz of voices that resulted from the announcement was loud, leaving Rolf and Cecile to wonder what in the world had happened. Cecile's intuition kicked in, and she told Rolf, "It's Maddie. I know it is." And with that, Cecile started frantically pushing her way through the crowd, almost knocking over a few of the Nazi elite women who stood with their mouths agape, like they were collecting flies. She shouted, "Out of my way, move!"

Cecile made her way through the crush of people, threading herself between bodies, parting the crowd like Moses and the Red Sea, slipping in between Nazis, and she found the back corridor, pushing and shoving everyone in her path. She hustled like a jockey approaching the finish line, hot in her pursuit of Maddie, ignoring the comments of,

"Watch where you're going," and "Hey, don't push," "Who are you to push me?"

She had long left Rolf in the dust, but Cecile wasn't stopping as she searched for Maddie like a mama bear searching for her cub. Finally, she reached the door with a star on the outside and the words *Guest Artist*. Cecile barreled through the door, bellowing "Yes" triumphantly—and then took in a sight that stopped her dead in her tracks: a blood-soaked Maddie, the daybed, and its coverings.

Aghast, Cecile gathered herself. She tried not to hyperventilate as she rushed to Maddie's side and began shouting orders. She was a volunteer nurse during World War I and remembered her training well. *Calm yourself. Assess the patient's present condition, check vitals. If a flashlight is available, check her pupils, find the source of the incident, wound, bone break, cut, rupture, bullet hole, or knife stab, and stop the bleeding by a tourniquet, if possible.*

Cecile shouted an order to the stage manager, who had followed behind her. "Towels, get me towels." Rolf entered the room just as Cecile checked Maddie's pulse against her watch, timing it, then put her head on Maddie's chest to listen to her heartbeat in time to hear Maddie say, "Yes, Miss Berk, I know what you told me. Clear out my pots of flowers and herbs. If the squirrels come to bury nuts, I've waited too long."

Cecile bolted straight off the side of the bed. She knelt, took Maddie's hand, and whispered, "Maddie."

Maddie opened her eyes slowly. They darted side to side. "Where am I? What's happened, Cecile? What are you doing here? How did you get to America? Where is Miss Berk?" Propping herself up, Maddie spotted the blood, and she screamed. "Oh my God, what's happened?"

Not So Fast

MAY 1939, HAMBURG, GERMANY

IN EARLY APRIL 1939, Minister of Propaganda Josef Goebbels announced that every German home would be given a radio that only received the Reich's programming. They chose the music, only airing shows and speeches involving Hitler. The Nazis ruled the airwaves. Coordinated with all media outlets, one continual message was repeated over and over.

Jews. Get out.

But they wouldn't go. While the Jews were drained from the constant onslaught of septic hatred, they remained true to the land—not so much the land as in a physical place, but more of a sense of historical endurance, for making it through centuries of living in Germany. The shock tactics of the Nazis couldn't dislodge them. Even the Einsatzgruppen couldn't drive them out. The Einsatzgruppen were the paramilitary traveling death squads that would abduct and then shoot them, allowing them to fall into the graves they'd dug.

The Nazis thought that surely, after Kristallnacht in November 1938, the Jews would depart in droves. But for the German Jews, starting a new life in a strange place with nothing to their names was more than just the turning of a page. No. It was the closing of a book. The end. They could never go back.

Still, life had become unbearable for the German Jews—

not just for them, but all Jews in Eastern Europe. The 937 Jews who purchased tickets and landing permits for a special voyage on a luxury cruise ship hoped to start a new life, even though the Nazis required the surrender of all their property, wealth, and possessions.

One such passenger cruise ship would take an unscheduled voyage from Hamburg to Havana, carrying these 937 Jews to their supposed freedom. Upon arriving in Havana, most would wait until it became possible to immigrate to the United States. Or so they hoped. The time spent in Cuba would be used to strategize how to gather funding to start a new life in the US.

To immigrate to the United States became the goal of many Jews, especially those who were former doctors, professors, bankers, and business professionals. Historically speaking, for the Jews of Europe, a change in status occurred in the late era of the Renaissance. That, combined with Jewish Enlightenment, the Haskalah, meant that Germany had one of Europe's most integrated Jewish populations by the 1920s, during the height of the Weimar Republic.

The Treaty of Versailles crushed the German economy and its people. Yet this stalwart community of Jews with an entrepreneurial spirit contributed significantly to the lagging German economy, featuring prominently in German society and culture. Soon after, Adolf Hitler became chancellor, and with this came a change in numerous policies aimed at the Jewish population.

In late September 1938, Reich citizenship, defined through the Nuremberg Laws, went into effect, distinguishing who was or wasn't a Jew. Family genealogy would elucidate the race laws. Jews were considered subjects of the state and not citizens. The Nazis developed techniques and methods to test "the Jewishness" of a person, not just by birth records, but by measuring the length of their noses, or by the size of their head, or the space between their eyes.

Many earlier codes and rules reached beyond the Nuremberg Laws. They were all strictly enforced, with threats of deportation to concentration camps if rules were broken. The Jews had no political rights. They were stripped of degrees and licenses. Doctors could only practice on Jews. In schools and universities, professors were dismissed, as were Jewish teachers in German schools, along with tax accountants and lawyers. Passports and documents would be marked with a capital "J." No mixed marriages. And a national boycott on all Jewish businesses.

Then, restrictions imposed by countries of refuge made it almost impossible for those poor souls with limited income or position to escape. They became Goebbels's chosen, the perfect specimen for his experiment. True victims. Goebbels was using the elegant and luxurious *S.S. St. Louis* as a backdrop, a canvas on which to paint a vivid picture in the minds and hearts of the world that the passengers of the voyage were a microcosm of the Jewish situation, illustrating Jews as undesirable and a blight. The same world that had utterly rejected the Jews, leaving their fate in the hands of those who wished them dead.

The Nazis would take one look at former Dachau resident Stefan Soutine and view him as undesirable. While he was dirty and unkempt—his head recently shaven, clothes the epitome of shabby—those exterior eyesores did not define him. Underneath his soiled exterior was a man of refined talent, and within the chambers of his heart lay virtue. While Stefan held no deep affection for Germany, he could relate to the plight of his fellow Jew.

He couldn't wait to board the ship and get to a world without the disease of virulent hate and Nazis. Standing on the pier, he asked his captor, "May I ask a question, sir?"

The man named Fritz nodded.

"Not to be impertinent, but why must you keep me here? I've broken no laws, I'm hungry, and I must relieve myself."

The man smiled. "I'll turn around if you're shy."

Stefan turned away and walked to the pier's edge to relieve himself. Feeling emboldened, he walked back to the man and asked, "Now, you know my name; what's yours?"

He neither smiled nor frowned. "Fritz."

Stefan looked the man over, noting he didn't resemble the average Nazi. While his hair was exceedingly blond and clipped like a Nazi's, unlike most Nazis, he had green eyes.

Stefan asked him a question in German, and the man answered perfectly. In German, Stefan said, "I'll tell you what, sir. I have an interesting object hidden here in Hamburg. It speaks of Nazi plans for a mission named Operation Sunshine. Have you heard of that? I'd be willing to part with it for my freedom. You let me go, and I'll tell you where it is. What do you say? That information could be dangerous in the wrong hands, wouldn't you agree?"

Flatly and with a blank expression, the man named Fritz replied, "No."

Stefan pressed more: "I think it might have to do with the ship I'm taking, a plot about Jews, and secret information gathered by operatives." He shrugged and added, "I guess I could turn it in to the ship's captain once I board."

Fritz again flatlined with, "No." He sized up his charge, looking him over. "I'm hungry. There are a few food stalls over there. I'll buy you breakfast." He nodded toward the stalls a hundred yards down the massive dock. "I'll always have my

9mm trained on you; you will remain in my custody. Is that clear?"

Stefan's stomach began gurgling at the words *food stalls*, and he salivated at the thought. He nodded excitedly, thrilled at the thought of food. "Yes, indeed!" Stefan's stomach growled even louder.

Keeping his word, Fritz aimed his 9mm at Stefan's mid-back. Stefan couldn't have cared less; his intuition assured him the man wouldn't shoot him. He tried to hide his giddiness over the provision of food, but he could hardly wait.

A southerly wind carried strong scents, emulsifying open sea and salt mixed with diesel fuel, but that was no match for the aroma of eggs and sausages cooking over an open fire in a food stall. The trade was as brisk as the service, since it was early Saturday morning. Two small plates of eggs, potatoes, and sausage were about to exchange hands with the counter person when someone knocked Stefan's plate of food out of his hand. He yelped and yelled, "Hey, what's going on?" in German.

Before Stefan could fully react, two beefy teenagers in Hitler Youth uniforms took out their bats and assailed him. Fritz stood by, calmly eating his breakfast. After six or seven bites and eight or nine swats with their bats, Fritz addressed the boys and shouted, "Heil Hitler," while flashing his Gestapo officer badge.

He took a slug of cold coffee while the hoodlums stopped beating Stefan and stood at attention, saluting back with "Heil Hitler." Meanwhile, Stefan lay crumpled on the ground, his hands bleeding from where he'd tried to protect his head from the heft of their bats.

Fritz offered the two thugs a cigarette, and the three stood there smoking, ignoring the groans coming from the bleeding, bruised, and battered Stefan. Pointing to the ground, Fritz told the youth in German that Stefan was his charge. "He's not a Jew but a former prisoner of Dachau, which is, of course, why you beat him. The shaved head. I know."

The three laughed together, the two thugs spat on Stefan, and one called him "a convict." Fritz had seen enough and waved them off. The youth saluted him with another "Heil Hitler" and departed in search of others to bully and abuse.

Fritz prodded Stefan with the toe of his wingtip. Expressionless, he said, "Get up. There's another plate of food waiting for you."

Stefan couldn't understand this man. *He's not like most Nazis, who could care less if I ate.* Stefan groaned and, after a failed attempt, returned upright. He assessed the tops of his hands—welted, bruised, and bloodied. Fritz waved to the stall attendant, asking for some water. He reached into his pocket, handed Stefan his handkerchief, and pointed to the water. "Clean yourself up. I'm curious. While you eat, I want you to explain how you found this object you have hidden. How did this come into your possession, and whose is it?"

Stefan checked his surroundings. *What have I got to lose— for some reason, I trust him. I can't say why, but I do.* He gobbled down his breakfast while moaning with delight, the food attacking his hunger and winning; he shoveled it into his mouth faster than he could chew it, saying between forkfuls, "I found it on the ground at Dachau. It must belong to an officer who visited the compound where I worked for the camp's commandant and his family."

The man toyed with his gun, looking away while the former Dachau resident finished his food. In a monotone, he stated, "Watching people eat disgusts me."

Stefan laughed, finished his coffee, and wipes his mouth.

"You'd really dislike my job."

Fritz handed his charge a cigarette, lighting it for him. He nodded at Stefan. "Tell me, Dachau prisoner, what is your profession?"

Stefan cocked his head, exhaling. "I already told you I'm a chef. I'm a classically trained French chef."

The man guffawed. "Sure, you are. Tell me another."

Stefan stayed silent. After a pensive moment, he said, "So, are you going to let me go and board my ship or what? Do you have a plan, or are you trying to provoke me into something we regret?"

Fritz scoffed at Stefan. "I'm the one with the gun. Settle down, so that I don't feel forced to shoot you like a dog. Tell me. Now. This diary, or whatever it is—where is it?"

Stefan took a casual stance, resting against the side of the food stall, away from the steady stream of customers, mostly dock workers and the like. Bolstered by confidence, his voice came across as introspective. "Well, well. We have ourselves a conundrum. I want to go free. You want the diary. We both want something. If you shoot me, you won't get the little diary. If you don't let me go, the same result: no diary. It looks like the wise thing to do would be to let me go. Simple as that."

CHAPTER SEVENTEEN

Scoundrel Times

MAY 1939, HAVANA, CUBA

WEEKS BEFORE THE *S.S. St. Louis* was scheduled to depart the port of Hamburg, Manuel Benitez, the director-general of the Cuban immigration office, came under scrutiny by the Cuban president for the illegal sale of landing permits. The sale of these false documents contributed to Benitez's growing wealth, leaving Frederico Bru, Cuba's president, fueled with resentment that none of the money greased his palm.

Bru and his cabinet were displeased over the huge sums Benitez was making, based on a loophole he'd found and was exploiting in Decree 55. The decree stated that each refugee needed a visa and was required to pay $500 to guarantee to the Cuban government that they would not become indigents. But the decree also stated that tourists were welcome and didn't need a visa. Decree 55 did not define a tourist or a refugee.

Quick on the draw, Benitez began selling landing permits for $150, which would allow refugees to land by calling them tourists. The permits looked official, like visas, and were individually signed by Benitez. Some people even bought large quantities of these, hoping to scalp them to desperate Jews for more than the $150 they'd paid. Even more egregious, Benitez double-dipped, as he also made money from selling passage to the *S.S. St. Louis*.

The ship was owned by HAPAG, who paid Benitez a portion of each ticket sold. HAPAG realized the advantage of selling a package deal through Benitez, and the tickets sold quickly, which meant a full ship—something the *S.S. St. Louis* hadn't had in many months. The German clamor for global cruises had dissipated, crushing the cruise line industry.

President Bru contacted Benitez and told him to share the wealth. He refused. So, Bru made a new decree, nullifying the previous Decree 55. The new one, called Decree 937, (coincidentally or not), had the same number of tickets sold to passengers set to board the *S.S. St. Louis* on May 13th.

On May 5th, Decree 937 passed, closing the loophole to Decree 55 eight days before the ship was to sail. Unknown to President Bru, every passenger on the *S.S. St. Louis* had purchased a landing permit except for twenty-eight. Twenty-eight passengers on the list of confirmed ticket purchases had proper visas. Among the few were a young female American musician, her traveling companion, a man traveling under the protection of a foreign government according to the confidential purchase record, and a released prisoner of Dachau Concentration Camp.

Rochester, New York

In late March 1939, Raymond Wellington received a notification from the US War Office that both sons, Wolfie and Buster, had completed their training and received their mission assignments. While Raymond knew what their training had been for, he had no clue as to the mission they'd be assigned. Until the mission was complete, no more information would be available, barring injury or death. Both boys dreamed of returning to Europe, having a penchant for fighting the growing Nazi machine.

Buckinghamshire, England

Buster and Wolfie graduated from Bletchley Park, Division D of the SIS, Secret Intelligence Service, as specialists in covert operations and espionage.

The Nazis' growing threat existed not only in Europe. Their lengthening tentacles stretched across the Atlantic to the United States, even beyond to South America. The German American Bund was a group led by Fritz Kuhn, a follow-up organization for the Friends of New Germany. The Bund established training camps for youth in New York, Pennsylvania, New Jersey, and Wisconsin. The zenith of their activities included a February 20, 1939, rally in New York City's Madison Square Garden. Over twenty thousand attended.

The Nazis funded the recruitment of Germans into the Bund by offering large sums of money for joining. However, recruits didn't receive the promised funds, and the money lined Fritz Khun's pockets. All of this Nazi activity taking place in Germany and Austria, and by The Bund in the US kept the Cipher Bureau at Bletchley on full alert, monitoring numerous potential escalations.

Along with Bletchley's Cipher Division, the Special Intelligence Service's Division D stood for Destruction Caused by Sabotage And Subversion. They worked diligently to develop counter-operatives, covert operations, and sabotage material, including training in incendiaries and explosives. Buster and Wolfie were selected for this program. It was a good fit for both of them, since they excelled in chemistry in college and were fascinated by incendiaries and pyrotechnics.

It was a spring day in April 1939, and Bletchley's grounds were vibrant with a palette of colors. The lush, emerald-hued lawns recalled the rolling hills not far beyond Buckinghamshire, and the pink crabapple trees and white blossoming hawthorns were filled with chirping birds.

Buster and Wolfie sat along the ancient stone wall that complemented the Victorian Gothic, Tudor, and Dutch Baroque styles of the buildings on the sprawling pastoral campus. The pleasant, sweet-smelling air refreshed them after being stuck inside a stuffy lecture hall that smelled of burnt rubber for six hours. The first two hours had been spent on the uses of celluloid film for incendiary purposes, and the next four on vital instructions for disarming and re-arming small bombs used for blowing through stone walls and heavy doors.

Smoking a cigarette, Buster said, "Can you believe how flammable celluloid film is? I'll think differently next time I take Maddie to the movies."

Wolfie took the cigarette out of his friend's hand and puffed on it. "Yeah, you can toss a lit smoke into a pile of film, and it will react like napalm."

He acted out the reaction to an explosion, throwing himself off the wall, then scrambled to his feet, still holding Buster's smoke. "Voila," he presented it, and Buster took his smoke back.

"Exactly my point. Hopefully, there's no smoking in the projection room." Buster pitched the cigarette butt to the ground, stepping down to crush it. Thoughtful, he gazed at Wolfie to be sure he had his attention, making eye contact with his friend and adopted brother. "Hey, there's something I want to express to you."

Wolfie grinned. "Go on, the suspense is killing me."

Buster began, "We've been through a lot together, especially our months here. We've grown through our experiences. Not to sound clichéd, but we entered here as boys, and we'll leave as men. As we depart to our assignments, I'm grateful for you and glad we can toss back a few and laugh now."

Wolfie nodded and glanced to Buster's right, watching a new group of enlisters cutting a path up the lengthy walkway, approaching the gabled Victorian brick-and-stone Main Building. He said in a low voice, almost under his breath, "Suckers," motioning to the recruits, then shouted, "Run, quick; there's still time to escape while you can. Run for your lives!" He waved his arms, jumping up and down.

Buster howled, pointing to the group. "And watch them pay you no attention! Ha! Let's go grab a beer before the pub closes at three."

Wolfie removed his cap, scratching his scalp. "I would, but I'm meeting Jeanine there. You can come too; it's a free country." He smiled at his friend.

Buster kicked at the ground with the heel of his shoe, his hands jammed in his pockets. He took a deep breath, breathing in the luxurious, English-countrified air. "I'm going to miss this old place, and I feel oddly sentimental. You know they're moving our department?"

Wolfie shook his head and poked Buster in the arm. "No. That must be the inside info only you're privy to, privileged boy."

Buster rolled his eyes. "Yeah. Right. I believe it's the other way around, Your Highness." He put his hands together and bowed, giving it back to Wolfie. The two shared a laugh and slapped each other on the back. "So, the brilliant British and American forces have concurred it would be expedient to move our Section D away from the cipher division, making the monumental decision that explosives and cipher decryption and encryption would be better-served miles apart. Aston House, near Stevenage in Hertfordshire, will be the new location starting next year. Glad we trained here amidst this grandeur."

Wolfie nudged Buster again. "Yeah, right. You're just glad you didn't have to train under Churchill."

Buster leaned back, laughing. "Hoo boy, you can say that again. Anyone would be glad not to train under him. They would be crushed!" he said, referring to Churchill's storied appetite and girth.

Wolfie and Buster had trained under Army Major Lawrence Grand of the Secret Intelligence Service's Section D. Grand led the war effort in the Balkans. His work involved researching the theory of secret offensives and how unconventional methods and non-military means could attack an enemy. Major Grand prided himself on his meticulous training methods. He had a quick and sharp wit; you had better be fully alert when in his presence.

The infiltration of spy rings and interception of documents from German spy agencies, most notably the Abwehr, was vital to Wolfie and Buster's training. Both young men spoke perfect German and could be inserted into several espionage operations, while working with the US Army. Before long, they'd be putting much of what they'd learned into practice, and it scared the daylights out of Wolfie.

Rochester, New York, May 1, 1939
On May 1st, while the boys were away serving the country and Maddie and Stani were in Europe, Raymond received another notice from the US War Department, Army division. After calling the State Department for approval, he decided it was time for a road trip.

Raymond placed a call to Wolferman-Wellington Motors, where Frederick answered the phone. "Wolferman-Wellington Motors, your place for all things automotive. How can I help you?"

"Frederick, it's Raymond. Do you have a minute?"

"Sure thing. Let me close the door first. Hold on." Frederick had learned that whenever Raymond asked if he had a minute, he knew it would be more than one. "Okay, go ahead."

The office was a smallish room filled with framed photographs and posters of race cars from the European Grand Prix. Floor-to-ceiling windows overlooked the showroom floor. Frederick settled into his desk chair, putting his boots on the desk. He had an affinity for boots, the western kind "like cowboys wear."

Raymond had used diplomacy to steer him away from wearing a wide-brimmed cowboy hat, saying, "It wouldn't be a good look and might scare away customers. This is New York State, not Texas." Frederick never knew if Raymond was joking or serious. After six years, he was still wondering, unable to figure him out.

Raymond said, "See if you can break away from the shop. Ask Denny if he can batten down the hatches while we take a short jaunt south. We've kept our shoulder to the grindstone with no time off. It's high time we kick back for a bit. So, tell Denny ten days. Keep the shop and showroom well-staffed in our absence. Tell him we'll check in from time to time and no closing early."

Frederick's interest was piqued. He lit a cigarette and asked, "Hmm. An adventure. What kind of adventure, or will you make me wait?"

"Come home, and I'll explain while you pack."

Frederick snickered, "Just as I suspected. You're becoming too predictable, my friend. See you later."

Raymond set about packing while Hollenius followed. He squatted down to scratch the cat behind his ears, activating the switch to his extraordinarily loud purr machine. "And what will we do with you, dear boy?"

Hollenius made himself at home in Raymond's open suitcase while his part-time master gathered clothes from the oak chifforobe and three-drawer dresser.

Raymond asked Hollenius, "Where are my swim trunks? Do you know?"

CHAPTER EIGHTEEN

The Worst That Could Happen

MAY 6, 1939, THE VIENNA MUSIKVEREIN

INTO THE BACK hallway leading to the dressing room plodded the stage manager. Tagging behind was a man best described as unkempt. Even the spectacles resting on his pockmarked nose were dirty. He carried a black bag.

Hustling into the room, pushing past the stunned SS trio, he waddled up to the daybed, leaving an invisible trail of pungency behind. Turning, he gesticulated and shooed the Nazis out of the room. The Nazis seemed to be familiar with the doctor, so they left without issue. Then he pushed Cecile out of the way with condescending words when she attempted to share Maddie's vital signs and that mentioned that "the bleeding has stopped, at least for now."

The doctor waved his hand and dismissed Cecile. "Madam, please leave. You're not needed here. Now go at once." He spotted Stani and Rolf and told them to leave as well. They ignored his order, as did Cecile.

Rolf raised his hand to cover the smirk on his lips, withholding a chuckle at the doctor's less-than-cordial greeting. Under his breath, he said, "Uh-oh," knowing his wife would not take kindly to being dismissed.

Cecile would have breathed fire and consumed the man if possible; instead, she adroitly lacerated him with her words. "You useless tub of waste, don't you dare speak to me in such terms with that tone. Now take care of my niece immediately and remember what you are and your place here." Cecile continued to fume under her breath.

Mostly ignoring her, the doctor asked for another blanket, and the stage manager appeared with one. The doctor folded the blanket, using part to cover Maddie and the blood, while he half-sat and half-kneeled by the daybed at Maddie's side. She was propped up against the head of the bed, sipping tea, resting quietly amidst the tense atmosphere, observing everything.

The doctor pulled a stethoscope from his bag and listened to Maddie's breathing while taking her pulse with his free hand, eyeing his stopwatch to check her beats per minute.

"What is your name? Can you explain what happened to me?" Maddie looked him over, from his chin that rested where his neck should be to his faded gray suit and a tie that didn't go with gray. His body odor and sloppy appearance concerned Maddie, and there was no way she would let him touch her or perform any kind of examination. She would have inched away from him, if possible, but the wall was on her other side, leaving her no room to move. He asked her, "What's your full name?" She didn't answer his question.

The stage manager left to wait outside the door. Rolf and Stani waited inside but stood facing the door, with their backs to her. Cecile stood close at hand, glaring at the balding doctor.

"I'm Dr. Theodor Morrell. I have questions for you first. Tell me your name."

"My name is Maddie Ture-er-Wellington, Turner-Wellington." Due to her lightheadedness, she'd almost slipped. "My married name is Wellington. I've not felt well for some time now, and...well..." Despite her shade of pale, Maddie blushed and squirmed in the bed. She wasn't used to speaking to a man about her women's issues, let alone a man who was revolting by his very nature.

The doctor said, "Go on."

Maddie whispered, "I'm late for my, you know, cycle." She hung her head in shame, embarrassed to speak of such things.

"Is there any chance you're pregnant?"

Maddie's face reddened at the thought. She was still intact there but knew why he'd asked. "Well, no. My husband is enlisted, and we haven't seen each other in six months. So, no. No chance."

The doctor lifted the blanket to get one last look at the volume of blood lost. "Judging from the volume here and your symptoms, I'd venture to say an ovarian cyst burst. You shouldn't have any more pain, but if you do, I will leave you with some Eukodal. Take one every six hours. I will print a doctor's name if you need one while you're here in Vienna."

From his pocket, he pulled out a small black leather diary with a pad inside. It was engraved with a swastika and his initials in gold lettering. Taking a pencil, he scribbled a name on a piece of paper.

The doctor waved the paper at Cecile. "Here, make yourself useful." She snatched it from his hand. Rolf took Cecile's other hand, hoping to assuage her fury, worried she'd slap the doctor on his head for his moronic behavior. He pulled her closer to his side.

To Maddie, Morell said, "Young lady, you're going to be fine. But you must rest and allow your body time to recover."

Cecile piped in, "She will. I can assure you of that."

Like a bullet, the doctor shot back, "You had better." As an afterthought, he asked, "Will she be traveling soon, or will she have the luxury of a few days' rest prior?"

Cecile nodded. "She'll have three days to rest before she travels—"

The doctor finished her sentence, "Travels to Hamburg to board the *S.S. St. Louis* on the 13th?" The room was silent, with everyone but the doctor staring, dumbfounded.

Cecile asked, "How did you know?"

He gave no answer. Instead, he patted Maddie on the arm, then left for the door, sliding to the side to allow Elzbieta into the room, who yelped upon seeing Maddie and rushed to her side; then the three SS slunk back into the room, to Stani's disgust. Elzbieta, quick as a deer, peeked back at the Nazis and then spoke Polish to Maddie.

Maddie put her hand up weakly and asked the maid to speak English because she couldn't understand Polish. Elzbieta's face showed her confusion, her eyes darting to the three SS and then back to Maddie. Stani observed all this, understanding why Maddie wasn't replying in her native tongue. Rolf and Cecile, on the other hand, looked completely bewildered.

In her usual fashion, Cecile was ready to take charge and get Maddie back to their home and to bed. She clapped, announcing, "There are four too many people in this room; you all leave and let her alone. We must get her to rest. Go now."

Stani had begun to herd the group out the door when the short SS officer who'd addressed him before said, "We'll be watching you." To which Stani retorted, giving them a three-finger salute from the brow, "Thanks for the warning, won't be the first time. Auf wiedersehen!"

While Maddie was on bed rest, Stani planned to spend some time enjoying Hamburg before going to Werner Kempler's house to collect the Amati—or whatever he had for

Mrs. Genhart.

———✦———

After a short taxi ride back to the house, a bath, and pajamas for Maddie, Cecile made tea and toast for all. They sat together in the kitchen. Maddie gazed earnestly at Rolf and Cecile. Dark circles sat beneath her deep blue eyes, and her skin tone was pallid from blood loss, but she was excited to hear their opinion about her performance, knowing what comfort their words would bring.

"I'm my worst critic, and Stani isn't here to critique it for me." She smiled, lowering her eyes, and said softly, putting her hands together as if in prayer, "Please."

Cecile bubbled on about "the sweet yet melancholy section of the canzonetta," and Rolf added, "I almost got up and danced for the finale. I loved the folk-like melody and the pace; oh, if only room existed between the aisles." He stood, taking Cecile by the hand and spinning her.

"Rolf and I adore dancing. We used to go so often in our youth, didn't we, my sweet?" She touched his cheek. He took her hand into his and kissed the top of it. But the phone rang before Rolf could respond to his wife, and Maddie jumped, startled by the harsh tone.

Rolf shouted, "I bet it's Stani! He made it to the train station!" He answered, "Hello." Cecile and Maddie watched intently as Rolf nodded and answered the caller, "Yes, okay, that's fine; we'll get her there. Yes, Saturday, May 13th, 6:00 p.m. We'll be there. Be safe, my friend. Call if you need anything. How can we reach you? Hello, hello?"

"Damn it. He hung up. Ah, well. What can we do about it now?"

Maddie asked, "Did he mention his plans, any changes?"

Rolf leaned against the counter, stretching his long legs

before him, and munched on a cold piece of toast. Between bites, he yawned and said, "Just as he planned, Stani said he will spend some time in Hamburg, see the sights, drink some beer, eat some schnitzel, pretzels, and bratwurst. Next, he'd go to Werner Kempler's place to pick up whatever it is, the mystery gift for Mrs. Genhart, and meet you at the dock before boarding the ship."

Cecile tucked Maddie into the four-poster bed on the second floor of the two-bedroom cottage, in the same room where Wolfie stayed when he visited. Maddie snuggled under the covers. "These sheets are delicious. They are so soft."
Cecile pulled the patchwork quilt her Bubbe had made for her wedding trousseau up to Maddie's chin and sat on the bed's edge. "Now that you're all bathed and comfortable, I will tell you the story of the patchwork quilt. Since Rolf and I had no children, I'd like to commemorate this time with you by telling you the story. Would you like to hear it?"

Sleepy-eyed, Maddie confessed, "I may doze off, but would you at least begin and tell me? Maybe if I sit up a little, I won't fall asleep in the middle of your story."

Yielding to Maddie, Cecile told her, "We'll save it for another night. I can see many more nights ahead." She kissed Maddie on the forehead.

"Mmm. That's nice." Maddie looked around the cozy room. The upstairs smelled of pine, cinnamon, and spices, thanks to Cecile's handmade sachet pillows for each room in the house. Maddie adored the slanted ceilings that mimicked the roof's external lines, covered in boldly patterned tiles. The walls were paneled in pine, and the furniture was pine as well; rustic pieces decorated the room, and across from the bed was a large wall hanging portraying Austrian scenes from the Alps, various lakes, and an alpine-looking inn. The candle on the dresser illuminated the wall hanging, giving the scenes a golden hue.

Cecile nodded in the direction Maddie was looking. "Do you recognize that inn?"

Maddie tilted her head, eyes clear. "Yes, I think I do. The inn in Salzburg, is that right? Your cousins'?"

Cecile spoke softly. "Yes, that was the Lehenerhof Inn that belonged to Josef and Minka Ross, my cousins." She reached into her apron pocket to retrieve a hankie and dabbed at her eyes. "You know, it's been six years since their murder, and I still can't talk about it. Maybe one day."

Maddie reached for Cecile's hand, taking it in her own. "You know, she was so kind to me. She gave me one of her frocks, seeing as I was dressed as a Boy Scout when I first met her! Both Josef and Minka were lovely, so kind—and their food! Oh, just heaven. Stani adored it all and was thrilled to have as much as he wanted after almost starving to death while imprisoned in Dachau." After a moment, Maddie added, "You must miss them. I'm so sorry."

The two sat there quietly, and then Maddie said something that finally convinced Cecile, removing all doubt about leaving her beloved Austria.

Maddie told Cecile what the Nazis were doing. It had never crossed Cecile's mind that she'd be at significant risk, thinking the Wolferman name would be her cover. Maddie told her, "The Nazis are collecting all records of individuals to root out Jews that may be hiding."

Cecile's family records and her marriage certificate revealed her maiden name, Rosenberg. Since the annexation, all Jewish residents were required to register with the Nazi government in their towns and villages. Maddie told Cecile emphatically, "It's not if, but when. They know about you; it's just a matter of time before they come for you."

Meanwhile, Stani settled into his sleeping berth aboard the Deutsche Reichsbahn, barreling ahead into the impenetrable darkness. He hoped to rest or sleep most of the one-thousand-kilometer, nine-and-a-half-hour train ride to Berlin, then to Hamburg. Stripped down to his underwear and an undershirt, Stani washed his face in the wash basin, grateful for the warm water provided by the train attendant. *I remember when there was no warm water, only ice water, and Jakob, after he died, was ice cold. Dachau, you never leave me. You freeze me with your memories, and you torment me with Jakob and the pit.*
Hanging on the wall was a hook with his coat. Reaching into the pocket, Stani pulled out a small candle, his cigarettes, and matches. Easing down onto the bed, he lit a smoke, exhaling every bit of air he could squeeze from his lungs. Before retiring, he lit a small candle, part of his ritual. He placed it on the floor, reached for his well-worn Tanakh and Bible in his suitcase, and propped it open next to him. Reading from the prophet Isaiah, a portion that brought him comfort—*Surely he hath borne our griefs and carried our sorrows and acquainted with grief*—Stani bowed his head to pray.

My dearest and most precious Lord and heavenly Father Adonai Elohim, there is no grief you didn't bear, Lord, no pain you didn't feel, no loss or sadness you didn't experience. You felt it all; you lived it. We share the fellowship of suffering. You know how fragile humans feel, and you are familiar with the pain and grief we suffer, with times of broken-heartedness and despair. Only you can comfort us. There is no human pain you haven't felt. Therefore, it is only you who can bring us what we need. You are the only one who understands because you've been there. You've carried it all. And you help us by lessening our burden with your words of hope. My yoke is easy. My burden is light, comes to mind.

Thank you, Lord, for helping me with my burdens. I feel a deep one for Maddie. Be with her tonight, comfort her, cause her to rest well, let that event be a one-time thing.

I no longer feel a connection with this land. It has turned into a type of hell. How long will you allow our people to suffer, or is this just the beginning of sorrow? It makes no sense to worry about things not in my control, so I leave them in your hands.

I ask your blessings over my family, especially Maddie and my boys, Wolfie and Buster, Raymond, Frederick, Rolf, Cecile, Mrs. Genhart, and Hollenius. Bless Wolferman-Wellington Motors. Help our people here in Germany, Lord. Give them hope, courage, and strength to leave and start anew. Help me, Lord, bring your light of hope and understanding to those I love and to this lost world. Brighten their spiritual eyes so that they may see you in everything. May I walk worthy of my calling—yielded, trusting, loving, and hope-filled. In thy name, Yeshua. Amen.

Stani's sleep was sound until it was impossible to sleep. The serene quiet was interrupted by the scream of the train whistle as the machine steamed into the Berlin Station. Sleepy-eyed, Stani reached for his watch. *Hmm, 4:20 a.m.. I think I'll sleep more.* Sleep hovered and never quite landed, trapping him in the in-between place of consciousness and repose. Half-sleep.

There was a knock on the wall outside Stani's curtain-drawn berth—once, twice, then a persistent knock. Stani heard it but couldn't delineate whether it was part of a dream or real. He snuggled into the mattress, pulling the covers over his head. The knocking persisted. *This must be real.*

Someone pulled the string to the light, illuminating the small space. Startled and bewildered, Stani attempted to stand, but a man pushed him back down. Standing before him, under a single incandescent bulb that cast a ghastly glow, was a man in his mid-thirties with pockmarked skin and beady gray eyes. He wore civilian clothes, but Stani knew better, recognizing a Nazi, whether in uniform or not. A putrid odor permeated officers of death. Standing beside him was a uniformed Nazi officer.

Stani asked, "Would you lovely gentlemen tell me your names and what you're doing waking me up? What do you want?"

The man with the beady gray eyes replied, "Schiendick. Otto Schiendick. I'm a Jew hunter."

CHAPTER NINETEEN

In Search of Freedom

MAY 7, 1939, ABOARD THE DEUTSCHE REICHSBAHN

IN FEBRUARY 1938, before the annexation of Austria, an act concerning trains and railways in Germany came to pass. The Act for the New Regulation of the Conditions of the Reichsbank and the Deutsche Reichsbahn made the Deutsche Reichsbahn-Gesellschaft the National Railway of Germany, placing them under Reich sovereignty and renaming the railway simply the Deutsche Reichsbahn. Even before coming under the Reich's jurisdiction, the Railway had a long history of anti-Jewish policies and followed the political rhetoric of the day.

In August 1933, the German labor board supported the Deutsche Reichsbahn decision to take part in the conversation surrounding the conflict of intermarriage in Germany, adding to the growing support that paved the way for the Nuremberg Laws.

One of the laws, called the *Reichsbürgergestz*, deprived Jews of citizenship, designating them subjects of the state. The other, called the blood protection law, or *Blutschutzgesetz*, was the Law for the Protection of German Blood and Honor. It forbade sexual relations or marriage between Jews and citizens of Germany of kindred blood.

The laws helped define what constituted an acceptable German marriage in the all-important eyes of the Reich.

The local Order Police, the *Ordnungspolizei,* enforced such laws, keeping records of employees who worked for the largest German companies. The German railway was one of them. The records listed personal information, disregarding employee privacy. Employees had few rights, if any.

The Order Police worked in conjunction with other police agencies on local levels, monitoring social and political behavior while enforcing Nazi racial policies. The more numerous the rules, the more enforcement was required. Germany was quickly becoming a police state, run by a fascist, quasi-totalitarian government.

In 1939, following the annexation of Austria and the Sudetenland, the Order Police numbered over one hundred thousand. Adolf Hitler appointed Heinrich Himmler in charge of it all, including the SS, Gestapo, and the Order Police. So, it came as no surprise to Stani to find trains frequently searched for Jewish passengers, looking for a reason to take them into custody and then strip them of money or valuables. Harassment of the Jews was a priority.

No one loved harassing the Jews more than Otto Schiendick and fellow Nazi Gunter Brumbach, who just happened to be on the same Vienna-to-Hamburg train as Stani. Checking the passenger logs for unusual names that sounded Jewish or Slavic was de rigueur for Schiendick. Night trains provided the perfect atmosphere for his shenanigans. As he'd perused the log that night, a name had caught his eye. Wellington.

He knew of Wellington, an American who worked for the US government under the State Department as senior counsel. He'd recently read his name on a list of US government State Department agents that had visited Germany since 1933.

Schiendick told Brumbach, "I'm curious. Why would an American lawyer working for the US State Department be on this train, not in first class? Hmm. I've got some interest in this name, Wellington. Time to investigate." He pulled out a small black diary with an embossed swastika and his initials, OS, in gold, and printed the name Wellington.

Schiendick's favorite tactic was to show up late at night or in the wee hours of the morning to question passengers, catching them off guard and half-asleep. He relied on their momentary forgetfulness and the potential to tell half-truths to draw conclusions that implicated them in some way, connecting the unsuspecting Jewish person to his fabricated malfeasance. Once information, false or not, was obtained, he'd divulge his findings to the Gestapo, filling him with an immense sense of satisfaction.

It was 4:30 a.m., and the sleeping car with its roomette berths was dark.

Schiendick knocked with his bat outside roomette #7, and after the third knock, pulled the curtain back, his flashlight leading him to spot the string for the light. He pulled it, the light clicked on, and he ripped back the blanket on one Stanford Wellington.

Stani was startled by the apparent disruption but was sharp-headed and ready with his papers, even before Schiendick demanded them. Stani slept with his papers, eagerly anticipating a request for them. Beating a Nazi to the punch made him happy.

Schiendick grabbed the papers from Stani's hand. His accomplice, Nazi Brumbach, glared at Stani like he was a repugnant creature while Stani watched as Schiendick pored over his credentials, searching for something to call into question. "Hmm. American passport. Tell me, just how does a dirty Jew like you have an American name and passport?"

"Wellington is my family name. You think it's a misnomer?"

Schiendick scrunched up his face and sniped, "Just what the hell is that?"

At the Hamburg Port, Warehouse District, The Speicherstadt
Fritz considered Stefan's offer, knowing he had no real jurisdiction over him, but kept it up for appearance's sake. He pursed his lips and looked Stefan over, saying, "Okay. Give me the diary, and you're free to go." He shook Stefan's hand to seal the deal.

Stefan flashed a smile, turned his back to the man, and reached down the front of his pants to retrieve the small diary. Sheepishly, he shrugged. "It was the safest place for it; I knew it had value."

The man's face showed his surprise. "I thought it was bigger than that," he said, taking it from Stefan. He fingered the leather-bound pocket diary and the swastika embossed on the cover with the initials, 'JG.'

Giddy at the thought of freedom, Stefan considered taking off in the opposite direction but instead, stayed. He offered insight as Fritz thumbed through the few pages of writing. "I think that belongs to Heir Goebbels, the Reich Minister. He visited the camp commandant one day."

Fritz asked, "At Dachau?"

Stefan nodded, "Yeah." Smiling, he watched a flock of birds fly over the gray-brown waters of the Elbe. "It feels good to be free. Maybe I shouldn't say that to you because you're a Nazi, and we are in Germany, and I must, as a citizen, respect your authority, but I'm just talking with you, man to man, person to person. Do you understand that?"

Fritz offered Stefan a smoke, lit it. He blew out a few smoke rings and answered, "Yes—man to man." He took his time to finish his thought. "Were you not a former prisoner, wrongfully accused or not, and I not an officer of the Reich, things might be different, and we'd get a beer and talk about our families. But some rules and protocols must be followed. I find no wrong in you, but perhaps you should leave before I do."

Stefan did not need to be told twice. He hightailed it out of the storage shed, running all the way to the dock where passengers ascended the gangway of the most incredible ship he'd ever seen.

Aboard the Deutsche Reichsbahn
Considering the hour, Stani thought twice about displaying his usual sarcastic wit when dealing with Nazis. He asked, a sober expression on his face, "How can I be of further assistance to you, gentlemen? I am, after all, an American citizen, as you so kindly recognized, so if I may say goodnight or good morning to you..."

Prickled by Stani's uppity attitude, Schiendick sniffed, wiping his nose on his coat sleeve. "How is it you have the name Wellington? Tell me why you are on this train and where you are going. Are you staying in Hamburg or leaving? What is the purpose of your travel?"

Not wanting to spar with the Nazis, Stani simply said, "I travel with a violinist who performed last night in Vienna. She fell ill and stayed behind for now; we plan to meet in Hamburg, where we will take the *S.S. St. Louis* to Cuba and be transported to the United States. I told you. Wellington is my family name."

Schiendick sized up Stani. "But why Hamburg? Why not Bremen to New York or Miami?"

Incredulous, Stani couldn't believe these two were unaware of the financial strains facing the nation, let alone cruise lines and the pleasure ship industry. He stared first at Schiendick and then at Brumbach, who, up to this point, had remained silent, with his leather coat collar upturned, chain-smoking, dropping his ashes and cigarette butts on the floor, his eyes vacant like that of a ghoul.

Stani cleared his throat for emphasis. "Ahem. I assumed you'd be familiar with the crushing economic blows that have hit your cruise line industry, making it economically unfeasible to sail ships with less than half-full capacity." Stani shook his head, muttering, "I just don't understand how you wouldn't be aware of that. There is so much propaganda out there nowadays; you just don't know who or what to trust. And to answer your question regarding the date of departure, it worked out well with the artist's performance schedule."

Schiendick looked at Stani suspiciously. "Well, today is the 7th. When does the ship depart? And who is this artist?"

Stani could see the Nazi working to trap him, try him by his words. He spoke quickly, his German crystal clear. "Out of an abundance of caution, I cannot divulge the artist's name. The ship departs on the 13th, giving the artist time to feel better and travel and, for me, time to explore Hamburg. I've never been. Have you? Of course, you have. Can you recommend any sights, restaurants, or galleries? Oh, I suppose you wouldn't know about those, ah no."

Stani capitalized on his offensive stance, putting Schiendick on the defensive. He shifted his eyes from man to man, sizing them up and seeking signs of intelligent life. "Well, what say you? Any recommendations?"

Schiendick couldn't tell if Stani was mocking him or being sincere. His tone biting, he responded, "I'm not your damn tour guide. We also are scheduled to take the *S.S. St. Louis* as crew stewards. We'll board before you and will be watching for you."

The men turned to leave, and as they did, Stani delivered a

barbed parting shot. "Of course you will. I would expect that, at the very least, from goons like you. Good night and sweet dreams!" Stani had dealt with cretins like Schiendick before. The guard at Dachau, Dukolf, came to mind like a sour taste, reminding him that he'd made it through a treacherous time by the grace of God.

Stani whispered, "Oh Lord Most High, watch over Maddie, Buster, and Wolfie, all of our family. Where would I be without them?"

When Stani departed the train in Hamburg, it was 10:00 a.m. He spied Schiendick and Brumbach speaking to a station official, most likely trying to assert some authority over a lowly station worker. Stani made sure he caught Schiendick's eye, making it a point to wave with enthusiasm, angering Schiendick. "That smug Jew. I'll take care of him; don't you even think about it, Gunter. We'll have him aboard the ship. He'll be a captive audience for two weeks. A lot can happen." Both men snickered in the way bullies do, pleased with the potential of two weeks aboard the ship. Gunther said, "He'll have nowhere to run. Except, perhaps, overboard?"

Armed with his small travel bag and a few days of clothing, Stani meandered through the Hauptbahnhof, the central rail station, with its platform hall's seventy-meter-wide roof construction boasting impressive architectural finesse. It was Germany's largest unsupported station hall. The food stalls emitted various aromas, causing Stani's stomach to growl. A stall with a simple handwritten sign in front, "Deiter's Breakfast Bar," attracted his attention, and he walked up to the stall, where six metal stools in front of a counter for patrons to sit and enjoy their breakfast.

A surly-looking pudgy man, wearing a too-tight shirt that revealed abundant sprouting black hair wherever there was skin, was wearing a sloppy, stained apron. He inspected Stani's profile, grunting at him while pointing to the sign, "We don't serve Jews."

This presented a moral and physical conundrum for Stani. Should he deny his identity for the sake of his stomach? His stomach growled in agreement as it gnawed against the insides of his guts. Stani thought of Esau and the story in the book of Genesis, where Esau denied his birthright for a morsel of food. *And then, in Dachau, where we had no food.* Stani could flash his passport at the man but decided that preserving his conscience was better. He stepped out into the brilliant sunshine, causing his eyes to burn, tired from the early wake-up call.

Now. Where to go to find Werner Kempler? Let's see what that address is... and he fished in his coat pocket for a small address book.

CHAPTER TWENTY

Give Me Your Tired, Your Poor, Your Huddled Masses

MAY 13, 1939, SHED 76, HAMBURG PORT, GERMANY

AT 7:00 P.M., the *S.S. St. Louis's* silhouette loomed against the darkening blue-violet heavens, moored in shed 76 while choppy seawaters licked the ship's painted sides. The Port of Hamburg stretched along the southern shore of the River Elbe, which branched into numerous natural river arms leading to the mouth of the North Sea, 110 kilometers away. The ship would prepare to launch at 8:30 p.m. after the passengers had settled in and enjoyed dinner.

Beginning at noon on Saturday, May 13th, passengers for the *S.S. St. Louis* filtered in from the customs sheds that led to the docks; many had lined up and waited over ten hours before the ship's departure, queueing behind the gold braided rope. Several passengers were Orthodox and needed to board the ship before sunset. The captain made an exception, allowing them to board first. The gangways were in place, and the natty crew looked dapper in their uniforms and shiny shoes. They exuded poise and took pride in their appearance.

Next to the ancient wooden pier where the vessel moored and passengers boarded, a six-piece band played traditional German national songs, a not-so-subtle insult to the passengers. Yet the passengers were not the only ones offended by this crass display of German nationalism. More than a case of bad timing, this appeared intentional.

The captain watched from the ship's top deck at the scene below, his steel beam-straight posture and tense jawline confirming his annoyance with this attempt to intimidate the Jewish passengers, knowing this would be the Nazis' last chance to stab at them and give them an added layer of suffering. The passengers wore signs of defeat, marked by sadness that couldn't be averted. These were people without a country. Orphans. Homeless.

Many of the adults trudged up the gangway like it was a death sentence, some cowed, some with eyes that wore fright and fear, their faces forlorn with worry and care. The children ran, not aware of what their parents faced, blissfully oblivious. The ship offered these passengers a place of respite for two weeks while trying to determine how to spend the rest of their lives. They would not see Germany again. It was a sobering thought for so many whose relatives had spent a millennium there, working and raising their families.

The Nazis told every single person leaving Germany on the *S.S. St. Louis*, "If you leave, you may never return, and if you do, you will suffer the consequences." To make matters worse for those boarding the ship, Prime Minister of Propaganda Goebbels had a photographer stationed at the pier with a two-fold purpose.

The first purpose was to take photos of more affluent passengers for Goebbels to use as propaganda, portraying to the world the beneficent goodness of the Reich: "We are allowing German Jews to leave, putting them on a luxury liner. Look how happy they are, dressed in finery even!" The second purpose was to photograph those who seemed less fortunate than other passengers to try to portray them as poverty-stricken savages and fugitives.

The photographer could not find many passengers that fit the description of poverty-stricken or savages because there weren't any, except a few men and teachers, who had been interned at Dachau, and, somehow, by miracle, had been released. So, the photographer took pictures of anyone on the dock, seamen and scavengers that either worked or haunted the environs.

The captain's patience ended as he viewed the nonsense below on the pier. Using a megaphone, he ordered the photographer to cease. "You, on the pier, taking pictures, you will leave this instant."

The man shouted back, "I'm under assignment from the Reich." The captain nodded at two stewards standing by; they scrambled down the gangway in a split second to remove the man.

Behind Schroeder was an ever-changing, limpid, purple-hued sky, clouds painting the background with angels' wings appearing as cloud wisps. A subtle mist nestled in the atmosphere, causing the shiny brass knobs and rails on the ship to glisten. The sun assumed its sinking position in the west, a precursor for the voyage, a hopeful harbinger for good: an irrevocable ending and a fortuitous beginning.

The last of the ducks and gulls announced their departure in search of an evening respite, quacking and squawking just moments before the ship gave three short blasts of its horn, alerting ships in the area that the 574-foot black-hulled, white-striped behemoth was preparing to leave port. Crew members had attached two tow lines, called hawsers, fore and aft, to the port tugboats. The tugboat engines sputtered and spat as they churned out black smoke from their stacks, expertly navigating and maneuvering the ship along the complicated web of canals and waterway traffic, leading it to the mouth of the North Sea, where they would bid the *S.S. St. Louis* farewell with a few toots of the tugs' horns.

Stretching beyond the canals, the ship entered the vast ocean beyond, aligning the ocean and skies, causing them to mingle and meld together, becoming one for as far as the eye could see.

Captain Schroeder walked down the ship's starboard side at a brisk clip to the aft and then to the bow on the other side of the ship on his way to the bridge, nodding at passengers and crew along the way. His steward, Leo Jockl, hustled to catch up with the captain's vigorous pace. He coughed to get the attention of his boss, who turned to see him. As he did, Leo announced, "Sir, your quarters are prepared as you requested. Is there anything else you'd like me to do? Shall I bring your dinner to your cabin at 2200 hours?"

Schroeder smiled at the sight of his young steward, whose father was a maritime sailor. *Oh, to be young and carefree without worries about the future. He'd be conscripted into the Wehrmacht if not aboard this ship. I will be grateful for small blessings.*

But the corners of his mouth turned downward, not in a frown, but concern, reflective of his commitment to his passengers' well-being. "Yes, Leo, that will be fine. First, I'd like to ask you a few questions about the passengers. How do they seem to you, the general spirit overall?"

Leo was not one to mince words. "Sir, I sense melancholy. Some women cried as they boarded, their husbands guiding them up the gangway, looking around with concern, hoping not to draw any attention. Yet you can see the fear, the defeat in their eyes. While I'm young and don't have much life experience, I can feel other people's sadness; it attaches to me for some reason. The good news is the children seem carefree, as they should."

As the final sun rays faded to black, the ship lights outlined their growing shadows, revealing a troubling scowl on Leo's face. "Sir, not to be impertinent, and please forgive me if I'm speaking out of turn, but I cannot understand why they are forced to leave. Where will they go, what will they do, how will they live? They have no money. Forgive my ramblings, sir. Did I answer your question?"

Captain Schroeder knew what he had in Leo: a sensitive young man with a solid work ethic and a desire to serve passengers. Leo fit the bill, just the kind of steward he needed, one who had a heart for the well-being of the passengers. One who, like himself, was filled with compassion for the travelers of this specific voyage.

"Yes, Leo, you answered my question. Dismissed." The captain nodded as Leo saluted him.

On the bridge, the captain spoke briefly with his chief officer and engineer, ensuring everything was in order. The men stood at attention before the captain relieved them. "Do you have any questions? If not, I'll head to my cabin. Leo is on duty until 0200 hours."

Gustav Schroeder made his way to his cabin, greeting the few passengers on deck who weren't already in the dining rooms, enjoying the culinary delights of the ship's chef, or dancing to lively music supplied by a jazzy five-piece band.

Captain Schroeder ate dinner in his private quarters, unwinding and focusing on his duties the next day. He wrote in his pocket diary each evening. Tonight, he wrote,

I am concerned about this voyage. There are forces at work that I cannot explain or describe. Like something sinister is taking place. I was told four times that this was a "special

voyage." An unplanned, unscheduled voyage. What does that mean or entail? I have no idea.

In the meantime, I will ensure my passengers have a pleasant voyage and that my staff attends to their wishes and needs. According to my steward, the passengers have a somewhat nervous disposition. He tells me some passengers seem convinced they will never see Germany again.

I witnessed touching departure scenes taking place. Some seem light of heart despite having left their homes. Others take it heavily. But beautiful weather, pure sea air, good food, and attentive service will soon provide the usual worry-free atmosphere of long sea voyages. Painful impressions on land disappear quickly at sea and soon seem merely like dreams.

Moments later, after making his entry, there was a knock on the door. "Enter."

Leo entered the cabin with a note from the ship's doctor. As he read it, Schroeder's brow wrinkled, and his eyebrows rose.

He instructed Leo, "We have an unwell passenger. Please go to the Weilers' cabin—Moritz and Recha—and see if you can do anything to comfort them. Please stress that we will help in any way possible. I'll follow behind you shortly."

"Consider it done, sir."

CHAPTER TWENTY-ONE

Hamburg, Hollenius, and a Fast Car

MAY 1939, HAMBURG

STANI MEANDERED THROUGH Hamburg's seaport, munching on a Franzbrötchen he'd bought in a bakery, soaking in the atmosphere of the elegant, ancient Hanseatic city.

The last time he'd left Germany was through Bremen, another Hanseatic port, when he, Maddie, and the whole group that was now his family sailed to his new home on a different continent, a different world, the United States. He'd never forget that first rush of exuberance at seeing the magnificent Statue of Liberty in the New York Harbor in September 1933, taken by how she'd towered over the bay, observing the expeditious goings-on below her. She stood guard over Liberty Island, dedicated by American President Grover Cleveland, her steel framework covered in sheets of hammered copper. The patina shimmered, catching glints of sunlight that showered the water below with her majestic reflection.

That September morning, forever etched in his memory, the harbor had been ensconced in a low-lying fog, the mist adding another layer to the solemn waters, while the sun peeked through the horizon, taking its time emitting its golden rays enough to illuminate the great lady of the harbor. Stani's eardrums had vibrated with the sounds surrounding him, other ships in the distance, and an occasional horn; salty air filled his airways, and he soaked it all in, fully immersing himself in this once-in-a-lifetime experience. Never again would the harbor of New York appear the same to him. The next time, it would be like the warm embrace of a long-lost friend; you haven't seen each other in a while, and your reunion will be pleasurable.

But on that particular September morning, the virgin voyage, Stani had shed tears of joy and danced on the deck, praising God, to the amusement of the sleepy-eyed deckhands scurrying about preparing the ship to dock. Stani had felt spry and vital as he danced the dance of King David, dancing with all his might before the Lord, as King David did after bringing the ark of the Lord into the city of David. Stani had shouted, "freedom!" at the top of his lungs while continuing to dance.

The deckhands hadn't known Stani's story or why he danced like he did. If they had known, they'd have learned how Nazis took Stani, condemning him unlawfully to Dachau, where he'd suffered daily abuse by the guards, who stripped him of all his clothes from the moment he arrived, where he was starved and carried rocks, naked, bruised, and beaten. They'd know how he held his friend Jakob as he died, beaten to death by the demon guard Dukolf, ordered to carry his corpse and drop him in the shallowly dug pit of decomposing bodies. But they didn't know what they didn't know.

By six o'clock, Stani found his way to Werner Kempler's house. He took his time, enjoying the blissful moments of walking down a new street in a new city. He approached the brick building, which appeared to hold several apartments, with varied window boxes on the first two floors of windows facing the street. Each apartment had a small terrace that overlooked the park across the way. Wrought iron fencing surrounded the property's grassy border, separating the yard from the buildings on either side. Daffodils and blue squill flowers filled a few pots, randomly placed along the base of the stairs leading up to the front door. Whoever owned the property seemed to care for it well.

Stani rechecked the address again: 140 Am Kratt, 22926 Schleswig-Holstein. He tapped the left breast pocket of his jacket, ensuring Mrs. Genhart's letter was where it should be as he climbed the four steps to the solid wooden door.

Standing at the entrance, he spied a bell; he pulled it, and it rang. A second-story window opened, and a bedraggled-looking man poked his head out, asking in German what he wanted. Stani told him he was looking for Werner Kempler. The man in the window said nothing. Stani put up his hands as if to say, *What's going on?*

The man grimaced and said, "Hold on."

Rochester, New York, En route to Havana with Hollenius
The day after Raymond announced their road trip, a slight problem arose during a discussion. While Raymond messed around in the kitchen, assembling sandwiches for supper and for their journey, he shared their travel plans with Frederick. "I figure we can take your sweet ride, break her in a bit. Lucky for us, I've got contacts along the way, where we'll be able to stay a night and continue on to our first destination, Miami. From there, we'll take a Coast Guard Cutter to Havana. We have a reservation at Hotel Ambos Mundos. Maybe we'll get lucky and have a daiquiri with Ernest Hemingway; I'm told he's a frequent resident there."

Frederick's eyes narrowed as he watched the assembly, smoking a cigarette. "I missed the part where you describe just what you intend to do with His Royal Highness while we galivant across the country."

His Royal Highness, Hollenius, perched on Frederick's lap at the kitchen table. The house was mostly dark, with the exception of the porch lights and the one light in the kitchen, which was bright and contained in a simple fixture. Frederick had a pet peeve about turning off lights when not in use, while Raymond would have every light in the house burning; "the place is lit up like a house of ill repute," is what Frederick would say. However, he insisted on leaving lights on for Hollenius when no one was home.

Raymond contemplated his next move while spreading mustard on a slice of bread. "Can't we just leave a lot of food down for him and let him roam the outside, coming in through the special door you fabricated for him? The weather's nice." Raymond turned to face Frederick, and their eyes met. "It seems like the optimal solution. He'll have free rein and can do as he pleases. What could be better or more convenient? So, let's move on, and—"

Frederick interrupted Raymond, something he never did. Raymond stopped, as requested, and waved his hand. "Frederick, the floor is yours."

"Your pragmatism is overwhelming. While you were busy pontificating, you forgot one specific detail, a feature of my fabricated door for him."

Raymond deadpanned, "What's that, pray tell?"

Hollenius hopped off of Frederick's lap, and Frederick walked to the back door, curling his index finger at Raymond to look. He squatted down, pointing to the two latch locks on either side of the unique swinging door he'd installed for Hollenius to come and go at his leisure. "After his dinner, he'll go out for one last evening constitutional. But be sure to stand to the side of the door, or he'll knock you down if you're in his way. He's afraid of the dark."

Raymond laughed. "Is that so, and how would you know? He told you?"

Frederick scowled. "Of course he did. Why do we lock the door after he comes inside? Yes, you know the answer: we lock the door, of course, to keep the bad guys out. In this case, other cats, skunks, raccoons, and various rodents. Note the sign. 'Lock the cat gate at night.'"

Raymond's pride wouldn't allow him to confess he'd never noticed the sign; he countered, "While you present a solid case, you leave out vital information, such as, how do you know they're not getting in at other times, like during the day?"

Frederick stood up and pointed to the cat's favorite perch above the cupboards, a vantage point that allowed him to gaze directly at the door. "The second that door even trembles to open, he's on it. He's displayed his hunter's prowess numerous times, and if one critter sneaks inside by chance, he'll smell it and dispose of it immediately. Too bad you're never around to experience the stealth action of this regal boy. He could be a real asset to the armed forces!" Hollenius purred loudly in approval as he wove between Frederick's legs. "I rest my case."

The following day, with Hollenius in tow, Frederick packed the luggage into his Aston Martin 2.0 Litre 15/98 Abbey Sports 2/4 tourer with a short chassis. She was a real looker. Her sleek body was tinted in striking silver with black and aluminum accents, and her lines were as fine as those of any other foreign sports car.

Frederick was twenty-four the first time he saw an Aston Martin in a photograph at a friend's home. That same friend had bought tickets to the French Grand Prix in 1922, bringing Frederick along, and the die was cast. Frederick was in love. From that moment on, he knew he'd not rest until he had his hands on one, experiencing the joy of owning and driving his very own Aston Martin. The beauty of the sound of her engine could calm seas and end wars; it was a vibrating roar with an indescribable pitch and whine that one must experience to appreciate. She was one of fifty produced, sporting five seventeen-inch wire wheels, the fifth on the trunk. Reaching a top speed of 137 kilometers, you'd feel a stable ride, benefiting from her Luvax hydraulic rear dampers. They worked in unison with the rear-wheel drive supplemented with Girling rod-operated brakes.

Raymond's jaw had hit the floor when Frederick revealed the price, "Worth every penny. It will hold tremendous resale value."

To help soften the blow of the cost, Raymond had decided on a marketing strategy: parking the car in front of the dealership to lure people in to view the automobiles for sale. The world was still locked in a financial depression. But thanks to the booming Rochester economy, Raymond's strategy had worked like a charm, boosting their auto sales by twenty percent over the past year.

Frederick slid across the premium calfskin leather driver's seat, turning the key and pushing the knob to fire the engine. He revved it, causing the throttle to drop, slowing the rpm, and then used his polishing rag to wipe the faces of numerous gauges before him on the dash. He yawned, tired from having spent the night fabricating a carrier for Hollenius. He situated the carrier so that His Highness could see out the window and simultaneously keep an eye on Frederick.

Raymond came out of the house with a thermos full of coffee, a road map with the route outlined in steps, a carton of Camels for Frederick and a few boxes of Marlboros for himself, his occasional indulgence in smoking, especially when drinking bourbon.

"I've got the addresses, contact numbers, and directions

to each place we stop."

Frederick responded with a salute. "I'd expect nothing less."

Frederick asked about the smokes, and Raymond waved the carton at him. Frederick whispered into the carrier to Hollenius, "That's a good thing. Ten hours with him in a car will make me want to smoke more."

Before getting in on the passenger side, Raymond watched in amazement while Frederick wound up Hollenius's leash. "Are you really going to put a leash on him like a dog and walk him when he has to do his business?"

Frederick put up his hands. "What else would you expect me to do, allow him to run wild?"

Raymond laughed. "For such a tough motorhead, you sure are a pushover for that cat!"

Using the voice tone he reserved only for the feline, Frederick said, "Tell Raymond, we understand each other, don't we, Hollenius? And you know, Raymond, he is a brilliant cat. Have you ever seen another cat come when they're called? He does; you've seen that."

Raymond yawned. "Big deal, it's not like he's doing tricks like a dog. And he only comes to you, Stani, and Wolfie."

Frederick shrugged. "He's fond of Germans. What can I say? He has good taste! But you did forget Buster. He adores Buster. Anyway, let's get going. We have a long road ahead."

Raymond sighed and removed his Ray-Ban Aviators to rub his eyes. "I can't believe we're taking a road trip with a twelve-pound cat."

"Consider yourself lucky! I think he's why we have good weather to travel, so less complaining would be appreciated," Frederick chuckled.

Once on the road, suspiciously eyeing his passenger, Frederick mentioned, "You know, you've never told me the purpose of this trip other than that it's for leisure and to collect Maddie and Stani. Is that all we're doing, or is there something more you're not telling me? I think there must be something else. And why Havana? Why are they going there, and why do we have to pick them up there?"

Raymond asked Hollenius, "Does he always ask this many questions?"

CHAPTER TWENTY-TWO

One Step Forward and Two Steps Back

MAY 1939, VIENNA, AUSTRIA, EN ROUTE TO HAMBURG

DURING THE HOUR-LONG ride to the train station, where the three were to board a train for Hamburg, Maddie commented to Aunt Cecile, "I cannot believe six days have passed so quickly. I feel like I slept most of the time, but I thoroughly enjoyed our walks along the Danube and visiting your farmer friends. I will never again have such delicious cheese. And the Viennese pastry shop. Stani will be so jealous. He loves anything with raspberry. I'm so glad we can bring him a piece of that incredible Linzer torte. If I don't eat it first!"

Cecile allowed Maddie time to ramble on without interruption, knowing she didn't often share her thoughts. Cecile cared for her like her own child. "Maddie, I've loved every minute, and so has Rolf. Haven't you, darling?"

Not waiting for him to answer, she continued, "Of course you have. Never having children of our own, we have always adored every opportunity to spend time with Wolfie. He's our only nephew. As you know, Frederick's wife died before they could have any more children. It's sad to think about because I think Frederick always wanted a big family of his own."

Maddie said, "He has a big one now."

Observing the drizzle threatening to ruin their travel day

and make the roads slick, Cecile worked on her crocheting project and quietly said, "That's not exactly what I meant..."

Rolf interrupted abruptly, "Cecile, change the subject. Why are you mentioning this? Don't start trouble."

Maddie sat quietly in the back seat. The three were silent for a long space of time before Maddie asked, "What did you mean, exactly? Do you mean because he's not married or that he didn't remarry and have more children?"

Rolf attempted to intervene, but Maddie put her hand on his shoulder; "Uncle Rolf, I know it's a difficult subject, but it's important for me to know more about my new family members. I know you avoid uncomfortable conversations. I do, too. So much so that Stani started to take note of every time I objected or tried to shut a conversation down. I became so good at it! Anything I didn't want to hear or discuss, boom! I shut it down. But no good comes from that. We sometimes have to speak of the difficult, painful things if we ever hope to change or be released from the things that hold us captive, like fear and the past. We cannot run from our problems; sometimes, we must seek strength from sources outside ourselves."

Cecile's posture straightened immediately. She turned around in her seat and focused on Maddie. "Where did you learn such wisdom?"

Maddie hesitated for a second but said, "Stani teaches me lessons from the Bible."

Cecile smiled knowingly, clapping and saying with pride, "Oh, he's teaching you Torah?"

Maddie shifted in her seat, holding herself tight, and hedged, "Well, not quite. We discuss Torah and the Prophets, the Psalms, and Proverbs." Then, spitting out the words so fast, "But the New Testament, too! The teachings of Jesus have helped me in ways I never could have imagined. I have come to understand he is the one the Old Testament prophets spoke of, the one who would come to fulfill the scriptures. My eyes have been opened to the truth. And it's a revelation to me because, for most of my life, I doubted if there was a God, or even a Savior."

Cecile turned back around in her seat without a sound. They rode in silence the rest of the way to the train station.

Hamburg, Germany
Stani walked down the steps to street level, observing children playing in the park across the way while waiting for the rumpled man from the window to descend the stairs.

The wooden door opened, and the man called to Stani, "Hey."

Stani ran up the steps to the building, entering and looking for his guide. "In here," came a shout, and Stani followed the voice to the back apartment behind the stairwell. His eyes adjusted to the dimly lit interior.

"Come in here."

Standing twenty feet from Stani, the man was short in stature, but that did not cause his appearance to be any less frightful. He was dressed in an old, moth-eaten military uniform, perhaps dating back to the Austro-Hungarian Empire War, a throwback to the establishment of Bosnia and Herzegovina. His red, craggy face was mostly covered with an unruly beard, much like his hair, which stood out from his head in a feat of anti-gravity. His scraggly eyebrows framed and shaded his sunken eyes. He coughed, and as he did, his lungs rattled.

It was evident to Stani that the man was not in good health, physically or mentally. Having spent time in Dachau, mental illness was familiar to Stani, and he was not wary of it; if anything, it caused compassion to well up in him. The building reeked of mold, and upon quick inspection, the stairwell leading upstairs seemed like it would crumble at the first step. *How odd. The outside appears perfectly normal.*

The man yelled, "Who are you, and why are you looking for Kempler? What do you have to do with him? Are you a relative, a long-lost friend?"

Stani began to take small half-steps backward, slowly, so as not to disturb the man any further; he stayed close to the front door in case a quick exit proved necessary. The man stepped closer to Stani; as he did, Stani saw he was holding a scarab or small commemorative-type knife.

Stani put up his hands. "Whoa, man. What are you doing, and why do you have a weapon aimed at me? Put that away, and we can talk."

The man debated with himself, talking out loud. "You could put it down, but what if he jumps you?" Suspicion narrowed his eyes, and he took another step toward Stani. "Tell me your name."

"My name is Stanford Wellington, and I'm here on a mission for a friend of Mr. Kempler's, a friend from the Conservatory."

This registered with the man. "Ah, the Conservatory, yes, the Conservatory. That place once held my love, that place that took her away from me." He began to weep, and as he did, he crumpled to the floor. With one convulsion, he shuddered and was still. After a moment, he stood, creaking to get upright. "She left me and took my heart; she never brought it back."

He eyed Stani suspiciously. "Did you bring me my heart back? Do you have it?" Then he shouted at Stani, "Tell me, do you have my heart?"

Stani flinched, and he started to sweat, anxiously telling the man, "No, I do not have your heart, nor did I bring it with me."

The man with the wild hair said, "Tell me who you are. Who are you? Why are you here?"

Stani cleared his throat. "My name is Stanford Wellington. I am here to pick up a gift for a friend. I have a letter to prove it. She was your friend from long ago." Keeping his eyes on the man, he pulled out the letter from Mrs. Genhart. "I have a letter of correspondence for Mr. Kempler."

"I am Werner Kempler. Who is the letter from? Who is this friend? I have no friends. Only ghosts. I'm in love with ghosts. Do you know what that's like?"

Stani said, "Yes, I have some experience with being in love with a ghost." *I wonder if this wild man knew my Elenena, my ghost.*

"What do you know of ghosts? You're too young. The letter. Read it to me."

I wonder if reading this will set this man over the edge. Am I wasting my time here? Perhaps I should just go, but that wouldn't be right. After all, I said I'd do it.

Kempler nudged, "Go on. Read it."

Stani began to read the letter, still eyeing Kempler, now fifteen feet away. "Werner, as you requested, I am here to pick up the Amati or whatever you have for me. Please give whatever you have to my representative, Stanford Wellington."

Kempler's eyes grew huge. "Who wrote that?"

Stani, his voice soft, said, "Your friend, Anatolia Genhart."

"Anatolia. Anatolia. Do you know what her name means? Her name means *to rise,* and rise she did. She rose and left. She abandoned everything. She never told me why. She took my heart when she left. Do you know why she did that? Are you her lover or her son? Did she tell you why?" Tears streamed down the man's face, and he wept, making sorrowful, guttural sounds of mourning. The sound of his crying reminded Stani of when a sheep gives birth.

Kempler turned away from Stani and walked through a door. Stani followed, unprepared to view complete squalor.

Stani gagged. His eyes grew large as he viewed rats chasing one another, decaying garbage, and the smell of an open sewer. He said aloud, "Oh my God, Dachau." *Oh my God. Please, God, take the thoughts away. I'm drowning in them.*

Kempler sat on a fruit crate and swigged from what appeared to be a bottle of vodka. Stani swallowed what felt like a liter of saliva and tried to regain his being; the stink of the place came close to causing him to faint. He wiped his forehead with his handkerchief. *God help me.* Hoping to lighten the mood, he offered, "Do you remember the concert you played at the Berliner Philharmoniker in 1932? That's the first time I experienced the celestial sound of the Amati."

Kempler turned, focusing on Stani. "You heard me play? I remember that night. I played Mendelssohn's 'Violin Concerto in E Minor.'"

Stani nodded, "That's right."

Kempler's eyes widened. "That was the night she left me, when she ran away and ripped out my heart. Did she tell you? Did Anatolia tell you? Is that why you're here, to torment me? What did she tell you?"

Stani stuttered, "W-well, I never have known much about her life in Berlin or Austria."

Kempler knowingly nodded. "Oh, I can tell you—she was wicked. She left a trail of destruction behind her. She was a hurricane, a monsoon of corruption. And she never brought me over. She promised she would. She said she'd get me a job but gave it to her friend instead. Could anything be more corrupt than the breaking of a sworn promise to a friend, a lover?"

It dawned on Stani that Mrs. Genhart must have offered the job to Elenena, not him, and that's where she was headed, to her new life in Rochester, when the SS murdered her in cold blood. "How have you kept in touch all these years?"

Kempler grunted in complete disagreement. "Hmmph. All these years, nothing. She only recently reached out to me. I don't know how she found me, but she did. She called me on that phone speaker right there," he says, pointing at the phone speaker. But it's not a telephone or a speaker. It's an overgrown, mostly dead houseplant.

Kempler turned away again and reached toward the floor, grabbing an ancient, holster-style violin case. He squatted down and opened it, putting the lid up to block Stani's view. Kempler reached inside as Stani stood by, choking back the saliva collecting in his mouth as he tried with every fiber of his being not to vomit. He swallowed hard and wiped at his eyes. *God help me not to throw up and tell me how to help this man. But what if he's beyond hope? What if he's completely off the bat? I suspect he is—then what?*

The thought had no sooner occurred to him when the answer to his question appeared. Kempler extracted a 9mm gun from the violin case and put it to his head. Grimacing before pulling the trigger, he said, "I thought she would come. Not you. She promised she'd come; she promised." He wept in a high-pitched whine, "Cut out my heart and give it to her."

CHAPTER TWENTY-THREE

An Ending and a Beginning

MAY 1939, ABOARD THE S.S. ST. LOUIS

RECHA WEILER'S CONCERN for her husband Moritz's health grew by the minute.

"Rechalah, don't worry. We have so much ahead to look forward to and much to think about. Let's focus on what we imagine our new life in Havana will be like. Let's dream a little."

Recha knew when her husband was placating her; after all, they'd been married for a long time. And she adored her husband almost as much as he loved her. They were a lovely match, an old-world blend of style and intellectualism. Well-to-do financially by virtue of hard work, both were highly educated, well-read, and able to speak at length on any number of topics, from Impressionist art to geopolitical issues.

In Germany, before the Nazis had claimed the rest of the Weilers' possessions and remaining cash, they'd bought visas, paying four times as much but not caring that they were charged exorbitant prices.

Moritz said, "They know we're Jews. They'll soak us for everything they can get." At this point, they didn't care. "After all, it's just money." They had spent the last of their savings on a first-class, twin-bed cabin. A long journey to Dusseldorf was followed by the train to Hamburg. Now, the two-week voyage.

They'd dressed in their best clothes for the trip, as was customary. Recha packed what she could, including her husband's favorite books on philosophy and religion. Moritz had never thought it would come to this. They were forced to leave their homeland, something Moritz had not imagined possible. For years, he'd argued with friends, basing his hopes on suppositions that were not accurate or practical. He'd been sure the Nazi party would collapse by 1936. Instead, that year, he'd lost his teaching position at the university, he'd been spit upon and had malicious names hurled at him, and a Nazi youth had thrown dung at him.

Recha knew the toll this had taken on Moritz. In a letter to her sister, she'd written, "Moritz grows more somber every day, and I'm so concerned for his mental state. No one should have to suffer such humiliation. If we can just make it to Cuba..." They clung to a shred of hope, desperate to survive.

But it would not be so; Moritz Weiler's last trip would not be to Havana. His last voyage would be to the bottom of the Atlantic Ocean in a HAPAG flag-covered casket, taking with him his wife's broken, anguish-filled heart.

Sorrow is really just love, all the love you want to give but no longer can.

Grief is love with nowhere to go.

Purser Ferdinand Mueller, who held the position of the ship's equivalent to a hotel manager, enjoyed a close and cordial relationship with the captain. After the first dinner was served, he reported that, after reviewing the inventory from HAPAG House, all had been fulfilled to his requisition levels, with priority in quality foodstuff and supplies, caviar, champagnes, cuts of meat—all the products one would expect on a luxury cruise ship. Even the toilet paper was three-ply.

The purser relayed to the captain the devious ways HAPAG had tried to fleece the passengers. The head office of

HAPAG, responsible for supplying inventory to their fleet, had attempted to substitute higher-quality products with inferior items. They'd tried to prohibit certain premium products, and to supply the ship as if it were a third-class passenger vessel. But they had failed, thanks to the purser's diligence and insistence.

While in his quarters, the captain offered the purser some of his cognac, a rare bottle the British prime minister had given him as a gift, but the purser politely declined. Schroeder swirled the cognac in the crystal snifter. "Why do they feel the need to undercut these people at every turn? They can't just allow them to get on the ship and go; they must torment them, and it is continual, down to the food they eat and the paper they use to take care of their private business. I wouldn't be surprised to hear those orders to use inferior products came directly from the Reich."

His purser nodded, "Indeed, sir."

Schroeder sat in silence, entranced in thought. He snapped out of it, asking, "What's on the agenda for later this evening?"

Mueller replied, "After the band and dancing end, movies are in the auditorium. I believe there is supposed to be a romantic film, a travel log, and a few newsreels, or so I've been told by Schiendick." Schroeder side-glanced at his purser upon hearing who was responsible for overseeing the night's festivities.

The purser assured him, "I'll check in on that. I will report back on any issues. Is there anything else, sir?"

Schroeder sniffed his cognac, then finished it in one last sip. "A man should always be aware of his limit and stay clear." He often said this about never over-imbibing, emphasizing always controlling one's self and senses. "How did the services go for the observant passengers? Was that portrait of Hitler removed?"

Smiling broadly to convey the success and good news, hoping to tamp down the captain's unease, the purser said, "I believe they went well. I heard some singing, which can only be taken as a good sign, sir," referring to the Assembly Hall being used for religious services for the passengers observing Shabbos.

Purser Mueller had compassion for the weight of pressure the captain carried. *I know the burden he feels for his passengers, so he went to great lengths to do everything he could to ensure a pleasant voyage for this load. None of us know how they feel or understand what they've gone through to this point, how it must feel to be Jewish and hated. And with that in mind, we must show them the utmost respect.*

※

Otto Schiendick went to the room of the man who was taking his position as the Abwehr agent on this voyage. The man named Fritz seemed agreeable enough but got under Schiendick's thin skin. Schiendick told one of his lackeys, "I long to pick a fight with him and knock him around." Schiendick was a former German welterweight champ and could fight with the best of them. He sized Fritz up, noting that the other man was a few inches taller and looked in excellent shape.

A steward carrying a dinner tray followed Schiendick as they made their way to B deck, cabin 373. Schiendick pulled on his keychain, which snapped to his belt, and unlocked the door with his master key. Fritz was lying on the single bed, his cabin comfortable and snug. Schiendick told the steward, "Put the tray down and leave. This will be the order for every tray you bring into this cabin. Understood?"

Fritz, wholly ignoring Schiendick, sauntered to the tray, peeking under the cover to see what culinary delights awaited him. He smiled. "Mmm."

If he looked up, he'd know the man he replaced was staring at him, burning with unbridled anger. Schiendick leered at Fritz, "Who are you, and why did you get my position?" He puffed out his chest; his fists were clenched as tight as his jawline, and he was itching to throw the first punch, awaiting any provocation.

Fritz stood directly in front of Schiendick, looking down on him. "I don't know who you think you are or what people you're used to pushing around but know this. General Canaris will expect my report, which will include *you*. So, keep that in mind, Officer Schiendick, when you come sniffing around here, looking for trouble. Oh, you'll find it all right. I assure you; you won't like it."

Fritz stooped and grabbed the suitcase containing the films, pushing the suitcase right into Schiendick's chest; the thirty-pound weight of the suitcase almost took him down. Fritz stifled a laugh. "Better hit the weights; you've got no muscle."

Schiendick stumbled backward, humiliated and ready to implode. He sputtered the words slowly, breathing fire with them, "I'm not done with you."

Fritz waved him off. "You've got your films. Bugger off. I want to eat my dinner."

He shoved Schiendick out the open door. Shaking, Schiendick slammed the door while swearing under his breath and fumbling with the keys. He locked Fritz in the room. Who cared if those weren't his orders?

Otto Schiendick stomped away from the room, mumbling flaming threats of vengeance and plans, recourse, for good. He stopped to gather himself. His hands shook as he pulled out a cigarette. Then, he sniffed the air and whipped around. "Who's there?"

Schiendick took five steps forward, seeing cigarette smoke

but no person. A thought caused him to stop, and he remembered the conversation with Fritz.

Bugger off?

———✴———

In the third-class dining hall, Stefan Soutine gave thanks for the spread before him, a feast of previously unknown proportions. He gazed around the room, taking in the atmosphere. The room glowed with soft lighting, golden sconces adorned the walls, and chandeliers sparkled, adding elegance to the simple crème walls and brown carpeted floor. During dinner, Stefan had his fill, which wasn't much compared to others at the table, who seemed to gorge themselves with no limit, while he ate small bites and took small portions rather than risk vomiting. It had been ages since he'd sat down to a proper dinner with all the accoutrements.

The other guests at the table chatted quietly. They seemed of the average sort, some educated, some nominal workers, but all exceedingly happy to be on such a grand ship. None seemed to notice or care about his shabby clothes or shaved head. He'd bathed in his cabin, hoping to wash away the stench and memory of Dachau. If only he could extract the horror he witnessed from his memory. The pit of decaying humans. The castrations. The senseless murder.

All these thoughts while seated around an eight-top. Stefan allowed himself to be distracted from painful contemplations; he noticed all the meticulous touches—silver salt and pepper shakers on the table, linen napkins, and tablecloths, surprising even for third-class.

Also surprising for third-class was the number of courses, one after another, leading to seven. Provoked by the thought of hunger, fearful of not having food, Stefan took two rolls and a few pieces of fruit, an apple, and an orange, shoving them in his pockets while he scoped the room, suspicious and worried that someone would stop him. Or report him. He had to remind himself: *You're on a passenger ship now, relax.* But he didn't know how; adjusting to newfound freedom would take a while.

A band played, but the music didn't interest Stefan. He was about to excuse himself from the table of diners when he caught a glimpse of a glitzy tray of golden, billowy-soft doughnuts, the yeast kind with the chocolate glaze, passed on a silver tray. Even though he knew he couldn't fit in another bite of food, he waited patiently for the tray to come his way, and he took a doughnut regardless, afraid he'd never have another opportunity for such lusciousness.

Stefan thought: *If this is the third-class food, I can only imagine what the first-class is like.* Even cooking for the camp commandant at Dachau, he had never seen an array of such a variety of foods, cheeses, pâtés and condiments, and wine for the table—not since working in Paris.

Stefan nodded at his tablemates and dismissed himself, leaving to wander the boat. *What happened to Fritz? Most Nazis would have first-class accommodations; why would he be different? How will I find him, if I want or need to? If caught strolling along the first-class promenade, I will have no reason or excuse to give.*

Stefan made his way back to his cabin. His accommodations reminded him of what he imagined to be the standard of the famed Ritz in Paris. His cabin was small but spotless, an obvious sign of high standards. It smelled clean; the linen on the bedding and pillow covers were crisp and sparkling. Everything was of superior quality. Even the towels were a revelation. He'd never had such a plush and luxurious towel, yet another good experience to replace a bad one.

Stefan knew this was the only way he would survive. If he held on to the new images, like the clean cabin and the plenteous food, would they replace the images from Dachau seared into his memory, tormenting him?

Living as a prisoner isn't living at all; it takes a toll on one's mind and soul.

CHAPTER TWENTY-FOUR

Déjà Vu

MAY 1939, HAMBURG, GERMANY

STANI HARBORED A permanent dread of seeing dead people. He witnessed many in Dachau. *Why God, today of all days? I have to board a ship.*

The sound and reverberation of a gun fired at close range manifested in the horror of the result. It is no less shocking to witness one death at close range than it is to witness three or ten. Death is death.

Stani claimed his past was never dead. He recounted his previous life to anyone who asked. He told them, *Most of my memory of 1933 finds me in Dachau Concentration Camp, wrongly arrested, then imprisoned the night I took Maddie to hear the Munich Philharmonic Orchestra. Here I am, naked, carrying rocks, the weight of them cutting my unprotected arms and midsection, a metaphor for what I witnessed, which had the same effect on my soul.*

The kapo took Aharon, Mordechai, and Wilhelm and delivered them to Dukolf. He made them kneel behind the garage right when Frederick first came to Dachau. Dukolf spattered their brains on the wall, then ordered Frederick to take the bodies to the pit and dump them, then clean off the wall and ground of any evidence. After murdering the three, Dukolf laughed and told Frederick, 'Welcome to Dachau. Get used to it.' Dukolf spat on one of the corpses, then unzipped his pants to urinate on all three. Zipping up, he said to

Frederick, 'Lucky for you, you're just a German criminal and not a stinking Jew.'

Stani temporarily lost track of time, in shock from what he'd just witnessed, obliging his memory to awaken the deep trauma that slept lightly, dwelling near the surface of his daily reality. That was when he heard someone knocking on the door.

Stani turned around to see two Hamburg Schutzpolezei. Dressed in black, with red swastika Nazi armbands, they appeared as ominous as their attire. Stani observed the men as their eyes scoured the scene, and then they gazed at Stani. They whispered to each other something about the size of his nose, causing them to make a snap judgment.

One shouted at Stani, the other telling him not to move. Both had their pistols trained on him. Without a single question, they surrounded Stani, putting him in handcuffs even though the weapon of destruction lay in the hand of the deceased. Stani was feverish to point this out when one of the Hamburg Schutzpolezei hit him in the head with the butt end of his pistol.

Aboard the S.S. St. Louis

In the ship's cinema, passengers could sit comfortably in upholstered oak chairs in lovely surroundings, complete with theater-quality sound, and enjoy the latest in cinema, with newsreels and sometimes cartoons or a travelogue. The room's gold molding and sparkling chandelier made for an atmosphere of modest refinement. The cinema was a return to civility for all who entered, especially those who bore the brunt of the Reich's criminal behaviors and policies.

Schiendick bullied the projectionist, pushing him against the wall and telling him, "You'll use the order I tell you. You'll follow my every instruction, written here, or you can expect to wake up at the bottom of the ocean. Is that understood? Nod yes. Good."

Schiendick punched the man in the gut for emphasis before storming out of the room, leaving the door open. Shaken up, groaning from the pain, the projectionist began to set up the reels in the order Schiendick had written down, though it made little sense to him.

Below the projection room, passengers filed in, some parents with teenagers; there were young adults, elderly couples, middle-aged people—the whole gamut. Some even breathed a sigh of relief. After all, this seemed like a return to a gracious way of life, where they could live without fear, without Nazi accusations drowning them up to their ears in hate. Overcoming those inherent feelings and emotions would take time. But good moments might procure more such moments; at least, Stefan hoped so. He didn't know whom to thank for this day's goodness, so he just whispered in his heart: *After a lovely dinner and a cinema, I will return to my warm room with an actual bed and crisp, clean sheets. Thank you, God, for your goodness. I know moments are fleeting, and I've learned good doesn't always follow, but for this moment, I'm grateful. Thank you for taking care of me and watching out for me.*

Stefan scurried behind a throng of passengers heading to the cinema, hoping to go unseen; he was about to enter when someone grabbed him violently by the arm and dragged him into a vestibule. Otto Schiendick held Stefan in a chokehold.

He whispered, breathing heavily in his ear, "Are you missing your concentration camp? Feeling a bit out of place here, hmm?"

Schiendick let go of Stefan, then kneed him in his privates, causing him to double over and moan in pain, the floor meeting him. Schiendick spit on Stefan and told him before leaving, "In a day or two, I'll shave your head for you." After a moment, Stefan pulled himself up off the floor. *Yes, and in a day or two, I'll beat your slimy face to a pulp, you bastard.*

Stefan would avoid Schiendick at all costs, but if he couldn't and there was a fight, Stefan had no doubt he would teach Schiendick a lesson. He wouldn't have to wait that long to do it. Being raised in an orphanage teaches you how to fight. You learn how to survive.

Stefan had found a seat away from most other passengers when a couple, most likely first-class passengers judging by their attire, overlooked his appearance and sat beside him. They said hello and he nodded at them and rose while the woman took a seat, out of respect.

First, a travelogue featuring French Morocco was shown. The film revealed the rich, fertile countryside and high-value crops like citrus fruits, vegetables, and olives, which thrive in the soil and heat of the arid summer. After ten minutes, the travelogue ended, and the feature film began: *Top Hat,* starring Ginger Rogers and Fred Astaire.

The story centers on wealthy Dale Tremont (Rogers) on a holiday in London and Venice. She falls for Jerry (Astaire), an American entertainer, whom she assumes is the husband of her friend Madge, unaware Madge is the wife of Jerry's business manager, Horace. The audience was thrilled with the orchestra's melodic translation of the Irving Berlin film score, which accompanied the duo's marvelous dancing. The two moved as one, smoothness personified, each movement timed, gliding in perfect synchronization, keeping time with the music while remaining slick and coifed, dressed to the nines.

As was customary with celluloid reel film, one machine arm projected the first wheel, and the projectionist switched to the projector's second arm for the film's last reel. Some in the audience gasped when they realized what they were watching was not the continuation of the movie; no, it was a newsreel with Adolf Hitler's face splayed over the screen. His voice shrieked the familiar invective, "Worldwide Jewry influences are clamoring for an interventionist war against Germany."

Waving his arms like he had a mouse or two running up his sleeves, he continued to excoriate the Jews. "They rule over all our banking institutions. Their influence is everywhere. We see it in education in schools and universities, their ever-reaching tentacles touching every aspect of life, even corrupting the pure with grotesque art forms, carnal films, and books. These people will bring down civilization as we know it and must be stopped at all costs. They are an existential threat."

Like numerous other passengers, the couple next to Stefan stormed out of the cinema. Otto Schiendick stationed himself at the exit, standing in the shadows, a viewpoint from which he could observe the expressions of horror and disgust on the faces of the people as they hurried away. Schiendick chuckled at first, then broke into a full laugh, knowing he got another dig in, a stab with an invisible sharp instrument meant to harm, maim, and kill, leaving him jubilant. This was how he repaid the unfortunate people he despised, not only by fulfilling his job requirements but by taking pleasure in every moment of the suffering he caused.

The newsreel ended, and the feature film continued, but the moment had transformed into something putrid. The nasty act of sneaking in a Hitler propaganda film intentionally stole the joy that the movie *Top Hat* had brought, extinguishing the flame and flattening the spirit like champagne with no bubbles remaining.

Stefan didn't have to think long to know who was behind such a heinous act.

After returning to his room, he found some articles of clothing and toiletries neatly folded on a chair. Stefan looked at the items incredulously. Who would be so kind and do this? He whispered, "Thank you, God."

Port of Hamburg, The Customs Shed
Rolf asked for Stani again, standing in front of an officer in the customs shed at the Hamburg dock. His impatience grew with each "uh" the officer made as he looked through check-in rolls.

"Uh. No. I see no name here."

Rolf almost roared at the man, "Did you spell the name correctly? You'd better let me look..."

He'd no sooner reached to grab the roll and look at it himself when a Hamburg Schutzpolezei pokes the barrel end of a machine gun in his back. The officer barked at Rolf, "Step away. Now."

Rolf took two steps to the side and turned to face the Order policeman, who must have assumed Rolf to be Jewish. The policeman couldn't be older than twenty. Rolf told him, his eyes peering deeply into the young Nazi's face, "You should think about a different career path. The one you're on is deadly."

The young man pondered the message, blinks, and told him to move along.

Cecile and Maddie stood six or seven meters away, observing the action but unable to hear the dialogue. Rolf walked away from the table toward the entrance to the shed, collecting the two women. He told them Stani's name wasn't on the roll.

Cecile wouldn't stop pestering Rolf for more details. "He had a machine gun in your back. What did you say that provoked him?"

Rolf sighed, "Oh, for God's sake, calm down. You should know by now that these goons need no provocation; they are chomping at the bit to cause an uproar, an excuse for their abuse. I'm sure he thought I was Jewish." Cecile winced at the words.

Maddie had been quiet until now, but panic caused her voice to rise to a brokenhearted whine. "What do you mean you couldn't find his name on the roll?" Tears welled in her eyes. "What time is it? Are we late or early? Maybe he hasn't checked in yet."

Trying to sound hopeful, Cecile chimed in, "Yes, that's it, something held him up."

Maddie said to herself, *What time I am afraid I will trust in thee. Oh God, please tell me he's right around the corner; please bring him here.* Wringing her hands, she felt perspiration gather on her neck and forehead. She told Cecile, "I feel ill, like something is dreadfully wrong. We never heard from him since that first call."

Rolf took Maddie's hand, stopping her wringing, and patted it. His voice was light and unusually optimistic. "Hey, listen, he said he'd never been to Hamburg and looked forward to exploring. He's probably got caught up in the excitement and lure of a new place and lost track of time." Rolf chuckled. "Who knows, maybe he met a lady who swept him off his feet!"

Maddie shook her head. "Highly unlikely. That's not like him. I've tried not to worry. Oh no. I think I'm going to be sick."

Maddie turned away and ran into a small alley between the sheds, and she retched. Rolf and Cecile followed close behind and approached her just as she searched for a handkerchief in her purse. Cecile had one ready. "Here you go, my love. Come here, over here where the benches are, see them? Let's walk over there while it's still light."

Cecile put her arm around the limp Maddie, holding her, with Rolf on the other side for support. Maddie couldn't hold back the tears. "What if something has happened to him? What if he doesn't show? I knew we shouldn't have come here! This is all my fault. I just had to play in Vienna for my foolish pride."

She blew into her handkerchief, wiped her eyes, and said emphatically, "I cannot get on that ship." She buried her face in Cecile's' shoulder, crying. They sat together on the bench, and songbirds gathered near their feet, chirping as if to encourage or cheer Maddie. Maddie turned to them and smiled. "That's a butterfly kiss from God; that's what Stani would say."

Cecile took her handkerchief, turned Maddie's face toward hers, kissed her cheek, and wiped Maddie's tears. "Everything will work out, don't worry. Stani will be here." She brushed a lock of Maddie's hair from her face, tucking it behind her ear, and told her, "chin up," as she touched under her chin as if to raise it.

Then she barked at Rolf, "Rolf, what's the time?"

Rolf looked at his watch, working to keep the concern from his voice, not realizing it was already getting very late. "It's 6:45."

Maddie sniffed, then blew her nose again and cleared her voice. With complete resolve, she stated, "I left Stani behind before, and I promised him, gave him my word that I would never do that again. I'm not leaving Germany without him. I'm not getting on that ship. No way."

CHAPTER TWENTY-FIVE

Halfway to Havana

MAY 1939, ON THE ROAD SOUTH

ON THEIR WAY to Fayetteville, Frederick and Raymond found a small gas station in Raleigh, North Carolina with a 45-seat cafeteria serving lunch and dinner. After filling up the car with petrol, both men observed the sign: "Home Cookin'." Raymond slapped Frederick on the back. "I'm in. How about you?"

This was Frederick's first foray into Southern cooking. Fried chicken, roast beef, fried pork chops, turnip greens, field peas, crowder beans, creamed corn, biscuits, and hot water cornbread were all a revelation for him. He almost hit the floor after tasting chess pie and banana cream pie, telling his travel companion, "This is the closest to German food I've tasted since moving to this country, outside of what Stani cooks. And the biscuits! Putting jam on them is just brilliant. Stani must try this food!"

Raymond got a kick out of Frederick's sudden enthusiasm. Excitement of any kind rarely got his blood up, only when necessary. Frederick said with an air of authority, "I believe in conserving energy. There is an exception to every rule. If you want to talk about food or race cars with me, that's a different story!"

Raymond said, "Or your cat!"

Frederick wrapped up some chicken. He tore it into pieces

and added some beef, which he quickly shredded. Raymond didn't have to say a word. His expression said it all.

"What? My boy is a hunter. He likes his meat, just like his poppa. I don't think he'd like cornbread. What say you, Wellington?"

Leaning back in the club-style chair, Raymond surveyed the humble interior. "I say we ask the lovely lady who so kindly served us whether or not there is the presence of bacon in the cornbread, as in bacon grease. If she answers in the affirmative, I say Hollenius will love that cornbread and relish it to excess; you may find him rolling in it."

A husband and wife owned the small restaurant; he cooked, and she served. Raymond posed the question, and she didn't have to ask her husband; she knew the answer. "Right, you are, sweetie. Bacon grease is in that there cornbread."

Frederick challenged Raymond as soon as the woman left the table, leaning in to ask, "How much you wanna bet that they fight like cats and dogs behind those closed doors?"

Raymond did a double-take. "Are you serious? Do you want to put money where your mouth is? Is that it?" He smirked at Frederick, made happy by the easy pickings.

Ever the deal-maker, he proposed, "I'll give you a fifty if you win, and if I win, I get to drive your car. Either way, it's a sweet deal; you can't lose." Frederick lost.

Raymond looked good behind the leather-wrapped wheel of Frederick's Aston Martin. Frederick sulked on the passenger side and reminded Raymond, "You're not a European. A certain sophistication and charm are necessary to accompany a proper European behind the wheel of a European auto, simple as that," snapping his fingers for effect.

"You're right. You are the epitome of soigné."

With a broad smile, Raymond said, "I sure do like the

way this baby accelerates," as he pressed the gas, but ever so lightly, like an egg was under the pedal. This was what German racing legend Bernd Rosemeyer had taught Frederick, who shared the wisdom with Raymond.

"So, tell me about Ft. Bragg and why we're headed there?" said Frederick, lighting a smoke.

Noncommittal, Raymond offered, "It's on the way. You know, just some old friends from college, a few bigwigs here I've kept in touch with. Contacts, say, if the boys ever needed extradition." R aymond considered the weight of his words. "Let me rephrase that—not that they would receive preferential treatment over the others, but let's just say I have eyes on them, looking out for their well-being while completing their mission."

At that pronouncement, Hollenius meowed loudly, voicing his approval. Frederick reached back into the door of his carrier, stroking his noble noggin. "You know when we talk about the boys, don't you? What listening skills! You'd make a good dog but are much more intelligent."

While Raymond zipped along the country roads, enjoying every hill and curve, Frederick admired the beauty of the red-tinged clay soil accentuated by clear blue skies. "Someday, I'd like to drive through this country and see it all."

Concerned, Raymond's brow wrinkled as he glanced at Frederick. "That's a grand dream and certainly obtainable, providing a war doesn't happen first."

Aboard the S.S. St. Louis

The hour was late; an almost full moon offered no consolation to those seeking her light to lead them. It was obscured by cloud cover, an omen for less-than-smooth sailing in the foreseeable future. The night air was twenty degrees south of balmy, hovering at sixty, but still quite cool. The music of the wide-open, watery expanses was not what Stefan could have imagined, hearing whales belching out their love song, their melodies crashing through the silence of the night. In the distance, the hollow knell of another ship announced its presence across the swells.

Stefan wandered through the tourist-class promenade, hoping for serendipity to occur, and he'd run into Fritz by chance when he heard singing. As he got closer, he recognized the lyrics and tune, a Horst Wessel song he'd listened to the guards at Dachau singing. He snuck in the door, and no one noticed. What he saw delighted him and his chef sensibilities: a formal dining room. The room was modestly accented, with wallpaper in pale blue hues and an elegant band of gold running along the middle like a chair rail. There were numerous rounds of ten, draped with white linen, with fabric-covered folding chairs pushed around the sides.

Stefan fantasized he was the chef, presiding over this beautiful room with stunning appointments. He imagined peerless table service and glorious courses. He plated each course, each one more magnificent than the last. The guests, in formal attire and expecting nothing short of superb, were overcome with excitement, swooning over each gourmet delight. But this wasn't a scene from *Top Hat*. Snapping back to reality, Stefan spied on the men deeply engaged in song. The Nazis stood on the risers while an officer pounded the ivories. Schiendick played the conductor and waved his arms as the men sang.

Ah, sweet revenge. Here's my chance to get back at Schiendick.

Returning to the promenade deck, Stefan spotted Purser Mueller walking toward him. He waved to get his attention and informed him of the crooning. "It could be exceedingly disconcerting to other passengers if they heard this, especially with what happened after the movie earlier this evening."

Mueller was puzzled. "What happened?"

Stefan recounted the dastardly prank Schiendick pulled, switching to a Nazi newsreel in the middle of the feature film, which upset many passengers. Mueller fumed silently. Stefan added, "I hate Hitler and the people that associate with him."

Mueller was a German, through and through, and technically a Nazi, but he didn't have any reason as of yet to hate Hitler. He shared this with Stefan, who said, "You should hate him. I've witnessed firsthand what he's done and know what he's planning to do, and it isn't good. There is a plan of deceit, something involving this ship!"

While he went on, Mueller listened. "Do you know that in January of this year, he gave a speech from the Reichstag? Six years to the day he became chancellor. At the end of it, he calls himself a prophet and calls for the annihilation of the Jewish race in Europe. Do you need further evidence as to why I hate him?"

Mueller assessed Stefan, pondering the weight and message of his words. *Does he know what he's talking about? How could a prisoner from Dachau have any idea of Hitler's plans, and how could he know anything about this ship or a dark plan concerning it?*

They walked together to the Assembly Hall and, peeking inside, spied Otto Schiendick, just as Stefan had described. Mueller had seen enough. They returned to the promenade deck, and the purser thanked Stefan. "You've done a great service to the other passengers by notifying me. Thank you. I'll take care of this at once. And know that I'm sorry for the plight of the Jews of Europe, but what can I do?" The men stood silently as Mueller added, "Please enjoy the rest of the evening, and let me know if I can be of any assistance."

Purser Mueller had continued toward the stairs when

Stefan stopped him, asking, his voice catching with emotion, "Was it you who provided me with clothing and toiletries? If you know who did, please thank them for me, or if it was you, I am grateful. Upon my release from Dachau, all I had to my name was on my back."

Purser Mueller blushed, moved by Stefan's humility and his impoverished condition. "We are here to serve you, sir, and ensure a pleasant voyage. Is there anything else?"

Stefan paused, wondering if the man knew of Fritz's whereabouts. Usually, he'd be afraid to ask a German. But the purser had shown him undue kindness. "I'm looking for a passenger I was friendly with while waiting to board. We spoke at length about many topics and had a stimulating conversation. I'd hoped for more once we boarded. I believe he's traveling in tourist class. His first name is Fritz."

Purser Mueller responded, "It is a HAPAG policy to keep all passenger information private, but I don't see a problem in this case. If you stay here, I'll get the passenger log, review it, and return with an answer. How does that sound?"

Stefan beamed, and flashed a brilliant smile, doing the heart of the purser good, causing him to sigh in relief.

In pursuit of the captain, Mueller found him in his office at his desk, entering information into a logbook. The captain was known for his meticulous record-keeping.

"Sir, if you please, there is a disturbance in the Assembly Hall, where you gave orders to the crew to set the room up so the passengers can hold their religious services in the morning. From what I could see, they set up the room as ordered, but now a huge portrait of the Führer hangs on the wall next to the piano. The crewman Schiendick and others are drinking and singing songs of the Reich."

Schroeder rolled his eyes upon hearing Schiendick's name;

he massaged his temples, hoping to ward off a migraine. "Did any of the passengers hear this singing?"

"Yes, sir. A male passenger first notified me, and I went to see for myself."

"Do you know the passenger? A name?"

"Yes, Stefan Soutine, he's a prisoner from Dachau."

The captain shrugged. "Dachau?"

"Yes, sir, Dachau, the concentration camp outside of Munich."

The captain tilted his head, squinting. "And how would you be privy to the knowledge of him serving time there?"

"To be specific, sir, the shaved head, the raggedy threads he wore, his passport papers. Some of us gathered together, took a collection of donated civilian clothing, washed and folded it, and put it in his room during dinner, not as a judgment against him but as a respectful offer of help, seeing he came aboard with no belongings. In addition, sir, we also outfitted him with some personal essentials: a suitcase, a razor, deodorant, tooth powder, and a toothbrush."

Moved by his purser's actions, Schroeder came from behind his desk to address his friend and colleague. He put his hand on the purser's shoulder, looking him straight in the eyes. "That is precisely the intentional attitude I hope for every crew member. You practiced compassion with this magnanimous deed, and I am grateful to you and the others. I'll be sure to include this in my logbook. Do you, perchance, have the staff assignments with you?

"No, sir. I'll get them."

"Good, you do that, and I'll have a cognac before facing that devil Schiendick."

Mueller hurried to the bridge, where he looked on the passenger list for Fritz. *Fritz, Fritz, ah, here we are, Fritz Effinger.*

B-Deck Cabin 373. He grabbed the crew assignment clipboard and returned to the captain.

While the captain perused the list to see who was on or off duty, he muttered under his breath, "Schiendick. It figures." Wearily, he told his purser, "I will see what's happening. Alert the chief mate of my whereabouts and say I'm taking care of an issue. Then come to the hall immediately after."

Finishing a small pour of cognac, Schroeder grabbed his uniform coat from the stand and put it on, buttoning it up. He also put his hat on straight, believing that tilting it disrespected the position and added a casualness instead of the decorum it deserved.

He reviewed his image in the full-length mirror. His steely blue eyes peered back at him.

You look like a thin and tired old goat; it's time to get away from this Nazi-fueled madness for good if we can just get to Havana.

Captain Schroeder was a proud German. As a boy, he grew up adoring the Westphalia region, swimming in the Rhine, Weser, Ems, and Lippe rivers. As a young man, he'd hiked the majestic Langenberg, Rothaar, and Kahler Asten mountains before enlisting in the army, where he'd become a man. He'd gone to great lengths to ensure dignified treatment for his passengers and given strict orders to his crew, repeating that "the refugees are paying passengers and must be treated as such."

And now I have to deal with this piece of excrement who defies all orders.

He grabbed his megaphone on his way out of his office and started down the hall to the promenade deck. As he passed, he nodded to passengers, tipping his hat to the women, and contemplated his strategy.

Walking half the length of the promenade, he drew closer to the Assembly Hall and heard the men singing one of the anthems of the Nazis, a song about stormtroopers, swastikas, and Hitler.

The captain spied the men through a window in two swinging doors that opened into the Assembly Hall. Crewmen and officers alike formed an unholy alliance. One man pounded the piano keys while ten others held beer steins, clenching them firmly in one hand while pumping their fists in the air and singing at the top of their lungs. The place reeked of hops, apparently from being slopped over the sides of their steins onto the carpet. The scene made Schroeder's blood boil, knowing this vacuous display of thoughtlessness was intentional insubordination.

Captain Schroeder slammed open the double doors with force, barking, "STOP!" through the megaphone. The music abruptly halted.

Schiendick, who was serving as conductor, jumped at the thundering command, his face beet-red. The room was so silent that you could have heard a rat scurrying across the carpeted floor.

The captain approached the ship's Nazi representative and stood face-to-face with him. He was no taller than the captain but seemed inches shorter. Through clenched teeth, Schroeder hissed, "What is the meaning of this? I said and repeated, do nothing to incite or antagonize our passengers. They've been through enough. Why do you directly disobey me?"

Schiendick, a slimy depiction of a man with greasy blond hair and pockmarked skin who stank of cigarette smoke and beer, said with a syrupy tone, "We are merely enjoying each other's company, singing songs of the fatherland. That shouldn't offend you, Captain. Do you need to be reminded you *are* part of the Reich?"

Schiendick looked at the men before him, and some obliged

him by nodding in agreement.

"And you, Nazi Representative Schiendick, do you need reminding you *are* impertinent?" Schroeder growled an order, "Now, all of you, straighten up. You're all unpresentable, bordering on insubordination."

While standing with the straightest posture, the captain surveyed the men, holding up his index finger and spitting out the words, "One more act of fomenting or a display of such misconduct will land you in the brig. That warning goes for all of you. This will be the last time I say this. Do not provoke or intentionally agitate the passengers. That's an order."

Captain Schroeder stared at the lot of them, ensuring eye contact with each man. He turned, glaring at Schiendick. "So help me God, I'll jail every single one of you upon our return to Hamburg if given a reason."

But Schiendick knew the captain couldn't put him in the brig. He was the Nazi representative on board, which entitled him to some privileges.

The captain made his way to leave and spotted Mueller and another man standing by the double doors. Captain Schroeder nodded at them, and the three left the area. Schroeder and Mueller ducked into a deck restroom while Stefan stood guard outside, but first, Schroeder handed the megaphone to Stefan, encouraging him not to be afraid to use it. Neither man spotted Schiendick, who peered around a corner, and observed Stefan with the captain's megaphone.

Mueller and Schroeder spoke quietly. The captain gave an order. "Get rid of that picture of Hitler."

"Where should I store it, sir?"

A rare, mischievous grin came across the captain's face. "Overboard."

"Yes, sir."

"And by all means, be discreet."

The captain and purser departed the restroom and took the megaphone from Stefan. The captain left for the bridge. Purser Mueller told Stefan, "I have a job to do and must attend to it. I was scheduled off-duty an hour ago, and the hours are precious; you only get four hours, maybe five if you're lucky," referring to sleep. "Oh, and by the way, here's Fritz Effinger's room number, B deck cabin 373."

Stefan jumped at the opportunity. "Wait a minute, tell me what the job is, and I'll do it myself as a thank-you for your kindness. I'd feel that would be an equitable exchange in the sight of God and man."

Surprised by the eloquence, Purser Mueller commended him, "Well said. Hmm. Let me think, well, I—hmm, I guess it would be okay, seeing not another person in sight due to the late hour..." Mueller reasoned with himself, with exhaustion making up his mind, *It's not like a job that involved the ship or its command, I guess it would be okay.*

Mueller explained the job to him, after which Stefan said, "Consider it done. You be on your way for a good bit of rest."

Stefan smoked a cigarette, a gift from the purser, kind enough to bestow a pack. He checked out the scene. The moon was hidden by clouds, allowing the black of night to encroach. No other passengers in sight. He slipped into the now-dark Assembly Hall and felt against the wall for the portrait. He grunted, trying to lift it and surprised by its weight.

Stefan struggled with the considerable portrait framed in dense, dark wood. Propping one of the double doors open with his foot, he dragged the portrait along the carpet and out the door onto the smooth deck. He peeked around a corner before bringing the picture to the railing. The coast was clear.

Using every muscle in his arms, he hoisted the portrait to

the edge of the railing, tipping it just enough for the painting to take flight. It did so for a moment before it alternated to a speeding nose-dive into the somber gray sea below.

Schiendick watched silently and took notes, adding to the list of who got paid back and who got sent to a concentration camp. He stepped out of the shadows and said to Stefan, not even ten feet away, "Almost time for a camp head-shave, wouldn't you say, Jew-boy?"

Frightened, Stefan hightailed it away from Schiendick, who laughed and yelled into the wind, "You can run, but you can't hide; we're on a ship! Sooner or later, I'll get you. I know where to find you." And he bellowed into the tenebrous night; his evil laughter reverberated on the gusts.

CHAPTER TWENTY-SIX

One Prison Is No Worse Than The Other

MAY 1939, THE HAMBURG SCHUTZPOLEZEI

STANI WAS BROUGHT down a long corridor into a room with a man behind the desk who gave him a pencil and a piece of paper, telling him to print his name and then sit down until his name was called. He pointed to four unoccupied chairs.

Stani watched as the man wrote his name in a small black book, then on a list. As one might expect in a mausoleum, silence was also here, giving Stani the creeps. He couldn't hear a thing, or feel anything for that matter, outside of his knees shaking and sensing the presence of something sinister.

Lord, I've done nothing wrong. I see it now; I'll be falsely accused like before, they will not believe me, and they'll bring me back to Dachau. I cannot fight them, but you can. I will trust you, Lord; You, my Father in Heaven, will not fail me. You see the beginning and the end simultaneously; the answer is already told, and only time prevents its revelation. You view your created world from the Alpha to Omega in real-time, a perpetual view.

What will Maddie do? Oh, Lord, please help her. Keep watch over her and the words of truth she's come to accept as her own. Let not the evil one pluck up those seeds of truth, plant them deep inside her heart. Amen.

———❊———

Stani heard his name called. The guard calling him looked to be around sixteen or seventeen, with barely enough peach fuzz to cover his unattended acne. That and a peculiar haircut with shaved sides and a close cut on top made a severe statement.

Stani followed him down a hallway to another room, where a man dressed in black with a patch over his eye—typical Nazi attire—sat behind the desk. The drab office was sparsely furnished, with a desk, a chair, a file cabinet, and the ever-present aroma of stale cigarette smoke so strong it made Stani gasp.

The man looked up from the book he was reading and leaned back in his chair, keeping his eye on Stani. Only a haze of smoke separated them.

Stani stood before him, not flinching a muscle except for his throat due to the smoke, silently choking from the smell. The chain-smoking officer lit another cigarette, which he inserted in a holder, then, clenching it, puffed on the cigarette. He viewed a piece of paper, gazed at Stani, and then returned to the paper. He let out a full belly laugh, almost choking himself on saliva and smoke, bent forward, and laughed until he had to wipe the tears from his eyes.

"Tell me, Stanford Wellington, who in God's name did you pay to give you such a preposterous Anglo-Saxon name? Look at you. Clearly Jewish. Pale. Slight. Vacant ice-blue eyes. Huge nose, ears, eyes set apart. Rat-like." He stood up and walked to the small window, peeking through the blinds, then squinted at Stani, his tone flat. "How do you expect me to believe that is your name for one minute?"

He pressed a small button on his desk. Without a word, the teenage guard led Stani away, down a dark, narrow hallway that transitioned from walls of cement to walls of stone and cement grouting. The deeper they ventured into the cave-like setting, the more sparse the fractured light became. Stani turned his ankle on the uneven stones of the floor. He limped the rest of the way. His nose twitched, picking up the unmistakable scent of mold. And death.

The guard locked him in a damp, cold stone cell, with no window or light except the minuscule amount filtering through a tiny slot in the door.

The Hotel Atlantic Hamburg

The hotel was owned by the same company that owned the passenger line, HAPAG.

The Hotel Atlantic Hamburg was inextricably linked to Hamburg's history. It began with its rise as a Hanseatic trading hub and was exemplified by the entrepreneurial talent of its ship owners. One of the most important of these, Albert Ballin, was responsible for the hotel's opening in 1909 when maritime tourism flourished. Ballin's creation was the first highlight for first-class passengers: an exquisite place to stay before embarking on a journey with the famous HAPAG Hamburg America Line.

After Rolf asked the HAPAG representative about arrangements, the man recommended the Hotel Atlantic, a reasonably new luxury hotel between the auBenalster Lake and the Hamburg Hauptbahnhof in the St. Georg district. Maddie, who did not use her first-class ticket for the *S.S. St. Louis*, could apply the funds toward a hotel stay. Then the representative directed them to the ticket agent, who refunded the money to use for the hotel, enough to cover a full-week stay with meals, all-inclusive for the three of them.

Meanwhile, Maddie cried, Cecile complained, and Rolf's nerves frayed. While standing in the lobby, off to the side of the desk, awaiting a bellhop to escort them to their room, Rolf delivered a brief lecture to lift everyone's spirits, focusing on the positives. "We're going to stay here and search for Stani. Here we are in this lovely hotel, and from the looks of this place, we're going to enjoy it as best we can, okay?"

Rolf spoke of the exquisite lobby, which featured a sunken lounge with a marble fireplace and floor-to-ceiling windows with silk and sheer drapes, augmenting the view of a scenic lake. Throughout the hotel, numerous arrangements of fresh flowers, each uniquely designed, were displayed.

Rolf told the two, nodding toward the fireplace, "I'd love to sit over there, read a book, and have a beer. But there's work to be done." Both women nodded, concentrating as much as possible. Still, the constant flow of guests and employees distracted them, especially Cecile, a fashion maven whose eyes followed the fashions worn by other women.

Rolf continued, "We could fall down the rabbit hole of panic, but we must refuse that. There is a logical explanation. We're here. Let's look for him. We can do this, and three is better than one. I'll make a list; we must check the hospitals, the synagogues, anywhere you think he may have wandered to, a museum or art gallery. I'll get a map, and we'll plot out our way, and we will cover every base.

"Now, Maddie, Cecile, look at me. We will find him. Stay calm. Take a deep breath; let's get on with it."

Cecile was more than happy with the arrangements. She'd sweet-talked the hotel manager, who'd given them a three-bedroom suite. As long as she could put off the inevitable and color her mind with luxurious distractions, this would give her husband some quiet instead of pestering him twenty out of twenty-four hours, which she admitted to being capable of achieving.

It began to rain that night, lulling them all to sleep. The downpour during the early morning mirrored Maddie's grief over Stani. It was more than she could face.

"The rain came at a good time," said Aunt Cecile. "Rain is good for the soul; it washes away the things that need to go." Then she lamented, "If only it took all our suffering away."

Rolf reminded her, "If there were no suffering in the world, how would we value or appreciate times of goodness and happiness? We need darkness to separate the days. If it was always light..."

Cecile blew her husband a kiss. "Very eloquent, thank you. I was speaking metaphorically, of course."

Rolf mimicked his wife, "Of course."

After three days of tedious rain and never-ending tears, Maddie was cried out and ready to face the world again. During her disconsolation over Stani, Cecile watched over her. Rolf made good use of the time, first searching directories at the mayor's office and looking for an address for Werner Kempler. There was none.

Rolf did his due diligence, checking the hospitals, jails, police stations, and synagogues for any lead. The police were no help, but they told him to check back; maybe they'd find a clue, and perhaps Werner Kempler would come to the rescue.

Rolf enjoyed being carefree to wander without his wife snapping at his heels. Not that he wouldn't miss her company, especially if he discovered something that would captivate her. It was more that he liked having a job.

Rolf tried Raymond, and still no answer at the house. Because of the time difference, he'd been unsuccessful in reaching the car dealership; they must close on weekends. Ever the encourager, Rolf told Maddie to keep her chin up and not give up too easily.

After enjoying a simple breakfast, Rolf savored coffee while reading the local papers, a joy for him. Maddie paced back and forth in the reception area of the suite, close to the door. Using the hotel's phone operator, they attempted an overseas call to Raymond but could not get through.

Maddie fretted but stopped herself short of wringing her hands. Instead, she remembered what Stani had told her: *At what time I am afraid, I will trust in thee. Oh, God Most High, please help us—where is Stani?* At that exact moment, she thought of calling Mrs. Genhart for Werner Kempler's address or phone number. *Thank you, God!*

They placed the call, and it finally went through. "Mrs. Genhart, it's Maddie. Yes. No, I'm not; it's a long story." The reception wasn't the best, causing both ends of the phone call to sound garbled, especially with the five-second delay. "Yes, all is well. Wait. There's a delay, I, yes. I'm calling because I need your friend Werner Kempler's address and phone number. Yes, well, no. It's a long story; if you could just, oh, okay, I'll hold on, thank you."

Maddie flashed a smile and fingers-crossed sign to Cecile, who lounged on the upholstered chaise lounge while reading a magazine on interior decorating. "Okay, yes, I'm here. Let me get it; yes, I should have thought of that. Please hold on," she waved frantically. "Aunt Cecile, get me a piece of paper and pencil quick."

Cecile ripped off a corner of her magazine and gave Maddie her eyeliner. Maddie's exasperation showed as she points to Cecile, a wild look in her eyes, covering the mouthpiece while holding the earpiece, snapping her fingers, making writing motions. "I'll repeat it to you, you write, not me, no, you write it down, just listen, shhh."

Then she heard garbled sounds. "Yes, Mrs. Genhart, I'm

right here, what, oh, okay, it's 140 Am Kratt, 22926 Schleswig-Holstein, okay, and the phone, oh, he has no phone."

Her hand over the mouthpiece, she said, "Cecile, did you get that?"

Her aunt nodded.

"Yes, thank you. We will, indeed. Goodbye." Maddie breathed a sigh of relief, and collapsed on a comfy chair. *Now we have a starting point. Kempler will know what happened; I just know it."*

Rolf stood before Maddie. "The queen on the chaise looks happy. Are you happy, Cecile?"

She stuck out her tongue at him. "You know I loathe rhetorical questions. I'm quite content right here, if you don't mind if I occupy this lovely room while you explore Hamburg. Does that answer your question, my dear?" She batted her eyelashes at him, smiling sweetly.

Rolf nodded. "Completely. Maddie, what do you say?"

Aboard the S.S. St. Louis, B Deck, Cabin 373
Bathed, shaved, and dressed, Fritz awaited the day's breakfast selection, served promptly at 6:45 a.m. Food—the one small pleasure he had to look forward to, the one thing that broke up the last thirty-six hours of confinement. The four walls could close in on him, but at least he had the sea and the sky to view from the portholes.

There was a knock at the door, startling him. He went to the door and asked, "Who is it?" *Schiendick always opens the door. Who could this be?*

"Forgive me, Mr. Effinger. My name is Mueller. I'm the purser. Would you mind speaking with me for a moment? I know I've come unannounced. Forgive me."

"Quite all right, I would, but we have a conundrum. I'm locked in this room."

Within seconds, Mueller used his master key and unlocked the door. "I'll see to it you get a key right away; how did you get locked in your room in the first place?"

Fritz was about to answer when Schiendick stormed into the room, his face like a thundercloud, ready to tear into Fritz. When he saw the back of the high-ranking Purser Mueller, Schiendick was forced to stand at attention. He pleaded his innocence, telling the purser, "Fritz is a courier who works with me, and we certainly wouldn't want to upset Admiral Canaris. I'm here to discuss vital information, which is confidential."

The crewman that had followed Schiendick into the cabin left the breakfast tray on the small table next to the bed and departed. Mueller's eyes passed from man to man. He was open to considering something, a sign or signal from Fritz, anything to make him doubt Schiendick. After all, why should he be believed? He was a liar, and that was a known fact.

Mueller questioned Fritz, "Sir, is this correct information? If so, I'll make myself of better use."

Fritz nodded. "All is well. Thank you."

Mueller bowed. "With that, I'll say goodbye."

Schiendick eyed Fritz while Mueller left, but not before touching the outer handle to feel gently if it was set to lock. Then Mueller remembered he'd forgotten to ask Mr. Effinger if he'd seen Stefan. *Did he even come to Mr. Effinger's room?*

Schiendick paced the floor, his eyes downcast. "I can take care of myself with him," he said, nodding toward the door.

Fritz tried not to laugh. "Sure thing."

Glaring at his adversary, Schiendick said, "You have only one purpose on this trip. That's it. Your orders are to stay put. I'll continue to ensure that."

Fritz offered Schiendick a cigarette. He took one, and Fritz lit it for him, then his own. He reminded him, "We're on the same team, fighting the same cause. I understand you're angry with me, but your anger should be directed at the person wanting you off this voyage."

He smoked his cigarette, letting his words sink in, then added, "Canaris only tapped me because it was thought you'd be put off the voyage if Schroeder got his way, but he didn't. It was too late. The plans to replace were already in motion, and you're more a victim of circumstances than anything." Fritz looked Schiendick up and down, smoking his cigarette while examining the Nazi before him. "I'm told you've got some strikes against you; why is that?"

Schiendick got up in Fritz's face. "Says who? Look, punk, keep your opinions to yourself." With that, he shoved Fritz. A mistake. Fritz was ready and gave him a bone-crushing left hook, but Schiendick countered with a vicious right, a left uppercut, and a jab right on the nose, knocking Fritz backward onto the bed and scrambling his thoughts.

The black pocket diary marked JG, and his pistol fell beneath Fritz's socked feet. Schiendick wiped his brow, then picked it up, thinking it was his. He stood over Fritz, still woozy from the jab, saying matter-of-factly, "I may be short, but I was a welterweight champ." The breakfast tray came into focus. "Your breakfast is getting cold."

Schiendick pulled the cover off the plate, grabbed a sausage, and shoved it into his mouth, then stuck Fritz's 9mm pistol into his waistband. "Have a nice day." Schiendick left to head back to his room but first tossed Fritz's pistol overboard. *He won't be needing that.*

CHAPTER TWENTY-SEVEN

Men Overboard

MAY 1939, ABOARD THE S.S. ST. LOUIS

THE SHIP WAS making excellent speed, cruising over relatively calm seas at twenty-two knots per hour. The weather was agreeable, but as all seamen know, storms can materialize without notice; you sail into a front, and before you know it, you've lost your tail, and the fight follows.

Chief Engineer Schmidt, First Officer Ostermeyer, and the captain had sailed through many storms and now discussed the possibility of weather. Days ago, while passing the Azores Islands, they'd encountered strong winds, but the crew had kept her steady, and now, they were discussing what steps would be implemented based on the timing of the weather and determining wind speed. Reassuring his crew, the captain told them, "We know the ropes; we've been here before." The men departed for their respective positions while the captain returned to his office to enter the madness from the night before into his log.

0230 Hours

The deck received a call from one of the firemen: MAN OVERBOARD. The boatswain's watch officer got the order from the officer on the deck. He sounded the horn, resounding with three long blasts. The watch officer ordered the helmsman to make provisions to come about.

The man overboard was a kitchen helper, who I'm told suffered from bouts of depression. I'm also told he had run-ins with Schiendick because of his supposed ethnicity; he was a Russian emigrant with a Jewish-sounding name.

We began a search. The decision was made to drop illuminated buoys while the ship quartered the area systematically. The search occurred amidst distressing news, a coded cable from Hamburg. Three other ships will compete with the S.S. St. Louis, all racing to reach Havana first. At 1:00 am, I officially ended the search, and the ship resumed course shortly afterward.

The captain put his head in his hands.

This is a bad omen for our voyage now: two deaths. First Moritz Weiler, now Uri Berg. May they both come to their place of rest, and may it be in peace. All procedures were followed, and the passengers returned to their rooms with no issues. No harm came from this incident.

This morning, at 0800, a fire alarm was activated on the B deck. It was apparently a prank, a false alarm. All B deck cabins were checked for fire. The all-clear signal was given at 0830. No injuries resulted.

Just then, Purser Mueller appeared at his office door. He'd come directly after searching for Stefan, to no avail. The captain motioned to him. "Yes, what is it?"

The purser was slow to approach. Hesitantly, he began, "Good morning, sir. Last night, when you requested I dispose of a certain portrait, perhaps using poor judgment due to the late hour, I allowed the young man from Dachau to dispose of the piece."

Schroeder's face turned crimson. He slammed his fist on the desk, causing his teacup to jump, his eyes scorching

Mueller. "You had a passenger perform a task I assigned to you? There had better be a good explanation for this!"

The purser wasn't used to being on the receiving end of the captain's legendary ire. "Sir, the man approached me asking in humility how to repay me for this kindness in procuring clothing and some essentials. I was slow to agree; his insistent request was humble and sincere, and I couldn't refuse him. So, I told him what to do, and he said he'd take care of it. I know exhaustion is no excuse, but it factored into my lack of judgment, and for that, I fervently apologize."

Despite the explanation, the captain's anger peaked. He barked, "Purser, There is no excuse. I'm shocked at your lack of good judgment; personal familiarity with passengers is forbidden. You crossed a line, and I must consider a suitable response." Softening, his face losing its deep-red shade, he asked, "What made you think it'd be okay? I cannot understand your lack of decorum. I don't care that he was a former prisoner. He's still a paying passenger! Dismissed."

The captain waved him off, disgusted with his right-hand man. The purser left, crushed by the dressing-down he'd received. In their five voyages together, never once had there been a cause for the captain to speak to him in such a way. But he knew he'd been wrong, out of line, breaking policy.

Mueller didn't mention that Stefan was nowhere to be found.

Hamburg

Equipped with a map and Werner Kempler's address, Rolf and Maddie took to the sidewalks, choosing to walk and savor the springtime atmosphere of a busy port city. They walked silently, enjoying the rhythm of the streets, the sounds, and the traffic. Urban living reminded Maddie of residing in Munich and Berlin with Stani and Elenena.

Maddie waved her arms, wafting the air toward them. "Oh,

take all that in if you can without an allergic reaction." The ever-present scent of blooming trees and sea air filled the space around them, inundating them with the scents of spring.

The sun felt warm on Maddie's face after days of being cooped up in the hotel due to rain and weeping. She asked Rolf, "Is today a good day?" His smile was her answer.

While they walked at a good pace, Rolf pointed out sights to Maddie, having traveled to Hamburg a few times prior. "The architecture throughout the city is eye-catching, with beautiful structures. Of course, there is the Speicherstadt, the largest collection of warehouses in the world, all connected by water, which provides a liquid history. Observe how the warehouses stand in unison in rows like citadels. They are fierce, proud keepers of mysteries."

He mentioned this as they crossed over one of the many canals woven throughout the city. Rolf pointed to the series of canals in the distance. "There's a lot of water. But water connects us; Bremen and Hamburg are called the gateway to the world!"

Maddie listened only partially to what he was saying. "Rolf. What if we can't find him?"

Standing on the sidewalk, Maddie squinted and shook her head. Rolf observed the pain in her blue eyes, now watery with tears brimming; Rolf told her, "It's going to be okay—one step at a time. Do you know mountain climbers never look up when climbing a steep peak? They only look at the next step. If they look up, they'll lose perspective, even their balance, not to mention the task before them, which would feel overwhelming. So, we will do as the mountain climbers, one step at a time."

After almost an hour's walk, the whistle from the local firehouse sounded, signaling the noon hour. Maddie told Rolf, halfway joking, "I hope he's not out to lunch." They arrived at Kempler's. Both stopped walking and gasped at the sight. Maddie's voice caught. She whispered, her voice hoarse from constriction, "What does this mean?"

Rolf held up the paper. "This is the address, but I don't understand why Order of Hamburg Schutzpolezei boarded it up." Both were confused until a moment of sobering clarity came simultaneously; Rolf verified what they both knew. "We've got to call Raymond."

Aboard the S.S. St. Louis

Purser Mueller hot-footed around every deck, speaking to crew and searching for Stefan Soutine's whereabouts. His cabin was empty, and everything he had collected for Stefan was nowhere in sight. *Hmm. There was no trace of him—almost like he was never here. Who would do that?* A sinking suspicion filled his mind, and beads of perspiration covered his forehead above his shaggy dark eyebrows.

Thirty-nine-year-old Ferdinand Mueller was married to the ocean. He was also husband to a woman and had two daughters. When he was a young lad growing up in the St. Pauli district of Hamburg, the sea had become his best friend, confidant, lover, and salvation. Many a night found him deep in observation, perched over the primeval swells while studying the vast seas or skies for answers, as if an ocean gypsy would appear speaking the truths he sought, or an angel would trumpet the answers he needed from the ethereal world. But none of that otherworldly dreamscape could quell the dread in the back of his throat, like acid, rising from his gut, a tide of distress. *Where is Stefan Soutine?*

It was past 10:00 a.m., and Mueller decided to go to B Deck and Fritz Effinger's cabin. *There* was *something about Schiendick's reaction to seeing me like he didn't expect me. And the locked door. Usually, I wouldn't get involved with anything to do with the Abwehr, but I must take the risk in the case of a missing passenger. At least Schiendick is off-duty.*

Mueller knocked lightly on the door. "Mr. Effinger." When no answer came, he unlocked the door using his master key and found the cabin empty. The bed was still made up from the day before. He checked the bureau for clothing or personal belongings. There was no trace of him.

But if not here, where? *He was just here a few hours ago! This is a disaster. Two passengers are missing.*

Mueller was assured of facing a court martial over his lack of judgment. He gave one last look around the cabin, hoping to find a clue, something to indicate where Effinger could have gone, and spotted a Nazi lapel pin on the floor, just the pin with no backing. *Who would have dropped this?*

CHAPTER TWENTY-EIGHT

An Unlikely Sanctuary

MAY 1939, FAYETTEVILLE, NORTH CAROLINA

WHILE HOLLENIUS SAT on Frederick's lap as he drove, Raymond gave the background on the newest addition to Ft. Bragg, Fayetteville, North Carolina.

"In 1932, the Army built an eighty-three-bed, three-story hospital. It served a post population of nearly 2,500 and was named the USA Station Hospital."

Frederick asked, "Is it a general practice of the United States to build an Army base without a hospital?"

Raymond pondered the question. "We are not at war here, and we are not like Germany; you've had wars on your soil often, so that would make sense, but here, not since 1865. However, as one of the programs developed by the US Army Medical Department, they'll train medical personnel to operate mobile and fixed medical installations and field units. Like triages or mobile facilities for more serious injuries."

Frederick listened carefully, concerned about where this was leading. Raymond continued, very matter-of-fact, "They'll focus on the organization and administration of training, changes in scope and emphasis, the development of doctrine and technique, and responses to personnel and supply problems, all the while treating local soldiers and staff while in preparation should a war break out, the chances seeming more and more likely, but you never know. The one thing I'm sure of is Hitler cannot be trusted."

Frederick's expression was one of worry. He glanced at Raymond, almost hesitant to ask, but knowing he must. "Do you think there will be war?"

It pained Raymond to acknowledge that question with a truthful answer, but he was compelled to be truthful, especially knowing a future war would involve the boys. He tightened his lips and nodded.

Frederick hit the steering wheel with his palm, an action rare for him; he tended to withhold his anger. "Damn it. I thought I could escape war living here, so far from it, and yet it's like the subterranean roots of a tree, grasping ground across the miles and miles of water, so far-reaching until they pop up and dig in the fertile soil of the United States." He lit a cigarette, blowing out the match. Bitterly, he said, "My new home."

"Hey, light me one of those."

Frederick glanced at Raymond. "Is there a secret bourbon stash I'm unaware of? Are you fortifying your coffee?"

Raymond chuckled, shaking his head. "Give me one, please. A Camel sounds better than a Marlboro."

Frederick did as asked, then pointed to the sign, "Ft. Bragg: Two miles."

Raymond took a drag off the lit smoke, telling Frederick and the listening Hollenius, "My friend, the chief administrator, told me of a recently admitted US Army officer, a young man serving and working with Division D of the Secret International Service in Buckinghamshire, England. He was transferred from the burn unit of the Stoke Mandeville Hospital after treating the lower extremities for second and third-degree burns.

"The patient will convalesce at Ft. Bragg until other arrangements can be made to transport him home now that the fear of infection is past. That's the greatest concern with burns of a severe nature, especially when flammable liquids or materials are involved. Oftentimes, the burns caused by the liquid or flammable materials are severe, burning deeply through many layers of the derma, causing a great chance of infection, which can be deadly."

Frederick eyed Raymond carefully, knowing there was something behind the information. It was a cat-and-mouse game they played. Frederick wouldn't ask for more details; he'd wait for Raymond to offer it, providing him an opening to pounce.

The three arrived at Ft. Bragg and headed straight to the inpatient part of the hospital. Raymond instructed Frederick where to park the car. Frederick turned off the engine, asking Raymond, "Now what?"

Raymond finished his cigarette and said, "Put Hollenius in the carrier, or if you prefer, on a leash; we're going on a short walk, and I'll tell you all about the purpose of our visit."

Frederick watched Raymond, who carried his poker face and used it. He went about attaching the leash to Hollenius's collar. "Oh? Now you're going to tell me. So, is there a purpose for our visit? I thought this was supposed to be rest time, a vacation." Frederick shook a finger at Raymond and said, half-mocking, "You lawyers always try and change the story. Now, hold on, we need to take care of something."

Frederick walked the cat onto the grassy area of the property. "That's my boy, king of the forest you are, the Black Forest. Please, do your business."

Hollenius took his time sniffing the grass, giving Raymond more time to work on his severe lack of courage. *Should I say it like this or like that? How do I tell him?*

Aboard the S.S. St. Louis

Stefan told Fritz, who followed close behind, "We'll be safe down here. Schiendick would never come to the belly of the beast; he'd be afraid." While Fritz had heard stories of passengers riding in steerage, that is, in the belly of the ship, the lowest part, a type of hell according to some, he was not prepared for what he'd face for accommodations. Stefan pointed to two bunks that had not yet been claimed. "We're lucky to find these. A steward told me this isn't even near full for steerage. We're packed in here pretty well, but not like cattle."

Having changed into the clothing the purser provided, the two were adequately disguised. Stefan wore a wool cap covering his not-so-bald head. His hair was beginning to grow back, short blond strands sprouting up like the season's first wheat. Nothing identified Fritz as a Nazi other than his Aryan good looks, his blond hair covered by a leather cap he'd bought off another passenger for three Deutschmarks.

Sitting next to each other on the lower of the two bunks, they were on equal ground. At the very least, a single light was sufficient to provide enough illumination for the men to see each other. Speaking low and guarded, Stefan said, "Okay, tell me now, why was Schiendick so angry with you? I thought you were on the same side. What happened?"

Just then, a young girl, no more than ten, unabashed, asked if either of the men had matches. Fritz reached into his pocket and extracted a matchbook. Smiling at the pretty blue-eyed girl, he said, "Here, you can keep it." She smiled sweetly and commented on his green eyes, then left. Fritz thought it odd but shrugged it off.

"At least everyone's not out of sorts," he said as a baby cried in the background. "Oops, I spoke too soon!"

Stefan nodded. "Go on."

Fritz began, "I work for the German Military Intelligence, the Abwehr. Schiendick is the Abwehr agent onboard this ship. He picks up secret information at a specific location and returns it to Berlin on the return trip. I was tapped to do the job, and it made Schiendick angry. There's nothing more to the story."

Stefan considered whether or not Fritz was telling the truth. "Yeah, well, there will be more to the story when someone finds him." Both men snickered at the thought of what they'd done to the Nazi and Abwehr Representative, literally leaving him tied up in knots, locked in his room. "Aren't you the least bit worried there will be hell to pay for this?"

Fritz straightened his stance. "Absolutely not. He locked me unjustly in my cabin. There were no orders for that, just his vindictiveness, a payback." He reached into his shirt pocket and retrieved two smokes, offering one to Stefan.

"No thanks. Bad for my tastebuds."

Fritz grinned, saying, "I've got to commend you; sounding the fire alarm was brilliant. You knew the stewards would open my door! How did you find my room?"

Stefan laughed. "I never reveal my sources. Now, you no longer have a weapon to order me around. Seeing I sprung you from your cabin prison, you owe me. We're on the opposite side, I know. I have no shame left, but if you have some money, if you have any, it would be appreciated."

Standing up, Fritz turned to Stefan, tilted his head, crossed his arms across his chest, and said, half joking, "What do I look like, a bank?"

Stefan asked what he knew to be a rhetorical question: "Does Schiendick know about the diary?"

Fritz snapped back at him like an unexpected lightning strike. "No, why would he? Why would I tell him about that?"

He quickly realized his mistake; he and Schiendick were supposed to be on the same team, and he hoped he hadn't blown his cover. Fritz didn't see Stefan pick up the diary with JG inscribed on the cover. Stefan spotted it on Schiendick's bed, carefully lifting it and putting it back in his pocket while Fritz ensured their captive was securely tied. "I mean, maybe he knows the voyage is a sham, or maybe he doesn't. We don't always tell the left hand what the right hand is doing."

"Isn't that a Bible reference, 'The left hand doesn't always know what the right hand is doing'?"

Fritz shrugged, about to answer, when a creeping stink filled the air. "Good God, what is that smell? What on God's green earth is that?"

One of the passengers familiar with such odors and the procedures associated with its cause announced to the group, "The sanitation crew just emptied the contents of one of the ship sewage bins into the deep. The excess gas caught in the line flushes through the air filter system in the ship's bowels, leaking a small amount into the steerage atmosphere. It wafts through our airways and our lungs."

Another passenger shouted, "No extra charge for the poison."

Fritz turned away. "God, that's putrid, horrid." He pulled his t-shirt up over his nose like a masked man.

"Let's get back to our discussion," Stefan said as they walked away from the air filters. "Where were we?"

Then, he suggested telling the captain about the diary and the 'special voyage.' "I don't know why. I just think it's the right thing to do."

Fritz put up his hands. "Not so fast. That book is now my possession, and I'll decide what to do with it."

Stefan sneered, "Is that so? I'd like to see the book; I have a question about something that was written there. I think the captain would want to know. From how the purser treated me, I can only assume he is of the same stock. And, after all, aren't you on the same team as them?"

Fritz told him, "I'm going to look around, see what these fine fellows do for food if something is provided, and if so, when. Despite the wretchedness of this place and its poisonous atmosphere, I'm hungry."

"You're not going to give me the book, are you?"

Fritz rubbed his chin, then walked away in pursuit of food. Stefan yelled after him, "Okay, then, I'll be right here, holding down the fort. Don't worry about me! You get the food!"

But Fritz had other plans.

The Hamburg Schutzpolezei
Rolf inquired again at the front desk of the Order Police Unit in downtown Hamburg.

"We've told you. We questioned a man regarding the death of a Hamburg resident. It was a suicide. While the weapon was in the victim's hand, we are not allowed to give out the name of the deceased until the next of kin are contacted. But the other one, Wellington, we let him go, he left."

Disappointment struck again, and Maddie whispered a cry and a plea, "When? Where did he go?"

The guard, the same smug seventeen-year-old punk, turned away from Maddie, providing no answer. Desperate, hot tears rolled down her cheeks, and she cried, unraveling, "Oh, no, where could he have gone? How are we going to find him? We're never going to find him."

Rolf told Maddie, speaking to her like he would Wolfie and putting an arm around her, "Come on, now, straighten up. You're tougher than this. We'll find him; I promise we will!"

He faced Maddie with both hands on her shoulders, trying

his best to reassure her. Then a wry smile crept across his face, and he snapped his fingers, "I know! I know what we'll do! Let's return to the hotel; we'll make an overseas call to the US government; that's what we'll do. We will have them track Raymond down. If anyone can find him, the government can!"

Maddie smiled weakly, hoping he was right. "You really think they can find him?"

"Maddie, trust me. The US government knows how to find its employees, without a doubt."

Maddie's crystal blue eyes reflected more than uncertainty. "Trust is a foreign word to me." *Trust? What does 'to trust' really mean?* She scowled, saying under her breath, "How can you be so sure?" *How can anyone be so sure about anything? God, why is my first thought to always doubt instead of trust? I trusted as a child. When did this change? When did I stop trusting?*

Engrossed in their thoughts, Rolf and Maddie walked in silence, enjoying the breeze from the nearby water, bringing the sound of honking and chattering as the bigger birds came ashore, announcing their arrival, preparing to scavenge for their dinner. The city's sounds filled Maddie's ears while she tried and failed to control her fear.

Then Maddie recalled her last conversation with Stani about how to find God when she was distressed. *I have to seek him and love him with all my heart, all my soul, and all my strength. But what does that mean?* She took a deep breath and recollected Stani's admonition; she breathed in and breathed out, *At what time I am afraid, I will trust in thee.*

Many of the teachings Stani had shared with Maddie for so many years came rushing back. Filling her mind, Maddie finally began to understand the mystery of faith. *Lord, I realize what Stani was telling me. I can talk to you like a friend, recognizing you are holy; no one is good enough to stand before you. I'm beginning to comprehend what Stani told me about laying my burdens down, realizing I'm helpless to fix certain things in my life. The broken and violated places. You alone are perfect; no one can measure up to you, walking this earth yet without offense. I need you as the bearer of my well-deserved punishment. Not just for what I've done but for what I am, and I, like all humanity, fall short; I'm on the outside looking in, asking you to knock on the door of my heart, and I will welcome you in begging your forgiveness, my heart is cut to the quick. Forgive me. I know you died for me, the Perfect Lamb of God who takes away the world's sins. And mine. Take my life, help me to live for you, walk with you, like Stani.*

She breathed the words, almost pleading, matching them with her steps, unaware of the tears rolling down her cheeks, repeating the words, asking for forgiveness until, like Stani had promised, something happened, a change, so subtle and gentle. She was aware of tranquility washing over her, like a wave that washes a deck clean or reminiscent of a beach when the shore is left free of shells and rocks, swept back out to sea, and for the first time in her life, she knew what it felt like to have peace. If Stani were there, he would have told her, *"The fruit of surrender, its byproduct, is peace."*

Without hesitation, she confidently told Rolf, "I know everything will work out as it should. We must stay on course and keep taking the next step."

Rolf stopped and clapped approvingly. "Well, that's a change and welcome relief. We both believe all will be well, so it must be!"

Back at the hotel, Cecile opened the door, dressed, perfumed, her hair done and makeup on, and greeted the two weary explorers. The recharged Cecile chirped, "I just had the most luxurious bath. I feel refreshed and ready to go." Vivacious and exuberant, she asked, rubbing her hands together, "What's on the agenda? Dinner, the theater, a movie?"

"Aunt Cecile, how can you think of such things when Stani is God knows where? We don't know if he's alive or dead, safe, beaten, hungry..." Maddie's words trailed off, and she collapsed on the small settee, her heartache seeping out through her tears.

"Shhhhhh now, Maddie." Bending down, Cecile collected Maddie into her arms. Pushing the hair off her eyes, rocking her ever so gently, and stroking her forehead, she said, "While hate may be stronger than love, there is something stronger than both." She took a deep breath and expelled the word *hope* with a full rush of oxygen behind the word, making it sound even more powerful. "Our disappointments are God's appointments. Sitting around thinking about how sad you are about anything never improves one's mood; however, in your case, you must be exhausted in every way."

Rolf's eyes were glued to his wife. He reveled in this gentle side of her personality, seldom seen, *but boy, what a good time for that side to show up!*

Cecile helped Maddie up, asking what she'd like to eat or drink, to which she responded, "Nothing," then helped her undress and get into bed. Cecile ran to the bedroom she shared with Rolf, who started to speak. She put up her hand and told him, "In a minute," then returned to Maddie with her silk eye mask. She whispered, her voice soothing, "This will help you sleep. Now rest, my love. We'll be right here waiting for you when you wake up. We won't go anywhere. Don't you worry about a thing." She leaned down to kiss Maddie's forehead, pulled the covers up to her chin, drew the blinds, and closed the drapes.

Maddie lay in bed, and just before the slumber reached

her eyes, she whispered a prayer: *God, will there ever come a time when I feel secure? If I have a home of my own that no one can take from me, then will I feel unafraid? Then will I fit in?*

CHAPTER TWENTY-NINE

Some Came By Flight, and Some By Fight

MAY 1939, FT. BRAGG, FAYETTEVILLE, NORTH CAROLINA, USA STATION HOSPITAL

WHEN THE SECOND notice came from the State Department on May 1st, informing Raymond of an accident involving Wolfie during training at Bletchley, Division D of the Secret International Services, he realized it was time to implement a plan. Raymond had felt it prudent to make the travel arrangements and then tell Frederick what had happened when they arrived at the hospital. He saw nothing profitable in telling him before they arrived.

There was a room for consultation at the hospital, next to the chief surgeon's office. Raymond knew he must fill Frederick in on Wolfie's injuries; it was just a matter of how.

Entering the consultation room with Hollenius in tow, Frederick put the carrier down on the floor and began to pace. He looked at Raymond and then away, his voice rising. "I've had enough of this." He turned to face Raymond, pointing a finger. "Enough of the intrigue. Why are we here? What is the reason?"

Frederick waved his hands, almost shouting. "For the length of this trip, you've beat around the bush; your lawyer-ish practices serve you well. Until they don't. I need to know now: why are we here? And what the hell does Division D stand for?"

Raymond jammed his hands in his pockets to fend off any emotion that might break through in his tone. He exhaled, saying evenly, "I received a notice from the War Department that Wolfie had been injured in a training exercise. His injuries are no longer life-threatening. To answer your question, Division D stands for Destruction; the boys are in this unit, and they work and train with incendiaries and explosives. This is top-secret information that is on a need-to-know basis. You need to know." Raymond's voice hedged and he shrugged. "And, well, quite frankly, luring you here was intentional. I confess." Raymond lights a cigarette, hoping to calm his nerves. "I didn't know what to do. If I came out and told you while we were in Rochester, imagine your distress! We had to come here if we were going to see him and bring him home. What could you have done from Rochester? Nothing!"

The color leaves Frederick's face, but slowly his cheeks begin to flush. Frederick snaps back, "Yes, but that's my distress, and I am the one who should decide how to deal with something, not you do it for me. If I wasn't so angry right now, I'd snap you in two. No more lying to me, Raymond, no more. This was wrong of you. You should have told me. Now, when can I see him?"

Raymond nodded. "We're waiting for the surgeon to come in and report how the surgery went. Wolfie was healthy and strong enough to undergo skin grafting."

The shock caused by the word *surgery* caused Frederick to sputter. "I can't believe it, my boy. What happened? Surgery? What did he need surgery for?" His eyes filled with tears, surprising even himself. He hadn't cried since Dachau, when first seeing Wolfie limp toward the garage, the kapo leading him, beholding his only son, battered and broken, his eye bashed in, his body, covered with welts, bruises, and gashes.

"What is this procedure, and why does he need it?"

"The surgery takes skin from other parts of his body and transfers it to the wounded place, where burns were worse than others. From what I was told of the procedure, there's a period where they must ensure nothing becomes infected and the area can be cleaned, making the removal of dead or burnt skin possible. He'll need time to heal, of course, but all in all, he was fortunate the injuries were kept to a minimum due to the diligence of the doctor and the fast action of another soldier to extinguish the fire. The unit the boys are in, like all units, are prepared for such emergencies."

Frederick growled, a low, guttural sound becoming a roar. He flushed, jabbing the table with his index finger. Looking Raymond square in the face, he barked, "I have one question. Just one. I want to know why they didn't contact me. I am his father."

Raymond winced. He tilted his head to one side, then the other. "Well, yes, you are his blood relative, his father, but legally, in the eyes of the government and US Army...I don't have to spell it out for you. It was part of the agreement to immigrate to the US, putting me under obligation, making me the person of responsibility."

Frederick folded his arms over his chest as he leaned against the table, his back toward Raymond. "I remember, of course. Why did you wait to tell me?"

Raymond sighed. He walked back and forth in front of the door, hoping to spot the surgeon, but Frederick's question caused him to stop, putting his hand to his cheek. "That was tough. I've known for weeks since it happened, but like I said, he was in a critical, fragile place; they couldn't send him on a flight overseas."

"Flight? Did they fly him from the place in England to

here? Oh, my God, who will pay for that?"

"Relax, the Army takes care of their own," Raymond said. "Once they could transport him, they flew him on an Atlantic flight from London. They brought him here for several reasons, mostly the surgeon here, specializing in burn injuries."

"What's the other reason?"

"Dr. Jeffrey Silberstein felt it would be beneficial to go somewhere closer to home to convalesce, once the skin grafts heal. Dr. Silberstein works as a plastic surgeon, famous for implementing procedures to help burn victims and those with severe facial injuries."

Frederick gasped. "Does Wolfie have severe facial injuries? Where are his injuries?"

Still calm, Raymond promised, "Frederick, have no fear, that handsome young man suffered second- and a few third-degree burns over most of his legs and the tops of his feet. His face is fine."

Frederick paced the floor, his face twisting in horror at the thought of his son having to endure such pain. "I burned my hand once on a car engine; my hand had a blister out to there," he illustrated the size of it. "I thought I was going to die. It was winter. Elise, my wife, made a poultice with burn salve and then made me sit with that for hours, then I was forced to sleep with my hand in a bowl with snow she'd fetch from outside. God, I adored that woman. There was no lying down in bed and no sleeping, and the pain was excruciating! I can't even imagine what Wolfie's going through." He looked down at his own legs. His eyes watered.

Raymond assured Frederick, "I'm sure they've pumped him full of morphine to combat the pain. He won't be feeling anything for a while."

Frederick sat down; his long legs stretched before him.

"My poor boy, my poor boy." He ran a hand through his dark brown hair.

After a moment, Raymond lit two cigarettes, offering Frederick one, and said, "I regret withholding the information from you. I did it with the best of intentions. Not knowing when he'd be able to be flown, it was an unstable yet fragile situation. Forgive me. I did what I thought was best."

Frederick glanced at Raymond. "Yeah, well, I'm not happy about the information being withheld, but what could I have done, anyway? Couldn't have seen him. I'll disregard the desire to label you as controlling. I still can't believe what happened to my son. I've been here before when Elise became sick. I'm brought back to that place of inescapable pain."

Raymond ruminated on Frederick's words; the mentioning of his wife's terminal illness caused Raymond's own emotions to bubble to the surface. *I've lost two wives. But this isn't about me now. It's about my friend's concern for his son.*

Aboard the S.S. St. Louis

Leo Jockl did as the captain ordered, searching the crew's common areas while seeking Otto Schiendick. He stopped and asked a couple of crew called Firemen, who served as the Nazi representative's lackeys. None had seen the man they emulated in hatred of the Jews.

There was no love lost between Schiendick and Leo Jockl.

Standing outside Schiendick's cabin, Leo knocked, putting his ear to the door and listening for any sound. Using the passkey, he opened the door and immediately spotted Schiendick; his mouth was taped while his extremities were tied tight to the back of a folding chair. Schiendick's hair stood on end, and his eyes looked like those of a madman. His expression was one of shame and anguish. Tears of frustration and anger streamed from his eyes.

Leo's eyes trailed down to the floor, where he saw a pool of urine. He contemplated whether he should untie Schiendick or get the captain first. Reaching into his pocket for a cigarette, he saw a lighter on the table next to Schiendick and took it. Schiendick grunted, emitting a muffled, high-pitched whine.

Leo shook his head. "I'm sorry, I can't understand you." He blew the smoke in Schiendick's face.

Leo tossed the cigarette into the pool of urine beneath Schiendick. "I'll get the captain first; he'll want to see this. I'll be back." Leo blew him a kiss and slammed the door, locking it. When a crewman asked if he'd seen Schiendick, Leo shrugged, replying with a resounding, "Nope."

The Hamburg Schutzpolezei
The prisoner in the last freezing stone cell, cordoned off from the other six cells, was Stanislaw Birnbaum, a former German citizen. In 1934, his name was changed to Stanford Wellington, and he lived in the United States of America as the adoptee of Raymond Wellington III. He no longer was who he had been—he had a new name and country but the same old lies.

The lies weren't his; he wouldn't claim ownership over them. The lies were from another source of the devilish sort, the tool of the enemy—the kind that attacked your mind, whispering untruths. He recited scripture to combat the enemy that stalked him like a roaring lion, seeking whom he might devour. "'Let not your heart be troubled: ye believe in God, believe also in me.'"

There were times when Stani would speak with Elenena, imagining her to be alive—like now. She sat there on the cold cement with him, holding his hand. She comforted him. He told her, "I always thought it would be Jesus himself who would comfort me; I'm always surprised to see you."

She answered, "He uses those we love to communicate at times. You recall that he made stones speak and a donkey talk in the scriptures. After all, is there anything impossible when your name is I AM? Truth heals wounds."

There were no other sounds to compete for Stani's attention, and the quiet was unnerving. He envisioned Maddie on the great ship, safe and warm, somewhere at sea, or maybe even in the New York Harbor now, viewing the ineffable Lady Liberty herself. He didn't know, he had lost track of time. *Am I mad? What is reality, this? I do not know.*

Aboard the S.S. St. Louis, The Bridge
Leo Jockl, the captain's steward, knocked on the door requesting permission to enter after observing Captain Schroeder and Purser Mueller immersed in a heated conversation. From what he could see, he saw a radio wire in the captain's hand—received or sent, he couldn't tell—it could be the source of the conflict. He knocked again, and the captain waved him in, nodding to his officer. "Excuse me, Purser. Perhaps Leo has some answers."

Leo said, "I went to Schiendick's cabin at your request. The door was locked, so I used my passkey. I found Nazi Representative Schiendick gagged and tied to a chair in his room."

He almost stopped speaking as he observed the shockwave reaction on their faces but went on, "I-I thought perhaps you might want to see this for yourself—that is, the predicament Schiendick finds himself in, and take photographs as evidence, view what kind of knots were tied, which could reveal whether or not it was a passenger or crewman. I think it's not far-reaching to imagine a scene that could involve the fractious Officer Schiendick in a fix with a passenger or crewman. After observing him in action, I can say with full assurance that both are possible, sir."

The captain appraised his steward. "Not much love lost between you two, eh, Jockl?"

Leo tried to cover a smile with his hand, but the captain was onto him. "Hmm. Thought so. Purser Mueller and I shall pay a visit to our entangled Nazi representative. Please inform the first mate and chief engineer that I'm handling an issue. Next, enter into the log the event we're investigating, all pertinent information, and the time. Dismissed."

While walking to Deck D, Captain Schroeder shared the troubling news he'd received earlier that morning from Havana. He whispered, but the purser could surmise his anger from his urgent tone. "Rabble-rousers are protesting, I'm told, with professional-looking signs. Upwards of forty thousand protesters oppose our arrival just days before our landing. And the landing permits sold to each passenger are worthless. The president of Cuba revoked them, forbidding passengers holding them from coming to shore, even though each one of these passengers purchased, in addition to their ticket, the insurance fee in case the ship has to return." The captain fumed in silence, chewing on his lower lip. "I don't know what the hell they expect me to do. We have a ship full of passengers, ready to begin their new lives."

Purser Mueller couldn't devote his full attention to the captain; the growing anxiety over the whereabouts of Stefan Soutine and Fritz Effinger paralyzed him. The captain rambled on about "possible solutions once we dock, or hold the ship in the harbor, send wires, contact people..."

"I'll need you to make a list...contact the JDC..." He stopped and peered at Mueller. "Everything all right, Purser?"

The fog in his mind didn't quite lift, so he put his head down. "Sir, please forgive me..."

The captain raised a white-gloved hand. "Not another

word about it. We'll discuss these details later."

They descended to Deck D, a rare sight to see the captain and the purser *down below*, as it's called in the vernacular.

Mueller said, "Let's see, ah. Here we are." He silently unlocked the door, revealing the sight Leo had described, with one exception: Otto Schiendick had turned his chair over in an attempt to escape from his bonds. Schiendick wailed in a high-pitched whine, his eyes red with fury, watery from crying. He was exactly as Leo had said: "Seconds from implosion."

The captain finally addressed Schiendick after the men set him upright in the chair. Holding the confirmation of the wire Schiendick had sent to HAPAG agent Robert Hoffman in Havana, Schroeder questioned the other man about its meaning. Schiendick had been so full of hate—fantasizing about murdering Fritz had occupied his thinking—that he'd forgotten to retrieve the confirmation, leaving it behind for a first mate to find.

Even though he stood just a foot away, the captain shouted, semi-reading off the confirmation wire, "What does this mean, ABORT—KILL CONTACT? I want you to think long and hard about your answer because anything less than the truth will land you in jail when we dock." The captain reread the confirmation. "What is this in response to? Are you authorizing an employee of HAPAG to murder someone?"

The captain nodded at Mueller to untie the rope that bound Schiendick. Once his hands were free, he ripped off the tape that covered his lips and expelled the handkerchief stuffed in his mouth. Sputtering and out of breath from hyperventilating, he told the captain, "That half-Jew steward of yours better watch his back."

Schiendick's trousers were soaked, his hair was on end, and he looked like a mophead. He continued to foam at the mouth with vitriol. "I'll have my revenge on him; just you wait." He wiped violently at his eyes and nose, using the tails of his uniform-issue shirt.

The captain stood next to Mueller, eyeing Schiendick. Both were close to laughing at his meaningless threats as Schiendick added, "Regarding the wire. No. It means 'Kill the meeting, abort, don't attend.' That's all. But I shouldn't have to spell it out for you; remember? I work for the Abwehr?"

"Officer Schiendick, I do not appreciate your impertinence. May I remind you that you are also under my command while aboard this ship. Is that clear?

"Now, it would be very easy to accomplish a certain goal in several ways. It depends solely on you and your choices to obey or disobey. You have two strikes against you. A third would have severe consequences. Either you fulfill your duties on board in a respectful, sober, dutiful way with the most circumspect behavior, or you don't. If you step out of line, one iota, once, that's it. Your time remaining on this voyage will be spent below, handcuffed, where we coil up the chain to hoist the anchor, in the grip of hell, where the air is rank and foul, the rats are big, feeding on the unsuspecting, and the slop they'll feed you is not fit for man or beast. All this and more await you. Abwehr be damned."

The captain never asked who was responsible for confining Schiendick; he didn't care.

CHAPTER THIRTY

Healing, Wheeling, and Dealing

MAY 1939, THE HOTEL ATLANTIC
HAMBURG, HAMBURG, GERMANY

WHILE MADDIE SLEPT, Cecile arranged for room service for Rolf and herself. She ordered a fruit dish and a generous slice of German Butterküchen for Maddie. "You can tell her, should she wake up and find herself hungry for a little something, there's cake and fruit here." Cecile pointed to the separate tray for Maddie. "Now, wash your hands, and let's break bread before our dinner gets cold."

Rolf did as she asked. "The candles are nice," he said, "You look exceptionally pretty by candlelight."

Cecile smiled at Rolf, then sighed. She quietly uttered, "Well, we might as well have a delicious dinner, seeing we won't explore Hamburg nightlife tonight."

Rolf chose not to respond, knowing that his wife was baiting him. They were enjoying their dinner quietly, comfortably, in the well-appointed suite, both absorbed with whatever one thinks about when seated across from their spouse of thirty years when Rolf came out with, "Did you mean anything by your comment about Hamburg nightlife? Do you feel you're missing out on something?

Cecile grimaces, "Are you going to scold me for something

I'm unaware of?"

Rolf says firmly, "Remember why we're here and what our priority is. Maddie and I are doing the work, allowing you to lounge and do as you please. Isn't that enough for you, or do you need nightlife and entertainment to make you happy?"

Rolf knew Cecile's calculating ways; like a leopard, she would never change her spots. "Ah, at least you're predictable," he said as he finished the last bite of Bienenstich—bee sting cake. "They do a good job with this. It reminds me of your mother's version, but with more almonds." He said this as he finished a pot of coffee all by himself.

Cecile's stare turned to a glare, deftly changing the subject. "Why do you insist on staying up to the ungodly hour of 2:00 a.m. in order to get a call through? Why can't you place it now, leave a message, and call again first thing in the morning?"

Rolf closed his eyes and leaned back in his chair, choosing not to engage.

She went on, "Fine. You'll stay up until 2:00 a.m., but God forbid we go out just to enjoy the town, even for a little while."

Frowning at Cecile, knowing no good would come from addressing her selfish statement, he said, "I want Maddie to sleep as much as she can, and when she awakens, she'll have good news."

"How can you be so sure you'll have good news? Have you considered it might take time to find him, Mr. Know-It-All?"

Rolf smiled lovingly at his Cecile. "Go to bed, don't let me keep you. I'll come to bed after I place the call. Now go!"

At 2:00 a.m., Rolf had the overseas telephone operator place a person-to-person call directly to the US attorney general. The hotel switchboard operator told him, "Sir, we will call you when the overseas call goes through." So, Rolf had to wait for the callback, and wait, and wait. He fell asleep in the chair next to the phone.

The phone rang, and Cecile stumbled from the bedroom into the reception area, yelling at him. Rolf shot up from his slouched position, going from sound asleep to groggy. He shouted, "What happened?" Then he heard the ringing phone, stared at it, and answered, "Hello." The hotel operator told the long-distance operator, "The party is on the line; go ahead with the call."

"This is the office of United States Attorney General Homer S. Cummings, Mark Dance speaking. How may I be of service to you?"

Rolf began, "My name is Rolf Wolferman; I'm calling from Hamburg, Germany. I must speak to Raymond Wellington or get a message to him immediately. Can you help me with that?"

There was a problematic delay between the time one party was done speaking and the person on the other end heard it, which could cause a great deal of confusion. Dance pointed this out to Rolf, and he counted out loud the seconds so as not to lose track. "Please state your name and your relation to Mr. Wellington."

Thinking fast, he told the man, "I'm family, his brother-in-law, Rolf Wolferman. I'm with his daughter, Maddie, and we need his help." Rolf counted down the delay, waiting for an answer.

"Sir, please hold on while I confer with a superior. Thank you."

Six or seven minutes ticked by, and Rolf began to doze off. Sitting across from him, Cecile clapped her hands to wake him up. "Rolf, wake up, Rolf!"

Rolf shook off the sleep and woke up feeling grumpy. "Calm down. I'm awake, Cecile; I was simply resting my eyes."

The minutes dragged on while Rolf waged war against his eyelids. Then Mark Dance came back to the phone. "Forgive the lengthy delay, sir, but I'm sorry, there is no record or anyone here to confirm your relation. Good luck, sir."

The line went dead until the hotel operator came on and asked, "Would you like to make another call, sir?"

He slammed down the receiver. "Damn it," Rolf yelled. "Why didn't I think to have Maddie call? If we call back now, that will reinforce their idea that I'm a lunatic. Damn it." Rolf fumed.

Ft. Bragg, Fayetteville, North Carolina, USA Station Hospital
Dr. Jeffrey Silberstein asked Frederick about his line of work and his favorite hobby, to which he answered, "Restoring classic cars."

The doctor explained the procedure of skin grafting to Frederick. "It's much like the bodywork on a car; you've got to prep the surrounding area, then focus on the most damaged parts, prepping as you go."

Frederick's shoulders drooped. His usual German bravado evaporated as the doctor reassured him, "Wolfie's prognosis is good. He did well during the surgical procedure of skin grafting, but healing some of his wounds will require between six months and a year of convalescing."

Frederick stared at the wall, slipping into the whiteness of it like a sphere of nothingness. "Can I see my son, please? May I see him now? I can't hear anything else or think at all until I see my son."

The doctor nodded. "This way. But you'll have to leave that here," he says, pointing to the mobile hotel housing Hollenius. "I'll lock the room."

Frederick frowned, raising his hand in protest. "Not so fast. Let me give him some food, and would you mind if I let him out of his carrier, seeing this is only a conference room?"

The doctor led the two travelers down the hospital corridor, not unlike the roads they'd traveled to get here to see Wolfie. They all seemed long.

They entered a private room. Stark white was everywhere, accented by a stainless-steel cart that doubled as a table and two simple wooden chairs. There was no window. Clear plastic sheeting hung down from the ceiling to the floor surrounding the bed, with a slit opening at the foot of the bed. The doctor said, "That's in place to minimize germ exposure."

On the hospital bed lay Wolfie, his legs and feet covered in moist gauze bandaging that made him look like a mummy, wrapped tight from the legs down. The doctor whispered, peering over the top of his glasses, "He's still sedated with painkillers. He'll be disoriented at times, so fair warning."

Frederick stood with his back toward the bed. He was afraid to see his son, fearful of the unknown. Tears streamed down his face.

The doctor dismissed himself, and Frederick slipped inside the sheeting, moving awkwardly around the bed, unsure what to do. He hesitated, then tenderly touched Wolfie's forehead, pushing back his blond bangs, which had grown out from the traditional Army haircut. "My boy, my boy, you're so pale." He put his hands to his face, crying, "Oh, Wolfie."

Raymond stood quietly at the foot of the bed. He touched Frederick's arm, and said, "I'll wait out there."

Wolfie continued to sleep while Frederick did something he'd never done before. He prayed over Wolfie. "Dear God, or Jesus, or Holy Spirit, I don't know how to talk to you, whoever is there. Do I call you sir? Stani, my friend, tells me to call you Abba, which means Daddy, I'm told. I don't believe I have that kind of status with you, to call you Daddy.

"If you are who Stani says you are, please. I have nothing to bring you; I am not a perfect man. Stani says I don't have to be perfect, just humble. I am here trying the best way I know to humble myself and ask you to please help my son.

He's only a boy, look at him, he's so beautiful. I've never told him that. Please help him in any way you can. I promise to be a better man. Thank you."

The Hotel Atlantic Hamburg
Cecile watched her husband, who sat motionless. "Darling, you didn't make a mistake. You did what you thought was the right thing. Everything is out of our control, and this seems like one of those moments. What else can we do? Who else can we contact?" After a moment, she suggested, "Why don't you try the business again? It's Monday, so they must be open."

Rolf's eyes darted to his wife. "You are a wonderful woman, and I'm so glad I married you. The smartest move I ever made." He stood before her, bending down to kiss her. "Thank you for keeping your head while I'm losing mine."

Cecile smiled. "I love you, darling. Now, make that call. It's 3:30 a.m. here; they must be open by now."

After placing an overseas call to Wolferman-Wellington Motors, Cecile and Rolf sat, eyes glued to the phone. They were still waiting for a call when Maddie emerged from the bedroom. "What's going on?" she asked.

Sleepy-eyed, Maddie sat beside Cecile on the small settee, putting her head on Cecile's shoulder. Her aunt stroked her head, saying, "We're working on contacting Raymond."

Maddie yawned. "I'm hungry."

Cecile jumped up and brought the tray to her. "We ordered you a little something just in case."

Maddie dug into the Butterküchen. "I haven't had this in years. We must have Stani make this." Saying his name brought reality back into focus, and she stopped eating. Her eyes awash with tears, she asked Rolf, "Can we check back with the police today as soon as we can get there?"

Rolf nodded. "Of course we will. Don't worry, Maddie, we

will find Stani."

Maddie lowered her head, whispering to herself, *God, help us.* Just then, the phone rang; Rolf answered on the second ring, and the long-distance operator put the call through. Denny, the manager for Wolferman-Wellington Motors, was on the other end.

"Denny, my name is Rolf Wolferman. I'm Frederick's brother. Yes, yes, it's nice to meet you, too. Listen, Denny, do you have any way to reach Raymond or Frederick? I've tried the house; we have an issue, an emergency, and we must speak to Raymond immediately. Are you able to get a message to either of them?

"Well, no, that's a private matter if you please, yes. Here is the name and number: The Hotel Atlantic Hamburg Room 160. Hamburg, Germany. Yes, that's right, yes. Thank you, haha. It might be sooner than you think! You as well. Thank you, goodbye." Rolf stared at the receiver in his hand, then replaced it on its hook and tapped the top of the phone. "Hmm. Great invention."

Feeling self-satisfied, he returned to a comfortable position in the chair while Cecile and Maddie stood up, wondering what had gone on with the conversation. Cecile's hands were on her hips; she meant business. "Uh, Rolf, are you going to fill us in or leave us standing here, wondering what took place?"

He glanced at them. "He said, *Hope to meet you one day*, and I told him that might be sooner than you think!" She rolled her eyes at him, her sign to get to the point. "Yes, well, he was very nice, sounded very professional, and all; he said he'd get a message to them. That's it. Oh, and, of course, the kind comment."

Cecile laughed a little. "Rolf, do you seriously think he meant that? Wouldn't that be the polite thing to say?"

"You know Cecile, the trouble with you? You're a skeptic, not cynical, but skeptical. I would think you, who preaches to me about what the scriptures say...perhaps it's time to put some of that to practice, give people the benefit of the doubt, expect good and not bad."

Maddie stood quietly, observing it all; when Rolf noticed her standing in the shadows, she quipped, "My favorite place."

He chuckled, "You'd make a good spy."

Maddie yawned again. "Not for now; maybe it's my next career. It's almost 5:00 a.m., and I must return to sleep for a bit; please wake me if anything happens, if someone calls, you know."

She kissed them both and crawled into her bed, grateful for soft, cool sheets and a heavy blanket to shut out the world. *This feels so oddly reminiscent of our time running from the Nazis after the concert when they took Stani, and I ran to the hotel and hid under the bed. I'm now on top of the bed instead of under it. What's the same is that the Nazis have Stani, and I'm alone. How I wish Buster were here. I miss him so much I can't stand it.*

Maddie whimpered in the dark, crying herself to sleep, just as the sun began throwing fragments of brightness over the horizon's edge. She pulled Aunt Cecile's mask over her eyes, shutting out the world.

Complicated Relationships

OTTO SCHIENDICK CLEANED up the mess in his room, then showered to wash off the stench, but the water did nothing to quell the rage smoldering within his gut. *Revenge is the fuel that stokes my engine. I will end them.*

A knock on his door broke him from his malevolent reverie. He shuffled to the door in his bare feet, dressed only in a t-shirt and trousers. Opening it, he found a fireman, Nazi Peter Von Hegler, and a little girl with blue eyes. Von Hegler had instructed her to look for Fritz.

Otto bent to her eye level. "Well, aren't you the most beautiful little girl? You're in steerage, is that right?"

She nodded.

"And you saw a man." Again, she nodded, and he asked her, "Did he have green eyes?"

A big smile crossed her face; she said, "So green."

Otto patted her on the head and stated, "He gave you something?"

Von Hegler handed him the matches, and he read the name on the cover, "Edwards Pub, Buckinghamshire." The two men's eyes met, and they shook their heads knowingly, confirming what Schiendick already suspected: this man was an imposter. This prompted Schiendick to wire Hoffman that the cover might be compromised.

"The confirmation went through, the captain knows, but so what?" To the girl, he said, "Here."

He handed her one deutschmark. "You can buy candy at the ship store; my friend Mr. Von Hegler will escort you there. Bye-bye."

Schiendick nodded at his associate. Grabbing a cigarette, he lit it and released a triumphant exhale of smoke. *Bugger off. A phrase only the English use. I've got that English bastard now.*

Ft. Bragg, USA Station Hospital
While Frederick sat with Wolfie, insisting on not leaving until he woke up, Raymond went about making plans. A hospital orderly unlocked the conference room, where Hollenius was perched upon the table, expecting a human to be at his beck and call. Raymond entered, and the cat looked away.

He sat, addressing the furry boy. "He's going to be fine. Don't you worry. Now, I have some work to do."

Hollenius, quickly bored of Raymond, lit off the table, and hunkered down in the corner. "Oh, no, you don't. Don't you even think about doing your business here! Damn cat, where's your leash? Where's your dad when you need him?"

Raymond sighed, grabbing the leash and putting it on the cat. *I can't believe I'm walking a cat. Oh, if they could see me now.*

Hollenius led Raymond to walk along the grassy grounds outside the hospital and then to the parking lot. The cat deliberately strolled to a parked car and sat down behind the vehicle. "Huh. Well, that's peculiar. I thought you needed to take care of business."

Hollenius meowed loudly, standing on his hind legs, and rubbed his head against the car's bumper. Then Raymond saw it. "Another car from New York here." Raymond snapped his fingers and looked down at the cat. He squatted next to him, rubbing his head. *Was this on purpose? Seeing this license plate stirred my memory. Did you do this because you know we haven't called Denny? We haven't checked in on him or the dealership in days.*

"Why did you walk specifically to this car and sit down?" he asked Hollenius. "How did you know?" Raymond scoped out the grounds; a few people were strolling around, and the weather was warm—*lovely grounds for a hospital.* The cat weaved between his legs, purring loudly. "Well, do you have to use the facilities, yes or no?"

Back inside the conference room, still empty, Raymond decided to use the time to organize his to-do list, a habit he'd had since adolescence. Sitting at the table, he went over his checklist: *Call Denny. Check on the business. Have him pick up Frederick and Wolfie at the Rochester Airport—more details to follow. Call Major Davis, arrange for a military doctor to assist Wolfie's flight to Rochester next week, and arrange his care once he returns home. Arrange for my flight to Miami, where the cutter will take me to Havana. The cutter will return to Miami on May 29th for Maddie, and Stani, and me. Flight home for Maddie, Stani, and me. Arrange for a driver to bring Frederick's car to Rochester. Notify the State Department of my transportation requests, under: Family.*

Inside Wolfie's hospital room, Frederick sat on the floor, his back rigid against the wall, where he could see Wolfie's face, his eyes, should they open suddenly. The floor's tile was cool, and the room was lit enough for Frederick to observe his son.

Dr. Silberstein returned, speaking in a low tone. "The nurse mentioned you had questions for me. Would you prefer to go to the conference room?"

Frederick swallowed hard, his hands twitching. "I don't want to leave him; in case he wakes up, I want to be here."

The doctor nodded. "Of course, although he still may sleep a few more hours. He's on some very strong painkillers and a sedative. Be aware, it may take a few days for him to become lucid, the effect of the drugs. But of course, we can speak right here."

Frederick smiled. "Thank you, Doctor. I have to admit, when I first heard about his injuries and saw him, my brain went blank. I couldn't think of a thing to ask you until after you left. So, now I have questions regarding how it happened and how we can get him home."

The doctor leaned against the wall, facing Frederick, and began. "His injury was caused by celluloid film, an experiment gone wrong. The film is highly flammable, and its flames can spread quickly to anyone or anything nearby. This is what happened with your son. His Army-issued uniform protected him to an extent, but it was not inflammable. And his shoes, the leather, caused third-degree burns on the tops of his feet. However, he has a greater chance of fully recovering because of the skin grafts."

Frederick raised his hand. "Where did the skin come from for the graft?"

The doctor said, "Here, these places," while pointing to the inside of Wolfie's thigh, his buttocks, and the inside of his biceps.

"That seems like many places on his body that must recover." Frederick glanced at the inside of his bicep and tugged at the skin. "It heals fast?"

The doctor smiled at Frederick. "It sure does. It has to. It's the largest organ in the human body! Plus, Wolfie has youth on his side."

Frederick wrinkled his nose. "Skin is an organ. Hmph. You learn something new every day. Oh, one more thing? When can he travel?" Frederick rubbed his hands together in anticipation and partly as a nervous response to his son's surgery details. Too much information left him queasy and pale. "Big men, squeamish stomachs, my mother taught me."

"I'd like to keep him here for another week to monitor his progress and ensure he's completely out of danger, fully on the road to recovery. We'll do a medical transport. Sound like a good plan?"

The doctor turned to leave, but before he did, he told Frederick, "I'm assuming you're not completely acquainted with the work your son is involved in within the Army."

When Frederick acknowledged this, the doctor continued, "Rightly so; confidential procedures must be adhered to, that's how it's done, and better for the family not to know. It won't be easy to persuade your son to switch to what you may think to be a safer vocation, like a desk job. I've worked close by him in the field, observing him and his superior character. It takes a great deal of commitment to work in the field he's been chosen for—he has an elite-type aptitude, and his testing competency is off the charts. You must be proud of your son. He is a courageous young man."

He left Frederick standing in place, mouth agape. *And I thought I knew my son.*

Aboard the S.S. St. Louis

Midnight approached, and the ship cruised at twenty knots; the seas were relatively calm. The moon revealed a sliver of itself, heaving as much brightness as possible onto the radiant carpet of stars. Due to its shape, one could describe it as a luminous image of God's toenail. So far away was this ghostly light, its shimmer reflecting on the salty waves, whispering secrets that only whales heard and man desired. This pale lantern in the sky broke the grip of darkness while soothing the weary hearts of sailors and captains across every sea.

The captain recorded it in his logbook.

0100 hours.

We have an epic challenge. As soon as we set sail, we received an urgent wire from the HAPAG office to make all speed, don't delay in Cherbourg, and reach Havana as soon as possible. Other ships were carrying German Jewish refugees heading to Havana as well. However, these ships had fewer passengers than ours. The Orduña carries only 154 passengers, while the Flandre carries 104. It is clear to me there is more to this "special" voyage than meets the eye. There is confirmation from the British Consul office in Havana that the ship is for propaganda purposes, confirming my worst fear that something far more sinister is taking place.

While some may attribute our departing day, May 13th, as a harbinger of evil, I'd like to think that has no effect. Certain passengers expressed concern over the ship departing on the Sabbath. The staff and crew must do an impressive job caring for our passengers. I must stay aloof to be a fair judge should issues arise.

Regarding arising issues, Crewman and Nazi Rep. Otto Schiendick should be dismissed from service at once. Unfortunately, I do not have the authority to do so. My paramount concern is my passengers' comfort and safe arrival at their destination. Before retiring from the bridge, I received another wire telling me the landing permits sold to my passengers were invalid; only those with an official passport could disembark the ship, perhaps thirty at the most. I've wired the JDC in Havana, the US, and Paris offices, explaining the potential quagmire. HAPAG officials are working with the Cuban government, and there is no guarantee of resolving the issues. It is as if forces are working against us to delay us or something along those lines. I retire this evening feeling less hopeful than I can remember.

At his door was Purser Mueller. "I'm just checking in with you. I'm on the night shift. All is well. Smooth seas, the weather forecast looks clear for tomorrow. Any requests, sir?"

The captain nodded at his purser. "Nothing I can think of. Thank you. See you at 0700 hours."

Ferdinand Mueller considered throwing himself overboard if passengers Soutine and Effinger were not found. It would be his fault and a greater penalty because of Effinger, who worked for the Abwehr. *I'm in deep; oh, God, what am I going to do? I've got to find out what happened to them. Schiendick is full of revenge, and he won't tell me if he murdered them. To him, there is no moral obligation to the Jews, even though the passengers are German Jews. It's over for me.*

Below in Steerage

Stefan wandered around the dungeon-like space, which was swamped with bunks, steamer trunks, suitcases, and clothing strung up after washing in the communal sinks. Various cats and dogs chased each other, and the occasional rat dared to show its hoary head.

Stefan's ears perked up when he heard the language of his homeland spoken. Behind a blanket that hung to shield two bunks came the words, sweet to his ear, "Mon amour, il me reste encore quelques jours." *My love, only a few more days to go.*

Stefan peeked behind the blanket, his cheerfulness spilling past the boundary of the makeshift curtain, greeting the strangers with, "Bonjour mes amis. Je suis si heureux d'entendre vos voix." *Hello, my friends. I'm so happy to hear your voice.*

Stefan assumed they would be as happy to hear another Frenchman and invite him into their space. But that wasn't the case; they were furious he'd interrupted their brief interlude. Embarrassed and red-faced, Stefan skulked away.

At that moment, he spotted the little girl with blue eyes and ran to catch up with her. "Hello, do you remember me?"

She shook her head, and Stefan squatted to her eye level. His voice was soft. "Sure, you do. You came and asked my friend for matches, and he gave you some. You see, I've lost him and cannot find him; I was hoping maybe you'd help me look for him."

The little girl's eyes widened in fear, and she furiously shook her head. "Edwards Pub, Bucking something?" she said, then ran away before Stefan could react.

Edwards Pub, Bucking—hmmm. The matches? What would he be doing with matches from...Well, that does it. I'm going up top to find the captain. Fritz is gone. I guess I'm on my own now.

Stefan returned to his steerage bunk and gathered Fritz's belongings and his few gifts of clothing and toiletries. He had no mirror and had no clue as to his appearance. *I just need to get back to my room. I'll wear all the clothing at once, giving me a stockier appearance, and I'll wear the cap.*

Uh-oh. Schiendick. I haven't considered him or how to avoid him.

CHAPTER THIRTY-TWO

Land in Sight

MAY 1939, FT. BRAGG, USA STATION HOSPITAL

RAYMOND, WAKE UP. Wolfie is awake, his eyes are open, and he's speaking. Wake up; you have to see him right now."

Raymond rubbed his eyes and blinked at Frederick, asking, "What's happening? What?" For the past two hours, Raymond had slumbered in the consultation room, sprawled out in an easy chair with a stool for his feet. A kind nurse had also brought him a blanket.

Frederick went to the carrier, bending and looking in. "Hello, my boy, come to Poppa." He stood up straight, his eyes wide. Frantic, he says, "Where is Hollenius? He's not in the carrier!"

Raymond smiled mischievously. "This cat is like a miniature oven."

Frederick took a step back. "What are you talking about?"

Raymond gave a sneaky smile and pulled back the blanket, revealing Hollenius curled around his waist. Frederick yelped, "What? You traitor, you two-timer! I thought it was only me you loved to sleep with!"

Raymond shook his head. "Purely an act of expediency; you were nowhere to be found." He laughed, "Never in one million years did I think I'd be charmed by a cat."

Frederick smiled knowingly. "I know. It's like you get bit with cat love and suddenly adore these furry creatures. Okay, so let's go. Wolfie is asking for you." He picked up the cat. "I'll take him out for a quick constitutional and a snack while you wake up. Just go right down to Wolfie's room; he's waiting."

Raymond stretched, then dropped to do a few pushups. *Ugh, you are old!* He trotted down the hall to use the men's room and to wash his hands and face. He assessed the state of his attire, which was decidedly wrinkled. *Oh, well, this will have to do.*

Raymond hustled down the hall to Wolfie's room, waving to nurses he recognized along the way. One of the nurses said to the other, "He's so handsome, suave. I wonder if he's married. I didn't see a ring."

The other nurse scoffed at her, "A man like that? He's tied down. Rich men don't always wear a wedding ring. But just look at him. Gorgeous, with an air of sophistication, like Cary Grant. I'd bet a week's salary he's attached!"

Raymond came to the room, pausing at the doorway. *Thank you, God, for saving his life and not allowing a worse result.* He walked into the room, over to the bed, and peered inside the curtain. "Anyone home?" He flashed Wolfie a wide smile.

Wolfie lifted his arm weakly to wave. "Hi! Fancy seeing you here." He tried his best to smile back.

Raymond took Wolfie's hand in his. "I'm so happy to see you and your wonderful face. How're you feeling? Are you in much pain?"

A sly smile crept across Wolfie's face, and he motioned with his free hand. "Smooth sailing, boss, no pain." The drugs did the talking, but Wolfie was surprisingly lucid.

Raymond felt Wolfie's forehead. "You're cool as a cucumber, too. Is there anything you need or want?"

Wolfie's face lit up. "How about some vanilla ice cream?"

Raymond smiled at the boyish request. "I'll check in with your doc, but I'm sure it will be fine. Are you getting good sleep?"

Wolfie shrugged. "Well, they wake you up a lot, so, no, not great, but I can sleep through almost anything, as you know from experience."

Raymond threw his head back, laughing. "Like the day you were supposed to fly to Europe. We chased the plane down the runway, it was pouring rain, you were yelling and swearing in German, I was trying to keep up with you, I dropped your duffel bag, and finally, the plane stopped. The 82nd Airborne Division did right by you, soldier."

Wolfie laughed. "That was a crazy start, right? I thought they'd take off without me! And by the way, it's Private Specialist First-Class Wolferman."

Raymond beamed with pride. "I would expect that and nothing less. Congratulations. We will celebrate when we all return to the homestead or Pultneyville, wherever you like. Miss Berk says the trout and bass are biting, feasting on the live bait of flies, and crickets. So, it's your call, sir." Raymond clicked his heels and saluted. His smile faded, and solemnly, he asked, "How is Buster? Oh, I know, you can't say. We just pray all is well, right?"

Wolfie nodded as Frederick bounded into the room and peeked his head into the curtain. Wolfie made a face. "Dad, why is your jacket zipped up so far?"

Frederick came close, and Wolfie heard it: the motor, the maniacal purr. "No. You brought the boy?"

At the sound of Wolfie's voice, Hollenius poked his head out of the neck of Frederick's bomber jacket. Wolfie reached to scratch the cat behind his ears. "His favorite spot. One of them."

Raymond cleared his throat. "I hate to break up this party, but it's 8:00 a.m. and Denny will be at work. Hollenius reminded me. He did one of those unexplainable things where he communicated with me and reminded me to call

Denny. He didn't say 'call Denny,' but he led me to a place where, I...well, oh, you know what he does, who am I telling? We haven't checked in with Denny, so the cat *is* smarter than I knew. I confess!"

Both Wolfie and Frederick applauded Raymond's conclusion. "I told you so," Frederick said. "I'm going to put the boy in his carrier before a nurse kills me for having him in here."

Wolfie reached out to touch his dad's arm. "Pop, you're always here for me. Thank you for bringing His Royal Highness here to see me; that must have been tough to wrangle, seeing you drove here and all. You really cheered me up and made a difference." Wolfie's eyes became wet with tears. "I'm going to work on being more grateful and less of a jerk, a clown, you know what I mean."

Leaning down, Frederick kissed his son on the forehead and then touched his cheek. "My beautiful boy. You rest. I'll be back soon."

Aboard the S.S. St. Louis

At 0100 hours, two men from Schiendick's Nazi cabal found Fritz in steerage and grabbed him. With the point of an eight-inch hunting knife pressing against his back, Fritz was careful not to make any false moves that would warrant a plunge of the knife.

They marched silently. The low lights on the ship shone adequately for them to see where they were going but were dim enough to shield their identities. When one is out at sea, the ship's lights and a full moon are the only illumination to guide you.

Across from the Assembly Hall, standing in the shadows, awaited Otto Schiendick. He chain-smoked and intermittently stifled a sinister snicker, placing his hand over his mouth to muffle the sound. The three marched up the stairwell, swaying with the ship's movement. Reaching the top, they turned left to the appointed location, next to the rail and the ship's side.

Schiendick slunk out from the shadows, smoking, first walking behind Fritz, taking the knife from his henchman; he walked around to face Fritz while the other two men held him. "Well, here we are. Now that I have this nice knife, I'm just itching to test the blade, its sharp edge." He ran his fingers up the blade's side, plucking his thumb against the edge. "Ooh, yes, sharp it is. Now. First, tell me who you are." Schiendick put the blade's edge against Fritz's cheek. "I'd hate to have to carve up your pretty face. Are you a Jew? I know a way to find out involving a knife. Did you know Nazis are famous for performing the simple task of circumcisions? Hmm. Perhaps it *would* be better if you were a Jew in this case."

Schiendick mulled it over while he munched on an apple. After a few bites, he wiped his mouth with his gloved hand and pitched the apple into the sea. "Wow. Hey Fritzie, did you see how fast that apple dropped?" Schiendick whistled, decreasing pitch to mimic the sound of a bomb falling, his hand dropping like a bomb would. "Now, tell me your name. Who do you work for? Are you a spy?"

Fritz smiled and said nothing.

Schiendick's eyes narrowed as he sized him up. "Goodbye, Fritz. I will be the last face you see." He reached into his pocket and pulled out a rag to gag him and a hood to put over his head. Then he took the knife and handed it to one of his firemen, who stabbed Fritz in the back of his head and his neck, then plunged the knife deeply into his back.

The two firemen cast him into the sea while the vessel traversed the waters, leaving Fritz in its wake. The British SIS operative and a peer from Bletchley, who because of Wolfie's injury had assumed Wolfie's role in the field, sank quickly, never to be seen again.

Ft. Bragg, USA Station Hospital
Raymond waited for an answer, and on the ninth ring, a familiar voice said, "Wolferman-Wellington Motors, for all your automotive needs. How may I be of service to you?"

Raymond breathed a sigh of relief. "Denny, it's Raymond."

There was a pause. "Was that you making a big sigh? I didn't know if something was wrong with the phone. So, was that you?"

Raymond sighed again. "Yes, Denny. I'm relieved you answered and that all is well. Do you have any news or messages?"

Raymond could hear papers shuffling, and then Denny came back to the phone. "Well, yes. Frederick's brother Rolf called from Hamburg, Germany; he needs to talk to you; he said it is urgent about something, and uh, I have a phone number and hotel address here. Hold on..."

Raymond bent at the waist, his stomach cramping. *Don't think the worst, don't think the worst.* He braced himself, took a deep breath, then exhaled. Reaching for a cigarette, he stopped. *I need a pen and paper.* He fumbled in his coat pocket for something to write on and found a receipt and his fountain pen.

"Okay, Mr. Wellington, here's the hotel name and the phone number."

Raymond repeated the number and name. "Okay, now, Denny, listen." Then he thought better of telling him about Wolfie and Frederick; instead, he said, "I need you to hold the fort for a few more days. Can I count on you to do that?"

There lewas silence on the other end, and then Denny said, "Yes, sir, you've been awfully good to me. I couldn't turn you down. All is well here, don't you worry."

The men hung up. Raymond talked to himself: *Keep*

composure; everything will be okay; don't panic. He looked at his watch. *8:00 a.m. here, 2:00 in Germany. Thank God. Now, how do I make a long-distance call from a hospital?*

Aboard the S.S. St. Louis
Purser Mueller walked the walk of a marked man. *Will I be court-martialed? Brought before a firing squad? Hung until my neck snaps? No telling what the Abwehr will do to me. What will they tell my wife and my kids? How will they be provided for if I'm dead?* His wife had married him despite his numerous peccadilloes, choosing to love him, despite his poor judgment, and not learning from his mistakes. *How can she stand me? Perhaps it would be a relief to her if I were gone.*

The ship's light flickered, catching his attention and breaking him out of his pre-suicidal ideations. Up ahead, no more than fifteen feet, shadows flickered, and then they were gone.

He walked to inspect the spot where he'd seen the shadows but heard nothing except for the steady hum and rhythm of the steam engines and the ever-present sloshing of the sea, enduring and inescapable, its waves hammering against the flat and curved surfaces of the ship. He breathed in the salt-filled air, clearing his sinuses. *It's better to jump when the sea is torrid than calm; I'll wait.*

Disconsolate, he went to B Deck Cabin 373. The hallways were empty, so he unlocked the door, inspected the space, and left. *If I could only have a heart attack, just kill me now, please.* Then, up ahead, he spied the captain's steward, Leo Jockl, who motioned him to follow. Leo jogged to the stairs; Mueller followed, jogging behind much slower than the fleet-footed, twenty-year-old Jockl. Finally, catching up, Mueller came to D deck and the door of Stefan's cabin.

Hotel Atlantic Hamburg, Room 160

Maddie and Cecile were resting when a knock on the door made Maddie jump. "I'll get it." She trotted to the door and opened it. Before her was one of the hotel's bellmen.

"I have a message for Rolf Wolferman."

Maddie smiled at the young bellman. "Thank you; I'll take that." She reached for the message he had presented on a small, round silver tray.

He pulled it out of her reach. "Are you Rolf Wolferman?"

Maddie's brow furrowed. "What? Do I look like a Rolf?"

A voice boomed behind her. "No, but I do. Give me that." Cecile reached past Maddie, grabbing the note off of the tray. "Be gone!" She closed the door.

"Wow, that was impressive."

Cecile laughed and winked. "Age teaches you things. Now let's see what this message is all about. Oh, it's from Raymond!" Cecile shouted out the blessing, "Baruch Adonai l'olam amen v'amen."

She did a little dance, handing the paper to Maddie. The note had a phone number and the name *Raymond Wellington.* "Should we wait for Rolf to call him? When did he leave for the police station? At two? He should be back soon, dinner time. Let's wait for Rolf."

Maddie hedged, pulling at a string on her bathrobe. "Well, you know, there's the time difference, and we don't want to somehow miss him." Looking at the number, she didn't recognize it. "Whatever number he called from isn't our home phone number. Who knows how long he'll be there? We should call him now."

Maddie walked to the phone to place the call and waited for the connection while Cecile huffed, steam building between her ears. "Well, it's not like Rolf can just easily call him back;

that's two long-distance phone calls across continents; that's going to be expensive. I say we wait."

Maddie's spine straightened and she stood stiffly while she chewed the inside of her cheek. "Aunt Cecile, I love you, but I'm going to call him. He's my father, and I'm going to..."

Cecile cut her off. "Well, he's *not really* your father."

Maddie ignored her and spoke to the operator. "Yes, I'd like to place a long-distance call to this number. Raymond Wellington. Thank you."

Cecile pouted, marching to her bedroom and slamming the door. Then, two minutes later, the door flew open, and she barreled out of her room, red-faced. She shouted at Maddie, "Why are you so obstinate? Does everything have to be your way? Is it because you are a star and used to getting what you want?"

CHAPTER THIRTY-THREE

Search and Rescue

MAY 1939, HAMBURG SCHUTZPOLEZEI

ROLF WOLFERMAN WAS a few inches taller than his younger brother Frederick. Like Frederick, he loved foreign automobiles, loved to race them, and was thrilled to see them race. A man who tinkered with engines, he enjoyed taking them apart and putting them together. *At least if we moved, I'd have guaranteed employment, and Cecile could adjust. I just don't know. I've never asked Frederick how he felt about surrendering his citizenship. It pains me to think of it, even more so to do it. And then there is the issue of her passport. Will it be a problem?* Rolf sorted out the issues plaguing his thoughts while he hurried up the steps of the building that housed the Hamburg Order Police.

The inside of the building was as drab as the atmosphere. Standing next to the front desk, Rolf towered over the youngster behind it—a mere child dressed in the typical slate-gray Nazi uniform, who seemed to think he could use his position to smart-mouth Rolf. "You've been told we released that man. We have no more information, nor will we have anything more for you."

Rolf looked doubtful and shook his head. "Now, how can you say you won't have anything more? How would you know that? Do you have a crystal ball?"

The youngster fumed at being questioned. "You will respect my authority!"

Rolf waved his hand at him. "Says who?"

The officer unsnapped the lip of his side holster, reaching for his pistol. He gritted his teeth and hissed, "Show me your papers at once."

Rolf guffawed, thinking the kid was joking around until he had the barrel of a 9mm aimed between his eyes. He raised his hands. "I can't give you my papers. They're at my hotel."

The officer narrowed his eyes and spoke in a monotone. "You should always carry them. What is the name of your hotel?"

Aboard the S.S. St. Louis, Deck D

Purser Mueller strode through the open door with all the expectations in the world. *This has to be a good sign; his door is open!* Inside the cabin, he checked to the right and left of the door before closing it. Muffled sobs came from the corner. Mueller flipped the light switch, and a voice cried out, "Off, please."

Mueller cut the lights, but before he did, he saw Steward Jockl standing over a sobbing man, huddled on the floor. "Is it Stefan?" Illuminating his way with his penlight, Mueller squatted next to the man on the floor and gasped with relief. "Mr. Soutine! Sir, you are a sight for sore eyes; I'm so glad to..."

Stefan cried out, "He, he, stabbed him in the head with a knife, a long knife, leaving it in, I couldn't see where the knife struck because his head was covered, but they gagged him first, then covered his head and stabbed him, and then..." He broke down, weeping more. "I saw the whole thing. I followed Schiendick. He and his goons. They put weights in his pockets, tied his hands, and threw him overboard; he's gone, he's gone."

The purser told the steward, "Jockl, please, get the captain. But wait." He asked Stefan, "May we turn the lights on now?"

"Yes, yes, and the captain. I have to speak with him." Stefan gathered himself to stand.

Mueller paced. "Can I get you anything, food, something to drink?"

Stefan's eyes went dark, and he whispered, "How can you think I care about food now? My friend is dead." And with one movement, he ripped the left corner of his shirt.

The purser was unfamiliar with the ancient tradition of Kriah, the Hebrew word for *tearing*. The tradition, performed while standing, signified showing strength during grief, as practiced by the Patriarch Jacob when he believed his son Joseph was dead, and King David after he learned that he and Bathsheba's son had died.

Stefan sniffed, and the purser offered him his handkerchief. "You can keep that."

Stefan blew his nose hard. "When the captain comes, I'll tell you everything." He sobbed again, speaking of Fritz. "He was so kind; even though I am his enemy, he showed me kindness. We connected. We were joint sufferers of similar circumstances where pedigree is of no consequence and has no place. Just like-minded, discussing the world, like we were friends."

Hotel Atlantic Hamburg

Maddie stared at Aunt Cecile's closed door. Her aunt's caustic remarks stung like a rough slap in the face, the words leaving a mark on her heart and mind. *Did she really mean what she said, is that how she views me? I thought I was special to her. Why would she say such things?*

Before she could worry about this further, she heard voices in the hallway outside their suite; keys jingled, and the door opened. She greeted Rolf, barely looking up. "Hello, Uncle Rolf. Aunt..."

Rolf coughed, and Maddie raised her eyes. She spotted the

stranger, a Nazi. Panicked, she used her robe to shield her face and ran to her room. Peeking out the door, she yelled, "I'm sorry, I'm not suitably dressed for company. Give me a minute." *At what time I am afraid, I will trust in thee.*

The stout Nazi perused the environment; his eyes grew big as he took in the suite outfitted in art deco-style furniture: zebra wood hutch and side tables, rich leather club chairs, and a glorious velvet chaise lounge. He asked Rolf, "How much does a place like this cost?"

Rolf was busy rifling through his leather satchel for his papers. He answered, "If you are a lover of luxury, which I can see you are, how would you like this?" He turned and tossed a pack of Marlboro 'America's Luxury' cigarettes to the youngster.

The punk grabbed for the pack with his pudgy hands, missing it. He stooped to pick it up. "Do you know what these are worth? I could sell the individual cigarettes or the whole pack to black market profiteers and take off two weeks from work!" He fondled the pack like it was pure gold; to him, it was.

Rolf knew of the financial situation of entry-level police and guard work in Hamburg and throughout Germany and Austria. It was well-known and written about in German conservative underground publications that the SS paid the lowest rate, especially to guards, and many worked second jobs to make ends meet.

Business experience would have been a plus for someone in Hitler's position; firm, confident leadership demanded it, operating from the gut instinct of knowing how the real world functioned instead of ideologies and utopian pursuits that had no place in the modern world. But Hitler lacked even a modicum of business acumen, depending on a war machine that governed by inflicting fear. The Reich's socialist practices crushed the low- to middle-class worker. Instead of quenching the public's thirst, the Nazis deprived them of what they needed to survive.

"Are you giving me these?" the boy asked.

Rolf smiled magnanimously. "Of course, and here are my papers."

The Nazi shoved the pack in his pocket, snatching the papers from Rolf's hand. "This says you're married to Cecile Rosenberg. That's a Jewish name. Is she here? Was that her when we came in?"

Rolf paused before answering. "No, that was a friend of my family, a musician unrelated to the man we're looking for at your station."

The Nazi squinted. "Hey, wait a minute, she's a Jew, so you must be Jewish! Okay, I've seen enough," he barked. "Everyone's papers—put them here now, for all three of you." He pounded on the end table, causing the lamp to tip.

Not to be outdone in the bombastic bullying department, Cecile launched out of her room, marched up to the Nazi, and told him, "You had better watch yourself, shorty. The man you're holding captive is the brother of a high-ranking United States State Department official with the last name of Wellington. How does that sound Jewish to you? If you want to live to see another day, you will back off, unless you want to be brought before a United States court that will find you guilty of subversion and hang you by the neck until it snaps and you're dead!"

Cecile's eyes flamed with fury. The kid tugged at his collar, tongue-tied, not knowing what to do or say. He left without checking Maddie's or Cecile's papers.

Maddie opened her door, glancing at Cecile, who sat on the small sofa with a face of shame. "Maddie, please, come here."

Maddie sighed and, with her head down, trudged to her. Cecile reached out to hold Maddie's hand, but Maddie refused to make eye contact with her.

"I have no excuse, my dear; please forgive me. I just get crazy and say the wrong thing. My face flushes, my whole body heats up, and I blow my top! The doctors don't know what's wrong with me. Why do I do this? I haven't always been like this, have I, Rolf?" She appealed to her husband's better angels.

He walked over to the two women and sat down on a chair. Rubbing his temples, he straightened and gazed lovingly at his wife. "Cecile, after that magnificent display of bravery, cutting the boy down to size, I have nothing to say but words of love and admiration." He took her hand in his, his eyes shining at her.

He looked at Maddie and nodded toward his wife. "She could have made Napoléon back down, Atilla the Hun even!" He kissed her hand. "Ladies, let's have a nice dinner, and you can fill me in on your day, as I will with mine."

Just then, the phone in the reception area of the suite rang. Rolf hustled over to it. "Hello, yes, yes I will. Hello, Raymond. Hello, can you hear me? There's a delay of six or seven seconds, yes. Okay, go ahead. Yes. We need help. Stani is missing. No, they did not take the ship. Maddie is here, safe. Yes. No, we don't need anything; wait, can you bring a few cartons of Marlboro cigarettes? Yes, exactly. Okay, see you soon. I will. Yes. Goodbye."

Maddie and Cecile stood on either side of him, waiting. "Well, he wants us to sit tight. He'll come here as soon as possible. Thank God for him. We don't need anything, just Stani. But in the meantime, Cecile, I'll have to pay for another week here. I know I won't get any complaints from you!" He took his wife in his arms and kissed her. "You really are a force of nature; I'm glad you're my wife, my friend, and not my enemy!"

Havana Port, Cuba

Along the walkway at the pier, a handsome man turned women's heads as he passed by, cool as a mojito. He was dressed in civilian clothing: a wheat-colored Varadero fedora, a Panamanian-style pale yellow shirt, silk tan slacks, and huarache shoes.

Buster Wellington donned his sunglasses—not his traditional Ray-Ban Aviators, associated with men of the US Armed Forces. He'd picked up a pair of cheap sunglasses after landing in Havana. The tropical air wafted an unfamiliar cacophony of scents toward him. *I can't wait to tell Maddie about how different the air smells here.* Havana was much closer to the equator than Rochester or Bletchley. The sun provided penetrating warmth, quickly turning his skin tone from pale to bronze.

Buster's assignment was to steal back the stolen documents that Hoffman would pass off to the Abwehr agent on board the *S.S. St. Louis.* He was here to monitor the passing of documents and plan how to retrieve them.

Inside the Hotel Ambos Mumbos, he strolled over to the bar to order a beer. No one was in a hurry in Havana, as illustrated by how long it took to accomplish anything, let alone get the bartender's attention. After five minutes, Buster whistled between his teeth, "Cerveza, por favor."

Weeks earlier, Buster had written a letter to his dad after Wolfie's accident at Bletchley, which had put the kibosh on the plans for them to work together on this scheme to trick the Nazis. Raymond had yet to respond.

His beer arrived, and Buster re-read the carbon copy of the letter as he sipped it.

Hi Pop,

I wish this were a note of good cheer; alas, it is not. You will hear soon from the War Department, probably even before this letter arrives, that Wolfie was injured in a training maneuver. He's now in a burn unit in London. I can't go into the details except we are hoping for no infection and for his organs to function as they should. His legs and feet are burned; the legs are mostly second-degree burns, and the tops of his feet are covered with third-degree burns. He was in shock for quite a while. Once he is stable, they'll transfer him to a regular hospital room, and days later, if he's still holding steady, transport him to the US to a hospital where they have a specialist who can perform skin grafts to help assist with healing and scarring. I was given a special leave to visit him. The travel was brutal, yet of no concern to me because I had to see him.

To be honest, I was scared to death when I got the okay for a visit. He was knocked out with pain medicine, and we never got a chance to speak. I could only pray over him, which Stani would have liked. Praying over him made me consider, what if he died? I was overcome with emotion. We might fight like animals, but none of that matters. He is always my brother first.

I was not present when the accident occurred. Poor guy. Surprisingly, it was not due to any shenanigans. It was an honest mistake. His captain told me if this had happened in the field, on assignment, he would have died. Thank God it happened during training.

Wolfie will be discharged for up to a year for full recovery. As for me, I hope to have a leave in July.

What have you occupied yourself with, the business, government, dating, what? Fill me in. I know my girl is in

Europe, and I miss her fiercely. My best to all on the home front, especially Frederick and Hollenius. That's all for now.

I leave you with an ask. Please, do what you can to keep us out of war. Please.

Your son,

Buster

The day before the scheduled meet-up with the HAPAG/Abwehr agent Robert Hoffman was to occur, Buster performed one of his daily duties: surveilling the dock, which stretched to the other side of the piers for non-commercial ships and the harbor side for commercial vessels. The harbor-side pier also housed the HAPAG offices where Robert Hoffman, assistant manager and undercover Abwehr agent, could be found. Buster had tailed him for the past two weeks, discreetly collecting information about him. Tracking his patterns when he arrived at work. Photographing him with the people he met with and noting the locations.

After strolling around the environs, Buster returned to the Ambos Mundos Hotel on the corner of Calle Obispo and Mercaderes, where he would await his next step. At the bar, he ordered a beer. The bartender, Carlos, a Panamanian, lit Buster's cigarette. "Sylvanna has been asking for you. She says, 'Where's that good-looking American, Ben?'" Buster was going by the name Ben while in Havana.

"I told her I didn't know."

Buster sipped his beer, then set it down on the bar, faced Carlos, and took a lengthy drag off his Marlboro. He made direct eye contact with Carlos and shook his head. He continued to sip his beer with his back to the bar, facing out, overlooking one of the numerous piers.

Carlos stood facing Buster's back and whispered with confidence, "Ernest Hemingway was in love with her."

Buster drained his beer. "Then Mr. Ernest Hemingway can have her. I hope she likes cats," he said, making reference to the numerous six-toe cats that the author had brought to the island. Finishing his smoke, he ground it out in the ashtray. Then giving a little farewell bow, he addressed Carlos. "Goodbye for now."

The bartender replied, "Yes, Mr. Ben."

CHAPTER THIRTY-FOUR

So Close and Yet So Far

MAY 1939, ABOARD THE S.S. ST. LOUIS

INSIDE CAPTAIN SCHROEDER'S office, Stefan held an audience with the captain and Purser Mueller. Leo Jockl stood guard outside the door, watching to ensure there were no interruptions. Especially by Schiendick.

After a shot of cognac and a cup of coffee, Stefan gained enough composure to recount last night's and that morning's incidents. The captain sat behind his desk, pondering how all this had happened without one crew member noticing.

"Well, we knew once Schiendick broke free, he would come after us," Stefan said. "We overtook him and subdued him, tying him to the chair with the rope he was going to use on me or Fritz. We took our belongings and went below to steerage, doubting he'd come looking for us there, but somehow, while Fritz wandered looking for food, one of the Nazi firemen must have told Schiendick, and they got him. Possibly identified by a little girl who asked for matches—Fritz gave her a book from Edwards Pub in Bucking...something. She told me this when I was looking for Fritz, and I found her walking around steerage. I came up from there, first going to my cabin to remove some of the clothing I wore and to, you know, clean up a little. I was looking for Fritz when I spied Schiendick and two of his cohorts."

Stefan put his hand up. "I have to stop for a moment; the

rest is so dreadful." His voice caught, and he lowered his head, wiping away tears.

Purser Mueller offered, "I can fill the captain in on the part you already told me if it is easier for you."

Stefan considered the offer. "No. I—I must honor Fritz by telling the story." He took a sip of coffee and a deep breath after. "Okay. So, this is what I witnessed. Schiendick put a rag in Fritz's mouth, then a hat or hood of one sort or another. Then, Schiendick or one of the men, I couldn't see well enough, but he took the knife and, and stabbed him repeatedly in the head or the face, his back, I don't..." His voice trailed off. He took another deep breath. "After that, they filled his pockets with weights, like from a scale, tied his hands, and threw him overboard."

The captain paid careful attention to the details, making notes in a small black book. Stefan saw it, his eyes widened, he swatted at his tears, and said, "Hey! That's what I have! I have one like that, it has the initials JG on it, and the plans written inside are called Operation Sunshine, about this ship, this voyage. It's being used for a propaganda tool, the passengers are not meant to depart the ship, but to be brought back to Germany."

Stefan explained, his volume rising with excitement. "It's all a trick, a sleight of hand by the Propaganda Minister and the Reich. They also use the voyage to transport espionage secrets between sources in Havana and the Abwehr, but Schiendick accused Fritz of being a spy from a foreign agency."

Mueller caught the captain's eye. "Sir, if I may, I can attest to that. The man allegedly thrown overboard said he worked for the Abwehr and was taking Schiendick's place as a courier; as you know, outside of his duties as Nazi representative aboard, he is also a courier for the Abwehr."

The captain nodded. "Yes, I'm aware of that, but I'm curious how you know this other information; how was it obtained?"

"I came upon their conversation and asked Mr. Effinger point-blank if it were true that he was replacing Schiendick on this voyage. He affirmed he was."

The captain sharpened his sights on Stefan. "I'd like to see the diary in your possession if you don't mind."

Stefan reached into his pockets, searching for the diary, then hit his forehead with his palm. "I shed some clothing in my room. I left it in another pocket."

The captain nodded to the purser. "Purser Mueller will escort you to your room to check. Also, I'd like to keep you from harm's way. A member of the crew will be with you at all times. Schiendick won't try anything during daylight hours; he operates in the dark like the devil. I'll make arrangements."

———❋———

The captain returned to the bridge but was anxious to return to his office. He checked in with his first mate and chief officer. "What's the forecast, have the dock master and pilot been wired?"

First Mate Lang showed the captain the report and confirmation of the wire.

"Very good. Thank you." He quickened his pace to his office, entering and pulling the shade down over the glass pane in the door. He had one thing on his mind—a book on ship protocol he knew was amongst his collection.

The captain was an avid reader and a collector of books. On every voyage, his office bookcase was full of books on maritime rules, the history of all continents and waters, maritime boundaries, and books that were required reading from the Reich. A few books for pleasure also made it to the shelves, mostly on history, counseling, and religion.

He thumbed through the handbook provided by the Minister of Propaganda Office. *Their grubby hands are in everything, mucking up principles and moral dictates. Let's see, ah, here it is. Here we are in the 'Chain of Command aboard Sea Vessels regarding Military Entities and Abwehr officials: They receive Immunity.'*

It figures. Of course, Goebbels set it up this way to castrate the captain's authority when it came to anything in question regarding his Nazi representatives and Abwehr officials. There are always two sets of rules with the Nazis. That clever bastard knows he's above punishment, that I have no power over him. I can no sooner throw him in the brig than I can myself.

The captain bellowed, "Damn him." He continued to look for something about at-sea disciplinary actions, searching to find a way to punish Schiendick for killing a man, even though the man in question had been a spy. The Abwehr would side with Schiendick, calling Effinger an enemy of the Reich, and would laud Schiendick for ending him. *There must be something!*

Then, an idea came: how to deal with and outsmart his troublemaker. He knew exactly what he had to do.

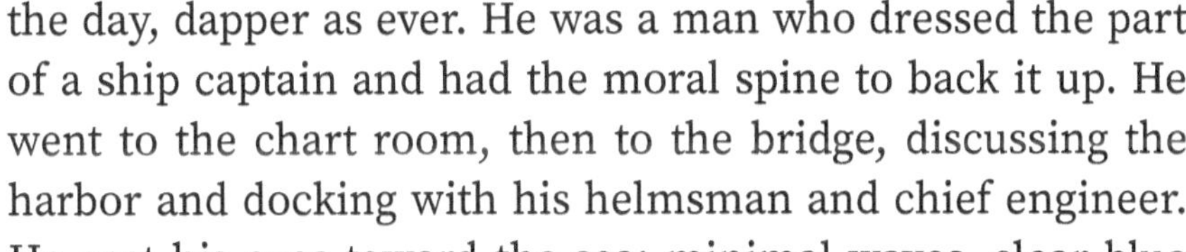

By 6:30 a.m., Captain Schroeder was ready and dressed for the day, dapper as ever. He was a man who dressed the part of a ship captain and had the moral spine to back it up. He went to the chart room, then to the bridge, discussing the harbor and docking with his helmsman and chief engineer. He cast his eyes toward the sea: minimal waves, clear blue skies, magnificent ocean air, and land in sight. *What could go wrong on a beautiful day like today? Plenty.*
Back in the captain's office, First Mate Lang tried to cheer his

superior with the news, "Well. We made it before the other two ships. However, we have yet to receive a response from the marine superintendent, Claus-Gottfried Holthusen."

The captain removed his hat and scratched at his scalp. He shook his head and replaced his cap, noticing First Mate Lang staring curiously at him. "An affliction," he explained. "My scalp raises at the hint of bad news as I fear its arrival. My scalp twitches as a tell-tale sign. If I had a fork I'd tear at my skin. It's nerves, or so I've been told. Please continue."

Lang marveled, "That's like a warning system. Simply brilliant!"

The captain scowled at the idea. Lang went on, "Regarding the marine superintendent, there's a deafening silence from his office. We've sent two wires. Not a word. We did hear back from the Jewish Joint Distribution Committee. They've contacted every national and international alliance and private citizens, hoping to raise the outrageous amount of money the Cuban government now requires as a security deposit on each passenger, in case of indigency."

The captain grimaces at the last four words. "It's a curious paradox. Here, these poor, tortured individuals are allegedly given freedom only after giving up everything they own, virtually penniless. Yet, they are fearless enough to take a chance for a new start in a foreign country, only to be hamstrung by new policies that seem deliberate. First, the wire tells us the landing permits are invalid after we've set sail, and then there is the threat of other ships arriving before ours. Then massive protests and threats days before our arrival, and now, this!"

He whipped around, and fury propelled his words. "You tell me this isn't intentional?"

Lang's expression gave way to a question. "Isn't this like

blackmail by the Cuban government?"

The captain nodded. "It's blackmail, yes, but something more sinister is taking place—like an intentional ploy to give the appearance of good, only to crush the people whose hopes of freedom lie wasted in the cruelest way possible."

The first mate and the captain's eyes met. Schroeder added, "We're being used."

The captain sighed. "When Purser Mueller returns at 0700 hours, have him report to me. Dismissed."

Purser Mueller and Stefan Soutine returned to his cabin on Deck D. The purser unlocked the door and flipped on the light. Stefan immediately sensed someone had been in his cabin. Then, he saw the evidence. "I didn't leave my clothes in a pile on the floor; I left them folded neatly on the bed. I'd worn them all to disguise myself, traveling from steerage to here, and then I removed most of them, except for what I'm wearing. After that, I went topside only to find...well, you know."

Stefan searched through his other pair of trousers. He reached into the pockets; his anxiety rose as he became frantic, searching through the clothes, tossing pieces aside and going through them all again. "I know it was here!" He threw up his hands. "Now, you and the captain won't believe me."

Just then, Otto Schiendick walked into the room. The door hadn't closed, allowing him to slide in unnoticed. He reached into his pocket and retrieved the pocket diary. Grinning a smile that would sicken a dog, he taunted, "Looking for this?"

The purser turned to face Schiendick, who smirked in the most insolent of ways. "Give it here. Now. That's an order."

Mueller put his hand out, expecting to receive the book. Instead, Schiendick laughed in his face. His putrid breath caused the purser to wince and step back.

"As the Nazi representative on this vessel, anything having to do with the Reich is under my control. This diary is the property of the Reich. Therefore, I am under no obligation to surrender it. It's not mine. The initials on the front are JG. All members of the Reich carry one, a gift from the Führer. And since it contains surreptitious information, especially about Operation Sunshine and my connections in Havana for the Abwehr, I will be forced to destroy it, and there's not one damn thing you can do about it."

He sashayed to the door and turned around, leaving with a parting shot aimed at Stefan. "Got my knife good and sharp for your haircut and other things not presently in view."

Schiendick gave a sickening, high-pitched, hyena-like laugh. He walked out the door and down the walkway to the side of the ship, then to the rail and the water's edge below. Without ceremony, he flung the diary into the abyss and returned to his duties, leaving Stefan more strung out than ever.

Mueller comforted Stefan, putting an arm around his shoulder. "Like all cowards, he's an evil bully of the worst sort."

———✼———

Purser Mueller and Stefan Soutine walked the promenade deck toward the wheelhouse and the captain's office. The seagulls squawked their morning songs while a low-flying colony of gulls competed for the best selections, seeking a meal close to the water's surface.

A few passengers were up early to greet the day. The dazzle of the rising sun helped whisk away the mist accompanied by the proverbial chill that arrived with the morning. The ocean's roar echoed in the ears of passengers and crew alike, decreasing the closer the ship came to land. The passengers walked briskly, nodding and offering a perfunctory, "Good morning." Well-dressed, carefree children ran up and down the main decks and promenade, squealing, laughing, and having a grand time.

Stefan walked with his head down, desiring not to make eye contact with humanity. Along the way, Mueller said, "I am shocked by that man's behavior, and I hope you know he does not represent the bulk of us; we do not feel as he does. Instead, we have sadness for your plight. And I apologize regarding the portrait. I shouldn't have enlisted you to do a job that was my responsibility."

Stefan waved him off. "It was nothing. I was more than glad to help." He offered his hand to shake with the purser.

"I'm so sorry you've had to experience this behavior by a crew member. He is the Nazi representative aboard this ship and is literally above the law. There is nothing we can do to curtail his behavior except humiliate him. By the way, you and Mr. Effinger did a marvelous job of that."

Stefan winced at the memory but softly laughed without tears for the first time since Fritz's death. "Yes, that was a bit of fun."

"Well done. I'm sorry for the horrors you've suffered; I only hope the future will be bright for you, as lovely and warm as the sunshine that bathes us in golden light."

Stefan gazed out over the sea. "Do you mind if we stop, just for a moment? There's so much beauty to take in, so much for my eyes to behold. I want to record every good moment in this journey to freedom to use it to recall when other memories try and cloud my mood."

Mueller asked Stefan to explain what he meant, and Stefan ran his hand along the steel-rung railing, thinking. "It's like the bad memories are joy thieves. You could be having a nice time, and a bad thought or memory gets triggered by something you see or something someone says, and the bad thought or memory creeps into your mind, ever so slowly, darkening your spirit and changing your mood. You have to fight back. In my case, if I don't, I feel like I'll be swallowed alive by those bad memories. So, it's good to have weapons to fight with, like a storehouse of good memories."

The purser nodded. "I understand well what you mean, and I commend you for finding ways to extricate yourself. I say *extricate* because I find myself stuck often, with no clue how to get unstuck."

The purser lit a cigarette and relaxed for a moment, placing his foot on the last rung of the railing. He looked out over the deep, remarking to Stefan, "The billowing sea, a liquid remembrance of what time forgets, but the retention of the sea is eternal, memories and tragedies alike, rich or poor, all come to the same end, lodged below in a watery grave. It is quiet there, peaceful, I would imagine."

He gazed at Stefan and smiled. "You know, before this voyage and meeting you and some of the other passengers, I never considered what it must be like to be Jewish, to feel like the world is against you. That must be difficult, isn't it?"

Stefan's eyes got misty. "I was raised in an orphanage but had good hand skills, so I became a kitchen commís at a young age and worked my way up through kitchens to become a sous chef. The closest I ever got to having a father figure was my chef in Paris. He would tell me, 'Stefan, you never know how another man feels unless you get in his skin and live life through that viewpoint.' So, I think that unless someone can understand the challenges of another person's life, they need to have a little experience of that life to gain a better perspective. I believe this journey has achieved that for you and possibly your captain."

Purser Mueller took a drag on his smoke. "You know, you've got a wealth of wisdom for such a young man."

Stefan lowered his head and said quietly, "Tragedy will do that to you."

The men marveled at the blueness of the sky. The depth of color presented an unending view into the heavens, searching for a touchpoint while getting lost in the intensity of color. Stefan posed the question, "Do you think that there is a heaven beyond that blue and a God who cares about us, his creation?"

Purser Mueller, not a religious man by nature, said, "That is the big question. I'm not equipped to answer, but I hope so. Everywhere you look, there is intelligent design to everything down to the smallest of organisms, giving man the brain power to build immense structures. There has to be more; there has to be. But in my mind, I believe everyone has a responsibility to find out those answers." He checked his watch: just after 0700 hours. He was due to be off now but indulged in the simple joy of Stefan's company.

Stefan nodded in agreement. "Yes, we do have a responsibility. We owe it to ourselves to not leave something so important to chance." He cleared his throat. "Sir, thank you. Your kindness humbles me. You've been exceptionally good to me."

Embarrassed by his emotions, Stefan covered his face. "I'm strung so tight, I'm emotional by nature, an artist of sorts. To witness another person die like that is just too much. I have to think about the good things. Like every other passenger, I've gone through a lot to get here. You're a German, as are all the staff and members of the Party, and except for a few bad ones, you've changed my life with your kind actions."

Color rose in the purser's cheeks. "Sir, we are only doing

what we should do. I can guarantee a pleasant voyage for everyone who purchases a ticket aboard a ship with Captain Gustav Schroeder manning the helm. Thank you for your words; they mean a lot."

Stefan frowned at a thought, then voiced it. "Sir, do you believe me now about the black pocket diary? Will the captain believe me?"

———✦———

At the captain's office, Mueller explained what had happened with Schiendick. He validated Stefan's story about the pocket diary and that Schiendick had stolen it. "He even mentioned the initials JG and the same name Mr. Soutine used, Operation Sunshine."

The captain's ears turned hot as his blood pressure increased. After consulting with his boss, Mueller retreated to his cabin, leaving Stefan with the captain, who called for his steward.

"You keep watch over him," he told Leo Jockl, nodding at Stefan. "You're his shadow. Tonight, you will switch and stay in each other's quarters. I hope that won't be too inconvenient, but we must do whatever it takes to preserve your life until we can just get you to shore." The captain added, "And Jockl, you know who to trust if you encounter any issues. Don't hesitate."

Leo nodded at the captain.

———✦———

First Mate Lang checked both dining rooms, speaking to passengers, greeting others, posing for, and taking pictures with the passengers' cameras. Several young girls, dressed in lace and bows, crowded around him, posing with him for a picture, and when one girl kissed his cheek, Lang wished he'd shaved closer. He maintained decorum, unhanding himself from the grasp of two sixteen-year-old girls who told him he was "dreamy."

He told a few young people, "For the final night of the voyage, after the religious services, the Assembly Hall will be transformed into a party complete with balloons and streamers, a band, and all kinds of fun foods and beverages, so we hope you'll all come and make a memory for your last night aboard the ship." Numerous older passengers told Lang they planned on getting to bed early, ready to prepare their "going ashore clothes." He wished them well and proceeded with his tasks.

Lang looked in on the Hall. Crew members were busy at work, setting up chairs. Other crew members scurried past him as he strolled the deck. He waved at a few children getting in a last swim while others played shuffleboard before lunch.

Back at the captain's office, he recounted his survey of passengers. Lang said, "As we steam toward Havana, the overall mood is good. Passengers have planned out their day and evening. Many mentioned that by tomorrow, we should be safe in harbor and port, waiting to depart the ship."

That very thought caused a rush of throat-tightening anxiety for the captain. He thanked him and dismissed Lang. In the captain's hand was a cable, ordering him to anchor at the roadstead, confirming his worst fear—he was not to dock and release his passengers. A roadstead is an area of safe anchorage while waiting to enter a port to dock a few hundred yards from the actual port. *No wonder Holthusen never replied. Could the story Soutine told me about Operation Sunshine be true? Is this voyage all a scam, and are the passengers pawns? If so, I believe this to be the pinnacle of evil acts I've witnessed.*

CHAPTER THIRTY-FIVE

Catch and Release

MAY 1939, HAMBURG SCHUTZPOLEZEI

THE EARLY-MORNING SILENCE was only broken by the sounds of the nearby port and deep-throated blasts from approaching ships and ferries. The sound of a distant train chugged away in sync, a repetitive choo-choo-choo-choo. The city awakened, sluggish and gray after a restless night, or perhaps that was how Maddie imagined it to be—like her night, unrestful. Fully awake, Hamburg, with its late-spring abundance of flowers and trees, their leaves and blossoms past bloom, would appear beautiful to her if not for the disappearance of her beloved Stani, skewing her appreciation of simple pleasures.

While Rolf and Cecile slept, Maddie bathed and washed her hair. Before dressing, she spritzed a floral and breezy scent over her washed body, a gift from Buster while he was stationed in Europe. She then dressed in a feminine Austrian frock Aunt Cecile had made for her, accentuating her assets. Cecile had embroidered tiny edelweiss along the hemline and curving neckline, with an appliqué of thin gold ribbon just above the flowers.

Maddie checked the mirror and adjusted her lipstick. She brushed her silky dark tresses, deciding to leave her hair down. She slipped on pale yellow heels, French-designed, and another gift from Aunt Cecile. Then she picked up her sweater and scarf, jotting a quick note that read: *I'll be back soon. Love, M.*

She left the suite without waking anyone. Maddie had a plan and intended to make a strong impression. Armed with the directions to the Hamburg Schutzpolezei and using Rolf's hand-drawn map, she glided out of the Hotel, nodding and smiling at the doorman.

She welcomed the low-hanging sky and wind-swept, cooler morning. The weather reminded her of eastern Poland, near the contested, sometimes German, sometimes Russian border, and the hopeless dreary skies that went on forever. She sniffed the air, still redolent with flowers, salt, and sea, just like the other day. *Ah, Poland, with the Baltic Sea to the north and the Carpathian Mountains to the far south, you still haunt me.*

Whenever a thought of Poland arose, the recollections flooded her: indelible memories of the Laurent sisters, Marcella and Elenena, Aunt Noelle, and the orphanage. Maddie's familiar friend, melancholy, attempted to land on her mind while dark thoughts riddled a new aspect of her conscience. *Well, I've burned down an orphanage to get people out. Why not a police station?* Then another thought bested the previous one: *No more destruction, Maddie. Go the way of peace.*

The thought seemed almost foreign to her; it was so simple a thought that even a child could understand, like a new way of thinking without doing anything. Then she remembered. *Stani told me that once I really believed and trusted in the truth of God's word, letting go of everything else, I would begin to think differently. He's right, and I can't wait to tell him!*

A newfound confidence caused her to breathe in deeply, filling her lungs and exhaling in a rhythm that whispered, *'I will find him. I'm not afraid!'* *This is all so mysterious to me, but I'm not afraid because I trust you, God. As Stani taught me, I breathe in your name and exhale at the same time I breathe, YAHWEH, YAHWEH, YAHWEH.*

Maddie spied the station's entrance. The relatively new building must have been designed by an architect with little imagination. Its brick exterior lacked a facade, leaving the building nondescript. *Hmm, nondescript and boring, like the Nazis that designed it.*

She entered through the glass doors and spotted the same Nazi guard who had come to the hotel with Rolf yesterday. He looked up, unable to take his eyes off Maddie, glued to the radiant beauty she possessed, as well as her curves. She walked up the four steps slowly and deliberately, her hips swaying as she approached the front desk. Breathless, she moistened her lips and said to the kid parading as an Order officer, "Well, hello there! I remember you. You're the handsome officer who escorted my friend Rolf Wolferman to our hotel yesterday."

She batted her eyes at him, using her feminine charms to her advantage. He could barely speak; he squeaked out an impotent "Yes."

Maddie went on, "You are just so handsome in that uniform. Do you like wearing it?"

The kid pulled at his jacket, nervous, and smoothed over a few wrinkles caused by his girth. Receiving compliments was foreign to him.

"You must be what, twenty-four or twenty-five?" she said, batting her eyes again for full effect.

He stuttered, "H-huh? I mean, Oh, sure, yeah, I'm twenty-four. Almost, yeah."

Sweat trickled down his face to his jowl as Maddie leaned over the desk, giving him an up-close view of her assets.

"Hey, um, what time are you done here? I was thinking we could get coffee or something. But wait, you must be married, a handsome man like you…"

His eyes enlarged, his mouth hung open, loose on its hinges, and he blinked back into reality. "Um, well, n-no, I'm not married, and I'm done at noon. Coffee would be good…"

"Great, well, how about if I just wait here while you work until you're done? We can get to know each other. Tell me your name unless that breaks protocol."

She smiled a flirty smile, and he stuttered again, "M-my name is Henrik Kempler."

Maddie raised her eyebrows. "Do you mean like the famous musician Kempler?"

The kid backed up from the desk. His neck stiffened, and his face flushed. Softly, he said, "He was my father. How would you know him or anything about him?" The kid looked away- his eyes watery.

Shocked to hear he was the son of the man who Stani was to see to get the gift for Mrs. Genhart, Maddie probed deeper still. "I know someone who knew him. I wonder if you know her?"

The kid smeared his face into his coat sleeve, wiping away the fast-accumulating perspiration. "Know who? I don't understand what you're asking."

A genuine frown crossed Maddie's face. "Oh, I've upset you. I'm so sorry. Please forgive me." She sorted through her pocketbook and found a hanky. "Here, you may keep it."

Before he used it to wipe his eyes, he saw that it was it embroidered with the initials MTW. He wiped his eyes and nose, then glanced at the initials again; he smirked at her suspiciously. "What do the initials stand for?"

Maddie grinned, "More Tear Wiping, of course."

He didn't buy it. In a monotone, only inches from her face, he says, "I told you my name, now what's yours?"

Ft. Bragg, Pope Air Force Base, Fayetteville, North Carolina
Two military medics transported a lightly sedated Wolfie on a stretcher to a Douglas DC-2 aircraft parked near the runway. The two medics and a doctor would fly back to Rochester with Frederick, Wolfie, and Hollenius. Before leaving the hospital, the attending doctor at Ft. Bragg, Jeffrey Silberstein, had given Frederick a full report of Wolfie's condition and his steps to full recovery.

"You know, Doc, I sure am glad to see the words *full recovery*. It's possible, right, no doubt?" A world of worry had been reflected in the deep-set lines of Frederick's face, adding to his haggard, sleepless appearance.

The doctor had comforted Frederick, "Your son was extremely fortunate. The other soldier with him acted quickly, implementing a proper procedure to reduce the severity of the burns."

"I'd love to thank this young man in person. Would it be possible at some point for me to meet him and thank him for saving my son's life?" Fredrick ran his hand through his hair, which continually drooped into his eyes, adding to his "puppy-dog look," as his older brother Rolf always said when describing his brother.

The doctor sighed. "I'm sorry, that won't be possible. He is not in the country at the moment. I believe he's on a ship. I'll gladly give him a handwritten note if you so choose. I work with the men at Bletchley, training them in on-field medical procedures. These men work with flammables, among other substances, and must be prepared for something to go wrong, which, incidentally, it always does. This gives an added layer of protection and on-the-job training. They need to know how to respond correctly for any given occasion."

The doctor had lit a cigarette and offered Frederick a smoke. "Your son is an exceptional young man. He's disciplined and hardworking. His sergeant calls him 'Can-do Wellington.'" He'd smiled, recollecting a memory. "We've all agreed there's nothing Wolfie can't do; that's quite clear."

Frederick had turned around, craned his neck to the right and then to the left, and stared at the man head-on. With all seriousness, he'd said, "This is my son you're talking about, right?"

The doctor had laughed at the incredulous look on Frederick's face. "Apparently, your son has grown up while he was with us. You can write to the soldier who saved Wolfie, Second Lieutenant Martin F. White, and send it to me here at the Ft. Bragg base. I'll see that he receives it."

Standing just outside the cockpit while waiting for Wolfie to be loaded into the medical transport, Frederick spoke with the pilot, asking about flight times, speed, and altitude. His eyes absorbed the plane's instrument panel, which contained numerous gauges, dials, a tachometer, fuel indicators, and switches.

Frederick came alive when speaking with another person who understood engine nomenclature. "Oh, yes, one day I will take flying lessons. I've always wanted to, but I've been busy with cars. Sports cars mostly."

The pilot's face broke into a grin, "Sports cars? Now you've got my attention!" Racing was a sweet spot with the pilot, an Army Major with an affinity for sports cars. They discussed the finer points of the latest Aston Martin model, and the pilot, Major Matthew Russo, lamented, "I'd rather be driving your Aston Martin Abbey Sports tourer back to Rochester than flying this tin can. We'll land on the grass there, no paved runways. But they've landed bigger planes than this, so we should be smooth sailing. We'll take good care of the precious cargo."

He lit a smoke and offered Frederick one. "My son will take perfect care of your baby," he said, referring to Frederick's precious Aston Martin parked at the hospital at Ft. Bragg. "He's military, and if he's good enough to drive generals, he's good enough for your sweet ride." He winked at Frederick.

Irked by the major's cavalier attitude toward his car, Frederick's eyes narrowed. "He'd better." Frederick retreated to the back of the plane to see Wolfie and Hollenius. "You don't look too comfortable. Is there anything I can do to help?"

Wolfie squirmed around on the makeshift mattress. "Ugh, thank God you're here. I'm *not* comfortable. Those guys went to eat, and I'm here fending for myself."

Frederick softened. "You've been through a lot. We're almost home." Hollenius meowed loudly in acknowledgment. The feline reclined in his fenced apartment, perched on a seat across from Wolfie so they could see eye to eye.

"Pop, fluff and straighten my pillows, then pull me up so I sit more than lie down. And can you get me a clean t-shirt? I think I stink. And then, put Hollenius here with me," he pointed next to him on the mattress.

Frederick came close to his son and sniffed. He tilted his head, wincing. "Yes, you're ripe." Then he grinned and tousled his hair. "Aww, it's not that bad."

"I don't want those goons washing me. Would you clean me up before they return, and we can take off?"

Wolfie gave his father a meaningful glance, and for a moment, Frederick saw the little boy who'd lost his mom, now a grown man of almost twenty-three. "Sure, I will. Hmm.

We'll have to sponge-bathe you, even if it's with a rag, soap, and water." He grinned and told his son, "Pretend you're camping."

Frederick looked through the bag the department at Bletchley had sent home to the States with Wolfie. "Here we go, one white t-shirt coming up." He put it in Wolfie's lap. "Now hang on, let's see about soap and water," he shouted as he walked down the aisle to the back of the plane.

He returned with a wet towel rubbed with soap, helped Wolfie remove his shirt, and wiped his son as gently and tenderly as possible. "Under the arms now!" Wolfie obliged, laughing as his father tickled him, knowing that was his sensitive area. Even as a kid, Frederick could always make Wolfie laugh until he cried if he got him in the armpit.

He dried his son off with the other t-shirt, then helped him into the clean one. "Well, it's not perfect, but at least I pass the smell test. Thanks, Pop." Wolfie winced as he adjusted himself. "You know, they still have the catheter in me. I can't get up and walk to the bathroom yet."

Frederick stroked his hair. "Are you in pain, son, or is the medicine still enough?"

Wolfie shook his head. "It's still enough. But I sure will be glad when I can get this garden hose out of me." He rolled his eyes, unable to cloak his frustration. It was unlike Wolfie to complain; by nature, he was even-tempered, much like his mother.

Frederick took his son's hand. "Not much longer; the good news is, a few days after we return home, hopefully your bandages will come off once and for all. One step at a time."

Frederick looked into his son's eyes and swallowed hard, choking back a sudden wellspring of emotion. He turned away to hide it, busying himself with taking Hollenius out of his carrier. The cat meowed loudly, not ready to be disturbed, until he saw Wolfie, who patted the space next to him. He snuggled close to his youngest charge, who stroked the side of his face near his ears, activating his purr engine.

"Oh, how I've missed you, crazy dear boy. You're going to help me heal, okay?" Hollenius must have agreed; he nestled even closer.

The warmth of the moment touched Frederick deeply. He told Wolfie, "I haven't felt this much emotion in years," as a single tear rolled out of its border.

Wolfie nodded. "Since before Mom got sick and died?"

Frederick took a deep breath. "Yes, since she first became sick. I couldn't cope with it; I had to erect a wall; the pain was so intense that I thought I'd die from grief if I didn't shut down my thoughts and my feelings. And then, Dachau, seeing you limp across the yard with the kapo, your eye bandaged, the bruises, well, that put a crack in the wall I erected. Then this happened with you, and you know, the funny thing is, the wall came crumbling down when I first saw you sedated in the hospital bed."

His smile was fractured, but a smile, nonetheless, adoring his son. He told Wolfie, "We'll get there. We'll get better together, okay, buddy?"

Hamburg Schutzpolezei

Maddie said, "I'm very selective about whom I give information to; you can't be too careful. Why, just the other day, I was close by, at the cafe, across the way from here, and an officer like yourself was having coffee with another officer. I wasn't eavesdropping but couldn't help but overhear them speaking about the prison below this floor, and it's almost ancient. They built this new structure on top of the old prison. Is that right, Henrik?"

He offered a blank stare in response, then said, "Yes, that's true."

Maddie gave him a brilliant smile; she moistened her lips, lowered her eyes, and then slowly raised them to focus on his. Tilting her head, she said coyly, "You wouldn't know this, of course, but I am an archaeology student at the University of Cambridge. We study such places, ancient prisons, and buildings built before the turn of the century, and use them in research, not for the public, but you could be cited by name in a doctrinal paper as an asset to this researcher. Would you like that?"

Henrik nodded, his head bobbing up and down like a fishing bobber.

Maddie grinned. "Wonderful, oh, and look at that smile. You should smile more; you have such a handsome face. For research purposes, can I take a quick peek at the prison just to see the composition of the rock, the formations and grading?"

Henrik scrunched up his face and hesitated. "Well, I don't know if I should. But no one else is near the station. It's still early…I guess I could. There's only one prisoner in there now, a Jew, that's his only crime," he said, forgetting that Rolf had come looking for the man, and that Maddie was in the apartment when he followed Frederick there in search of his papers. Maddie had heard what she needed to hear, her intuition confirming it must be Stani being held in the prison cell.

He unlocked the door to the prison below. Even before they descended the stairs, Maddie began to sneeze and did so four times in a row. Her eyes watered terribly, and she covered her mouth. She shook her head and told Henrik, "Mold, there must be mold present. The dampness makes me sick. I have to go."

Maddie trotted up the steps, leaving Henrik with his mouth agape as she hustled through the small lobby, her high heels clicking down the stairs and out the front door. *If only I could run in heels! Oh please, God, let him follow me!*

CHAPTER THIRTY-SIX

Day–Tripping

*MAY 1939, THE TRIP HOME TO ROCHESTER
FROM FT. BRAGG, NORTH CAROLINA*

AIDED BY MORPHINE, Wolfie slept soundly for most of the flight home to Rochester. According to the pilot, "Clear skies all the way to New York, ceiling unlimited." Frederick chain-smoked to calm his nerves. He couldn't take his eyes off his son.

The doctor on board, Dr. Jamie Anderson, sensed Frederick's anxiety. "Sir, your son will recover; he'll be fine once he has enough rest and allows time for the burns to heal. He'll be as good as new!"

Frederick scowled. "How can you say, 'good as new'? You don't think his mind is harmed by this accident? And furthermore, why the hell won't anyone tell me what happened to him, how he suffered such life-threatening injuries?"

Anderson hemmed, "Well. Not necessarily life-threatening. Your son was treated immediately; they were on a maneuver, and thankfully, Dr. Silberstein was present. However, regarding the severity of burns, left untreated, an infection could set in, and it *would* be life-threatening."

Frederick chuckled wryly, gesturing toward the doctor with a wave of his hand. "You're joking, right? My son is fried like an apple fritter, and you say, 'not life-threatening'?"

Anderson shook his head. "Sir, we have guides that categorize injuries. Second-degree burns only qualify as life-threatening if left untreated, and infection sets in."

Frederick lit another cigarette, exhaling his frustration with the smoke. "You people, whether Army or government, always have slippery excuses and strategies to shut down inquiries that don't match your agenda. My son is done serving in the Army, and that's that." His eyes narrowed as he viewed the doctor, and Anderson squirmed in his seat.

"Well, sir, it's not as easy as a dogmatic answer. He signed up for enlistment and will not be discharged until that time is served. And sir, Private Specialist First-Class Wolferman is a fine soldier. He was top of his class at Bletchley."

Even that didn't convince Frederick to change his stance. Regardless, the doctor was correct, and Frederick hated to admit it, knowing Wolfie was obligated to serve his time. Anderson added, "Conscripted service will begin soon enough, especially if war breaks out."

Frederick shook his head, lamenting, "And I thought I'd protect us here, living in the US. Is it any better than Germany at this point?"

Anderson shrugged. "Well, sir, at least we don't have a tyrannical extremist running our country."

Frederick didn't respond. He viewed the world below as the plane reached its nineteen-thousand-foot cruising altitude. The smooth flight, made possible by the powerful Wright Cyclone Engines churning out 710 hp, kept the 18,569-pound ship buoyant on the whims of the atmosphere, a silver bird skimming the brilliant blue skies.

While Wolfie and Frederick flew home, Raymond arrived in Hamburg.

Hamburg Schutzpolezei
"Why, that little..."

Order Police guard Henrik Kempler ground his teeth in anger. He spits out words, laced with venom, "Just who does she think she is, running off like that?"

He walked the narrowing hallway down to the last cell, which was beyond repugnant and dark. He removed his nightstick and banged on the door, speaking through the small opening. "You have a visitor."

No response.

"Hey, did you hear me?" He pounded on the door with his stick, waiting for a sign of life, something. No response.

Now, where is that flashlight? Here it is. He grabbed the flashlight, harbored in a space between two rocks. Henrik pulled his belt-latched key ring forward, fumbling for the key to the cell. He began to sweat; droplets dripped into his eyes. *Where is the damn key?!*

In frustration, he tried all the keys until he found the right one. Henrik opened the door and shone the flashlight, seeking the captive while simultaneously knocked back by the pungent odor of human waste. He shook off the stomach-wrenching stench and spotted the prisoner in the corner, held now for fifteen days. Still standing in the doorway, Henrik repeated, "You have a visitor."

Weakened, Stani struggled to raise his hand to block the light in his eyes. Standing was an impossibility.

Henrik continued, "She has dark hair and blue eyes and is very beautiful."

Stani cried out in anguish, "Maddie, my Maddie." He wept and gulped air, his throat parched from lack of fluids.

Henrik asked, "Is her last name the same as yours?" Stani didn't answer, prompting Henrik to beat him with his nightstick. Standing over the helpless victim, huffing for air, Henrik spat out, "That's okay. You gave me enough information. I know how to hunt Jews. She'll be easy to find because I already know where she's staying." With that, he left, slamming the door and locking it tight.

Stani croaked out, choked with tears, "Maddie, my Maddie."

Hotel Atlantic Hamburg

In Room 160, Cecile and Rolf awaited Raymond's arrival. Cecile fussed with her hair and corrected the lines on her hose, ensuring they were straight. "Do I look all right, Rolf?" She batted her eyes, pursing her lips for him.

Her husband grumbled, "Why are you going to so much trouble? We haven't even had our coffee yet."

Cecile rolled her eyes at him and stuck out her tongue. She continued to fuss with her stockings and then began the same treatment with her makeup, viewing herself with her hand mirror. She put the mirror down and stood in the doorway to the bedroom, where Rolf sat up in bed, reading the papers, waiting for his wife to free up the bathroom.

She stomped her foot to get his attention. "Rolf, if you must know—"

He interrupted her, "Hark, is that the sound of Juliet's voice?"

Cecile was about to answer when Maddie came through the suite's door. She scowled at her niece. "And just where have you been, dressed up like you're going on a date at eight in the morning?"

Maddie's eyes met Rolf's, pleading wordlessly, *Please remind her I'm twenty-three, I'm not eight.* But like a dog with a bone, Cecile refused to give up her line of questioning. "Well?"

Rolf interceded, "Sweetheart, she's a grown woman. She doesn't have to answer to you or me." He reflected for a moment, then asked, with a smile, "Where have you been?" But his delivery was soft, curious, not intimidating or accusatory like Cecile's.

With the door to the suite still open behind her, Maddie said, "I went to the Order Police where Stani was held. His only crime is…"

From behind Maddie came the voice of Henrik, finishing her sentence for her while jabbing the barrel of his 9mm pistol into the middle of her back. He hissed in a sing-song voice, "'His only crime is being a Jew' is what you were going to say, wasn't it?"

After Maddie had taken off from the station, she hurried back to the hotel, with Henrik not far behind. He'd left in haste, leaving behind his hat—a code violation. A superior would punish him if he was spotted capless, revealing a curious razor-cut scalp.

Henrik pushed Maddie into the room, in full view now of Rolf, in his blue-striped pajamas, and Cecile, dressed like she was going for a photo shoot. Rolf made eye contact with Henrik and deadpanned, "Oh. Not you again."

Before Henrik could speak, Maddie informed every one of his origins. "He is Mr. Kempler's son, whose home we visited while looking for Stani." Maddie turned to face Henrik, pleading with him, "You told me you're holding him, with his only crime being a Jew, so why won't you let him go? Haven't you tortured him enough?"

An evil smile crept across Henrik's sizeable face. Squinting, he said, "I don't answer to you, Miss. You lied to an Order Police guard, which makes you guilty of a crime. You're coming with me now. I'm taking you into custody," he said as he gestured with his pistol for her to head toward the door.

Cecile lurched forward, stopping short of coming between Maddie and the pistol's nose. "Just wait one minute. Who do you think you are, arresting American citizens? You are holding her family member unlawfully, confining him in prison."

Cecile's bluster didn't move Henrik as it had the first time. Gritting his teeth and speaking through them like a wolf baring his canines, he said, "Madam, you take one step closer, utter one more word, and I'll shoot you all like dogs. I carry multiple magazines. Is that clear? I set the rules. Not you."

Cecile took a step back, so astounded that this young kid would speak to her in such a way that she didn't care if he had a pistol. She approached him with her hand out. "You give me that gun this instant; how dare you speak to me in such a tone? I don't care who you are or your position. You will not, I repeat, you will not speak to me or anyone in this room with disrespect again."

Berlin to Hamburg

Either by luck or serendipity, Raymond flew first to Berlin with the new ambassador to Germany, Alexander Comstock Kirk, before going to Hamburg. With a quick turnaround in Berlin and the handoff of documents to an Embassy aide, the two men boarded the Army plane again and headed for Hamburg.

Alexander was a few years Raymond's senior. The two had a history: several years of traveling in the same DC circles, with law degrees from Harvard, both employed by the US government, working at the State Department. While Alexander was in the center of those DC circles, Raymond intentionally stayed on the outskirts.

Traveling en route to Germany, Raymond explained to Alexander over cocktails, "My adopted daughter, Maddie, is a brilliant concert violinist, having trained in Europe and under the tutelage of Mrs. Genhart and the Eastman School of Music."

Alexander finished his martini and waved for another. "And this time, just let the vermouth blow a kiss to the gin." He turned his attention back to Raymond. "Is that George Eastman's place, connected to the theater? He throws mad parties, wild affairs, simply over the top, the stories!" He whispered, "Scandalous affairs." Alexander threw his head back and laughed.

Raymond smiled. "Yes indeed, that's right, George Eastman." He expertly steered the conversation away from gossip and returned to discussing Maddie. "She's a senior in the program, which made her eligible for the lottery to play with Wilhelm Furtwängler and the Austrian Philharmonic Orchestra as a guest artist. She was chosen out of one hundred other eligible students." He nodded yes to another cocktail, a bourbon old fashioned. "I have to admit, she's a remarkable talent. This was a once-in-a-lifetime offer for her; it will undoubtedly advance her career. The performance was at the start of the month. She became ill and needed a few days of bed rest to recover."

Alexander suggested, "Maybe she'd consider a command performance once I settle in Berlin. I have a fabulous home, a huge mansion in the Grunewald neighborhood. I'll create a comfortably elegant home, my penance for accepting a position at such a time, a nation on the brink of war. We'll throw luxe parties to chase the blues away and hobnob with the few intellectuals that remain, and some of the nominal Berlin Nazis can be fun; they're wicked. Oh, can they drink!"

Shifting gears, the ambassador asked, "Regarding your daughter, tell me what you need, and consider it done."

The two men clinked their glasses in a toast and continued to make small talk. After four martinis, Alexander confessed to Raymond, alcohol loosening his tongue, "I've always found you wildly attractive." Sitting across from Raymond, Alexander first ogled but then blushed when Raymond met his eyes with just as direct a gaze. Alexander looked at his shoes, his face scrunched, and he said, droll as ever, "I've gone and stepped in it. I'm sorry."

Raymond quickly waved him off, assuring him he was flattered more than anything. Apprehensively, Alexander asked, "You are?"

Raymond chuckled, "Alex, you have remarkable style and understated elegance. I'm not a Neanderthal and can appreciate beauty in any form."

Raymond drained his drink, signaling he was done. He handed the glass to the Army steward serving them. Then to Alex, he said softly, "You're safe with me." He extended his hand for a shake, and the men nodded to each other, confirming their friendship.

"I've got a plan in mind," Raymond said. "Rolf, the brother of one of the adopted men that I spoke of, tells me the men we're dealing with are unfortunate individuals, lacking in education and everything that goes with it."

Alexander nodded. "I see. What do you propose?"

"Cigarettes. Marlboros, to be exact, carry a deceptively devious weight of value here, sold as you would imagine on the black market. They've provided much-needed assistance in the face of perilous events."

Standing up to stretch, Alexander asked humorously, "Really? Tell me about it."

With that, Raymond recounted the trip with Ambassador Dodd, his driver, and Raymond's whole clan in two cars on the way to Bremen from Austria in August of 1933 when stopped on the road by Nazi police. He detailed how they'd demanded papers from everyone and there were four passengers without papers. "I was smoother back then. I hope I haven't lost my charm." The ambassador assured him that he hadn't.

Raymond offered Alexander a cigarette, then lit his own. He inhaled, scratching his forehead. "Man, that was a hell of a moment—tense, you know?"

Alexander's utterance of "heavens!" made Raymond laugh. "I may need you as my bodyguard if trouble happens in Berlin," the ambassador said. "I think you could smooth-talk your way out of any circumstance. Hopefully, I'll be safe, and the Embassy provides their internal security, right?"

Raymond raised his eyebrows, placing his hand on his chest. "Are you asking me? I do not know the arrangements, but I'd substantiate your claim that you need security. We're closer to war than we've ever been."

Alexander signaled the steward for service and, to his discouragement, was told, "I'm sorry, sir, we'll be landing soon."

To this Alexander answered smugly, "So?"

He waved off the young man and rolled his eyes at Raymond, who understood well that Alexander was the type of diplomat that the DC elite found haughty, elegant, and overrefined—the type they became suspicious of because it caused them to evaluate themselves as the hypocrites they were. They deemed themselves perfect while regarding lesser beings as plebians.

But what the elite didn't understand about Alexander Comstock Kirk was that underneath the mask of urbane, frequently exaggerated sophistication lay a wealth of intuitive perceptiveness and dry, biting wit, capable of impressing Winston Churchill with a well-placed, acerbic comment. Like Raymond, Kirk vehemently opposed the Nazis and would do what he could to disrupt their madness in any way possible, even down to the smallest act—subterfuge at the ground level.

Alex readied for arrival, putting on his Homburg, a classy complement to his London drape v-cut wool suit, like the ones that Fred Astaire and Cary Grant might have worn. Dapper and groomed, Alex would have once wowed Berlin with his style. Now, the days of the wild Weimar Republic were a memory, an oft-forgotten eclipse of gaiety, frivolity, and artistic expression conjoined with the extremes of rampant debauchery. Like a song left unfinished, while the wine was poured and the candles burned, the fascists moved in.

CHAPTER THIRTY-SEVEN

Missing Persons

MAY 26, 1939, ABOARD THE S.S. ST. LOUIS

THE SHIP'S ASSEMBLY Hall was decorated to the nines, prepared for the final night of festivities. After a grand celebration of food, drink, dancing, and general merry-making, an unfamiliar specter of melancholy skulked around the edges of the celebration. Almost like a virus, the initial spread was slow before becoming pervasive. Moods went flat as fast as corked champagne while hope capsized for some due to worry about an uncertain future. Leaving the safety and comfort of the ship dredged up ambivalence, especially for a suicidal passenger who cut his wrists and jumped overboard into the harbor, where the Cuban authorities retrieved him from the water. The man tried to strip his cut arms of their veins and ligaments, pulling them out like strands of spaghetti.

Yet, for a few others, uninhibited freedom beckoned. They celebrated the release from Nazi horror. The band played on as the remaining couples danced, hoping to assuage the trepidation of the looming unknown. Even the children danced together, copying the steps the adults made, boys trying to tango and foxtrot with their partner, often only to step on a poor girl's toes.

———✻———

At 10:30 p.m., Leo Jockl and Stefan Soutine played a final game of cards in Leo's quarters. Both felt secure in the cabin behind the captain's quarters, well out of Otto Schiendick's sight and reach of revenge. Leo said, "I've got a record player, and I can play some records if you like." Stefan smiled and nodded.

For safety reasons, and concern for Stefan's life, as not to be spotted by Schiendick, Jockl had a steward assemble covered plates of food from the buffet served to the passengers to be brought to the captain's quarters at 8:30 p.m. He'd brought succulent slices of tender carved steamship round of beef, plates with roasted turkey with all the trimmings, and, for the passengers that did not keep kosher, plates of seafood, chilled shrimp, crab legs, lobster. He'd also brought every accoutrement to accompany all the dishes. Then came the desserts: an assortment of cookies, cannoli, napoleons, pies, tortes, and petit fours.

The young men entertained themselves, playing cards. Stefan threw his hand down. "Gin. Good game." His eyes surveyed what remained of the food and desserts. "Man, that was some spread. You know, I'd like a job like that!" He chuckled at the thought, using his hands to illustrate a banner. "I can see it now. How does this sound? 'Jewish chef cooks for the masses under the Nazi flag!'"

Leo laughed. "Not a chance."

He became suspiciously quiet, and Stefan wondered why. "Did I say something wrong?"

Leo shook his head. "No. The irony of your banner strikes me. And at the same time, convicted by it." He fumbled in his pocket, digging for his cigarettes and pulling out a smoke.

Stefan fiddled with a half-eaten piece of pie on his plate, then grabbed a cookie from the dessert platter and asked, "What's ironic?" while nibbling on the shortbread.

Leo took his time to answer. Finally, he looked up at Stefan and said, "If shame could cover me like a prayer shawl, it would now." His eyes cast down, Leo said, "If you must know, I'm Jewish."

⁕

Captain Gustav Schroeder paced in his room, often consulting the clock on his desk. It was almost time. He sent for his steward. "Leo, are we ready to go?"

"Yes," Leo confirmed. "He's all set in my cabin. We can proceed, sir. As we discussed, I'll go first, and you will follow behind. I will give the signal if I spot anyone."

The captain shook his steward's hand. "Thank you for your assistance. This would not be possible without you. You're doing mankind a great service." He winked at Leo, his eyes twinkling, pleased with the concocted scheme. "Let's hope all systems go as planned."

Later that evening, stewards scuttled about, bringing the passengers' suitcases and luggage to line up on the top deck, to be paired with their rightful owners once the ship docked. The moon's light was obstructed by cloud cover, creating a low ceiling; it was almost as if the sky and ocean met, if you strained your eyes to see it. A gentle south-by-southwesterly wind blew at eight knots, or a three on the Beaufort scale, which is used to assign a numeric to wind speed while at sea. A solo whale cried in the distance, its cry perhaps happy or despondent.

First Officer Ostermeyer was on duty. Along with the helmsman, he would bring the ship to the specified place that the harbor dock pilot desired and then hand over the reins to the well-trained maritime pilot once the command came to leave the roadstead. The command order was a day late. Before engaging in the plan's next step, Captain Schroeder checked in with the first officer, who voiced his concerns.

"Sir, with this being the last night on the ship before

docking with no order, what do we do? How should we proceed?" Distress filled the atmosphere in the wheelhouse as the crew awaited the command from the docking pilot. With no command, they would be left to tread water at the roadstead while anxious passengers waited to disembark.

"Mr. Ostermeyer, patience. We'll hear from them. We are all aware of the consequences of docking in a roadstead. On another subject, be ready on my signal to have First Mate Lang and two crewmen come to Deck D, the cabin of passenger Stefan Soutine. The door will be open."

The captain left the bridge knowing if the order did not come, the ship would be forced to anchor away in a roadstead, hundreds of yards away from the dock. The distance would seem cruel and insurmountable to anxious family and friends awaiting the return of their loved ones.

Captain Schroeder was in his office, writing in his log, when the order arrived from the local HAPAG official in Havana, and he was summoned to the bridge. It was the message they'd been waiting on, but not the answer they'd hoped for. The order insisted the ship anchor at the roadstead instead of docking at the HAPAG Pier. So, the captain gave the order to dock there, and the ship docked there, dropping anchor and awaiting further instruction.

Luis Clausing, the HAPAG official, stated that the president of Cuba had made a concession but still would not allow the passengers to land. He demanded a large sum of money, $500 per passenger. Unless the Jewish Joint Distribution Committee or private sources could produce that money, totaling nearly one-half million American dollars, the passengers would not be allowed to disembark the ship in Havana.

A groan escaped the captain's lips. He sighed, "I have a matter to attend to, then I'll be back."

Before Schroeder left, the first officer reached into the breast pocket of his uniform and handed the captain a telegram intended to be sent by someone. "It just never went through for a confirmation."

The captain scanned the contents of the telegram. Wordlessly, he tucked it in a side pocket and nodded to his first officer. "Carry on," he said, then left to embark on his next mission.

Leo Jockl led the way to Stefan Soutine's cabin; the captain followed four or five meters behind. Leo used the master key to open the door. He stepped inside. Finding it untouched from his last visit, he scoped the room and beckoned to the captain, who slipped inside. Nodding to his steward, the captain got under the bedcovers and waited.

Hotel Atlantic Hamburg
Alexander Comstock Kirk and Raymond Wellington decided it was better to keep a low profile, opting not to ride in an embassy vehicle. They took the commuter train from the airport to Central Rail Station, which deposited them close to the Hotel Atlantic Hamburg, between the station and AuBenalster Lake.

They walked to the hotel after Raymond and Alexander arrived at the station. As they rounded the corner, they saw the hotel's unmistakable calling card: a figurehead of two bare-breasted women on the bow of a gigantic ocean liner, with a globe of the world between them and the word ATLANTIC beneath them, displayed in large block letters.

The US ambassador shouted, "fabulous!" as the hotel came into view. As they walked to the grand entrance and beyond, Kirk marveled at the superb landscaping of the tree-lined front, the architecture, and the luxury appointments of the hotel itself. He spun around, pointing to the various exquisite features. "Look at the crown molding, the inlays, the draperies, and marble floors. Is there some way I could serve my appointment in this fine place? What are the chances?"

The ambassador smiled at Raymond, hoping for a positive response, but Raymond crushed his hopes. "I would say your chances are nil. It's obvious why the consulate is situated in Berlin. You'll be in the center of the action, on the pulse of each move by the Reich."

Kirk frowned. "I know, that's what terrifies me."

They walked silently down the hallway to room 160, and as they approached, Raymond noticed the door ajar. He put his finger to his lips. "Shhh. Stay here." Hugging the wall, he peeked around the corner of the entrance. He spotted a woman approaching a Nazi, who had his 9mm trained on her. *If I surprise him, he might shoot her.*

That's when he noticed a door chime. He pressed it, and it *ding-donged.* He cleared his throat and waved to the ambassador to proceed, telling him, "That must be Cecile, Rolf's wife." The two men entered the suite. Raymond kept his eye on the Nazi, who hurried to a strategic vantage point where he could train his gun on everyone in the room.

Standing behind Raymond, the ambassador pulled a sterling silver, Tiffany-crafted badge from his breast coat pocket, identifying him as Diplomatic Security Service, Special Agents Division, Department of State. As a US ambassador, he carried credentials for times such as this.

Raymond stepped softly toward the Nazi, noticing he was only a boy and couldn't be much older than seventeen or eighteen. "Son, we're here on business from the United States. Tell me your name." He nodded toward Kirk. "This is the US ambassador to Germany, Alexander Kirk, and I'm Raymond Wellington, State Department of the United States."

"Yeah, so what? I'm Officer Henrik Kempler." He squinted to see the words engraved on Kirk's badge. "You are free to contact the Reichsführer, Henrich Himmler, with your questions. For now, I'm taking this woman into custody."

He waved the pistol at Maddie, motioning toward the door.

CHAPTER THIRTY-EIGHT

Traveling Is a Delight On the Hamburg–American Lines

MAY 1939, ABOARD THE S.S. ST. LOUIS

THE MESSAGE FROM one of the Nazi henchmen caused Otto Schiendick's voice to rise to an ear-splitting screech. "What do you mean you didn't wait for the confirmation? If you didn't wait, then where is the original? Don't you understand how important this is? The Reich must demand that the *S.S. St. Louis* returns to Hamburg as soon as I get the documents from Hoffman; now you've gone and mucked up the works. Get out of my face before I murder you!"

Schiendick threw a beer stein at the wall, shattering it. His cabin was in general disarray, like Schiendick himself. He pulled at his hair in frustration, knowing full well that the Abwehr axe would fall on his Saxony German neck if this operation failed. *Damn him!*

Schiendick motioned to his remaining henchman, Peter Von Hegler, and slowly drew his index finger across his throat, instructing Hegler, "Upon our return. He can't be trusted. Take care of him. In the meantime, while you're at it, find out what happened to the original document and see if the first officer has it in his possession. I'm going to take care of the other problem now."

Nazi Representative and Abwehr cohort Otto Schiendick

made his way to the D-deck cabin of Stefan Soutine. At the late hour, everyone on that deck had either gone to bed or passed out from inebriation, the result of the final celebration before landing in Cuba. He peered side to side using his passkey: the coast was clear. He silently opened the door, slipping inside, intentionally leaving it ajar, and pulled a small flashlight from his pocket. He reached under his left arm to retrieve his pistol. With the silencer attached, no one would hear the gun when it fired.

He shone his light on the body in the bed; the covers were drawn, and the room was cool. He could hear the person's soft, rhythmic snoring in deep sleep. Schiendick whispered to the form on the bed, his voice laced with venom and dripping with sarcasm, "We have ways of handling snitches and spies, especially Jewish ones and concentration camp prisoners. It's a pleasure to end your life. Enjoy hell."

Standing next to the bedside, he aimed his pistol. He was about to shoot when the room light flashed on, and Captain Gustav Schroder flung back the bedcovers. Jumping to his feet swiftly, the captain grabbed the gun from Schiendick and pointed it at him.

The captain nodded at Jockl, who made a call to the bridge. Then, he took the handcuffs that the first mate had given to him, snapping them around Schiendick's wrists.

The captain waved the unsent telegram. He held it up in front of Schiendick so he could see for himself. "Sloppy work again, Mr. Schiendick. Or is it intentional? Your way of telling me what you're up to, your next move?"

As soon as the captain lowered the unsent telegram, Schiendick spat thick mucus in his face. He glared at him, seething like a pot ready to boil over. "You're a disgrace to Germany, the German military, and that uniform you wear.

You will regret every action taken against me."

The captain's eyes bored into Schiendick, and he barked, "And you will regret speaking another word. You will be tried for attempting to assault and murder a ship captain, with witnesses watching. Your actions amount to mutiny, attempted murder in the first degree, and anything else I decide. While I couldn't put you in the brig for insubordination, I can for attempted murder. Game. Set. Match." He smiled audaciously at Schiendick and waved a small goodbye.

First Mate Lang and two stewards arrived as planned to escort Schiendick to the brig. The captain issued orders. "If he speaks a word, gag him; if he gives you any trouble, use the straitjacket."

"Not, that, please," Schiendick whimpered, his expression crestfallen. He confesses and stutters, "I get—I get claustrophobic."

First Mate Lang and the stewards saluted the captain, and he dismissed them. Leo Jockl applauded his boss. "Oh, how the mighty have fallen! Well done, sir. Can you tell me how you came up with this idea to trap Schiendick or how you knew what he'd do?"

The captain's wry smile told the young steward that there was no formula. Just sage advice from a man who had sailed the seven seas. He said with a twinkle in his eyes, "Know your men better than they know themselves."

Havana, Cuba

At the chosen location, it was easy for Buster to spot a man wearing a green Tyrolean alpine hat with a red feather and a Leica camera around his neck on the massive pier. It was 7:30 a.m., and the pier bustled with crusty dock workers, spiffy cruise ship crews, and suspicious hawkers of goods or souvenirs who encroached on weary travelers with restless children. And Nazis. Nazis were as ubiquitous as the brilliant sunshine.

The spring days heat up quickly once the equatorial sun assumes its position perched above Havana, adding to the humidity of the time of year. The rainy season is already in swing. There are only two seasons in Cuba: wet and dry.

Steam rose from the warmed pavement and the wooden planks. Grateful for the island breezes and cross-winds, Buster observed the man with the Tyrolean hat while he stayed at a distance, perched on a slight incline near a food stall. The man was at the right location, almost an hour early, but he looked nothing like the man Hoffman he'd observed for two weeks.

Buster smoked a cigarette and contemplated his next move. If he ventured down to the HAPAG Office to look for Hoffman, the assistant manager, he might miss connecting with the man dressed as the contact. *This is awkward. Who is this joker?* Buster spotted magazines under the man's arm, pens in a breast coat pocket, and an umbrella. He knew from his training that those would be the three most obvious places for his contact to hide the intelligence secrets to hand off to the Abwehr agent.

Perhaps Hoffman became ill, and this man is the stand-in. If so, there would be no point in going to the office to search for him there. But he can't know what I look like. How could he? So, I can stay here and watch him. Perhaps things will be revealed in time.

The contact milled around the general area, taking pictures or pretending to; Buster made sure to stay out of the camera's viewing area. After three cups of dark-roasted Cuban coffee, Buster threw the paper cup down as he saw a man dressed in a plain suit and trench coat approach the contact. *Who is this? This is not the contact!* They walked together briefly before the contact handed the magazines, pens, and umbrella to the man, who looked decidedly German.

My supervisors never discussed what I should do in this situation, but I need to follow the secrets. Buster followed the man for a few moments until he walked down the pier, where others were waiting for a tender to transport them to the cruise ship anchored at a roadstead. *What in the world? How did this happen? This isn't going as planned. I must contact my support. I better head back to the hotel.*

First, Buster stopped to ask a person on the pier what they were waiting for, if it was for a skiff or tender to the *S.S. St. Louis* moored at the roadstead, and when it would arrive. Since Buster had asked the question in Spanish, the man looked at his watch and said, "Sesenta minutos."

Great. One hour. Buster returned to the Ambos Mundos Hotel, bypassing the front desk and the bar until a bellhop caught him halfway up the winding staircase to the second floor. "Señor, a message for you." Buster slipped him some coins in exchange for the envelope.

The fan was on in his tidy room, causing the wafting aromas of food cooking in the restaurant below to encompass his space and make his stomach growl. The room had a wrought-iron balcony that overlooked an endless stream of drama: car accidents, bikers knocked off their peddler, a policeman's whistle, people yelling at each other, and the constant reminder of the feline empire that inhabited the Ambos Mundos Hotel.

Buster spotted a few of the hotel's felines. *Hollenius would not be happy here. He'd not care for the loss of the undivided attention of whatever human's fascinating him at present.* He kicked off his shoes and poured a glass of water from the pitcher that resided on the festive tray atop the table near the kitchenette. In the background, happy Cuban music drifted up to his windows from the street below.

He ripped open the envelope; all it contained was a piece of paper with a woman's lipstick kiss. He crumpled the paper and tossed it in the trash can under the bathroom sink. The kiss must be Sylvanna's, and he had no intention of returning her affections.

Contemplating his next move, Buster considered the time it took to get a call through to Europe. While placing the call to London, the thought occurred to him. *Suppose the stand-in for Wolfie didn't make it or was found out, and this was the real contact, the real Abwehr representative who met with the contact as originally planned? But what happened to Hoffman? And what happened to Wolfie's replacement? What would Wolfie do?*

With haste, Buster slipped his shoes on and raced back to the dock in search of the man in the suit who'd met with the man in the Tyrolean hat.

The Hotel Atlantic Hamburg

Raymond tried to reason with the youth. "My name is Wellington, Raymond Wellington. I'm a United States attorney and work for the government. My daughter tells me you're the son of a famous artist."

Henrik snarled, "Do you mean a famous dead artist? Yes, that was my father. What of it?"

Raymond pulled out his cigarettes and offered Henrik a smoke.

"No thanks. Let's go, you." He nodded at Maddie.

Raymond stepped in front of Henrik and his pistol. The others in the room stayed silent, motionless, as Raymond put his hands up in appeal. "Henrik. We can work this out. Diplomatically speaking, because our countries are not at war with each other, the United States ambassador here has legal jurisdiction over this woman, an American citizen. I'd hate for you to be court-martialed for such interference in international laws and rulings.

"The same holds true for Stanford Wellington, whom you hold captive without just cause and who is also an American citizen. Would you be willing to stand trial to defend your actions? I think not, so I recommend you release him immediately. May I add, Officer, I've noticed you're without your Schirmmütze." Raymond pointed to the top of the officer's head. "Isn't that a blatant violation of the rules of the Reich?"

Henrik's hand flew to his head while he deliberated. The young officer glared at Raymond, knowing he'd been outdone. He surrendered Maddie, and his eyes narrowed as he considered his next move. "You'll have to come to the station for the other one. But you'll have to trade me something before I let him go."

Raymond assured him, "That can be arranged. What do you have in mind?"

Hamburg Schutzpolezei

Henrik stood behind the nondescript desk, nestled next to a four-drawer metal filing cabinet. That, plus a telephone, rounded out the archaic office. Henrik filled out the paperwork to release Stani. "Fulfilled sentence" was stamped onto the form and filed in a drawer.

Raymond marveled that Henrik had the authority to grant Stani's release. "Well, of course I do; I'm usually the only guard on duty." To make a point, Raymond questioned, "So you're not an officer, you're a guard?"

Henrik disregarded the question and instead said, "Regarding the offer, you know, the trade I mentioned." His voice cracked, and he made a fist, punching the inside of his other hand. He looked down to hide his misty eyes. "I want to meet my mother. That's the deal. You're a big-shot American lawyer. You can arrange it. She lives in the United States with you. She works at the Eastman School of Music. I sent her a letter, pretending to be my father, hoping to lure her to Hamburg so that I could meet her."

Raymond had been prepared to hand over two cartons of Marlboro cigarettes. Caught wrongfooted, he asked, his voice overlapping with surprise, "Your mother? And whom would that be?"

Henrik spoke her name, almost sounding reverent. "Anatolia Genhart."

Doing what lawyers do, Raymond framed the situation, constructing an argument. "My goodness. Well, now, that presents quite a problem. For one, you're a Nazi; you've sworn allegiance to Hitler with a pledge to support and protect Germany and its people. You sign a pledge that states you possess no Jewish blood. You are commanded to hate the Jews. However, there's a small problem. You are, in fact, Jewish because your mother, Anatolia Genhart, is Jewish. How do you square that circle or work that out? How do you reconcile that with the Reich? Hanging or firing squad will appear to be your choice if you confess to falsifying documents. What say you?"

After seventeen days in an ancient, damp, and moldy prison cell, Stani was beyond weak, so Rolf and Raymond used a taxi to transport him back to the hotel, while Ambassador Kirk stayed behind to secure rooms for the three men. Rolf had brought a robe from the hotel to wrap around Stani. Henrik, the guard, told Raymond, "He came with no suitcase or belongings," which was a lie. Henrik had confiscated Stani's small suitcase. So, the ambassador was tasked with rounding up some clothes for him in the men's department of a store near the hotel.

During the taxicab ride, Stani was quiet. Raymond and Rolf engaged in small talk. Raymond explained to Stani how he came to Hamburg with the American ambassador and what took place at the hotel with Henrik. Then he broke the news of Henrik: who he was, and the deal he'd tried to make. Stani listened but stayed silent. He remained pensive while juxtaposed between shock and freedom. After fifteen minutes, while he chain-smoked, he told the men, "When freedom is taken from you, without cause or reason, once that freedom is returned, the feeling is...well, I'm overcome with so many thoughts. For weeks, my mind only had one thought: will I get out today? And I would think that every day, expecting to be released. I cannot tell you I did like Paul and Silas did when they were imprisoned."

Raymond told Stani, "And who would expect Herculean-type strength from you? You've been through more than we can imagine, and we are so grateful to have you back. The ambassador will have a room ready for you to shower and change."

Raymond added, his tone cautionary and eyebrows raised: "The ambassador is in charge of your wardrobe, so be prepared." He turned to face Stani, taking one of his hands in his, and said, his voice filled with emotion, "We are so happy, and we do thank God to have you back with us."

CHAPTER THIRTY-NINE

No Time to Lose

MAY 1939, HAVANA, CUBA

THE *S.S. St. Louis* was moored at the roadstead, hundreds of yards from shore. Out of 937 passengers that boarded the ship on Saturday, May 13, 1939, twenty-eight were allowed to disembark from the ship to enter Havana on Saturday, May 27th. These fortunate passengers had legal visas, a ticket for the voyage, a worthless landing permit, and ten marks per passenger. Stefan Soutine was the luckiest of all. The Dachau camp commandant, Theodor Eicke, had given him all the credentials he needed to secure passage on the *S.S. St. Louis*.

Eicke was fully aware of Operation Sunshine, that the ship was never intended to land in Havana, and that it would not allow the passengers to disembark. That's why he had ensured Stefan's credentials were above reproach. After all, Stefan had saved the lives of himself and his family, so for once, Eicke kept his word even if it was to a French-German prisoner who was a great chef.

Purser Mueller came to Stefan Soutine's cabin to bid him farewell. "If you're ever in Portsmouth, England, there's a pub named Wurst End. You'll find me there from July through September when I take over my brother's pub while he vacations in the Scottish Highlands. But I doubt we'll ever see each other again, so I wish you all the best, hoping your days are easier than they've been."

He stopped, raising his hand. "Let's see, there was something else. Oh, yes! Do you plan to stay in Havana? If you do, check out the Hotel Ambos Mundos. You can rent a room there; they always need kitchen help, maybe even a chef! Oscar Martinez runs the hotel and is a personal friend. Take my card and present it; perhaps he'll offer you a job. Also, take this, open it later." He handed Stefan a sealed envelope.

After Stefan bid him the same, the two shook hands. "I'm grateful for your help and friendship," Stefan said. "You made this voyage pleasant for me despite the problems with Schiendick. Thank you. And by the way, what was the name of the Hotel? Ambos Mu—something..."

The purser offered, "Ambos Mundos. One final word of caution and warning, speaking of Schiendick. He will have shore leave for four hours, ordered by the Abwehr. The captain is none too pleased; he should be in the brig, but the Abwehr operates by different rules. But do be careful and watch your back."

At the pier, the sun became hotter by the minute as Buster searched frantically for the man in the suit who'd met with the contact, supposedly Hoffman. He casually conversed with a well-to-do elderly woman waiting on the pier. Her perfume overwhelmed him, making his nose twitch. Ignoring the miasma, he asked the silver-haired woman, "Has the boat returned to take passengers to the ship?" He pointed to the *S.S. St. Louis*, moored at the roadstead.
She shook her head and gave Buster the once-over, side-eyeing him. He blushed and bid her farewell.

The temperature kept rising by the hour, giving way to intensifying humidity while the people on the pier were sucking up all the oxygen. Buster panted for air as he shimmied and slithered through the crowd of immovable people, no one willing to give up an inch of ground.

In such close quarters, Buster knew well to keep his hand on his wallet and credentials. For some reason, a bee was insistent on following him. He swatted at it, trying to coax it to change its course. *This is all I need.*

He peered over the heads of some gangly teenagers with binoculars, probably looking for family aboard the ship. Some people had even rented small boats and skiffs to try and get alongside the mammoth sea vessel, just for a word or a glimpse of their family or friend.

A larger vessel from the ship was heading for the pier, where Buster stood. That's when he spotted his man standing close to the water's edge. As he moved in, Buster saw the three pens in the man's breast coat pocket, the umbrella in his right hand, and the magazines under his arm. Buster got as close to the man as possible before considering and asking himself *what would Wolfie do?* After a moment, an idea materialized.

He screamed at the top of his lungs, "Bees, bees! I'm allergic to bees! Run for your life! Bees!" Buster pretended to trip, bumping into the man. As he did, he snatched the pens in a flash and nudged the man off the pier and into the murky ocean. Buster turned from the scene and pushed through the crowd, waving his arms like a madman, still shrieking, "Bees, Oh, God! Bees are everywhere! Get them away from me, help! Bees!" The crowd parted, making way.

Buster ran back to the hotel, making it to the entrance steps. He was out of breath but wasted no time scampering to his room and calling his superior officer, staked out in Cuba at an undisclosed location. The call and information would be coded as pre-discussed with a Bletchley contact. His superior officer would then relay the information back to Division D of the SIS at Bletchley.

After making the coded call, Buster learned the time and location of the drop spot, where he'd hand off the pens. Buster felt like celebrating. His first mission was almost complete. *Wolfie would be proud of me. Little does he know that he's inspiring me from afar. Perhaps it's not such a bad idea to think, 'What would Wolfie do?' He is, after all, brilliant.*

Otto Schiendick, in a state of panic, tried valiantly to retrieve the magazines and the umbrella that contained the secrets that were supposed to be delivered to Hamburg as part of Operation Sunshine. The incoming boat caused waves to lap at the pier, pushing his body back instead of forward. The water was too deep for Schiendick, who couldn't swim. The wake of the boat swept the magazines and the umbrella farther out into the deep.

Schiendick splashed about in the water as people on the pier concerned themselves with boarding the boat, ignoring the man in the water who was desperate to find his belongings. No one paid him a bit of attention except for an older woman who observed Schiendick and his frantic efforts to retrieve the irretrievable. She shouted to him over the confusion and noise, "You must be getting paid back for something!" She smiled and waved at him as the boat left the pier, leaving Schiendick to wonder if she was a prophet and if so, what would happen next: a shot in the back of his head or a hanging?

The *S.S. St. Louis's* horn blared so loud it rattled his head and vibrated his eardrums, announcing its departure to an unknown destination. But even that was no match for the thundering cacophony of panic-induced thoughts about the punishment due him, subjugating Otto Schiendick's mind and making him a terrified prisoner of his thoughts.

———✳———

Aboard the S.S. St. Louis

After five days of negotiations between the captain, the Joint Distribution Committee, and the Cuban government, discussions concluded in another stalemate, and no decisions were made. The ship was ordered to leave Cuban waters at once. It drifted up and down the coast of Florida awaiting word; something, anything to offer a scintilla of hope, but it appeared hope had been discarded. The captain yearned to get an answer that would bring optimism to his woebegone passengers and, perhaps, catch the world's attention.

Captain Gustav Schroeder sat behind his desk and massaged his temples, trying to stave off a cortex-splitting migraine. He noted in his log the lack of results after the week-long negotiations with the Cuban government and the Jewish Joint Distribution Committee representatives. By writing, he was able to unload his thoughts privately.

June 3, 1939, 0400 hours

The Cuban president demands $453,500 from the Joint Distribution representative. Five hundred dollars per passenger, knowing full well the Nazis bankrupted each person before leaving Germany. There was no way to extract any more money from the passengers. The Nazis had already taken everything. Will private sources be willing to fund this money?

Then we have the American president, who will not respond to the pleas through telegrams sent from desperate passengers or phone calls from his biggest donors pleading with him to help. Nor will his wife, Eleanor, when sent telegrams from passengers entreating her to at least help the children on board. There is no response, no reply to the passionate pleas for help. Is it because they're Jewish? It's been said she is a 'champion of children.' Perhaps, but with the condition that they're not Jewish? The same can be said for her husband regarding his lack of concern for hundreds of Jewish adults.

As of June 5th, the United States has made no effort to help my passengers. The same response from the Canadians. Add that to the Cubans. It seems we are abandoned at sea, and there is no safe refuge. I question the kind of message and optics this sends to Berlin and the Reich. It howls, 'Jewish lives are expendable. Their lives don't matter, and they don't possess any redeeming value, as confirmed by every country that rejects them.' Does this three-country rejection play into the Nazis' hands?

Orders came today from Berlin to return the ship to Hamburg. I have yet to respond. I will most likely lose my commission over this; damn them for forcing my hand. Meanwhile, the mood on board is fragile at best— primarily sullen and depressing. The anxiousness and expectation of imminent departure transform into anxiety and suspiciousness as the waiting is prolonged from hours to days, contributing to a growing hopelessness that permeates the once-jovial atmosphere aboard. A group of passengers, over one hundred souls, have signed a petition promising to commit suicide by jumping into the sea if the ship returns to Germany. We are rationing our food, fuel, and water, knowing these shortages could become critical as we were forced to leave Cuba before we could fully restock and refuel.

The once-jubilant, hope-filled passengers are now left to

stare at the sea, wondering what will become of their lives. I wonder the same thing. I contemplate the emotional state of my passengers as they see the lights off the coast of Florida as we come close to Miami. Could anything prove to be more painful than being so close yet so far? As for Otto Schiendick, the Nazi representative and Abwehr courier, my superiors ordered me to permit him to go to shore despite the charges against him. He has yet to appear on board. One of his henchmen contacted the Abwehr, who responded with a threatening telegram directed at me. It is beyond evident now that this "special voyage" was nothing more than a sham for propaganda purposes and the transport of culled espionage. The Nazis NEVER intended for the ship to land and for the passengers to begin a new life—a hoax of the cruelest form.

My poor passengers. Haven't they been through enough already? Laurence Berenson and Morris Troper of the Joint Distribution also seem to think so. They are allies. Perhaps they will further assist with placing my passengers anywhere but in Germany. They report that one member of the president's cabinet has done all he could, striving valiantly to make a headwind with the man in charge, but to no avail.

I'm stunned by the antisemitic attitudes of the good people of the State Department of the United States. If, they will provide no help, other actions must be taken, and I'm willing to take them. I cannot and will not allow my passengers to be returned to Nazi hands. I'll crash the ship first off the coast of England and set the ship ablaze, using the reef to get them ashore. In such an emergency, the passengers must be evacuated and rescued as shipwreck survivors. I'm willing to do whatever it takes to procure a safe destination for my passengers—that is my number-one duty, Germany be damned.

Hotel Atlantic Hamburg

Maddie was as quiet as a cat. It was still early in the morning, but she had to see her Stani. She'd been asleep when he returned from the prison with Raymond and Rolf but had seen Rolf's coat on the sofa in the front room when she awoke, confirming their return to the hotel.

Still dressed in her pajamas and robe, her long dark locks bundled in a neat braid, she was wearing the comfy slippers Aunt Cecile had bought her. Sunlight ebbed through the windows, taking its time to rise on the horizon, as she left the suite and the sleeping Rolf and Cecile, hustled down the hallway to the end, to the last room, and knocked softly on the door.

"Stani," she whispered and knocked again. She tried the door, but it was locked.

"Maddie?" Stani's raspy voice barely permeated the thick door, but Maddie heard it. She knocked harder, pressing her ear to the cool wood, listening for movement inside the room. Finally, Stani flung the door open, ecstatic; he struggled to shout, "My Maddie!"

At a loss for words, she embraced her dearest friend, who felt slight and bony in her arms after weeks of near starvation. She nuzzled her nose in his neck.

As if sensing her thoughts, Stani broke the embrace. "Come inside and sit; we must catch up." He took her by the hand and led the tearful Maddie to a chair. "You sit." He took a step back from her, shaking his head, smiling that loving smile he reserved for only her. "Look at you, more beautiful than the last time I saw you."

She laughed at him. "Now I know you're lying!" Maddie took a deep breath and dabbed at her eyes with a hankie. She shielded her eyes with her hand and told him, her voice cracking with emotion, "I've missed you beyond words. My heart was breaking. I've been so worried, even to the point of being sick, especially knowing the Nazis had taken you captive."

He patted her on the shoulder and gave her a winning smile. "I'm here now, and that's all that matters. We are together!" Stani turned on another light, revealing a room with everything in its place. Stani was a model of neatness and organization. He clapped his hands, his pale cheeks slightly blushed with color, his voice brimming with excitement. "Oh, goodness, I can't wait to show you! Just feast your eyes on this." He slid open the closet door to reveal the clothes and suits the ambassador had purchased on his behalf. "I'm a fashion plate! And shoes, look at these shoes!" Looking upward, he said, "God is only good to me."

Maddie blinked away her tears, perplexed by his gratefulness.

Stani handed her beautiful, caramel-brown leather wingtips, "Like the kind the boys wear!" referring to Raymond and Buster. "Look at the craftsmanship! And the fit is perfect!"

Stani stopped, noticing Maddie's expression. "My love, you're pensive; what is it?" She gazed at his face. His blue eyes searched hers. "Tell me, what is it?" He smiled at her, coaxing out the words, as her eyes filled with tears.

"I'm just so thankful. God has done something in my heart. I'm no longer afraid. I understand. I know who I believe in! Yet, you must explain something to me. I cannot understand how you can be exceedingly grateful after being locked in a dungeon for weeks. How can you be so happy? I think I'd be angry and fit to be tied that I got locked up in the first place!"

Stani sat in the chair beside her. "Wait a minute. What's this?

Tell me everything, oh this is what I've prayed for, that your understanding would be opened, and you'd see how much God loves you, how He sent His son to bear the cost of our sinful nature, and by accepting Him, giving us a new way, a new life, and for the blessed hope of eternity with Him and our loved ones! How do you think I've survived such imprisonments, Dachau, here, without the One who gives me hope? The strongest souls are sometimes sent to the darkest places."

Maddie wrinkled her brow. "But I don't understand how that works. How can you be so cheerful, holding no anger?"

Stani's smile was one that only came with experience, and it was a smile of wisdom. "My happiness is not contingent on location or circumstances. I trust that everything that comes to me comes from the hand of my Creator. He is the Alpha and the Omega, the beginning and the end. He knows the in-between too. He knows everything: the before, during, and the after."

He said, almost laughing, "Who am I to question He who holds the worlds together? Who spoke the world into existence? Trust. You need trust. It's a funny thing. Without hardships or trials, how could we ever develop trust? God gives us trials, hoping we will press into Him and seek His help. Remember? He is our Abba Father, meaning *Daddy*. This is why I can have peace in any storm of life. I don't worry about the details.

"Remember the twenty-four? There is no promise for tomorrow; we have all we need in this twenty-four-hour period, and if tomorrow comes, praise God! I know who I have believed in, just like you. That's faith. Believing in what you can't see. Like the wind. You can't see it, but you know it's there. Now. Enough about me. I want to hear about you."

Maddie stared clear through Stani, allowing his words to sink in before she spoke. Yet she was still stuck, not understanding the paradox of trouble juxtaposed with peace. "But Aunt Cecile became angry with me when I mentioned that I believed in Jesus; He is the Messiah. She is Jewish, you are, I am, but you know I know nothing really of the Jewish practices, the laws, the rules. We are born Jewish; we have no choice in the matter."

Like the warmth of the sun's rays, Stani beamed benevolent rays of love at Maddie. He looked at her tenderly. "You are hungry to understand, and I'm thrilled you have so many questions!" Stani used his hands as if to frame his words. "Know this: we will discuss your questions, backed up by scriptural references, by the authority of God's word. Are you aware the Bible is not just God's love letter to humanity, but a record of human development through the ages?"

Maddie cocked her head, questioning, "History is recorded, and the Bible validates it? Is that right?"

Stani nodded. "Yes! You see, it's important to fully understand the height, length, width, depth, and strength of God's love through his word; this is how we can know him! To do so, we study his word and other books that lead us to spiritual wisdom, building on our relationship with Hashem, the Most High. This is how we get to know Him and what is expected of our lives. Torah is the first five books of Moses, the first five books of the Bible. I know it's a lot; I'll try not to teach too much at once. We build upon your faith with each lesson, okay? But one step at a time, Rome wasn't built in a day."

Maddie scowled. "But I want to understand everything now."

Stani laughed. "How long have you played the violin?"

Knowingly, she shook her head. "I get it; I understand what you mean. Okay. I must admit, it's uncomfortable to know there is a vast world out there to discover, and I know so little about it." Her scowl faded, and she returned to her winsome look of love. "I'm on a journey, and I know I could not make this journey without you."

Stani stood to stretch and told her, "You're stronger than you think." He changed the subject, commenting, "This is a lovely hotel, and this bed is like a slice of heaven, especially after my former environs!" He winked at her, and she shook her head.

"I hope I can be like you one day. The word resilient comes to mind."

Stani walked to her and squatted down to her eye level. "You be you, and you'll be better than me. I promise. Tell me what happened to you after I left."

Maddie nodded. "While in Vienna recovering at Rolf and Cecile's, I read the Bible you gave me and spent most of my days trying to absorb it. First, I would pray and ask God to open my understanding so that I'd realize the truth when I read the parts you told me to read, the part about Jesus being the vine and we the branches, and if I trust him, he will abide with me, is that right?"

Stani's eyes brimmed with happy tears. "Yes, that's right!" He reached for her hands, and she stood. They danced a little waltz while he hummed, and Maddie twirled.

Stani's voice was soft. "Know that all God's creatures, great and small, face trials and difficulties. No one is exempt. The answer lies in where our help comes from. Remember that. Okay, so tell me more."

They sat down in the two easy chairs. Maddie began. She couldn't hide a smile. "Remember when you told me last spring it's more important to belong than fit in?"

Stani nodded and picked up his cigarettes, lighting one. "Yes, I do remember."

"For the first time in my life, I feel like I belong, and it's different than belonging to the Wellington family; while there are things that are similar, this is not the same."

Stani asked, "How so?"

"I've never felt like I fit in. Anywhere. Like I'm a square peg in a round hole. You know how I've felt about this. How it's different from being in the Wellington family is that there are times when I may argue with a member, and we'll be cross with each other, which may go on for a few days at a time. You're not concerned with fitting in with your family; they're supposed to love you. For me, fitting in involved how I felt about the world, about being accepted and using my talent to fit in. And in that world, the stunning reality is I never fit in, nor will I, and I don't care.

"The world, those I sought acceptance from, my peers, and Europe as a whole—they don't care about me. They only care about what they can get from me. Well, I know now that God does not treat me like that. I know that when I say I'm wrong and when I confess, I am forgiven. I belong no matter what. Therefore, I do not fear him turning his back on me or abandoning me when I do something wrong or out of sheer ignorance, which happens quite often, but I do hope that as I learn and grow, those moments lessen over time." And softly, she added, "I know I am loved with an everlasting, unconditional love, just like you said."

Stani nodded, encouraging her to share more. She went on, "The pain of my past was something I had to confront. I had to take it out of the shadows and remember it, bring it into the light, and confront the nightmares I've had since, well..." Her voice trailed off. "Most of my life. It was an introspective journey, nothing I could talk about except to God."

Stani was careful not to ask too much. He hedged gently, "Can you tell me what you remember?"

She tilted her head, speaking sarcastically, Which part? The attack or where I burn the orphanage to the ground? I'm sorry, I shouldn't be sarcastic about that."

Then Maddie smiled a smile that warmed Stani, and he told her, "Your smile, do you know how beautiful you are?"

Maddie's eyes narrowed, and she deflected his comment. "Do you want to hear what I remember or not?"

Stani laughed at her sharp response. "Oh, my Maddie." He nodded. "Please, go on."

Maddie took a deep breath. "It's not so much of what I remember. It's more like how much I need to forget. Does that make sense?" He nodded, and she continued. "Yes, what happened at the orphanage wounded me deeply; I didn't think I could ever let another man touch me, let alone trust a man."

She pushed the tears away. "I cannot change the orphanage and what took place. But I can change how I think about it, how I feel about it. Ignoring or constantly focusing on it is the same and changes nothing. I've used the violin and my music to hide in and to keep myself from everyone and everything. It was my shield of protection. And while I adore my music and playing, I feel differently now.

"All these things, the broken places, don't define me; they don't tell me who I am. I am a child of God, and my life has been made new. None of the past is in my new life. Those are the former things. You've taught me that, like a newborn babe, I will grow in time, and I desire that so much."

CHAPTER FORTY

All Creatures Great and Small

*JUNE 3, 1939, HAVANA, CUBA, HOTEL AMBOS MUNDOS,
THE OFFICE OF MANAGER OLIVER MARTINEZ*

IF YOU ARE a friend of Purser Mueller's, you are a friend of mine. I am happy to extend the famous Cuban hospitality to you." The words resounded in Stefan Soutine's ears as he surveyed the small, neat-as-a-pin room on the hotel's second floor.

Tomorrow, Stefan would meet again with Martinez, who would take him to meet the chef of the hotel's restaurant. Stefan walked around the sparsely decorated and simply furnished apartment. He was joyful and could say what freedom felt like for the first time in a long while. No weight of worry, no fear, no bondage to keep him chained in a prison or to a habit. Nothing was holding him down or back. That was freedom.

After getting a pen and hotel stationery, Stefan opened the windows, soaking in the sounds and aromas of cooking, cigar smoke, and the sea. The light streaming in was warming, and his skin felt good after months of dank Dachau and days in the innards of a ship.

It was said of Havana that festive music could always be heard from morning until the wee hours, like a city that never slept. The hotel was conveniently located close to the pier and mercados, and little shops were lined up and down the street. There were areas of Havana that had twenty-four-hour activities, entertainment, restaurants, and seedy speakeasies.

Stefan sat at the table with a foldout leaf, making it a table for two. He wrote to Purser Mueller and then sealed the envelope. He'd drop it at the front desk, and the manager would know how to get the letter to the Purser.

The aroma of luscious grilled meat filled the air, whetting his tastebuds. *I think it's time to celebrate, enjoy my freedom, and have a drink and a nice dinner. Not since my days in Paris have I felt so alive, so free!*

After a shower and changing clothing, Stefan was ready to face his new world. He observed his image in the mirror. *At least my hair has grown back, and the bruises have faded. I shouldn't scare too many people.*

The Bar at Hotel Ambos Mundos
Buster sat with his back to the bar, observing the foot traffic sauntering past the open spaces near the seating area cordoned off with a braided rope between two weighted stands. It was early, and the usual five o'clock drinkers had yet to show. It was virtually the bartender, Leticia, and himself.

From the vantage point of the street, the bar, attached to the western side of the hotel, sat back behind curtains that surrounded removable floor-to-eight-foot-high window panes. Surrounded by royal palms, the curtains hung on a frame and were tied back at the corners with thick, braided golden tassels. The bar had a definite speakeasy feel, complete with palm-leaf fans and dimly lit Naugahyde booths tucked away behind the oval-shaped bar, which were favorite spots to gather late into the night for romantic trysts or after-hour rendezvous, not to mention business deals of all kinds, legal and not-so-legal.

Carlos, the bartender, came on duty, relieving Leticia. "Hello, Señor Ben. Can I get you anything? Another of what you're drinking?"

The lilt in his voice offered just enough encouragement for Buster to break his rule of only one cocktail or two beers. Bletchley had taught him to be clear-minded and sober at all times. Buster turned to face Carlos. "Yes, I think I'll have one more, seeing it's my last night here."

Buster intentionally omitted the details, and Carlos knew better than to ask, especially if he wanted a good tip. "A Beefeaters martini, two anchovy olives, right?"

Buster nodded. "Right you are, with just a kiss of vermouth."

Another voice rang out, one with a soft but definite masculine tone. "Hey, that sounds good. I'll take one too."

Carlos and Buster's eyes met. Buster tilted his head toward the outspoken man. He said to Carlos in Spanish, "No slow play," referring to the slow-moving Cuban style when a new customer came to the bar; the service typically slowed to a snail's pace. "Give him a drink. We're celebrating."

The stranger spoke again. "What are you celebrating? I'm celebrating, too." He extended his hand toward Buster. "My name is Stefan."

Buster shook with him. "I'm Ben. It's nice to meet you." He nodded toward Carlos. "Our barkeep is the ineffable Carlos, maker of delightful potions and libations. Your drink is on me. I take it you're new to the island?"

Carlos delivered the martinis, and Buster made a toast, "To going home!"

The men clinked their glasses, each almost draining their cocktail. Buster offered Stefan a cigarette, but he declined and asked, "Where is home for you?"

Buster sniffed. "'Going home' is more of an expression than a truism. How about you? Where do you hail from, and what brings you to this fair island?" Buster took a deep drag on his cigarette and studied Stefan's face, hands, and attire.

Stefan noticed. "Yes, I'm here to work, hopefully in the hotel kitchen. I plan on living here as long as I'm happy."

Buster straightened up, leaning in. "Sounds to me like you're free as a bird. Is that right?"

Another voice chimed in, coming from behind them seated in a booth. With a recognizable bone-chilling quality, the voice said, "Oh, he's not as free as he thinks he is, and neither are you."

Unsung Heroes

JUNE 13, 1939, ABOARD THE S.S. ST. LOUIS

CAPTAIN SCHROEDER, WHO had yet to arrive, had called together a group of passengers, hand-picked for the qualities exhibited during the voyage as observed by Steward Leo Jockl and Purser Mueller. They had picked stable, even-minded souls to break the news about the ship's direction and their hopeful destinations. Purser Mueller and First Mate Lang were present. Missing from the observers was Otto Schiendick, who, as Nazi representative, would certainly include himself in such meetings. No one lamented his absence.

Stewards prepared the Assembly Hall like they would for a business meeting, using u-shaped seating, put together with three six-foot, rectangular tables draped with white tablecloths. Stripped of its usual decorations, the room was comfortable yet stark. The captain would stand at a podium before the composed group of passengers. Each place had a glass, a water pitcher for every third person, and ashtrays for every two people. There was seating for twelve passengers.

———❋———

Captain Gustav Schroeder stood before his mirror every day after dressing. *I'm looking tired, like an old man. And weary. Well, why wouldn't I be? This voyage was supposed to end weeks ago, yet here we are. At least I have hopeful news versus no news. Some may ascribe to the belief that no news is good news; however, in this case, no news is bad. If we can only get them safe passage, then let the chips fall where they will, which will mean the end of my career at sea, but I take that as a harbinger for good if that's the case. Do I want to serve in the Nazi regime? Let them dismiss me. At this point, I couldn't care less.*

—————❖—————

The lights in the hall were dim; the captain strode into the room and immediately motioned to turn them up. To his first mate, he said, "Good. Now, we can see one another eye to eye."

He pulled Purser Mueller aside as he scoped the room, speaking in low tones. "I've just received a telegram from a US State Department contact. This was leaked, and I quote Franklin Delano Roosevelt's comment regarding the *S.S. St. Louis* to his secretary of state. The *S.S. St. Louis* and its stranded passengers, all German Jews: 'I don't want them in the Western Hemisphere. They have to leave.' The captain shook his head, placing the telegram in his coat pocket.

The United States government did not only refuse their entry; they even sent a Coast Guard cutter to keep the ship away from Florida's shore, firing warning shots, using their loudspeakers to tell the *S.S. St. Louis* to leave US waters.

The purser was not surprised by the news. "Well, we can certainly attest to the validity of that warning shot!"

"So much for American goodwill." Their moment of silence only further bonded them in duty and service. Their eyes met, and their steely exchange spoke of their dedication and commitment to the passengers' well-being and, if necessary, safekeeping.

The captain held a telegram with the latest information and numbers from the American and European Jewish Joint Distribution Committee. He stepped to the podium, and the chatter stopped. Not all the passengers had seen or met the captain in person. Many thought he'd be at least six feet tall based on his booming baritone voice, which could be heard frequently over the loudspeakers throughout the public spaces—part of a daily ritual, greeting his guests before Purser Mueller took over with announcements or events taking place on the ship. Did they think stern command and exacting standards could raise a person's height? Not height, but perhaps stature.

Captain Schroeder was dressed in spotless whites, looking like a royal commander, Napoleonic in height, with a matching roar. His graying temples and mustache contributed to the appearance of a wise and learned officer of the seas, wearing wisdom modestly. He cleared his throat. "Ladies and gentlemen, crew members, I bring good news."

As he spoke, the captain established eye contact to connect with the people in his care. "As you know, we have attempted numerous times to sort this out with various countries and diplomats. I've promised you that we will not return to Germany under any condition. Desperate pleas have been made on your behalf. Those efforts came to no avail until now. In my hand is a telegram from the European and American JJDC announcing the European countries have agreed to accept you with no conditions."

One man raised his hand, asking, hopeful, "Did the Americans come to our rescue?"

The captain refrained from cringing; his pained mien said it all as he quietly stated, "No. They did not. However, England, France, Belgium, and Holland did, and we can all be most appreciative. I'll read you the telegram from Mr. Morris Troper of the JJDC: 'Final arrangements for disembarkation of all passengers complete.'"

The group and the two officers began to clap, and the

passengers stood, cheering and applauding the captain for his efforts. Not once had he given in or given up on finding a port of safety for his passengers. He raised his hands to quiet the room. "The plans are as follows: we will steam ahead to Antwerp, Belgium, arriving June 17th, where we will dock, and all passengers will be sorted and transported with the help of the Red Cross. From there, you'll be delivered to your destination. I'll provide more information as soon as I receive it. There will be a division of passengers, with 288 going to Great Britain, 244 to France, 214 to Belgium, 181 to Holland. The Distribution Committee will make the assignments. I have no say in the matter, and all assignments are final. Now would be a good time for all of us to be grateful for a solution. Questions, one at a time, please."

He waited for a moment; a passenger asked one question. Joseph Karliner stated, "Antwerp is only a few hundred miles from Germany. Will we have protection when we arrive and await transportation to the next destination? Will we be placed together as a family or split up?"

The captain signaled to the purser and whispered something. Purser Mueller left the room as the captain turned to Karliner and said, "How many are in your family, Mr. Karliner?"

"There are six of us: my wife, my two boys, Walter and Herbert, and our daughters, Ilse and Martha."

"I'll look into that and let you know directly." The captain turned, his eyes narrowing as he scanned the twelve before him, their expressions carrying the weight of the world. "Are there any more questions? Then that is all. I'll say goodbye."

Purser Mueller returned and nodded to the captain, mouthing, "Done." The captain was the first to leave while his officers closed the doors, holding the group back to allow him to gain some distance before dismissing them.

Mueller told Lang, "At least give the man a running start. God knows how fast the news will travel. They'll chase after him. He's got enough on his mind."

Lang nodded at the purser. "I agree."

Mueller asked, "On a different note, I've yet to see Schiendick. Did he board?"

Lang pretended to consider, knowing Schiendick had never boarded. "I don't believe I have. Certainly, he would have attended a meeting between the captain and the passengers." Lang snickered to himself as the twelve passengers filed out of the room.

Mueller eyed Lang, observing his giggling. "Okay, Lang, what's so funny."

It took Lang a minute to regain composure, and Mueller became impatient. "Come on, tell me!"

Lang glanced around, making sure no one was within earshot. "I went ashore about the same time as Schiendick. We were allowed four hours, so my time was up, and I was at the pier waiting for the skiff to take me back to the ship."

Mueller offered Lang a cigarette. "Thanks." He leaned over for a light, puffing, and then exhaled. "So, I'm observing Schiendick from a distance when I see a man barrel into him. He tripped or something, and Schiendick is dropped into the drink. The funny thing was that neither the man nor any people standing around paid any attention to him, nor did anyone offer to help."

Lang blew a few smoke rings, as did Mueller, and for a minute, they played a game of the biggest and longest smoke rings. Mueller asked, "So what happened to him?"

Lang ground out the butt in an ashtray on a table. "That's the funny thing. He was flailing like a drowning cow in chest-deep water, trying to reach something, which could have been whatever he was holding at the time. But dare I say, he was afraid to go under the water; perhaps he's a land-locked Nazi who can't swim. The ship blew its departure horn, and still, no Schiendick. The captain should notify the land forces that we have a deserter."

Both men couldn't contain their laughter as they imagined Schiendick being carted away by local authorities for abandoning his post.

Rochester, New York

"Wolfie, lunch is ready. Come in and quit your sunbathing." Frederick laughed as he closed the screen door and returned to the stove in the sun-washed kitchen. He'd made his specialty: scrambled eggs with potatoes, peppers, onions, and Münster cheese with griddled bread.

Hollenius remained perched in his spot above the cabinet, spying on Frederick's every move and paying close attention to the pan with the goods as Frederick first dished up a plate for Wolfie. The cat knew he came next: just eggs. Frederick told him, "To make it a little German, we only need some Westphalian ham! Why cats like pork is a mystery. You'd like some of that, wouldn't you?"

Frederick deposited a spoonful of eggs in a bowl with a crown and the inscription "I Rule." Fur flew, and His Highness descended from the shelf to the counter to the floor, prancing like a king to his treat. Frederick stood beside the kitchen window, telling Hollenius, "He's doing pretty well on those crutches. It won't be long before he's running and playing soccer, like the old days."

Frederick scowled, catching himself. "Whoops. I didn't mean to mention old. We're as young as we feel, right, old boy?" He swooped down and scooped up his cat, his keeper of secrets. "Come here, you, big orange ball of fur." Frederick nuzzled his face in the cat's fur until Hollenius had had enough. A playful nip at a finger was his usual warning shot. Only one. It translated, "Put me down this instant, or I'll swat you as you've never been swatted before."

Frederick obeyed and put him down gently. The cat immediately wound between Frederick's socked feet and dungaree-wearing legs. Frederick bent down to scratch his head, and Hollenius responded with a "Purr-urrr-urr," making Frederick crack a grin. "What an engine. If we could only bottle that sound."

Wolfie came through the screen door, hopping on his one good foot over the threshold. "Mmm. Smells good. I love Sundays. Did you make your famous eggs?" Washing his hands, he said, "Sure hope there's more coffee. I could use it."

He sat at the table, and his dad took the food from the oven; an aluminum pie pan covered it, and Frederick removed it, setting the plate in front of Wolfie. "Great. I'm starving." Wolfie picked up his fork to dig in, then stopped. He glanced at his dad. "Uh. Hmm, Pop. Hey, until we hear any news, I'd like to continue the tradition of praying before we eat. I think it would make Stani happy."

Frederick irreverently lit a cigarette, waved his hand to cede all power, and told his son, "Pray away, I'll listen."

Wolfie bowed his head. Putting his hands in his lap, he began, "Lord, thank you for the food we are about to receive. Bless our loved ones and keep them all safe. Bring us together again soon, and please soften my father. Amen."

Frederick muttered, "Amen."

Wolfie plowed into the plate of food. "I'm pleased my appetite has returned, and food tastes good again. I could eat another plate of this!" he said as he munched away, happy and grateful. He wiped his mouth and took a sip of coffee. "So Pop, tell me the plan again and how this happened." Wolfie referred to what had started as a simple conversation with the pilot Matthew Russo on the flight home to Rochester and had turned into the creation of a race-car team.

Frederick was about to begin when the phone rang. "Hello? Raymond! Thank God. Is everything okay? Everyone safe?" It had been days since they'd heard from him.

Standing next to the phone's table in the little cubby space in the kitchen, he nodded and bit a hangnail. "Uh-huh. Yep, that's right. Okay. Sounds good. We look forward to seeing you then." And then Frederick said something entirely out of character. He wished him "Godspeed."

Too Good to Be True

A BELLMAN WAS WAITING outside the door of suite 160. "Any more bags, ma'am?"

Cecile gave the suite and two bedrooms a once-over, checking the closet, the drawers in the vanity, and the dresser. "That's it; please take them to the lobby, where my husband is waiting."

Cecile waited for the bellman to leave. She hesitated while she said goodbye to the suite. *I loved staying here, enjoying Hamburg, and experiencing a little bit of nightlife. I'm sad to leave. I regret that I will be heading back to Vienna on a train instead of a plane to America with Raymond, Stani, and Maddie.*

Why am I so stubborn? Why do I always have to have my way? Why can't I give an inch? I know Rolf's wanted to sell our place and leave, and I've fought him tooth and nail, even after the murder of Josef and Minka. I have nothing to lose and everything to gain by being honest. And I'll have to confess to Rolf he was right all along.

Rolf's voice pierced her silence and thoughts. "Hey, Cecile, let's get a move on." His tenor voice reverberated down the hallway, blatantly disregarding the hour or the other guests. Cecile modified her desire to shush him.

She said to the suite, "This is where we part and say farewell."

She was about to close the door when Rolf sidled up beside

her. "And just who were you speaking to?" He didn't wait for an answer. "Are you ready?"

He sensed her hesitation. "Okay, what is it? Do we need to go inside for a moment?" Cecile nodded. He said, "Okay, on one condition, make it brief. They're all waiting for us."

Cecile side-eyed her husband, kissed his cheek, and pushed the door open with her red, high-heeled shoe.

———❧———

Sitting in the roomy limousine provided by Ambassador Kirk, Raymond read the letter Kirk had left for him, explaining why he'd offered such an extravagant gift.

The envelope had contained two letters, one labeled "for all eyes," the other, "at your discretion." Raymond skimmed the second letter first, then read the first one softly, speaking the words:

I'm calling it a parting gift for the pleasure of your company and the privilege of meeting your Maddie and Stani. They are fearless warriors for the cause of good. I'm grateful they are sheltered under your wing, especially during perilous times, which I fear will only escalate. Know that I am at your service should any need arise during my stay as ambassador. The position could be short-lived, but I hope cooler heads prevail for your son's sake.

Thank you for entrusting me with the message he gave you, 'Please, do what you can to keep us out of war.' The sum of his words struck me as poignant and simple yet extremely powerful, just as a young man's words should be. I can see why you're proud of him!

I wish you well and safe travels across the skies for his sake, Maddie's, Stani's, and your extended family.

I remain yours,

Alexander Comstock Kirk

"Well, that's that," Raymond said aloud. Exiting the car with the second letter tucked in his pocket, he told the driver, "I'm going to have a smoke. When we depart, take the long route around the city to the train station." That would give him time to speak to his group.

Maddie and Stani came out the door from the hotel; they spotted Raymond, who waved them over. They walked to the limo, and the driver greeted them, taking their luggage, while Raymond explained it was a gift from the ambassador, "for our use, to get us all where we need to go."

Maddie told Stani, "I found the ambassador brilliant and highly entertaining. He also has marvelous taste in clothes. Look at you!"

Maddie watched Stani as he sat quietly reading a book, smiling at her. "His taste is impeccable. I'll give him that." He continued to read while Maddie chattered away.

"Honestly, I'm grateful for this little extra pampering because you deserve it."

Stani looked up from his book and over the top of his reading glasses. "I could take that rather literally, Maddie darling, but understand this: we should expect nothing and be grateful for everything. It's a simple way to live."

Maddie frowned. "I know, I never say the right thing."

Stani closed his book. "Maddie, is something on your mind?"

She shook her head, nodding toward Raymond. "We can discuss it later." Then she added, "Do you know I haven't picked up my violin once since coming to Hamburg? I've learned that when I'm upset, and I mean really upset, I can't practice. I can't even begin to think about playing or practicing. We couldn't find you. First, you're not at the dock. Then we can't find you at all. At one point, I almost threw my violin against the wall. I felt so much anger about your situation, knowing my stubbornness and false expectations caused this, as well as my pain and fear of not knowing where you were or what had become of you. Especially this being round two; our first go was six years ago in Munich."

Stani took her hand in his. "So, my love, what did you do?"

Maddie's eyes widened. "Oh. Wow." The realization hit her, delivering a concise moment of clarity. "That's when I cried out for help. You taught me, *Ask and it shall be given; seek, and I'll find; knock, and it will be opened.* That's what I did!"

Stani patted the top of her hand. In a sweet tone, he explained, "Oh, my girl. I know. He uses our heartbreak to draw us close. I laugh, thinking God is saying, 'There I go using that crazy paradox again, but hey, it works. If they call for help, I can answer them and show them great and mighty things that they know not.'" He paraphrased from the prophet Jeremiah.

Maddie giggled at the image drawn by Stani's words. "He waits for us to ask for help, really? The God of the universe, the Creator of all? No way."

Stani shook his head for effect. Lovingly, he told her, "He loves you, us, that much. Yes. The Psalms tell us the hairs on our heads are numbered; he saves our tears in a vial and even knows when a sparrow falls to the ground. For someone that pays that much attention, I'd say that's a big case of *I love you* written all over it! We are His creation, his children. As a responsible parent, he cares for us."

Maddie's face lightened momentarily, then grew stern. She whispered, "Okay, I can grasp that. It's a lot to believe at once, but I do believe." Maddie hesitated for a minute, then added, "What about Henrik? We've yet to discuss him and Mrs. Genhart."

Cecile, Rolf, and the bellhop came from the hotel to the limousine, and the driver opened the door for the couple. Cecile squealed, "Wow, fancy!"

Once the luggage and everyone was tucked in and on the way to the train station, Raymond shared the information found in the second letter. "I've just skimmed the contents, but I'll warn you, what I'm about to read you is terribly unsettling."

Cecile yawned, adding sarcastically, "Oh, it can't be that bad, can it?"

Rolf scowled at her poor attempt at humor. "Raymond, please continue."

He nodded, cleared his throat, and began to read out loud, leaving out parts that would not be suitable for all ears.

"In a strange set of occurrences, it is apparent now your family is beyond fortunate not to have taken the *S.S. St. Louis*. The ship was never allowed to dock in Havana. They could only anchor at a roadstead hundreds of yards away. Only a very few were allowed to disembark. There are numerous issues at hand, including reports of Nazis abusing the Jewish passengers, threats of mass suicide, and shortage of supplies, food, water, and fuel.

"As it were, the ship is now on its way to Belgium, Antwerp, to unload the passengers. It arrives June 17th, almost three weeks past their arrival date in Havana. The United States, I'm ashamed to say, turned the ship away. And I know why.

"The State Department is infested with antisemites who support the weekly radio broadcasts by 'Father' Charles Coughlin on Sundays, to which hundreds of thousands of Americans tune in. They listen while he preaches his Jew hatred. Then, there's the American Bund taking over venues in New York City, spreading their hatred, even to the youths of America with their Nazi youth camps in Long Island, Wisconsin, New Jersey, and Pennsylvania. They know if they can get their hooks into the minds of the American youth, they can grow their hatred exponentially. Meanwhile, you have Roosevelt turning a blind eye to the plight of European Jews, more concerned with winning another election. Forgive me. But what kind of message does this send to the world?"

Everyone in the vehicle listened with rapt attention as Raymond unwound the situation. After a few minutes, he asked, "Are you sure you want me to go on?" He lit a cigarette and opened the window a bit.

Stani watched the countryside fly by. "Raymond, please continue to explain."

Raymond grimaced. "Well, alright, I'm just worried I'm sucking up all the oxygen in here. We'll be at the train station soon and have yet to discuss other things."

Cecile petitioned quietly, "This is news to us. Please go on." So, he did.

"In any event, it's been discovered that the ship was never intended to land in the first place. The ship and the all-Jewish passengers were used as pawns to illustrate to the world there was no place of refuge for the Jews. Look at all the events launched by the Nazis in an attempt to get the Jews to leave Germany and Europe. But they wouldn't leave. They've tried almost everything to get them to go, bankrupting them, not allowing them to practice medicine, law, teaching, and accounting work. They've ruined their businesses and careers, destroyed their homes, burned down their synagogues, put them in labor camps, and still they would not leave.

"'The Nazis began searching for a final solution. Propaganda Minister Goebbels devised a scheme and implemented this plot using Havana, Cuba, and a docked ship when the cruise business had slowed to almost a standstill. He gauged that the cruise ship owner, HAPAG, would jump at a chance to sell a guaranteed nine hundred to one thousand tickets for an unscheduled, 'special' voyage. An almost-full cruise ship with paying passengers during trying financial times would be impossible to turn down.

"Enter Havana and the *S.S. St. Louis*. The setup begins first by installing paid propaganda pieces in local newspapers and magazines, describing the incoming refugees as criminals and the scourge of the earth. The Reich continued to supply propaganda pieces against the Jews, multiplying the reasons Havana wouldn't want them, then staged protests, paying thousands to protest, and providing them with signs to intentionally deter the Cuban public and government from accepting the Jewish refugees, even though they paid for landing permits. Where were these people supposed to go?"

He went on reading, "Because of the tepid response to the Jewish refugee crisis by thirty-two nations this past summer at the Evian Conference, Propaganda Minister Goebbels wagered that no one, not one country, would accept a ship of Jews. This left the Nazis free to implement any actions they deemed necessary to deal with the Jews. It's checkmate. The Nazis know no country can claim a moral high ground after openly rejecting them when they had the opportunity to save them."

Raymond's eyes began to glaze over, internalizing the weightiness of the letter. As he summarized, grief saturated his words: "No one wants the Jews. This creates a vacuum that leaves Germany and the Nazis to do what they will, seeing the world does not care. Their end game? Kill every Jew."

He folded the letter, put it in the breast pocket of his coat, and spoke the obvious. "Well, now that's out of the way, we're all left with sobering thoughts."

Maddie, quiet for most of the ride, said, "How can people hate so much? I can't understand why anyone, or any government would hate me because I'm Jewish. It makes no sense." She turned to seek Stani's face and his eyes, which she could read even before a word was spoken. "No one knows more about that than you, Stani."

Cecile, remarkably quiet for the ride, piped up, holding back her thoughts until the wall broke and they tumbled out. "I'm scared to live here, afraid I'll be found out, and then what?" She turned her attention to Rolf. "My darling, before our friends and family here, I'm admitting I was wrong. You were right all along, and we should be taking a plane instead of a train."

Her eyes immediately moved to Raymond's, and she pleaded, "Can you do anything to get us to safety, to the United States? I'm ready to go right now!"

Raymond was as encouraging as ever, giving Cecile hope. "I will do what I can as soon as we return to the US. In the meantime, get your papers in order and pack."

At the train station in Berlin, Stani, Maddie, and Raymond walked with Cecile to the benches to wait for the train's arrival, while Rolf purchased tickets. Stani, who had been primarily silent since his release, walked up to Cecile, taking her by the elbow. As they walked, she said, "You know, a train disappearing over the horizon, carrying those you love, can leave a howling gap in a person's day and heart. This one, especially so. I'll miss you all so much."

He whispered, "We can always connect through prayer now that our hearts are knit together."

Cecile marveled at Stani. "Do you always speak so poetically?"

Stani chuckled. "No, I don't, but God does! Now, I want you to do one thing for me that will only help you, okay?"

They were close in age, but that didn't interfere with Stani smiling at her with benevolence like Cecile was his daughter. "Memorize this and call upon the mighty name of God, Psalm 56:3, 'At what time I am afraid I will trust in thee.'"

CHAPTER FORTY-THREE

Familiar Faces and Troubling Spaces

JUNE 1939, HOTEL AMBOS MUNDOS

TUCKED AWAY IN a booth at the back behind the bar, where the lighting was dim despite the bright sunshine outside, a man in a dark suit almost blended into the Naugahyde. The only thing that seemed out of place was the Nazi swastika armband he wore around his left bicep. Buster hadn't seen too many of those in Havana. The majority didn't advertise, mainly when participating in "spontaneous" riots concerning the landing of the *S.S. St. Louis*. Because of the lighting or lack thereof, at first Buster didn't notice the other person with him, also dressed in dark clothing.

Carlos stepped from behind the bar, needing to restock the beer stored in the walk-in icebox. Refrigeration in Cuba was not up to the modern standards of the United States, so the hotel had installed a large icebox that could hold up to one hundred thirty-pound blocks of ice, stored inside an insulated metal box with drainage and a door to enter. Meat and fish were stored in a separate section of the ice box. The men who delivered the ice had an ice crusher and could provide crushed ice for the bar and hotel.

Carlos entered the tin-sided cooler, and while he was busy inside, the man from the booth jumped to his feet and jammed the metal bolt to lock the door. Moments later, the other person slid out of the booth and said to Buster, "Hello, Ben. You're looking dapper tonight. Who is your friend?"

Buster tilted his head, looking at her. "Hello, Sylvanna. I'll ask you the same question: who is your friend, and why did he lock Carlos in the cooler? A man could freeze to death in there." Picking up his glass, he said, "We'll need refills soon. What do you say we let him out?"

She threw back her head and exuded a throaty chortle, then zeroed in on his face. Her long dark locks cascaded down the back of her black silk dress. She could have passed for a black widow spider with a more vicious bite.

Otto Schiendick stepped into the light, and she nodded to him. "My friend Otto here says he has unfinished business with both of you. Is that true?"

Buster was stunned to recognize the man he'd tackled and sent careening into the water after he'd absconded with three pens full of microfilm with secrets stolen from the Americans. "Business with us both? What are you talking about? I've never seen this man before. How about you?"

Standing behind Buster up until this moment, Stefan stepped out into view. "Oh, yeah. I know this guy," he said, spitting on the floor for emphasis. He whispered to Buster, "He's worse than a bad penny that keeps showing up. He's evil, and he's deadly."

Buster kept his cool while sizing up the man; surging adrenaline infiltrated his bloodstream, dissipating any residual effect of the two martinis. He addressed Sylvanna, fighting off the urge to laugh loudly just to humiliate her. "My reliable instincts lead me well once again. I knew it was good to keep my distance from you; now I know why. I don't care for the company you keep." He glanced at Schiendick, who smiled his rotted-tooth smile.

Sylvanna moved within inches of Buster's face, so close he could smell the whiskey on her breath. His green eyes pierced her, as did the question he asked: "Are you a Nazi also, or just by relations?"

She blushed at the inference and stepped away from him. "Is that the best you can come up with? An educated man like you? I hoped for a more philosophical or intellectual discourse rather than a flat accusation."

Meanwhile, they could all hear Carlos yelling from within the cooler while pounding on the door. Schiendick motioned to Sylvanna; he removed his pistol, added the clip, then chambered and locked his 9mm. He handed it to Sylvanna. "Keep it trained on them, but discreetly, in case someone comes in the bar."

She scoffed, waving the gun and speaking dismissively. "No one comes in this place until five. The locals know they water down the liquor. Only tourists come here. If someone comes in, I can always go behind the bar, but you might have to muffle Carlos or speed it up and get it over with, whatever you're doing." She made a circular motion with her hand to convey her point.

Schiendick's head jerked at her words. His lip twitched, he glowered, and he eyed her long enough to cause her to say sorry. He took his eyes off her and slid in front of both men, speaking to Buster while staring at Stefan, who avoided his face altogether. "Isn't this nice and cozy, the three of us here, all connected in the most unusual of ways—wouldn't you say, gentlemen?"

Not waiting for an answer, Schiendick focused on Buster; in his sickeningly sweet, sing-song voice, he began, "I have a few questions for you. What is your name? Ben? Is that it,

Ben? Number one, who are you, and why did you steal my pens and push me into the water? Number two, where is the property you conveniently lifted from me?"

Buster chuckled. "Counting is not your strong suit, is it?"

Schiendick snarled at him, "Why don't you consider returning what's mine while I speak to Mr. Soutine, my former passenger and Dachau escapee."

Stefan shook his head, saying bitterly, "I'm no escapee. Commandant Eicke wrote my release papers. I have the guts to die. Do you have the guts to live?"

Schiendick reached into his back pocket and pulled out the knife—the same one his goon had stuck in Fritz's head, murdering the man before disposing of him in the deep. He felt the edge and held it before Stefan. "Let's see if you have the guts to die. But first, I promised you a haircut, remember?"

Buster scrunched his face. "His hair looks fine to me. Perhaps it's you who needs the haircut and a shower. Aside from that, I'm curious: are you not a crew member of the ship that left port a while ago after your swim? Why aren't you on the ship? Are you a deserter?"

Schiendick, Buster, and Stefan faced each other in a semi-circle. Schiendick snapped, "You think you're smart, don't you? Are you an accomplice to this man? I mean, here you are together, having drinks, toasting each other for your not-so-grand success. First, Mr. Soutine, you had the pocket diary of Minister Goebbels in your possession. You know all about Operation Sunshine. Then this man, your associate, conveniently steals property that is not his and pushes me in the water."

Buster yelled, "The property doesn't belong to you! You stole it in the first place!"

No one except Sylvanna paid attention to the four armed

guards of the hotel until one called into the bar, getting all of their attention. In Spanish, he shouted, "We are looking for a man, Otto Schiendick."

Buster answered in Spanish, "He's right in front of me."

Sylvanna cued Schiendick, waving her hands furiously. "He told them it's you."

Schiendick wasted no time. He moved to plunge the knife deep into Buster, but the shorter Stefan stepped in front of Buster, the knife hitting him in the chest. Stefan crumpled to the ground.

Two Havana police officers carted Schiendick away in handcuffs as he yelled and screamed enough to infuriate the officers, who responded by clubbing him with their sticks. Another officer apprehended Sylvanna, who screamed, "It's not even my gun. It's not mine."

Buster yelled, "Call for an ambulance! Get me something to prop up his feet and a blanket, bandages, or towels."

Time came and went in waves. The room moved in and out of focus amid a cacophony of voices, an officer calling for medical help and meows from cats milling about. Buster shouted, "Hurry! The feet need to be higher than the heart." Someone brought a huge sautoir from the kitchen to him, then turned it upside down and placed Stefan's feet there, holding them in place.

Buster knelt, removed his shirt, and pressed it against Stefan's chest to stop the bleeding, applying steady pressure with one hand. He continued to talk to Stefan, saying, "It's okay, buddy, we're going to get you through this. You're a hero. Help is on the way. Hold on to me, we'll get through this together."

The Havana police officers took over from the hotel guards, who handed off the apprehended Otto Schiendick, still woozy from the beating, without a struggle. "He'll be no trouble." The men laughed while Schiendick stumbled along, bringing him by the medics attending Stefan while Buster hovered nearby.

Schiendick sneered at Buster, getting in his last shot. "Don't waste your time on that worthless life. He's not only a Dachau prisoner; he's also a Jew."

Buster looked to the officers holding Schiendick. He spoke to them in Spanish, telling them he was in the armed forces too, and asked them to hold him, which they did. Buster stood eye to eye with Schiendick, said to him in perfect German, "I'm a Jew and proud of it, you Nazi bastard," and delivered a roundhouse blow square to the side of Schiendick's head.

The police carted Schiendick away, half-dragging him, bloodied and reeling from Buster's crushing blow.

Aboard the S.S. St. Louis

A noticeable change in temperature at sunset hinted at what was to come, piquing the mind to wonder what the canvas of the sky and the great artist of all would do next. Captain Schroeder stood outside the bridge, on the deck. It was brisk enough to cause him to don an overcoat. His black leather-gloved hands stretched out on the railing, mindful of the sky above him, which was painted with incredible strokes of color, a brilliance the eye hoped to hold in a singular view. As the sky unfolded with bursts of radiant hues, those witnessing it were gifted a delight to behold.

Leo Jockl stood behind the captain for a moment, not wanting to interrupt the peaceful moment, but the urgency of the telegram caused him to clear his throat. "Beg your pardon, sir. I have a telegram for you."

The captain sighed. He turned to his steward. "What's it say?"

Jockl cleared his throat again before reading, "This is from the Havana Authority Police. Deserter suspect Otto

Schiendick has been apprehended. Will hold while awaiting further instruction."

The captain sighed again. Jockl knew him well enough to ask, "Sir, aren't you pleased they caught him? He's a slippery devil."

The captain nodded in agreement. "That he is." He took the telegram and read it. Then he balled it up and tossed it into the deep.

His attendant stared at him wide-eyed, knowing protocol demanded keeping every telegram sent and received in the bridge logbook. The captain responded, his voice weary yet firm. "Hmm. I know. But what does it matter? My issue is that I know nothing will come from this, his desertion, and there will be no punishment whatsoever. The Abwehr will have him released, and he'll go on his merry way, wreaking havoc, making the lives of those he deems unworthy miserable. And that is why, Mr. Jockl, I am not pleased."

CHAPTER FORTY-FOUR

The Grief of a Goodbye

JUNE 1939, TRAIN STATION IN BERLIN

AT RAYMOND'S REQUEST, Stani and Maddie returned to sit in the limousine while Raymond discussed Wolfie with Cecile and Rolf. Observing Maddie's puzzled expression, Raymond said, "I'll tell you what's taking place after the train departs. For now, go, and I'll wave to you when it's time to say goodbye." Maddie hesitated but did as asked.

She slid close to Stani inside the limousine, linking her arm through his. "I know you haven't opened up about this yet, but maybe now is a good time for you to tell me everything."

Stani sighed. "You want to hear this now when we're in the middle of a goodbye with them?" He nodded toward Rolf and Cecile.

When she said, "Yes," Stani told of the events that had taken place at Werner Kempler's apartment, and what Raymond learned after questioning Henrick at the station jail where Stani was held.

Maddie's hands flew to her face; she held her cheeks in disbelief, her voice shrank, and quietly she asked, "Mrs. Genhart has a love child?" She fanned her face. "I think I might faint! And you, you had to endure his death at close range. Oh, my God, Stani. I can't believe this! What did you do? You must have been in shock—maybe you still are in shock? Oh my God, then they imprison you? This is too much for one person. How do you endure such things?"

When he didn't answer her direct questions, she knew he wouldn't speak until he'd processed it himself. Instead, he lit a cigarette. "I'll take one, please," she said.

Her pleading eyes softened Stani, and he lit one and handed it to her.

"Thank you," she said. "You must get these from Raymond. American cigarettes are so different from German smokes; well, you know this. I'm sorry, I'm babbling on about nothing. This is so much information. I'm just swimming with questions. Do you think he would have shot her had she gone? And did she have any way of knowing that was his plan, not to give her a treasured instrument but a gunshot to kill her?"

"There's no way of knowing that now. Raymond told me that Henrik wrote the letter to Mrs. Genhart, not his father Werner, asking her to come to Hamburg. He hoped to lure her to Hamburg, desiring to meet her."

Raymond sat beside Cecile while Rolf stood, knowing he had both their attention. He gestured, palms down. "Listen, there's no delicate way to share this news, so I'm just going to say this. Wolfie is home in Rochester, recuperating from an accident suffered while training. He's almost 100 percent recovered, so we give thanks. He has some scarring from the burns, but it's on his legs and feet."
Raymond continued. "He was working with flammables—you know about his love for pyrotechnics—and due to no fault of his, he was injured during a training exercise. A situation became dire, and that's all I know, except a brave young man helped him, and the medical staff, a great doctor and surgeon, were on scene to treat Wolfie immediately."

"What's his long-term prognosis?" Cecile interrupted.

Raymond smiled. "Cecile, it's very good, just some scarring. He's good as new!"

Cecile emitted a grunt. "Easy for you to say, good as new. You're never good as new once they cut you open. Oh, yes, they may repair you, but how well, for how long? Answer me that!" She folded her arms across her chest and tapped her foot like she was keeping time with a song that was playing only in her head.

Raymond peeked at Rolf for support, but the other man only shook his head knowingly. Raymond quipped, "Well, we can all be thankful there was no cutting open or surgery of that kind."

Rolf muttered, "Yes, thank God for that." Then, he put his hands together as if prepared to say something serious, moving his lips like he was talking to himself. "I'm veering off-topic, but I must ask, seeing we're about to leave you. We will do as you recommend. We will get our papers in order and pack. However, there's a small problem with Cecile's passport. It has a 'J' stamped on it. The Gestapo and the agents all require a show of identification at docks, train stations, and boats. The laws are changing quickly. We don't know how or when to leave, but can we even do that?"

The huffing sound of the engine rang in the ears of all who stood by, and slowly the ground began to rumble underfoot. In the distance, the banshee cry of the train whistle broke the atmosphere with its high pitch, increasing in volume with every mile of track it devoured. Rolf saw the tears form in his wife's eyes, and he eagerly handed her his handkerchief. She sputtered to say the words, finally getting them out in between tears. "This is the hardest of goodbyes."

Raymond waved to Maddie; after a moment, the door to the limousine opened, the driver got out, and Stani and

Maddie came to say their goodbyes. Maddie threw herself into Cecile's arms. She said, through her tears, "You drive me crazy, but I love your bossy, harebrained, wacky ways, and most of all, your good heart. Please come to New York. We need you; we all do. Rolf, Wolfie, and Frederick need you too, not to mention all of us here."

She hugged Cecile hard as if she'd never see her again, and together, they felt the train's reverberation as it glided into the station, squeaking brakes and all, with a considerable steam release. The doors opened, and passengers began to pile out, engulfing the group in a mad rush of people.

Maddie grabbed Rolf's jacket, pulling herself to him. He bent down to hear her say amidst the noisy platform, "You are Superman to me, like the man I read about in the American comics. You're a hero, and I'm so thankful for you."

He cupped her chin and said, "And I for you. God bless you."

Maddie's arms slipped around his waist. She hugged him, and big, somewhat clumsy Rolf became shy, tamed by a 5'4" brunette with a powerfully sweet way about her.

Stani and Cecile shook hands, and then she pulled him close in a hug. "I'm so pleased to know you, and I look forward to seeing you soon, God willing."

Stani whispered, "Don't forget."

Rolf and Raymond shook hands and embraced. "Thank God you came into our lives. I speak for my family. We are all so grateful for you."

Raymond blushed at the praise, waving him off. His eyes met Rolf's, and he said, in all seriousness, "You know how to find me. I promise to work on a solution and let you know soon."

As Stani and Rolf said goodbye, the conductor shouted, "All aboard!"

The driver handed Rolf his baggage stubs and came to

escort Raymond, Maddie, and Stani back to the vehicle. Maddie pleaded, "Can we just wait until they leave?"

The driver said, "Of course, Miss."

Maddie whispered to Stani, "I've made some decisions. I want to share with you where my heart is leading me. I've prayed about this, knowing it's the right path."

Stani smiled and squeezed her hand. "I know it's the right path because no double-mindedness exists."

Just then, the train whistle howled out its departure message. Slowly, the wheels moved, squeaking and squealing down the rail, gaining momentum. With that increasing speed, it chugged its way into the lonesome night. Billowy puffs of steam and smoke escaped from the train chimney as it headed east—once again, dividing a family just like in 1933.

At the Hospital in Havana

Buster paced back and forth in the waiting room, filled with helplessness and indecision. He knew nothing about the man he'd brought to the hospital. Due to his military status, he could speak to the chief medical officer on staff and ask for special provisions to be made, considering the circumstances.

The CMO, a Chinese doctor raised in Cuba named Glenn Zhao, spoke with Buster in his tiny, cramped office. There was a sizeable window that gave a fabulous view of the ocean. "Please sit down, Specialist Wellington. Your friend's injuries are substantial; his lung is punctured. If you can visualize, the knife was at an angle that caused a very jagged cut. There may also be damage to the heart, as the knife went between the ribs and not the sternum or breastbone. We hope for a correction and help for his lung.

"As I mentioned, the angle of penetration can affect specific structures. So, for now, we will wait and hope. In most instances, people want a number or a percentage of chance for survival, and I cannot predict. That is in God's hands. Mr. Soutine is in surgery now. Do you have any questions?"

Buster's head spun with the details, *punctures, jagged cuts, heart, and ribs.* The doctor's face came in and out of focus.

"Mr. Wellington, here, have some water, take a few deep breaths."

———✤———

Buster opened his eyes. He was on a gurney in a room with an attendant watching him. There was a cold compress on his forehead, which he removed and sat up. "Excuse me. Hello, uh, how long have I, uh, what time is it? Is there a phone I can use?"

He steadied himself, smiling at the attendant while his head pounded like a sledgehammer was hitting him. "I'll just sit here for a minute until my head unscrambles." *I can't even think who to call. Do I call my superiors? Do I call my dad?*

The attendant held him by the arm as he hopped off the gurney. "You've got quite a knot where your head hit the floor." She reached to touch the lump on his forehead, causing Buster to pull away. "You fainted."

His eyes grew big, "I what?"

She tilted her head. "You fainted. Now, there's a phone available for you in the doctor's office. Follow me, but please go slow."

Buster asked, "Is there an update about Mr. Soutine's surgery?"

Aboard the Flight from Berlin to New York
The mighty DC-3, with fourteen sleeper berths, stretched its wings wide over the bumpy runway, gaining speed. Finally, it lifted off before the runway disappeared, and the thrust of the engine's power pressed the passengers' bodies back against

the seats.

The eighteen-hour flight would refuel in Greenland and Canada before heading to New York City. An Army private served as an attendant aboard. He told the passengers there were sandwiches aboard, and the crew would refill supplies once they touched down in Greenland.

Stani's eyes widened. "That means three take-offs and three landings. Oy. I hope my stomach can take this." He squeezed Maddie's hand and shouted over the engines, "I feel like a space explorer!"

Maddie smiled at Stani and blew him a kiss. Raymond sat in the front to get a better view of what the pilots saw, while Maddie and Stani sat a row back, holding hands and hanging on for dear life. Never having flown before, neither knew what to expect.

The noise of the engines was loud, making communication difficult, and neither Stani nor Maddie cared to yell. Stani asked the Army private for paper and a pencil, which he provided, with the Douglas Aircraft Company logo at the top of the paper and stamped onto the pencil.

The higher the altitude, the less the engines roared. Once above the clouds, Stani remarked, "Maddie, one thing I've learned about life is nothing stays the same. We live in a constant state of flux, even if it doesn't feel that way. Everything changes. And we must be willing to change, too."

Aboard the S.S. St. Louis

On June 17, 1939, the coast of Antwerp came into view, and the passengers crowded the decks to view what they hoped would be a fortuitous beginning and the conclusion of a tragic five-week journey. The deckhands rushed about the ship, making last-minute adjustments to tow lines to be ready when the tugs came, and the docking pilot boarded the ship.

In the wheelhouse, Captain Schroeder stood before his senior officers, making eye contact with each one, and then spoke.

"Men. You have undergone a journey none of us expected or could predict. Little did we know that other governments in Cuba, the United States, and Canada would reject our landing. What they don't know is that their refusal would signal to the Nazis a green light that they could now do as they wished to advance with their plans against the Jews of Europe. Perhaps, the world.

"I do not relish speaking of such things. There were dark forces at work even before the start of the voyage. Was there any way to know this voyage would be used as a propaganda ruse while making the ship into a transport vehicle to share stolen espionage secrets for the Abwehr? Men, we've been hoodwinked by our government. Beware. Fair warning.

"Except for a few who are not in attendance, you've performed your duties above capacity, many of you going above and beyond for our passengers' sake. I am eternally grateful to you. In circumstances such as the ones we experienced on this voyage, showing compassion and gifting kindness to strangers is the greatest of all acts. I'm grateful for your professionalism. You did your job, allowing for me to do mine. Once I prepare my report, I will write commendations for each of you.

"As your captain, it's been a pleasure to serve with you, shoulder to shoulder, through this tumultuous journey. I hope that you'll come away from this voyage as changed men. You've witnessed firsthand what hatred can do beyond robbing a person of dignity. It scrapes at the very foundation of humanity and the implicit orders given by God to all of creation to be kind and care for others as you would yourself. You've witnessed firsthand the endemic and baseless hatred of the Jews by the Reich, contaminating the masses with their particular brand of contagion.

"Vaccinate yourselves against such toxic diseases. Do not allow yourselves to be swept up into the unintelligent masses that seek no answers for themselves, who find ease in complacency, recognizing it is acceptable in their masses to be spoon-fed pablum by the dictates of those in power. Power is fleeting, a self-contained vacuum of sorts. It will, eventually, consume itself." And then he said with all gravity, "We can only hope. I wish you all the very best. May God bless you all. Dismissed."

Unbeknownst to the crew, the captain had already received instructions from Berlin. The telegram excoriated him for disobeying orders by not returning the ship directly to Hamburg. His rank as ship captain had been withdrawn. He would serve his remaining commission behind a desk, pushing papers, removed from the sea travel he adored. He told himself, *So be it. I did the right thing regardless of the punishment. God help my passengers.*

CHAPTER FORTY-FIVE

Our Prayers Aren't Always Answered

JUNE 1939, ABOARD THE DC-3

IT WAS JUST past 3:00 a.m., and the final refueling was complete. The plane began its route to New York City. The cabin was otherwise quiet, with just the whirr of the engines as background noise. Only the cabin floor lights shone, creating a shadowed atmosphere. Outside the plane was a galaxy of enrobing obscurity dotted with the fluorescence of stars.

The plane reached cruising altitude, and the pilots lowered the engines' thrust power, reducing the roar. While Raymond and Stani rested in the side-by-side sleeping berths, Stani, on the outside berth, noticed Maddie was restless, tossing and turning, seemingly trying to find a comfortable position. Raymond snored softly, so Stani whispered, "Psst. Maddie. Do you feel like talking? Meet me in the back."

Maddie got up quickly and silently. She stretched, her back cracking, then padded back to the last two empty berths. Stani, already seated, wore the silk robe picked out by the ambassador. She sat across from him. "I wish I had light to see you in that silk robe. Not much light back here."

Stani smiled in the twilight and, reaching into the pocket of his robe, retrieved a small penlight. "Ask, and it shall be given." He chuckled, "Another gift from the ambassador." He placed the light between the two berths, securing it under a cushion. He could see the color of Maddie's eyes. She could see his face. "What's on your mind, my dear?"

Maddie fiddled with her hair, washed at midnight before retiring, giving herself a loose side braid. "Yes, that is a lovely robe. Very handsome on you." Stani knew Maddie's stalling techniques, but she came out with it. "I don't understand something."

He lit a cigarette while she contemplated her words. "Do all our prayers get answered?"

Stani enjoyed his smoke and told her, "I really missed smoking while I was locked up; now I'm making up for lost time."

Maddie slapped at Stani's slipper. "That's not what I meant, and you know it." She laughed while jabbing Stani in the side, hitting his rib bones. "Wow. We've got to get some meat on those bones of yours."

Stani giggled at her comment, agreeing with her assessment. Then he said, "Do you remember me saying the same to you? You were a skinny little imp of a girl. Then you came to Germany with Elenena, and we lived as one happy family. That prayer was not answered—quite the opposite. But you came into my life forever or for as long as God intends to keep me here."

Maddie said softly, "Yes, I remember." She asked Stani, "Does it smell musty in here? I think it does. Now, answer me, please, but first, light me a cigarette!"

While Stani did as requested, Maddie touched his cheek. "If I don't tell you enough, I love you, and I'm so thankful you're here now. You're the only one who really understands me. I know I'm difficult at times."

Stani passed Maddie the smoke and squeezed her hand. "I'm thankful to be here, too, and by the way, all artists are difficult, and can be overbearing, or uncommunicative. It's part of the package and comes with the territory."

Maddie winked at Stani. "Ah, so you're confessing to being difficult, too? Haha. I'm surprised."

Stani tossed it back. "No, no. I'm not an artist; you are an artist. Elenena and Kempler were also artists. Mrs. Genhart and I are instructors. See the difference? It's how the creative brain works at a different rhythm and pace than the rest of the world. How artists see, hear, and relate to the world around them is quite distinctive, a unique gift—not everyone has it. But, as a side effect, sometimes a degree of madness is involved, taking residence next to the creative force."

Maddie stared at Stani. She said with a degree of resignation, "Oh, yes. The madness." Then, with a comical expression, she asked Stani earnestly, "Do you mean we're all a little nuts?" Maddie couldn't hold back her laughter, and a "shhhh" from Raymond quieted them both, but they continued to giggle and snicker.

Stani added, "Sometimes it's like a curse and a blessing."

Maddie whispered, "Yes, I so agree. But how do we know if our prayers will be answered? I'm asking circular questions." She sighed and hung her head.

Gently, he said, "Maddie, if our prayers aren't being answered, it's not time for them to be answered. You must have faith and trust."

Maddie jumped up. "That's it, that's the question, how do I know I trust or even have faith?"

Stani tilted his head, gazing at Maddie. "Why is our first thought always to complicate what God has made simple? I'll never know. My dear, here we are, up almost twenty thousand feet, flying through the air in a musty tin can. Did it not take trust and faith to get aboard, believing the plane would go where it's supposed to go?" He blinked at her a few times for emphasis, a trick he used to do while instructing or tutoring her, desiring she give a particular note more attention.

Maddie giggled at Stani. "You know how to get your point across. You taught me I can't see the wind, but I can feel it. I can't hear a star fall, but I can see it. I can see a baby born, hold it, and feel it with the understanding that God knew that baby while it was in the mother's womb; God breathed life into the baby as He did with me. Oh, Stani, I believe, I believe with all my heart, and the crazy thing is I feel more Jewish as a result of believing in the Messiah. I see us as completed Jews. And like you taught me, 'Taste and see that the Lord is good.'"

"Yes, yes, that's it! He is good to those who seek Him! You are experiencing His extravagant love. Oh, and I like that, a completed Jew. You mentioned you decided something. What is that about? Will you tell me?"

Maddie took a deep breath, dropped her head, and said, "Better hold on. It's a shocker." She stated, "I've concluded: I don't want to play anymore—no more concerts, and no more travel. I've had enough. I never thought I'd say these words, but I've focused most of my life on the violin. At that last concert, in a few short hours, I grew years older! The funny thing is, I now understand that I've clung to my violin like it was my source of life, my lifeline, and hid behind it. I've felt like I'd die without it and without making music."

Stani inched closer to Maddie, focusing on her face and expression as she revealed her heart. He encouraged her tenderly, "Go on."

She let out a deep moan. "I've put so much pressure on myself these last four years, and after the Vienna performance, I determined I'd had enough. I wrestled with the thought for the last three weeks. With a clear heart, mind, and conscience,

I can now say that I'm ready to settle down with Buster, start our family, and live the life we hope for in Rochester. For now. My life feels oddly incomplete without Buster."

She yawned, stretching her arms, "As far as my career, I've reached a pinnacle I thought I'd never climb: to play in Vienna before my people, Europeans. But those were not my people. I've lived in a fantasy world thinking I'd somehow not feel like an orphan if I played all over Europe, seeking the love and adoration I never received as a child, that somehow I would feel whole, or, complete."

Maddie looked out the window of the plane. "How could I think those people could give me what I've found in God, my family, you, Buster? I know he adores me, and I him. I've held him off for so long."

Stani took her hand, patting it. "Buster understands you better than you know."

Maddie's face lightened. "I realized that I couldn't truly move on with Buster until I addressed my pain, let it go, and learned to forgive myself instead of pointing fingers at others."

Stani offers a broad smile. "Well, thank God for your tender, seeking heart. Some matters can only be solved by deep introspection and a release of the event or person that wounded you. Forgiving yourself is a true gift of God. To be forgiven is everything. And while I'm at it, I'm thanking God for your discovery regarding your career; it is a gift to receive clarity over a life-changing decision. The days of Jews making music in Europe are over, at least for a while. Who knows how long? The Reich has outlawed it. If they found out you were Jewish, you never would have performed! Tell me, Maddie, what was one of the things that made it possible for you to perform there?"

Maddie's eyes dropped to the floor. She sighed loudly. "The Wellington name. You were right. I think you might very well be a modern-day prophet!"

Stani affirmed her. "I support your decision 1,000 percent."

Maddie placed her hand over Stani's. "I can always count on you, and I'm so grateful," she said as she kissed Stani's hand. "Maybe I'll teach or give recitals, who knows. I'm almost twenty-four. I want to be young while my kids are young."

Stani laughed. "Kids? What's this? When did you have kids?" They giggled together like little children until another rousing "shhhh" came from Raymond.

Cautiously, she peered at Stani. "Sometimes the heart doesn't know what it wants until it finds what it wants. What do you think about that?"

"The greatest achievement in life begins and ends with contentment. Remember this, my darling: to be double-minded is soul-destroying and the thief of peace. That is a marker. When you feel conflicted, listen to that and don't ignore it. You took your time coming to this conclusion: some factors contributed to your decision; peace is the by-product of a good decision. Know that the peace of God, which passes understanding, will keep your heart and mind. Do you understand what I'm saying to you?"

Maddie kissed Stani on the cheek. "Yes. I get it 100 percent."

Stani clasped his hands for emphasis and stated, "I think my work here is done!"

As he began to doze off, he whispered, "*My heart, Oh Lord, my heart, help me.*"

At the Hospital in Havana

Recovered from his untimely spell, Buster called home long-distance. No answer. *Who can I call?* He tried the number again, asking the operator to allow it to ring past the customary seven rings. On the tenth ring, a woman answered, sounding sleepy, her voice reflective of a French accent, saying, "Hello,

Wellington residence."

The operator informed her, "You have a long-distance collect call from Buster Wellington. Will you accept the charges?"

The woman said, "Yes."

The operator said, "Go ahead with your call."

Perplexed, Buster asked, "And just who might you be, and why are you in my house, answering my phone?"

After a moment of hesitation, the sultry voice replied, "I'm Camille Gautier, Wilhelm's physical therapist and nurse."

Buster chuckled. *Wolfie with a French nurse.* "Where is Mr. Wolferman, either the younger or older? Are they available to speak?" He peeked at his watch. "Six a.m. here. Well, are they? Hello? Hello?"

After a moment, a sleepy Frederick answered, "Hullo." Buster swallowed hard. Emotion filled the back of his throat, catching him off guard. It had been months since he'd heard the sound of a family member's voice. "Frederick, it's Buster. It's a long story. How are you? How is Wolfie? Good, good. I can only imagine. Sure. Hey, have you spoken to my dad? Do you know where he is? Oh, okay. Huh. Sure. I'll try him again in a few days. Tell him to expect a call from me. No, I cannot say. Sure thing. Same to you and Wolfie. Punch him for me. Okay. Will do. Same to you, Frederick. God bless you, too."

Buster reflected on the conversation and Frederick's last sentence. *Frederick just said God bless you to me first. What's going on at home?*

Buster was marinating in his thoughts when the door to the doctor's office opened, and Dr. Zhao came in. "Mr. Wellington, I'm glad to find you here. Won't you please sit down?" Buster had anticipated this conversation; he bit the inside of his cheek, preparing for the worst.

The doctor sat behind his desk and used his hands to

illustrate his words, but his movements made no sense to Buster. Instead, he focused on the words coming from the doctor's mouth. They traveled in slow motion, floating through the atmosphere. Each syllable traveled to the location of his head, finding its way, and they hammered his ear one by one. The news he feared had reached him; he heard the words but didn't want to believe them.

If I ignore death, will it leave me? Or will it come like a thief in the night to rob me of the shred of hope I've held on to, praying this man lives? He was wounded for me. He took my place. He stepped in front of me, and now he's dead. It should have been me.

Vienna, Austria

Rolf was in the basement, sitting atop a packing container drum. He reached into the back pocket of his work pants and removed his handkerchief, which his wife, Cecile, had embroidered with his initials. Wiping the sweat from his brow, he lamented the lack of wisdom in making a move, especially during June, the rainiest time of the year. *Does it have to be so damn humid? Ugh.* He lit a cigarette, tilting his head back to exhale. *Is there anything better than a Marlboro?*

Cecile interrupted his thoughts. Her voice rang out. "ROLF."

Well, thanks to Raymond, I still have four cartons of American cigarettes. I hate it when she yells from another room.

"ROLF!"

"What now, woman?"

"Someone's at the door, and I'm busy. Would you see who it is, please?"

Rolf considered mentioning that he was busy, too, but let it go. He took his time, and the knock became louder and more insistent. *All right, all right, keep your shirt on.*

Cecile shouted from the top of the staircase, "Rolf, are you getting the door?"

Sighing, he shouted back, "Yes." Rolf turned to the door and peered out the small window at the top of the door to a sight he'd dreaded. No, *silently feared* was more like it.

Cecile shouted in the background, "Who is it, Rolf? Who's at the door?"

He hissed at her, speaking through clenched teeth, "Stay put. I mean it."

He opened the door, and two Gestapo agents barged into the house uninvited. They were dressed identically, like twins, in the trademark SS black, their jackboots shining like the black lacquered visors on their peaked Shirmmütze with the Totenkopf skull.

One of the twins shouted, "Cecile Rosenberg Wolferman, is she here?"

Rolf detected a Munich accent, asking the men, "Which of you is from Munich?"

The men looked at each other, puzzled. One answered suspiciously, "We both are."

Raising an eyebrow, he asked Rolf, "You and your wife, are you Austrians?"

Using the most cordial spirit he could muster, speaking in German, Rolf said, sounding jovial, "Of course we are. My brother lives in Munich and sounds just like you. Yes, he enlisted the same day as my wife's brother. They're both in a Panzer Unit training for the future. That's how I recognized your accent."

Rolf rubbed his hands together. "Are you hungry? What can I make you? My wife is upstairs. She'll be down in a minute. In the meantime, come to the kitchen, and I'll make you something fantastic to eat. By the way, do either of you like American cigarettes?"

Both agents smiled and nodded. Rolf led them into the

kitchen and babbled on with a constant flow of chatter. "Let's see what we have: roast chicken, bread, cheese, mustard, pickles, and beer."

After the men gorged themselves on what was to be Cecile and Rolf's supper, Rolf tucked a carton of cigarettes under each officer's arm while occupying their hands with almond Schnecken. Cecile came downstairs after seeing the men drive off. Astounded, she asked, "How in the world did you persuade them to get lost? I thought they'd never leave. I know you're charming, but Gestapo? What did you do?"

Rolf smiled sheepishly. "Trade secrets, my dear, trade secrets."

CHAPTER FORTY-SIX

To Expect the Unexpected

AUGUST 1939, PULTNEYVILLE, NEW YORK

IT WAS A gloriously sunny afternoon, with a light breeze blowing off the lake. Buster walked hand-in-hand with Maddie, away from the crowd, still gathered around Stani's graveside. Maddie said, "It's just the kind of day Stani adored."

The family had held the burial in June, within twenty-four hours of his death, honoring the Jewish custom of burying Stani before sunset. They had decided to wait to hold a graveside service until Buster could apply for leave and the Wolfermans could arrive from Austria. Raymond had ceremoniously cut through the boondoggle of bureaucratic malarkey and red tape, bringing the Wolfermans here on extended visas until he could work out citizenship details, which would take a few years.

Buster had arrived just last night. Maddie had told him after a soul-stirring kiss and welcome, "I have so much to share with you." They'd sat up until the early morning hours, kissing and making up for lost time while discussing what had happened in the last four months.

As Buster and Maddie strolled around the spacious yard, Buster commented on the grass, how lush and thick it was, and how it cushioned each step. "Would you look at this heavenly oasis you've created here? I'm so proud of you, darling, and I adore you and your numerous talents." He kissed her softly.

Maddie returned the kiss. "I know he'd love the location, the water to one side, land to the other, surrounded by the trees and flowers, across from his vegetable garden."

She broke down, turning toward Buster, her arms around his neck as she buried her face in his shoulder. "I think he knew, I really do. On the flight, after we talked, we spoke about many things," she took Buster's handkerchief and blew her nose, "I was sharing about things I learned, things I've shared with you," she said while stroking Buster's chest, where his heart is. "He told me his work here was done. How could I know he'd go back to sleep never to wake up? I can't believe he's gone, a heart attack. What am I going to do without him? Why now? His absence creates a chasm in me, emptying me and ripping through the fabric of my life. No one ever loved me unconditionally as Stani did."

Buster winced at the last statement. In a low voice, he said quietly, "I love you, Maddie, perhaps not as Stani did, but you can trust that my love for you is unconditional. Stani would tell you that unconditional love mimics the love of Christ."

Maddie wiped her nose and eyes. "Oh, my darling, of course I know that." She paused, and, thinking aloud, said, "I know this fear is irrational. This idea that I will be left alone with no one to love me is what I've thought my entire life."

Buster was bewildered; he grimaced, not fully comprehending Maddie's fear. That had never been his experience. He had always felt loved.

A thought stopped Maddie. She said, "Darling, I haven't even asked you about what happened on your last mission."

They walked up the steps to one of the verandas. Relaxing in the moment, leaning against the post, Buster closed his eyes and replied, "You know I can't talk about that." He took her in his arms. "But there is something I've realized. Want to hear?"

Sweetly smiling, she said, "Say on, my dear," then planted a firm kiss full of warmth on Buster's lips.

"I warn you; this isn't an easy topic to discuss, but I found wisdom in it, profound to me."

Maddie nodded in understanding, and he went on. "So, I experienced the passing of an acquaintance, and a week later, I heard the news of Stani. The acquaintance was someone who, through a series of events, saved my life. I'll go into that later. But I became acutely aware of already being immersed in a state of grief so that when the news of Stani arrived, the blow crushed me, but not in the way I thought it would, already being in that sad place, mourning my friend.

"Comparatively speaking, two losses close together versus experiencing those two deaths separately, like a year or two apart, or for two years in a row, I will suffer grief. However, when we lose friends or loved ones in a shorter period, I've found it's easier to accept due to being prepared by already experiencing the first loss. Not that we grieve our losses any less intensely. Or that all losses are the same. It's just that you're already in the place of grief. The shock isn't as intense. Does this make sense to you? I've gone and given it a name. I call this hypothesis 'The Economy of Grief.' I think there's truth to this, and I'm sure Stani would have liked the explanation. What do you think?"

Just hearing Stani's name caused Maddie's tears to resume. She smiled through her tears, telling Buster, "And he would have had scripture to back up your hypothesis. When I have more time to consider it, I'll agree because you are brilliant."

Cecile approached the two and, nodding to Buster, took Maddie by the hand to sit on the porch swing. They walked past the colorful and lush gardens; everyone who lived at the house pitched in. Maddie had taught everyone how to see, how to look for weeds, and if a tree or shrub needed pruning, or if aphids attacked the roses and needed treatment, to do it or ask for help. She'd learned what worked and what didn't through trial and error. Miss Ada Berk would tell her, "You see it, treat it." Then there was the cutting of the dead wood off of the trees that bordered the property. It was a twice-a-year job, and it took two weeks to do the pruning and then cut the wood for firewood and kindling.

Maddie told Cecile, "It was Stani who taught me discipline, to take care of a thing the moment I notice it or see it. He taught me everything. I don't even know where to begin."

Cecile sat with Maddie and held her hand, brushing a stray lock of hair behind her ear; looking into her eyes, she shared with her, "The measure of a friendship, a true friendship, of a precious heart bound by love, when it departs, the pain is best quantified this way, the greater the love, the deeper the hurt. You couldn't have loved Stani any more than you did. You made him so proud. And how he cheered you during your last performance.

"It's not ironic that your last performance was in Vienna, and you were with Stani. That is a treasure given to you, a pearl of great price. Always remember how special and treasured those memories are. Preserve them by remembering them and speaking of them often. You'll honor Stani at the same time."

Maddie gazed at the yard, thinking of the times she spent with Stani. She concluded, whimpering, "I've never felt so alone. The tempest of death has gutted my soul."

Cecile and Maddie sat together, swinging ever so gently, and marveled at the close bond formed between patient Wolfie and nurse Camille. Cecile mentioned, whispering in Maddie's ear, "Wolfie told me he's in love with the girl. Look at her; how could he not be?"

Arm in arm, Wolfie and Camille walked away from the graveside, with Hollenius following close behind Ninotchka, Camille's black-and-white tuxedo cat. Cecile observed them, Wolfie in particular, and told Maddie, "You two were closest to him. You'll need to support each other."

Maddie smiled knowingly. "Wolfie has all the support he needs from Camille. They're perfect for each other, and she's a match for Buster at chess. She's the only one who can beat him. They curse each other in French when they play. It's hilarious to witness."

She called out to Wolfie, "Do you have a smoke on you? Come up here, you two. Where are the Wellington and Wolferman men?"

Wolfie handed Maddie a Marlboro and then offered her a light. He sat on one of the chairs after seating Camille first. Hollenius jumped up on Wolfie's lap while Ninotchka sat at Camille's feet. Hollenius chin-bumped Wolfie, wanting his attention.

Wolfie told the ladies while scratching behind Hollenius's ears, "They're all in the kitchen, hunting around for things like mad. I think between the four of them, they're trying to get the food organized while Raymond handles the fire. They asked me first, of course, but I deferred," he said with sarcasm.

Cecile replied, "Ah, no more fire for you for a while, Mister." Something caught her attention, and she tapped Maddie's arm, asking, "And who, pray tell, is that bossy woman?"

Maddie giggled and said under her breath, "Takes one to know one!"

Cecile was commenting on Miss Ada Berk, who told Raymond, "You've built the fire all wrong." She hollered away while he fetched more wood. "You can't just stack it, you must set it properly, like the foundation of a house. Weren't you a Boy Scout?"

She shook her head in frustration and chastised Raymond, who looked desperate to escape her watchful eye. After starting the fire, he snuck away and found the group on the porch. He authorized Cecile, "I think you'll need to work on Miss Berk. You're probably the only person left on earth up to the job. She's a handful!"

Raymond said specifically to Cecile, "When you have a moment, I need a woman's opine on a matter; what say you?" Cecile looped her arm through Raymond's and beckoned to Maddie. "You come too, for moral support."

Maddie hopped off the porch and pulled the ends of her black lace shawl over her tanned shoulders. Raymond included Maddie on the subject of how to break the news to Mrs. Genhart that the Nazis had discovered her son, Henrik, was Jewish. He was now a prisoner at Dachau.

"The US ambassador to Germany in Berlin did some reconnaissance work for the State Department, including the whereabouts of the son of the famous violinist Werner Kempler. While searching his apartment, a State Department official found a copy of a letter Henrick had written to Mrs. Genhart asking her to come to Hamburg. He sent it to the Eastman Theater. Now, just how do you recommend I convey this information to Mrs. G?"

The three stood outside the kitchen's entrance. Maddie and Cecile exchanged glances, their eyes speaking a language foreign to Raymond, labeled as something like female intuition. Cecile pitched in with an agreed-upon answer: "Tell her the truth, flat-out. Don't break it to her like you're trying to protect her. You do her a disservice, discounting her ability to handle anything emotional; therefore, you feel like you must rescue her."

Raymond stared at Cecile with an expression as blank as a

chalkboard. He swallowed hard. "Well, don't I?"

Maddie gave her two cents. "Oh, I don't think so. You don't have to rescue her. She's a modern woman. She divorced herself from her past. Something tells me she's a lot tougher than we credit her. Especially after hearing Stani tell me about Kempler and what he was told about her. That could be hearsay or the meditations of a madman; who knows? I think I should be the one to tell her."

The thought of Stani and mentioning his name caused Maddie to become teary-eyed again. Cecile put her arm around her shoulder and hugged her. Maddie said softly, "I hope I can one day say his name or hear it and not burst into tears."

Buster came looking for Maddie while Cecile moved to rescue Raymond and the Wolferman men. He asked her to come and walk with him for a moment. "You know, I was thinking about what you said about Stani saying 'My work here is done.' Stani firmly believed in life after death and that for every death, new life should follow."

Maddie agreed and added, "Whether on a spiritual or physical level, it seems as soon as you hear someone dies, soon after, you'll hear of a baby being born."

Buster nodded, agreeing. "Regarding his work being over? Well, on today, of all days, I now know why he said that." Buster turned her to face him and put his hands on her face, but just below her cheeks, like when he went to kiss her. They stood at a stunning part of the lawn in front of the garden with the rose bushes of many varieties Buster and Maddie had planted together. The setting couldn't have been more perfect or the day more symbolic.

Gazing into her almost violet-colored eyes, Buster said, "Maddie. Stani knew the time had come. He could let go."

She smiled at her love. "What time is that?"

Buster got down on one knee on the soft turf, with the buzz of summer birds, crickets, and frogs serenading them with their evensong. "He could release you; he could let you go."

The breeze blew like a delicate kiss scented with jasmine and iris. He took Maddie's hands in his, and as the sun set over the lake, the sky vexed over two colors of red, Buster asked Maddie to marry him.

———❖———

Portsmouth, England, Wurst End Pub
Part-time barkeep Ferdinand Mueller prepared to attend to his afternoon banking chores, shopping, and picking up the mail. His job at the Wurst End Pub was like a holiday for him after being at sea ten months a year. This provided ample time with his family. He was content to have his feet on solid ground for a while. It suited him.

The pub was of the typical brick, thatched roof sort, dark wood inside, leaded glass windows stained with cigar and cigarette smoke that looked out onto a bonny sheep pasture. The counter was long, with bar stools for twenty hard-drinking patrons. Pitchers of beer and shots of Irish whiskey ruled the day and early night. The pub opened at nine and closed at nine. They served a limited menu and closed from two to four daily, and were closed on Sundays.

His wife and children were housed nearby in his brother's farmhouse, which was modern and lovely. His summer job provided a real vacation for the Mueller family by extracting them from the grime of Hamburg for two glorious summer months in bucolic England, the land of lush, green rolling hills.

His wife, Heidi, rang him at the pub. "Hello, love; I stopped by and picked up the mail. You had a special delivery package, so I'll drop it off. Bye for now." *Well, that's one thing off my list.*

After a plate of bangers and mash, similar to a German plowman's lunch, Ferdinand's wife brought the mail. "The special delivery piece is from HAPAG; it must be mail from the ship," said Heidi, familiar with the routine once her husband was landlocked. "Hmm, there's also a letter for you from Panama, from Oscar Martinez at Hotel Mundos. I remember you mentioning that hotel with all the six-toed cats belonging to Ernest Hemingway. All very mysterious!"

Ferdinand smiled at her and kissed her cheek dutifully. "Thanks for the mail. I've got some errands to run. Can you hold the fort, or must you run along?"

She yawned and stretched. "I didn't sleep well last night. But oh, yes, I can stay a while."

He gathered his banking and list as Heidi asked, "Don't you want to open your mail?"

Ferdinand shook his head and grabbed his coat. "Go ahead and open it if you want."

Heidi poured herself a small glass of beer and sat with the mail. *Hmm. Should I open it? Well, what else do I have to do? Let's see. Huh, both are from the hotel in Havana, but one is postmarked two days later. Isn't this mysterious?*

She opened the one with the earliest postmark letter, took it out, and read,

Dear Purser Mueller. I can't thank you and the crew enough for providing me with room and board for two months at the hotel. That is a kind act of great magnitude. Thank you for giving me a good place to land after a difficult time. I'm hoping for better days ahead for us all.

I still grieve Fritz, even though he was a stranger; we had a connection, thrown together, opposite sides of the coin, yet we understood each other. After time in a concentration

camp, it takes a while to warm up to normal life and the people in it. The camp, the time I spent there now, seems like a dream. It was not a bad dream because I learned some things and grew up. It is in the crucible of experience that we learn our greatest lessons. We may not have chosen to grow up, but the circumstances can make us do so.

I spoke with the Mundos Hotel manager, Mr. Martinez, a kind man. As your friend, he assured me of the full extension of famous Cuban hospitality, even taking me to meet the chef tomorrow. Does good beget good? I'm wondering if it does. If so, I pray it continues and never stops. For some reason, I think I could be very content living here. We'll see. I'll keep in touch. I hope you will as well. Your kindness left a mark, and I'm forever grateful.

May God bless you, the captain, Jockl, and your crew. I remain in your debt,

Stefan Soutine.

Heidi wrinkled her brow. *Hmm. Clearly, my husband must be a different man aboard the ship. What does this next letter say? Maybe I'll read more fascinating insights into my husband's ship-side personality.* Eagerly, she picked up the second envelope, saw the word *personal* marked on it, and debated opening it. *Well, he told me I could, so I guess I can.*

She opened the envelope carefully and extracted the letter. It was from Oscar Martinez, the Manager.

Dear Purser Mueller,

I regret to inform you of the passing of Stefan Soutine, the young man you temporarily subsidized here at the hotel. I'm unsure of the exact details, except the hotel guards said he was killed by someone he knew, perhaps from the ship. He seemed like a fine young man. My condolences.

At your service,

Oscar Martinez.

Also, you have a credit on record, or we can refund the unused amount you left for payment.

———✳———

Rochester, New York

Wolfie entered Raymond's office just as the clock chimed the five-note bells of Westminster like they did every hour. He waited for his adoptive dad to come from the kitchen, where he was preparing coffee for both of them. From the window with the scenic view, the start of fall was evident, with the final vestiges of summer hanging on at the end of August. The branches on the flowering trees appeared tired; they seemed to droop from exhaustion, resulting from a hot summer. The lawn was brown around the edges, begging for a thunderstorm.

Raymond came in, carrying two cups of coffee. "Ah, here we go. Have a seat." He sat behind his desk and sipped the steaming beverage, "Blast, it's hot. Ow." He put the cup down and waved his hand. "Dang it, I burnt my tongue. Now. Tell me, how's the leg, the feet, and news from the doctor?"

Wolfie put his coffee cup on the end table and, standing up, proceeded to jump in place. "Almost as good as new and cleared to report for duty. Light duty, that is, probably a desk job for six months. They did say it would take up to a year. Even I have realistic expectations, thanks, in part, to Camille."

Raymond tried to stifle a smile. "Well, you better follow

the doctor's orders. Camille's too. I have some good news. I heard from your CO today, and you and Buster will receive commendations, as will Specialist Martin White, the man who went by the cover name of Fritz Effinger. His will be awarded posthumously.

"Martin, as you know, was the one who helped you after the accident, saving your life. Your division at Bletchley thought he was best suited to take your place for the mission you were assigned. He must have stepped up bravely, especially after viewing your accident. The CO said when asked if he'd answer the call, he replied, 'Need seen, assignment given.' I'll never forget that. Brilliant attitude. His loss saddens me greatly, but I'm thankful to God it wasn't you, son."

Raymond lit a cigarette, offering one to Wolfie. "Martin, like you, was an exceptional asset to our side. You'll all be honored for your bravery. Buster will receive a special commendation for his heroics and his recovery of stolen information. He will also be promoted to lieutenant. You might have to take orders from him. Are you okay with that?"

Wolfie waved his hand at Raymond. "Aw, go on, Dad. We worked that out long ago, and we understand each other better. Now, seeing we'll be old married men soon, we'll be fine even before you know it."

That brought a smile to Raymond's face. "Camille is a special girl. I'm happy you found each other and Hollenius found Ninotchka. It's kismet for you all. I'm in awe of the timing and considering Stani...Hollenius would have been so lonely without him." Wolfie adds,

"Not that he doesn't miss him; he does. I see him sleeping on Stani's bed at night and leaving before anyone gets up. It's his silent nocturnal vigil. But now, he shares the bed with Ninotchka, and they sleep curled up together. It's a happy thought, isn't it?"

Raymond sighed. "Yes, it is."

Wolfie detected the hesitation in Raymond's voice. "What is it, Dad?"

Raymond tightened his lips. "It's nothing, really."

Wolfie stood and walked to the front of the desk. He observed the precision with which everything was lined up in Raymond's workspace. "Dad, I've got big shoulders. Now tell me what's on your mind."

Tilting his head, Raymond commented, "You have grown up." He stood and walked over to the wall of leather-bound books. "Uh, so yes. A problem. My mood is melancholy due to tomorrow, August 30th, Buster's birthday. I won't be able to celebrate with him. Then, we have the situation in Europe. It feels like war could break out any second. Intelligence reports show a massive build-up of Germans at the Polish border."

Wolfie knew what that meant. Buster was in Europe, working in Special Ops. Raymond lamented, "Buster asked me to try and keep war from happening, and I failed, can't do anything about it. But we got Rolf and Cecile out, at least." He approached Wolfie, putting a hand on his shoulder. "I didn't intend to cast a damper over the mood, so how about we go to the garage and see your father's new race car? Think he'll let you take it for a spin?"

Wolfie eyed Raymond. "Are you sure it's not you who wants to take a spin?"

The front door opened, and the men walked over to see who it was. "Here, let me help you with that." Wolfie grabbed the bags of groceries while Raymond attended to the door and Maddie's coat.

Maddie's effervescence was contagious, causing both men to hug her, happy for her visit. "I thought I'd come over and make dinner for us and break bread together. Cecile tells me the best way to remember someone you loved is to keep their traditions and honor their memory by participating in what they did and loved. That way, you keep their memory alive—and the spirit, too. So, gentlemen, what do you say? We preserve the tradition of dinner around the table like Stani would. He'd tell us to be like the Three Musketeers regarding our care of one another. Do you know what he'd say, Wolfie?"

He scrunched his brow, "Hmm, no, I don't think I know. Tell us!"

Maddie said triumphantly, her fist raised in the air, "All for one and one for all!"

EPILOGUE

AUGUST 1939, DAYS BEFORE WORLD WAR II BEGAN

CAPTAIN GUSTAV SCHROEDER remained a HAPAG employee despite Berlin's threats. However, according to a declaration by the German Embassy, the captain was forbidden to discuss the refugee trip of May 1939 in public or private.

On August 26, 1939, while under the jurisdiction and supervision of HAPAG, the *S.S. St. Louis* was scheduled to depart New York Harbor for Bermuda when the trip was suddenly canceled. The paying passengers were handled abruptly, and HAPAG had no further plans to accommodate them. The next day, at 8:00 p.m., sailing empty from the pier at Forty-Sixth Street, the *S.S. St. Louis* left New York and was at sea when war was declared just days later. History would show that HAPAG had information about the date and commencement of the war.

As for the passengers of the May 1939 voyage of the *S.S. St. Louis*, they were distributed among Belgium, Holland, France, and Great Britain. Only those sent to Great Britain did not fall under German occupation. The individuals tasked with organizing the passengers' onward journeys were unaware of the profound ramifications their decisions would have. Little did they know that the destinations they assigned would significantly influence the fates of the travelers, ultimately leading to life-altering consequences for some, including tragic outcomes. Over 250 passengers on that ill-fated voyage died at the hands of the Nazis, mostly in concentration camps.

The *S.S. St. Louis* was the final litmus test the Nazis performed on the world, assessing the political and moral fortitude of the world's nations, whether weak or strong, by their reaction to the voyage and the fate of the passengers aboard. As proved by three countries' rejection of the ship, one being the United States, the end game of Operation Sunshine could come to fruition.

After this voyage, the Nazis believed the world had given them the green light to do as they pleased with the Jews of Europe, creating the segue for the Final Solution: the Nazi plan for the extermination of the Jews, which resulted in the genocide known as the Holocaust or Shoah.

THE END

Questions for Discussion: Book Clubs, Study Groups, or Classrooms

1. The Nazis perfected the art of propaganda, as we see demonstrated in *Some Came By Ship*. We see how the synchronized message broadcasted through all media sources can contribute to gaslighting the public. How can you protect yourself from being gaslighted by the media?

2. We see a rise in anti-Semitism worldwide. How does 1939 differ from today? Have we learned our lessons or forgotten them? Can you provide examples for both arguments?

3. The Nazis indoctrinated their children from a young age to hate the Jews. How can you prevent this in your life? Learning about people, their cultures, their country, and their customs breaks down the barriers erected by hate. Would you consider spending time learning about people and cultures that are different from yours? What would you be willing to do to accomplish that?

4. Did this book challenge your thinking, and if so, in what way?

5. Did the US government fail the *S.S. St. Louis* passengers? What could they have done differently?

6. Could you imagine starting a new life in a foreign country after the Nazis took everything from you? What would you do? Does putting yourself in the passengers' shoes increase your empathy?

Thank you for reading *Some Came By Ship*. If you enjoyed it, please consider leaving a review at Amazon, Goodreads, Bookbub, or Barnes & Noble.

Cathy A. Lewis

CATHY A. LEWIS is an accomplished author of two novels and a graduate of the Culinary Institute of America. After a successful career as a classically trained Chef, she began writing in 2018, fulfilling her long-held aspiration of becoming a published author. Her passion for writing lies in historical fiction, focusing on reviving overlooked stories from Europe between 1933 and 1939. Lewis resides in Nashville with friends and her cat, Toute Suite. She enjoys attending Crosswalk Church, watching Syracuse Orange basketball, IndyCar racing, NFL football, the Buffalo Bills, and the Tennessee Titans, and Turner Classic Movies. Cathy donates to The SS St. Louis Legacy Project Foundation, Jewish Book Council, Nashville Jewish Federation, Homes for Our Troops, Save Them All Best Friends Animal Rescue, The Beat of Life, and other local and national charities.